D1275953

DATE DUE

NOV 0 2 2009		
NOV 1 2 2009		
NOV 3 0 2009		
JAN 1 9 2010		

| GAYLORD | | | PRINTED IN U.S.A. |

THE TEST

ALSO BY PATRICIA GUSSIN

Shadow of Death
Twisted Justice

THE TEST

A Novel

Patricia Gussin

Oceanview Publishing

IPSWICH, MASSACHUSETTS

ISBN: 978-1-933515-19-9

Published in the United States of America by Oceanview Publishing, Ipswich, Massachusetts
www.oceanviewpub.com

10 9 8 7 6 5 4 3 2 1

PRINTED IN THE UNITED STATES OF AMERICA

This book is dedicated to Bob

ACKNOWLEDGMENTS

Many, who will remain unnamed, have inspired *The Test*. So many of my friends have obsessed about how they would *finally* allocate their material possessions in a fair and equitable manner among their heirs. You may or may not know who you are, but I want you to know that I am grateful to you for sharing your insights.

Many thanks to my editor Barbara Phillips. I also want to thank the entire Oceanview Publishing team: Susan Greger, Maryglenn McCombs, Gayle Treadwell, Mary Adele Bogden, John Cheesman, Susan Hayes, George Foster, Joe Hall, Joanne Savage, Sandy Greger, and Cheryl Melnick. You are the best.

AUTHOR'S NOTE

None among us knows for sure how he or she will face death. Will it be with sadness as we leave our friends and family behind? Will we fear losing power or control over future events? Will it be with regrets or guilt that we have not righted our wrongs? Will it be with concern that our loved ones be protected? Will it be with worry that our material wealth be distributed as we have directed and have we directed it fairly? Or will it be with peaceful resignation?

In *The Test*, Paul Parnell, a man of great wealth, faces death with regrets. Paul has lived a successful life, full of professional and financial and personal achievements. But as he reflects on his life, he obsesses on a perceived flaw: he feels that he has failed to pass along to his children a strong moral code of values. Can he correct this flaw from the grave? To address this concern, Paul creates a "test" as his last will and testament. His intent is good and honorable. He wants to right a wrong. But his plan to propagate his moral value credo, instead, triggers a series of unforeseeable tragedies and invites evil influences that may well destroy the Parnell heritage.

THE PARNELL FAMILY

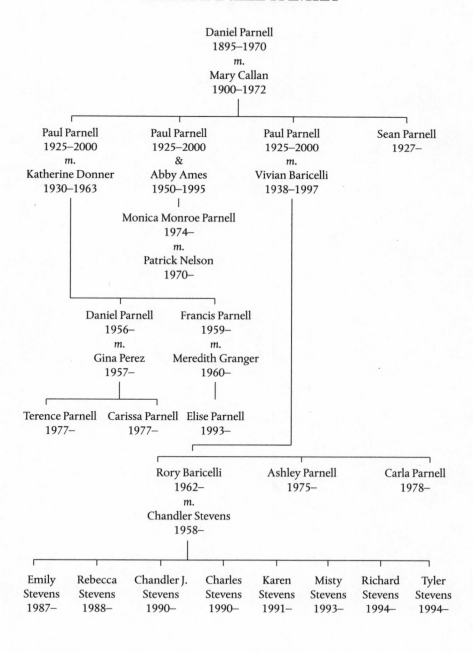

Daniel Parnell
1895–1970
m.
Mary Callan
1900–1972

Paul Parnell
1925–2000
m.
Katherine Donner
1930–1963

Paul Parnell
1925–2000
&
Abby Ames
1950–1995

Monica Monroe Parnell
1974–
m.
Patrick Nelson
1970–

Paul Parnell
1925–2000
m.
Vivian Baricelli
1938–1997

Sean Parnell
1927–

Daniel Parnell
1956–
m.
Gina Perez
1957–

Francis Parnell
1959–
m.
Meredith Granger
1960–

Terence Parnell
1977–

Carissa Parnell
1977–

Elise Parnell
1993–

Rory Baricelli
1962–
m.
Chandler Stevens
1958–

Ashley Parnell
1975–

Carla Parnell
1978–

Emily
Stevens
1987–

Rebecca
Stevens
1988–

Chandler J.
Stevens
1990–

Charles
Stevens
1990–

Karen
Stevens
1991–

Misty
Stevens
1993–

Richard
Stevens
1994–

Tyler
Stevens
1994–

THE TEST

CHAPTER ONE

The door to the psychiatry department stood ajar. Ashley Parnell dabbed her eyes and knocked. In a black cashmere suit and creamy silk blouse, she looked more like an MBA intern than a fourth-year medical student. But her shoulders were slumped, her eyes puffy and red. It wouldn't take a psychiatrist to tell that all was not right in her world.

"Dr. Welton?" She called beyond the door labeled Acting Chief, Psychiatry.

"Come in." The voice inside distinctive, yet annoyed.

Psychiatry had not been her favorite rotation. Talking to crazies all day had started to make her question her own mental stability.

"I'm sorry to interrupt —"

"I assume you're the medical student who called?" Dr. Welton glanced up, fixing ice-blue eyes on her. "I don't have much time. What can I do for you?" He signaled for her to take the chair across from his pristine desk.

For an instant, Ashley felt her eyelids flutter and her knees start to wobble. Why? The man inspecting her looked remarkably like her father. A trim, muscular build, tanned face, and silver-tinged sandy hair, so much like Dad, maybe fifteen years ago.

"The reason I'm here is that my father died yesterday, and I need to hand in my patient report so I c-can —"

"I see. Did you bring it with you?" Brusque, to the point, Dr. Welton held out his hand.

Ashley fumbled in her bag and pulled out a sheaf of papers. Once she submitted these reports, she'd complete her psychiatry rotation two days early, free to attend her father's funeral.

Important to make eye contact, Ashley reminded herself as she handed the professor the packet, one sheet for each of the seven schizophrenic patients she'd been assigned. Psychiatrists always make a big deal about eye contact, but when she tried to engage his eyes, a surge of new tears made her blink hard and clamp down her jaw. Even if this guy did remind her of her dad, she would get out of here without a crying jag.

She groped inside her purse for Kleenex, and when she looked up, Dr. Welton was staring at her. His index finger stabbed at her signature at the bottom of the first page.

"You're Miss *Parnell*?"

He rose from his swivel chair and came around the desk. He whisked a snowy-white, monogrammed handkerchief from his pocket and held it out to her. "I didn't realize. I am deeply sorry about your father. Such an admirable man."

He tucked the handkerchief in Ashley's hand. It felt stiff with excess starch, but she accepted it, wondering whether she should actually use it to blow her nose. Before she could decide, he grasped one arm in a protective gesture and assisted her across the room to a paisley upholstered couch. The couch symbolism didn't even register as Ashley fought to contain her tears. She had never considered herself overly emotional, but today she felt desperately alone.

"Miss Parnell, please. Let's sit for a moment." Dr. Welton's voice was now warm and comforting. "I just want to make sure you're okay. I'll get you some water."

"I'm okay." Ashley had intended to leave right away, but she found herself moving robotically under his touch. She clamped the cool glass of water in both hands as Dr Welton joined her on the couch.

"Do you want to tell me about your father?"

Ashley, always a private person, found herself pouring out her life to Dr. Welton: her father's two-year battle with pancreatic cancer, losing her mother to cancer three years before her father, how she had always wanted to be a cardiologist like her mother. When she finished, she found herself encircled in Dr. Welton's arms, sobbing uncontrollably.

There was a knock at the door and a muffled voice interrupted, "Dr. Welton, you have patients waiting in the clinic."

"I am so, so sorry." Ashley jumped up, wringing her hands. "I've taken too much of your time. I need to get home."

"Miss Parnell, you're too upset to drive. Let me run you home."

"Thank you, but my driver is waiting," she said. Again, he took her arm. "I'm so sorry. Naturally, I'll come back after the funeral and," she pointed to the stack of papers on his desk, "and f-finish."

"No need, Miss Parnell. I'll handle everything with the psych department."

She felt a slight shudder. "Thank you," was all she could think to say.

"Let me escort you to your car."

Ashley ignored the raised secretarial eyebrows as Dr. Welton walked her out of the office and down the corridor.

Under the flutter of wet snowflakes, Conrad Welton stood transfixed as the chauffeured, forest green Mercedes merged into traffic, Ashley Parnell ensconced in the backseat. Attractive, not stunning or sexy, but classy. Medium height with a bit of a slouch, average weight — maybe 120 pounds — light auburn hair pulled back, sad brown eyes behind gold-rimmed glasses. A conservative designer suit. No jewelry, but med students rarely wore rings or bracelets.

The girl had sounded intelligent, but introverted. From her actions, Welton detected a lack of self-esteem, quite unexpected given her position of privilege. Despite the frigid winter air, Conrad felt a surge of warmth course though his veins. An heiress had stumbled into his office at the most propitious of moments: she had an Oedipal complex at a most vulnerable stage; was under extreme emotional stress; and would be susceptible to imprints that defied her own logic and personality. There'd been no doubt that she'd felt the chemistry between them. He'd felt the quickening of her heart and the heave of her chest as he'd held her close.

After enduring a banal clinic session, Conrad hurried back to his office. He instructed his secretary to hold all calls so he could turn his attention to the Internet. The object of his study: the recently deceased Paul Parnell, world-renowned billionaire and philanthropist.

Paul had been the retired CEO of Keystone Pharmaceutical. According to the annual reports, he'd amassed stock worth close to a billion. He'd been a founding partner of Gene-Tech which went public, another quarter of a billion. He'd been a primary investor in Computer Appliances. When it went public, another quarter of a billion. Inheritance from his father's estate with appreciation, at least eight million. Real estate, an art collection, lots of other luxuries including a jet and a helicopter accounted for another eighty million or so. And there was that Nobel Prize, a status symbol to add to the money.

At six thirty p.m. when Welton logged off the computer, he found a haphazard arrangement of pink message slips taped to the back of his door. The usual trivia that plagued him. An admission to the psych unit — suicide watch. A consult request from the floor — panic attack — would he use hypnosis? A call from the dean: had he sent over the monthly department update? He hadn't. The dean had as much as told him he'd never be chairman of the department now that the National Institute of Mental Health had terminated his research grant. He didn't intend to play this demeaning game much longer. His reputation was second to none in the field of medical hypnosis since the passing of his mentor, Milton Erickson, and he had tenure, so the university couldn't fire him. But the whole field of psychiatry bored him now.

Crumpling the handful of notes, Welton tossed them into the trash.

The Cathedral of Saints Peter and Paul in Philadelphia was crowded with dignitaries, political leaders, and business icons. The day was brisk but sunny, the streets cleared of the light snow of the day before. A day much too cheery for a funeral. Welton debated whether or not to attend. He needed a natural way to reconnect with Ashley Parnell, and was anxious to glean as much inside Parnell information as he could. As a psychiatrist, he was trained to observe how people deal with stress, and today's insights could be valuable to his plans.

The vestibule was crammed with flowers and people. Conrad disliked crowds, but he calmed himself, nodded to fellow attendees, and wended his way toward the Parnell family. He found Ashley standing between her sisters. One was definitely older, and fat compared to Ashley. The other, who Welton knew from his research was a professional model, had that typical emaciated look. All three women wore black dresses and wide-brimmed black hats as they greeted the snaking line of mourners. Welton joined the procession, noting how the chubby sister slowed the process down, sharing the details of the old man's death, singing the praises of the hospice. Waiting to get to Ashley, he got a good look at the skinny sister. She didn't look anything like the glamourous photos he'd seen on the Internet. Leaning heavily on Ashley, she was either consumed with grief or she was stoned. The latter, he surmised.

Murmuring, "I'm sorry," Welton passed along the family in the line of mourners. When he stood in front of Ashley, he paused long enough to make sure she recognized him. This time she wore no glasses, he noted. Reaching to press her hand, he was rewarded with a gentle squeeze. He then abruptly left the cathedral, the stench raised by so many flowers sickening him.

The adulation of the masses, including the press, for the over-privileged, self-absorbed, pompous dead man disgusted Welton. All these people wanted a piece of the Parnell influence and money. Even a scrap would do. Well, no scraps for him, he had much more in mind.

Escaping the cathedral before the service began, Conrad had to step aside to avoid brushing against one of the two Parnell brothers, Senator Frank Parnell, junior U.S. senator from Pennsylvania, Ashley's half brother. The senator's face was flushed and his jaw clenched. An expression of anger, not grief, Conrad surmised. He was tempted to follow the senator back inside the cathedral, but the sickening floral odor deterred him.

As Welton retreated, his attention was directed to a stage-whispered conversation between a sophisticated-looking woman, whom he recognized from his Internet search as Meredith Parnell, the senator's wife, and a partner in one of Philadelphia's most prestigious law firms, and a frail old man with very black hair.

"Frank's upset, Carl," said the Parnell woman, as if defending a petulant child. "He expected Paul to be buried next to his own mother, not Vivian."

"What can I say?" The old man's shoulders slumped further forward. "Paul and Vivian were married for twenty-three years. It's been thirty-seven years since Frank's mother, Kay, died. It's what Paul stipulated."

Welton knew exactly what this overheard tiff was all about. Which wife to be buried next to: wife number one or wife number two?

"I know there's nothing that you can do, but Frank is irate," the woman said. "Maybe after the will is squared away this afternoon, Frank'll come out of his funk."

As Welton turned to watch the senator's wife and the old man return to the family, he noticed a look of panic flash across the face of the other Parnell brother, who must be Daniel, the oldest of Paul's children, reported to be a recluse in Florida. Following Daniel's troubled gaze, Conrad observed two dark-haired women, both attractive, one younger than the other, and a young man enter through a side door. Not much to note in and of itself. But why did the Parnell brother look like he'd seen a ghost? So much to learn about these Parnells. And learn he would.

CHAPTER TWO

Meredith and Frank Parnell, their daughter between them, rode in the stretch limousine from the cemetery to the Parnell home in Devon, on Philadelphia's Main Line.

"What a shame we can't have a gathering at the house," Meredith mused. "At least for the VIPs."

"Darling, you're nonstop when it comes to political opportunities."

Meredith reached over the little girl to take Frank's hand. "Every single vote counts. Just ask Al Gore."

It was no secret that Meredith was the brains behind Frank's political career. And Frank didn't deny it, basking as he did in her unabashed love for him, her extraordinary intelligence, and her unfailing political street smarts.

"Dad had his own agenda. Who would have guessed that he'd mandate the family return to the homestead immediately after the burial service to read the will?"

"He spent a lot of time behind closed doors before he died," Meredith said. "Ever notice that when men get older, they get more reluctant to talk to their kids about their money? I only wish he'd named me executor."

"Surprised me. Dad respected you. I don't know what got into him at the end. Maybe it's all in a trust and you'll get to be trustee. If not —"

"What are you guys talking about?" Elise grabbed both of her parents' hands and shook them.

"Just grown-up talk, honey," Meredith said, patting the seven-year-old's curly brown hair.

"Will you tell the driver to hurry? I want to get there the same time as my cousins."

Frank and Meredith rolled their eyes. The "cousins," not real cousins, but Paul had always insisted that Rory be treated like a Parnell. Rory, the daughter of Paul's second wife, had been twelve years old, and Frank had been fourteen, when their father married Vivian Barricelli and she and her daughter had moved into the house.

"Thank God, Dad never legally adopted Rory," Frank said, not responding to Elise.

Rory was married to a family doctor; they had five kids; they'd adopted three more. Thus the "cousins" that Elise so adored. Rory's reputation as a saint had long been a thorn in Frank's side.

"She may fool the rest of the world, but I've always known Rory for what she is, a leech trying to take what belongs to the Parnell family. And she spent a heck of a lot of time with Dad at the end," Frank said, strumming his fingers on the leather upholstery. "If Dad included —"

"Frank, not now." Meredith raised half-moon eyebrows. "We've been over that. Paul knew what we'll need and he wanted it for us. He took care of your senatorial race. He'll have taken care of your political future."

Meredith was right. That had been a shared dream — hers, his, and Paul's. Frank, president of the United States. Best case scenario: follow the second term of George W. In 2008, Frank would be forty-nine. Simply put, to make that happen, he needed the enormous amount of money now at stake.

"For now, be gracious," she advised. "Just act nice to everybody. No matter what happens, don't blow up. The media's still hanging around the family."

"You're a strange one to be giving me advice on 'being nice.' Your tolerance level for my family is zero."

"Except I always respected your dad," she said. And Frank knew that to be true.

For the rest of the trip, Meredith chatted with Elise. Frank didn't know how she could find so much to say to the kid. For him, Elise was a political prop. A nice enough child, very pretty and always dressed like she'd stepped from Saks' 'tween department. But Meredith truly loved the little girl and Frank respected that and never felt even the smallest twinge of resentment over the affection he had to share. At least Meredith didn't want more kids. Meredith didn't want Elise to have to share anything.

Frank used the rest of the ride to go over in his head the most pressing congressional issues. The screwed-up election in Florida was making Washington crazy. Bush was still not confirmed, although he was about to announce his cabinet nominees. The senate was looking at a 50-50 split. The Democrats had vowed to fight John Ashcroft's confirmation as attorney general. Committee chairs up for grabs. Politics in chaos. On top of that, a gunman had killed seven people in a Philadelphia row house and Mayor Street wanted Frank to join him for a press conference.

As Meredith and Elise chatted and Frank pondered, the car phone rang. The driver answered. "For you, Senator. Mr. Cleveland."

Matt Cleveland, Frank's young staffer and confidant, managed his calendar, making all decisions about allocating his time between the unending demands from D.C., and those back home in Pennsylvania.

"Bad weather tonight, Senator," Matt announced. The copter can't go. The Lear may make it out, but you'll have to take off out of Wings Field. Of course, if you're not in D.C. tomorrow, everybody will understand."

The car had arrived at the Parnell estate and lingered in the circular drive. "I'd like to get back tonight," Frank said. "But we just arrived at the house and I have to stay for the will. Call later with more specifics."

As the driver came around to usher them out, Frank wondered what would happen to this stately mansion. Surely Dad would have willed it to Ashley. She still lived here, commuting to medical school at the University of Pennsylvania. Commuting via chauffeur, that is. Ashley, over-privileged, but so studious. On her way to becoming a doctor, just like her mom. Taking everything in life for granted. Frank doubted if she'd ever paid a single bill. Now she'd end up with the house, the cars, and the Mendoza couple to wait on her. Dad would have figured that no one else needed the house. Dan lived on a farm in Florida. Frank and Meredith had an estate on a horse farm in Bucks County; Rory had her place in Doylestown; Carla stayed at the Parnell apartment in Manhattan. That left Ashley. Too bad, it would have brought a bundle on the market.

With Elise between them, Frank and Meredith headed inside the house where all four of the Parnell children had grown up — not counting Rory, the interloper. The skies were still blue, no sign of the snow that had been predicted.

Once inside the house, Mr. and Mrs. Mendoza, caretakers of the Parnell estate for over thirty years, murmured condolences and took their coats. Meredith turned Elise over to Mrs. M., instructing her to have the child join the Stevens' kids in the game room. Frank could hear the unruly chaos of kids chasing each other, squealing and giggling. You'd think that just this one day, Rory would insist on a modicum of decorum, but no, she believed in unfettered children at all times.

Frank took inventory of the priceless artwork displayed around the mansion, wondering absently whether he would dispose of Vivian's favorites, the Monets and Sisilys, and convert them into money. Dad had certainly indulged that woman. His own mother, Kay, had come from money, but Vivian had worked her way through medical school, a single mother and a cardiologist when she'd met Paul. For the millionth time, Frank thanked God that Vivian had died before Dad. He could only imagine the fiasco if she had been left with financial control.

Frank and Meredith entered the living room hand in hand. With a stab of pride, Frank marveled at Meredith's style: slim designer dress, black stockings, Ferragamo shoes with just enough of a heel to show off her legs. He'd often considered that her nose was a hint too large for her thin, oval face, but her large brown eyes, creamy complexion, and auburn hair swept dramatically off to one side more than compensated for that single imperfection.

Frank assessed those in the room. His brother, Dan, and Chandler Stevens, Rory's husband, chatted by the fireplace. Although older than Frank by three years, Dan was held in poor regard by his brother. Dan had dropped out of college and dropped out of family affairs, and Frank could count on one hand the number of times he'd seen his reclusive brother in the past ten years. Frank had to admit that both he and Dan were aging well. Tall, slim, wavy sandy-brown hair. Jack and Bobby

Kennedy look-alikes, people used to say. But unlike Jack and Bobby, Frank and Dan shared no common interests. Frank supposed that Dan would split as soon as the will was read. Dan had no interest in the family and no interest in the family's money.

Across the room, Ashley and Rory were speaking in low tones. Frank couldn't hear what they were saying, but he did note how horrible Rory looked. Eyes puffy, a frumpy dress that hung like a bag on her body, hair unstyled, no attempt at makeup. As Frank led Meredith toward them, Meredith leaned into whisper, "Rory could use a makeover."

"She's in bad shape," Ashley was saying to Rory. "Her drug habit is out of control."

They were discussing Carla, Frank's youngest sister, half sister really. Not wanting to join that conversation, Frank changed course, letting go of Meredith's hand. The front door opened and he heard the voice of his uncle, Sean Cardinal Parnell. For a moment, Frank felt disoriented. If it weren't for the black clerical garb and the scarlet sash, the cardinal could have been his dad striding into the room. When they were kids, they'd been mistaken for twins even though Paul was two years older than Sean. Frank had been very close to his father, but his relationship with his uncle was strained, yet cordial. Meredith was Jewish and that hadn't set well with the cardinal.

"Let's go tell Carl that everybody's here." Meredith had returned to his side. He knew she just wanted to get this over with, go home to her horses, settle in, and start planning their next political move. Carl Schiller was Paul's best friend, the founding partner of Meredith's law firm and, to Frank's chagrin, the executor of his father's will.

"Frank, before we get started, can I see you for a moment in the library?" Carl said as Frank approached him.

Frank exchanged an annoyed grimace with Meredith, then followed Carl into his dad's paneled oasis. The smell of old leather and pipe tobacco reassured Frank of his father's allegiance. Here is where they'd first plotted the course of his political aspirations.

"Frank," Carl said immediately. "Just so you know, with Paul's will, I am reading it exactly as he instructed. He left me no latitude. None whatsoever." Carl extended a frail arm to pat Frank on the arm. "I want you to understand that."

The old man looked so stooped, much older than seventy-six, and his hands shook with Parkinson's. But his voice still held that rich baritone and Meredith reported that, in the firm's infinite wisdom, he was considered mentally competent.

"Certainly Meredith can handle any legal issues," Frank said, perplexed over Carl's remark. "She's perfectly capable and since it'll all be in your firm —"

Carl's hands began to move as if he were rolling a pill. When Frank stared, he moved one hand to smooth his shoe-polish black hair. Meredith often made fun of the old man's ridiculous attempt at vanity. "No, Frank, I'm afraid your father was specific, very specific. After the funeral your father specified that all the children gather here as well as their spouses and any grandchildren over the age of eighteen. And your uncle and myself."

"Grandchildren?"

"Yes, Dan's children."

"Dan's?" Frank could not suppress a gasp. "What? He hasn't seen them since they were infants."

"That concerned your father greatly," Carl explained, but his normally steady voice shook. "He was very specific that of his eleven grandchildren, only those of age be present."

"For crying out loud, you mean he's counting Rory's kids?" Frank figured Elise to be the only *legitimate* grandchild. Dan hadn't seen his two kids in twenty-three years, and Rory's eight had no legal claim.

"Certainly, Frank, you realize that Paul always considered Rory as his own. Right from the beginning."

"Come on, Carl, what are you saying? One of his own? Not by blood. Not by adoption. Not by anything." Frank could smell his father's cologne, could recap all the discussions they'd had in this room.

"By intent, I would say," Carl paused. "Paul always treated Rory as his daughter."

Frank needed Meredith by his side right now. Should he call her in?

"We have to go back in now, Frank, but please understand. What happens this afternoon is as Paul insisted. I tried. Let's go gather everybody up."

Frank started to object, "This fiasco can't be legal." But he stopped as

Carl had already turned to go. Frank had a law degree from Yale. That's where he and Meredith met, but he'd never done civil work. Before going into politics, he'd been a prosecuting attorney in Philadelphia. Civil law was Meredith's territory. And Meredith would stop this nonsense in its track.

CHAPTER THREE

Dan Parnell hated the north. Give him the Sunshine State and his palm tree farm, his dogs, his tractor, his beer, and a sports channel on TV. He hated not just the weather but the hustle-bustle, the bullshit. And he hated family affairs. He'd flown up for his father's funeral, but he had no intention to hang around for the reading of the will. The darkening Philadelphia skies and freezing rain were enough to send him directly to the airport. But at the cemetery, just as he'd ducked behind a tombstone to sneak a smoke, Uncle Carl approached. He wasn't really their uncle, but the Parnell kids had always called him that. And they called his wife Aunt Phyllis. But when Dan had dropped out of the Parnell family, he'd left the Schillers behind too. Half expecting a lecture, Dan stubbed out the cigarette on the bottom of his shoe. "Busted," he said.

"Dan, you are coming over to the house afterward. Right?"

"Naw, I'm catching a plane back. Got new plants goin' in. Besides, I can't take this weather." He shivered. Not a fake shiver, a genuine one. "This shit's gonna turn to sleet."

"You can stay at the house. With this weather they may close the airport."

"Whatever. Need be, I'll camp out on an airport bench. No biggie."

"Dan, about the will —" Carl seemed like he needed to explain something.

"Look, I don't want anything. Dad knew that, so no hard feelings. Okay?"

"Your Dad wanted —"

"Face it. I never really knew my father. After my mother died, I figure he'd just given up — forgot he had two sons. I don't remember much about my mother either. So let's just forget it."

"Kay," Carl put an arm around Dan, "she died so young."

Katherine was her name, but everyone called her Kay. Dan had been seven when she was killed in a moped accident. She was thirty-five years old — eleven years younger than he was now. Vacationing with her parents in Bermuda. Dan and Frank had been home with a nanny, Paul had been on business in Europe. Kay's parents died soon after, of grief, everybody said. Dan and Frank were raised for the most part by their paternal grandparents as Paul revved up his career. By the time Paul married Vivian, Dan was seventeen and off to the University of Miami. Now Vivian, too, had been dead for three years. Dan had nothing against Vivian, he'd just never gotten to know the woman.

Dan jerked his head toward the dispersing crowd. "Shouldn't we be going?"

"Dan, it's urgent that you come back to the house. Your father insisted that you be there." Dan heard the pleading tone in the old man's voice, but he'd be dammed if he'd sit through a greed fest.

"He's dead, Carl. He can't 'insist' on anything anymore. The rest of the family may give a shit about his money, but not me."

Then Carl said words that shook Dan to the core. So stunned him that he started to shake.

"Gina will be there," Carl had said. "And your children, Terrence and Carissa."

Dan groped in his pocket for his pack of Camels. Carl reached to steady Dan's hand as he lit a cigarette, but backed off as his own tremor intensified.

For so long — twenty-two years — Dan had lived with his cowardice, his stupidity. It had only been the past few years in Lantana, Florida, working his palm groves, that he had made a sort of peace with himself. He'd gone through every excuse. He'd been young. Insecure. But what remained was the truth. He'd been a fucking coward.

Their love story — Gina's and Dan's — came flooding back. He'd been twenty-one and she a year older when they'd married twenty-five years earlier. Both students at the University of Miami. He, from an affluent family, all expenses paid, a generous allowance. She, number eight in a family of nine kids that had emigrated from Puerto Rico, supporting herself with a partial scholarship, the maximum in student loans, and a job in the university hospital's kitchen.

How many times had he revisited his decision not to tell Dad and Vivian about Gina? Sure, he'd had concerns that they wouldn't approve of her. But, when he was honest with himself, he blamed his own self-ishness. He'd wanted Gina for himself. Free of the Parnell family's grasp. And so he'd led Gina to believe he, like her, was a struggling student. He'd claimed he was an orphan, and she had believed him. Gina, the most gorgeous woman in the world in his eyes. Dark long hair, black eyes that smiled and teased. Funny and smart. She was all his and he adored her. Even now, looking back, Dan couldn't believe that he'd ever been so proud and so happy. Until it all fell apart.

Carl had been there on that day, and now here was Carl again urging Dan into the limo, telling him that he would today face her, face the depth of his shame. Dan puffed vigorously and hesitated, not sure whether to take the cigarette into the car. Finally he stubbed it out on his shoe bottom and flicked the butt into the bushes. Then he moaned, "Oh God," suddenly realizing that Gina would not approve. He hadn't smoked when they'd been together. She'd been such a health nut. What about his breath? Gina would find him repulsive. Fingers shaking, he fumbled in his pocket for one of those mint strips that disappear on the tongue.

"Dan? Are you okay?" Dan hesitated as Ashley met him at the front door. He stood, finger combing his hair, afraid to step inside.

"Yeah, I'm fine," Dan mumbled. "Not used to this friggin' weather."

"Come in. None of us are really okay today. I can't imagine living here without Dad. I still can't believe he's gone." Dan knew he should say something comforting to Ashley. Her eyes were so red and puffy and sad. Of all the Parnell siblings, she'd miss Dad the most. She'd always lived at home and it was no secret that she was Daddy's good little girl. Then Dan saw Carla standing beside Ashley with that faraway, stoned stare. Daddy's naughty little girl. But Dan ignored both girls as he looked around for Gina.

And there she was, walking toward him, holding a cup of coffee. The cup halted halfway to her lips and lingered there. His first instinct was to run. Run to her? Run away from her? Could she hear his heart pounding? Dan just stood, staring. Gina hadn't changed at all. Still that luxuriant black hair. Those dancing black eyes. Still so small. Behind

Gina appeared a young man. Lighter complexion, but dark hair, cut short and stylish, and with Gina's black eyes. Following him was a young woman who looked so much like Gina that day he'd met her on the University of Miami campus. Except his daughter's glossy black hair was short, a blunt, chic cut.

Gina made the first move, guiding the boy and the girl toward Dan as his mind fumbled with the greetings that he'd been rehearsing for twenty-two years. Yet no words would come. He could feel all eyes in the room on him, but he was beyond all ability to react.

"Dan?" The same mellow voice, tinged with a Latin accent. "Dan?" she repeated as he remained motionless, not even accepting the hand she held out to him.

Dan said nothing, petrified that he'd do the wrong thing, say the wrong thing, something that would make her go away again. When Gina withdrew her hand, he realized that she must think this was a rejection. He saw her glance toward the boy, who shrugged his shoulders as if to say, "So what did you expect?" But he watched the young girl inspecting him. Then he felt the shame and embarrassment of tears trickling down his cheeks. He could only blink when the girl reached into her purse, pulled out a white embroidered handkerchief and handed it to him with a shy smile.

"Gina, everything okay?" Carl had approached, wringing his thin hands.

"Just fine," she murmured, taking the handkerchief and patting away the tears on his cheek. The sensuous gesture caused everything in front of him to start to blur.

"Here's Carrie." She smiled at Carissa with obvious pride. "And here's Terry."

Terry reached out to shake his hand, and this time Dan was able to go through the correct motion.

"Hello," Terry said simply.

"I think it's time to sit down," Gina nodded to the rest of the family. Taking Dan's arm, she escorted him toward four empty chairs.

From that point Dan remembered nothing. Nothing about what followed; nothing about what was in that will. His mind was consumed with the mistakes of his past.

CHAPTER FOUR

Frank, his face a splotchy mix of pallor and angry red, grabbed Meredith by the arm as the family assembled in the living room. "For crying out loud, you're never going to believe what Carl's been up to."

Meredith faced him, her dark brown eyes flashing a warning that Frank knew meant, "not now." Then Frank realized that Chan, his nerdy brother-in-law, was moving into his conversational space.

"What's up in Washington?" Chan asked. "This election fiasco finally over?"

"Looks like it. Congress formally tallied the electoral college." Frank assumed his political speak, a reflex finely honed. He had no use for Chan, but for now had to put up with him for appearances' sake. "Let's hope the flack about butterfly ballots and mutilated chads is put to bed."

"You never told me what happened at yesterday's subcommittee meeting," Meredith said. Frank suspected that she wanted to avoid a rehash of the contested presidential race. "Frank chaired his first subcommittee meeting on Technology, Terrorism, and Government Information. It's an arm of the Judiciary Committee," she explained.

"What with the election debacle and Dad's funeral, I found it hard to concentrate on copyright infringement and online Internet issues."

"Think that Rumsfeld will be confirmed?" Chan asked. Frank wondered that his brother-in-law even knew that he was also on the Armed Forces Committee, now holding hearings.

"Probably," Frank said.

"Did Paul know him when he was CEO of Searle?" This, too, surprised Frank, that Chan knew enough about current affairs to ask that question. As a family doctor and the father of eight, all Chan seemed to do was answer hospital pages and wipe kids' noses.

"Yes, but they weren't close." Frank craned his neck as he spoke in response to unfamiliar voices at the front door. "Who are those people?"

All three turned as three strangers entered the room, flanking Dan, who looked wild-eyed and woozy. Could Dan have a drinking problem? Frank wondered. Then he realized that the strangers must be Dan's estranged wife and grown children.

Meredith scanned the room, her mouth an "O," her eyebrows raised. "Don't know."

Frank hadn't had time to brief her on his chat with Carl. Neither of them had met Dan's former family. Frank had to admit that the woman was a stunning Latin beauty and the young man and woman were attractive as well.

Dining room chairs supplemented the seating pattern in the vaulted living room to create a semicircle, and Carl asked that all take a seat. Meredith glanced at her watch, then leaned into Frank, "Showtime. With old man Schiller, 'on time' is late. But who are they?"

Frank shrugged, distracted by counting the chairs. He and Meredith sat down in two chairs next to each other. That left two empty chairs on his right. Carl took a place in the center, looking pathetically feeble. Frank figured that even with Dan's crew there should be twelve people. So why were there spaces for thirteen?

The room came to a hush as Carl opened with blah, blah, blah platitudes. *Get on with it, old man*, Frank mentally urged. All eyes turned toward the three strangers clustered next to Dan when Carl said, "Now, I'd like to make the formal introduction of Gina, Carissa, and Terrence Parnell. They were gracious enough to honor Paul's request to join us in blustery Philadelphia."

The two women smiled graciously, but the boy actually scowled. Frank noted that Dan's deeply tanned face now looked pasty and twisted.

"But before moving on, I have another family introduction," Carl continued. "Cardinal?"

Frank wanted to say something, to make a protest, to challenge this craziness, but before he could, his uncle rose to open the door leading to the library. Frank did not trust the old man and had always resented the close relationship he'd had with his father.

What happened next, Frank could never have anticipated in a million years. Stunned, he gasped as Cardinal Sean escorted a drop-dead gorgeous, young woman into the living room. The occupant of the remaining thirteenth chair? A vaguely familiar woman with long black hair and very black eyes? Very chic in a taupe suede suit, with matching stiletto heels and a triple rope of pearls. Frank knew how expensive they must be since he intended to buy something similar for Meredith. Then he identified her: Monica Monroe, *the* famous female vocalist, Grammy-award winner, and poster child of the media. The vocalist that Dad had specified for his funeral Mass. But there'd been lots of celebrities at the funeral: the Philadelphia cardinal, George and Barbara and Jeb Bush, Rosalyn and Jimmy Carter, Governor Ridge, Governor Pataki. So the superstar, Monica Monroe, did not seem out of the ordinary.

Frank glanced around at the others. Stunned faces all around.

"Cardinal, will you take over?" Carl broke the silence as Miss Monroe settled into the chair, crossed her incredible legs, and flipped raven hair off her face.

Cardinal Sean, renowned for his powerful oration, seemed uncertain, tentative. He stood, then he sat, then stood again. Finally he sat down.

What could this woman possibly be doing here? A woman whose latest CD release catapulted straight to the top of the charts. Whose performances were sold out as soon as they were announced. And just this morning, her stunning performance — "How Great Thou Art" and the "Ave Maria." After he'd given the eulogy, Frank had looked around to thank her for coming, but she'd already left. But what the hell was she doing here at the will reading?

"I know that this will come as quite a shock," Cardinal Sean began. "Why Monica is here. It may be difficult. I know it's difficult for her."

What was the old man talking about? We don't need a serenade.

"I'll get right to the point." Cardinal Sean's blue eyes lacked the usual sparkle, and he spoke shakily. "Monica is your father's daughter, by blood."

This was the limit — no way — this was absurd. Frank started to rise. Somebody had to put an end to this nonsense. He felt a surge of acid in the pit of his stomach. Then he felt Meredith tug at his sleeve.

"Sit down," she whispered through clenched teeth.

"She is the daughter of Nick and Denise Monroe by adoption," Cardinal Sean said. Frank squirmed under Meredith's hold, struggling to come to grips with this insanity. Then he sat back down. His uncle had the attention of all. Even Carla, who looked half-stoned, sat up straighter, staring in disbelief. As for Dan's Florida entourage, this was going to make the trip north more interesting.

"I've known Monica since she was an infant," Cardinal Sean resumed. "And now, at Paul's request, she's here as part of the Parnell family."

Cardinal Sean leaned over to pat Monica's hand as the superstar gazed silently ahead.

Was that smugness on her face? What kind of a fraud was she trying to pull?

Carl cleared his throat to speak. "I'm going to explain, as your father requested. Nine years after Kay died," he paused for Monica's benefit, "Kay was Paul's first wife."

Monica nodded her head in acknowledgment.

"Paul had an affair." Cardinal Sean looked first at Frank and then at Dan. "Frank and Dan, this was just after your grandparents died, and just before Paul met Vivian. The woman's name was Abby Ames."

Frank could feel his inheritance slipping out of his hands. He stiffened and Meredith pressed her shoulder into his as a gesture of support — or maybe warning.

"Miss Ames was a model in one of Keystone Pharma's advertising campaigns when Paul was president of the company." Carl spoke deliberately. "She was twenty-four, he, forty-seven. She became pregnant. Paul convinced her to have the baby. He provided for her until her death five years ago."

Frank's eyes bored into Monica.

"Abby realized that she was not cut out for motherhood," Carl continued, "and she left the infant with me. I contacted your uncle."

Cardinal Sean took up the story. "I had just been anointed bishop of Detroit, and had become acquainted with the Monroes. Nick and Denise were blessed with four sons. They had very much wanted a daughter, but Denise couldn't have more children. Well, let's just say that they were elated when I told them about the baby girl. They named the baby Monica, and as you can see she turned out to be a beautiful and incredibly talented young woman."

"Yes, she did," added Carl proudly. "And Monica, we thank you for being here today. I know you had doubts about coming."

The woman casually fingered her hair, but remained silent and expressionless.

"Monica has a marvelous family," Cardinal Sean continued. "Her father and brothers who adore her. And her fiancé. Someone you might know, the sportscaster, Pat Nelson."

With that Monica turned toward Cardinal Sean, her lips curving into the slightest of smiles. She uncrossed, then recrossed her legs.

"Although she has always known that she was adopted, Monica only recently learned that Paul was her father. She met him for the first time here, just after Thanksgiving."

"This may seem awkward for you all," Carl interrupted, "but I know you will welcome Monica into the Parnell family."

Silence from the assembled group met this announcement.

"So let's move on to your father's will."

"Excuse me," Frank interrupted. "With all due respect, this is quite a shock. Has anybody thought through the implications here? Miss Monroe is a big celebrity and I'm a senator. Paul Parnell, the perfect family man, having a secret affair, fathering a child he tried to hide. This could turn ugly. What about the public relations aspect of this story?"

"Frank, I brought that up with Paul." Carl seemed to have an answer for everything today. "He pointed out that with the right media spin it could enhance both of your careers."

"Right spin?" Frank clenched his jaw to keep from yelling.

"It was your father's dying wish," Cardinal Sean butted in, "to unite the family."

"Cardinal Sean? Do you understand what the tabloids will do with this? This woman's a paparazzi target."

"Yes, Frank, but maybe —" Cardinal Sean stopped mid-sentence. His focus seemed to wander and he grimaced. All were silent until he composed himself.

"Look everybody, this is not easy for me." Monica's voice rang crystal clear. "I didn't ask for this. I have a family. I'm here because of a promise I made to a wonderful old man, a man I just recently learned was my biological father. Yes, Senator, I think that our PR people should control this, but mostly I'm worried about my father. I don't want him hurt because of —" she scanned the room "— all of you."

"We understand," Rory gushed.

"I suggest we move forward with the reading of the will." Carl reached for a sheaf of papers. "I am going to do this exactly as your father instructed."

There was no response. No one stirred.

Come on Carl, Frank urged silently.

"I also want you to know that several attorneys have carefully examined the will. Paul was lucid when he signed this, and I can assure you he spent a great deal of time, energy, and effort on his Last Will and Testament."

What does that mean? Frank did not like the undertone here. But then he told himself to stop being paranoid, to just listen. His dad would not betray him.

"Once diagnosed with incurable cancer, Paul had plenty of time to consolidate his investments. He wanted execution of the will to be as straightforward as possible. The assets are clearly defined. Tax implications have been optimized for the benefit of the estate. He leaves no debt. He did not believe in life insurance. A ballpark analysis of the after-tax assets of the estate amounts to almost two billion dollars, excluding real estate and personal effects."

There was a low groan. It came from Dan who was slumped in his chair, head in his hands. What was that about, thought Frank After all these years, his reclusive brother gave a damn about money?

Everyone in the room tried not to stare at Dan as his former wife leaned over and whispered something to him. No one heard what she said, but everybody could hear his hoarse reply, "I'll be okay."

Carl proceeded to read the will verbatim, his hands continuing to shake.

His father kept two houses and an apartment, each with caretakers. Frank was not surprised as Carl confirmed that each would be getting a flat sum, much more generous than they deserved, but typical of his dad. To his brother, Cardinal Sean, Paul Parnell left fifty million dollars, which would no doubt go to Detroit diocesan charities. Then the will dealt with the grandchildren, naming each in order of age: Dan's two, the eight Stevens kids, including the three adoptees, and Frank's own daughter. Each kid — eleven in all — got a million dollars.

"What the heck!" flew out of Frank's mouth.

"Frank," said Carl, as if admonishing a child.

Frank glared at Rory and Chan, disgusted by the way they sat teary-eyed, holding hands. One million for my kid. Eight million for theirs. No wonder Rory had spent so much time with Dad. He'd been too sick to see through her motives.

Carl went on. Frank heard, "Gina Parnell, five million dollars."

"No," Gina said from across the table. "I want nothing."

Frank glanced at Meredith. She'd been waiting for Carl to name her next, but he hadn't. This was getting worse by the minute. Stay calm, Frank told himself. It's a two-billion-dollar estate. Less than seventy million had been dispersed so far. Only one of those millions was his, or at least his daughter's. Eight for Rory's family. Seven for Dan's. Fifty for Cardinal Sean. Then Carl read on about the money for the minor children being kept in trust. So he couldn't even get at that.

Frank calculated as he clutched the arms of his chair. One point nine billion dispersed among Dad's four real kids should add up to five hundred million each, give or take a few. Not a problem, Frank told himself, just hang in there while the old man reads on. Later you can look into the matter of Dad's sanity. But no way could he let Rory get away with this. From the moment she intruded into their life, she'd been manipulating his father. Dad, who'd never had time for him and Dan, just couldn't do enough for Vivian's daughter, Rory. And what about this Monica apparition? What was she trying to walk away with?

What was Carl saying about real estate? The Gulfstream aircraft and the A-Star helicopter? Going into a trust? Funded by an annuity to cover maintenance for each property, including three automobiles for each, except the Manhattan apartment. For use by all of us? Hiring a trust administrator? Somebody named Peggy Putnam? Next to him, Frank could feel Meredith tense up, and when he looked down he could see that his knuckles were white.

Frank didn't remember exactly what Carl said next. Something about Paul's having dispersed all of Kay's and Vivian's jewelry before he died. He vaguely remembered the exquisite pieces Dad had given Meredith.

"So what?" he heard himself mutter.

Carl, sitting there, looked too old, too tired, and too shaky to handle such a huge estate. Meredith should be Dad's executor, not that old goat. Outside, Frank could see that the clouds had descended and heavy blobs of snow had started to fall.

He leaned toward Meredith. "Can you believe this bullshit?"

"Not now, Frank," she said, meaning, *Don't lose your cool and say something you'll be sorry for.* Then she added, "Check out Dan."

Frank looked to his brother to see tears starting to trickle down his cheeks.

Frank shrugged his shoulder and pulled his concentration back to Carl, wondering whether the shakiness in his voice had anything to do with the Parkinson's. Could it be affecting his vocal cords? He had to pay close attention to what the old man was saying. His future was at stake.

"Before I go on, I want to remind you that the sheer magnitude of the estate will require probate. Once I am officially appointed executor by the court, guardians must be established for the minors. You will all get copies of the will and all probate documents as well as specifics of the hearing on the petition to probate the will. Soon thereafter, I will provide a list of assets as required and you will all receive a copy. I will also engage the necessary tax and estate attorneys."

A lengthy pause followed as Carl shuffled the papers in front of him. His dyed black hair accentuated the grayness of his skin. It occurred to Frank that he might not make it through the probate process.

"I have one other assignment in addition to executor, that of trustee. Paul has established a trust, which he has funded with the remainder of his assets."

Frank let out a low whistle, and all eyes turned toward him. Was this it? Would he get the whole thing?

"As you know," Carl continued, "a trust provides much more discretion for the grantor. It also provides privacy since, unlike probate, a trust does not need to be disclosed to anyone except the trustee and the beneficiaries. Nevertheless, Paul wanted the contents of the trust disclosed to those here present."

Frank and Meredith had each been in the top ten of their class at Yale Law. Frank had gone to the district attorney's office in Philadelphia as a jumping off point for politics, but Meredith, as a senior partner in Donnor, Clark and Schiller, was an authority on estate and tax issues.

"I am going to read verbatim as to how your father plans to distribute the proceeds of the trust." Carl fumbled to find the page.

"Plans?" Frank wondered why Carl was using the present tense.

"The assets of the trust will be distributed to the following beneficiaries according to the provisions so dictated and disclosed below. The beneficiaries are my six children, irrespective of blood or legal relationship. Specifically they are Carla Parnell, Ashley Parnell, Rory Stevens, Senator Francis Parnell, Daniel Parnell, and Monica Monroe. All are to be treated equally under the provision of the trust. Each is to receive outright a million dollars."

"What?" Frank blurted. "How ludicrous!" *One million of a two-billion dollar estate?*

He wanted to shout out that his father must have been totally nuts, that he vowed to contest this insanity, but again Meredith's firm grasp on his arm held him back. Without Meredith, Frank knew he would have blown his stack right there.

"Frank, please be patient. I'm not finished." Carl shifted his weight and slowly found his place in the document. Frank could feel the reproachful eyes of his uncle on him.

"What I'm going to read next are the words of your father. What is communicated here comes from the depth of his soul. Well, why don't I stop editorializing and get on with it?"

"Yes, why don't you?" Frank mumbled as he perused the semicircle. Dan didn't appear to be listening. Gina sat next to him, quiet and serene. Ashley appeared alert and interested. Carla shifted restlessly in her chair. Rory and Chan were trying to pretend they were bereaved. And beside him, Monica sat silently examining her new family. The woman must be worth millions; she didn't need more.

Carl started reading from an ordinary sheet of paper. Dad's last message. Drivel about contrition and hope. How after Vivian died and he was diagnosed with cancer that he had this epiphany. How he faced his failures as a father.

> For Dan and Frank, I wasn't there after their mother died — too busy with my career. For Rory, I should have pushed for a legal adoption. For Ashley and Carla, I won't be around to see them mature. And for Monica, I regret not being a part of her life."

Ashley and Rory started to sob. Chan put his arm around Rory. Meredith kept her hand clamped on Frank's arm. Carl read on:

> In the end, only values and character count. Not money, not fame, not career. Here's where I fear I have failed you.

"Weird," Meredith mouthed to Frank.

> I kept asking myself: is there a way to use my financial success to help correct my failures?

Carl paused for a sip of water. The room was absolutely quiet. Even Dan and Carla seemed to be tracking this ridiculous effort at a confession.

> To sort out a code of values, I created a personal credo. This will be my legacy to you, that these values be passed from generation to generation.

So much money at stake and his dad was going on about values? Smack in the aftermath of the Bush-Gore screw up? The inauguration just two weeks away? The one hundred seventh Congress in session? His committees — Armed Forces, Judicial, and Intelligence — all with hectic hearing schedules? And he was sitting here listening to drivel on family values.

Carl read slowly:

My value system has four parts God, family, community, and profession.

First, God. It wasn't until the last year of my life that I realized that faith is our most treasured gift, our absolute anchor. Faith is not just a private affair; its very essence is rooted in a public acknowledgment so that it can be passed from generation to generation.

Second, family. I should have spent more time with each of you in your formative years. I left too much of the responsibility to Kay, and then to Vivian. I let my professional ego interfere with dedication to my family. For this I beg your forgiveness.

"That's not true, Dad," Ashley sobbed. Carla leaned against her with a "Shush," and Meredith patted her hand.

Not you, Ashley, Frank almost said aloud. You were Dad's special little shadow. Remember the time he took you on that world tour in the company plane?

Carl read on:

Third, community, By founding the Parnell Foundation, I want to give back to the world community that had been so generous to me. I trust that the foundation will flourish under your leadership and that you will extend the abundance of the family widely and generously.

So far, no mention of funding his political career, Frank thought. How could he afford to worry about the world community? Maybe someday, but certainly not right now. Frank could see that the rest of them were eating this up, especially Rory who liked to consider herself the do-gooder of the century.

Fourth, professional, career, and financial responsibility. You have had access to the best in education and to the family's financial resources. Now you will need to demonstrate responsible management of your own funds.

Carl stopped for a moment. The women, with the exception of Monica and Meredith, were fumbling with tissues, and Dan still looked shaky. Frank watched aghast as Carl looked pointedly at Cardinal Sean. No, he wanted to scream. Could Dad have left all that money to the church? But the cardinal simply nodded and Carl continued to read.

It is my last wish that you embrace these values as your own. As an incentive, the allocation of all assets in this trust will rest on your demonstration of these values.

What kind of a scam was this? Frank's mind reeled as he watched the two old men exchange a knowing look. Everybody else wore a quizzical expression.

As further encouragement, I have arranged for a test to measure your personal acceptance of these four credo values.

Carl paused and reached for a glass of water.

Carl Schiller is the trustee of the trust. He has a thorough understanding of my intent, he will administer this "test" and score it according to the guidelines I have provided. He will also give you the personal note that I left for each of you.

Trust? Credo? Test? Personal note? Frank struggled to process what he'd just heard.

The test will be given one year from now. Remaining assets of the trust will be distributed according to the results.

Frank's mind flew to the date, January 6, 2002. He almost missed the next part.

Should collective scores not justify distribution of the entire trust, any remainder will default to the Parnell Foundation.

Frank, who hardly ever used obscenities, not even in his head, could think only, "I'm fucked."

Carl's hand's shook more intensely as he read further.

I hope you all know how much I love you and how deeply I hope to inspire you to embrace your legacy.

"That's the end," announced Carl, "except for administrative details."

Frank spoke first. He didn't care if he sounded sarcastic or obnoxious.

"Wow, what a reading, Carl," he began. "Is this real? Or some kind of a joke?"

"No, Frank, it's not a joke."

"Well, certainly it's not legal. Certainly it's not sane. Get your firm on this and get it sorted out. This is craziness."

Meredith increased the pressure of her hand on Frank's leg.

Nobody else said a word. Frank looked toward Ashley. She had more common sense than the other three. She sat biting a fingernail, thoughtful, but not upset. She wasn't going to jump into this.

"At the end," Cardinal Sean broke the stunned silence, "your father was desperate to go back in time and focus on the values that he now realized were so important. But of course, he couldn't, so he decided on this type of incentive to encourage you all to make positive change in your lives."

"Look, Cardinal Sean," Frank interrupted, in no mood for a homily, "Dad was obviously senile. You said 'desperate,' right? 'Wanting to go back in time.' That's crazy talk. All I'm saying is that this trust needs to be contested. Okay? Now I suggest we let Meredith handle it with Carl. That we sell the properties, and get on with our lives."

"Let me assure you," Carl stated. "that your father took every precaution against the type of allegation you're suggesting."

"Frank, I know you're unhappy, but Dad was not senile," Rory blurted. "His thinking was very clear until he lapsed into the coma at the very end."

"Look, Rory, I don't think you're the one to get involved here. Is this why you insisted on spending so much time with him the month before he died? I wouldn't be surprised if you concocted this whole farce."

Rory turned several shades of red.

"Frank, we're all in a state; I know you didn't mean that," Chan said, starting to rise from his chair. Frank wondered what the hell his stocky brother-in-law was going to do. Punch him out?

"It's okay, Chan." Rory tugged his arm and her husband sat back down. "Somebody had to stay with Dad. Ashley was in school. It wasn't about money."

"For God's sake," said Chan. "Don't you realize how tough it was on Rory? Spending all that time away from the kids to be with Paul at the end?"

"We all appreciated what you did, Rory." Ashley spoke up, "You were inspirational."

"Inspirational?" Frank couldn't hold back the sarcasm. "Don't any of you understand what's going on here?"

"Would it be okay if I said something?" Frank had almost forgotten that Monica was sitting next to him. She didn't belong here, he thought, and he planned to check out that story about Dad and this woman. Insist on DNA. No two ways about it, she was not raised as a Parnell. She had been legally adopted by another family, and she surely didn't need money.

"Certainly," said Carl, hoping, Frank guessed, that she might reverse the downward spiral.

"I came here today to fulfill a promise to a man I wish I'd known better. I think that what Mr. Parnell tried to do for his family before he died is so wonderful. To have thought all this through about how we can all become better people. I come away inspired and impressed."

You picked up a cool million bucks and are just greedy for more, Frank thought, but didn't say.

"But," Monica continued, "I want to make this perfectly clear. I am renouncing my inheritance. The money Mr. Schiller mentioned I will sign over to the Catholic Charities in Detroit."

Cardinal Sean beamed at Monica. His lucky day, thought Frank. Not a problem for the little lady, raking in megabucks from concerts and CDs. What a disingenuous gesture. It made Frank want to throw up.

"Monica, that's most generous," said Carl, putting down the sheaf of papers. "We have now concluded the official business."

Frank was too stunned to notice that Carla nearly tripped over his feet in her haste to leave the room. Ashley jumped up to follow as Carl concluded, "I will be in contact to give each of you your father's personal message and to answer any questions. Now, Cardinal Sean, would you please conclude with a prayer?"

Frank tuned out as his uncle droned on about Dad, his soul, and how we would all carry forward his brilliant legacy. At the final sign of the cross, Meredith steered Frank out of the house. Frank's parting remark: a mumbled, "I will bury Rory."

CHAPTER FIVE

Muting the Rolling Stones CD, Carla grabbed the cordless phone. "Yes, this is Carla Parnell."

The gravelly voice on the phone introduced herself as Miss Lopez from the New York City Health Department, and then asked for her confidential code.

Carla felt a surge of nausea. Maybe she should just hang up. Last week, Hank, a guy she used to boink — before Bunky — unloaded that he was HIV positive. A sweet guy — straight, or so she'd thought — trying to make it as a model.

"Face it, we're high risk," Hank told her with tears in his eyes. "What I understand, if you got the virus, you'd better know it. Like Magic Johnson. He's got it. Right? And he's gonna be okay."

Sex and drugs. Carla's friend, Jan, the one who'd taken her to her one and only Narcotics Anonymous meeting, had said that there was a connection — a cross addiction — between sex and drugs. Parties, drugs, sex, blackouts. Before Carla came into her million from her father, she'd been so desperate for money that she'd signed on to an escort service as "Roxie Randall." It hadn't been too bad, better than turning tricks in the streets.

So with Hank's urging, she'd had the HIV test, and a hepatitis test as the Health Department suggested.

"Frances of Assisi." It took her a moment to remember the code she'd made up. "Frances" for her middle name and "Assisi" for the patron saint of animals. "Do you have the results?"

"You'll have to come in to see one of the counselors."

Carla's knees buckled and her voice sounded tiny. "Why?"

"Routine protocol," said the scrappy voice. "We're open nine to noon and one to four."

Carla sank back against the pillows. Normally, she'd consider her private doctor. She had great health insurance — one of the Parnell family perks — but with that Peggy Putnam bitch, who managed all the Parnell affairs, sticking her nose in everybody's business, she couldn't take the risk. Just the thought of that Putnam woman made Carla cringe. What right did she have to tell her what she could and could not do? When Carla had complained to Uncle Carl, it must have backfired because Putnam started to make her life a living hell, scrutinizing every penny she charged to the Parnell house account.

But Carla knew that she could count on her housekeeper, Sara Waring, to stick by her. Sara had worked for the Parnells ever since Carla had been a kid. It had been Carla, not Ashley, who had been there when Dad interviewed Sara sixteen years ago. Carla would always remember that day. Her mom was supposed to do the interview, but she had an emergency with a patient. So Dad had picked up Carla at school, and they'd driven to Manhattan. Just Carla and her dad. Not even a limo driver.

Ever since, Carla knew she'd been Sara's favorite. A tiny woman with mocha-colored skin, deep brown eyes, and black curls that she always wore piled on top of her head, she lived with her husband and mother in the Bronx. She commuted by subway, and stayed in the maid's quarters if they needed her for evening affairs or over the weekend. Without Sara, Carla wasn't sure how she'd survive. Sara protected her from her family and the assholes in her building.

As Carla waited in line for the slovenly receptionist to check her into the health department, she had second thoughts. Fellow patients were slouched in rows of metal chairs all crunched together. She thought of her mother's cheery cardiology office. Mom wouldn't believe this shitty dump. But then again, she wouldn't believe many of the places where Carla hung out.

Waiting to be called into one of the cubicles, Carla almost threw up as the odors — disinfectant, body odor, urine — turned her stomach. Why hadn't she just used cash for a private doctor? But since Bunky had moved into her apartment, he handled the money and she didn't want to scare him. Unless she had the virus, then she knew that she'd have to tell him. Would she have the guts to do that?

"Miss Parnell?" She'd given the clinic her real name. Dressed like the other derelicts, shabby, and not too clean, she couldn't see anyone making a connection with the well-known Parnell family. "You can see the counselor now. Step right in."

"Miss Parnell." A plump, gray-haired lady pointed to a chair in a cubicle. "You're HIV test came out positive," she said straight out. "And you tested negative for hepatitis."

"Oh fuck," Carla slumped back into the chair. So Hank *had* given it to her. Or was it the drugs? "Are you sure? Could there be a mistake?" Floundering for the right question, the one that would give her hope, "A false positive? Oh shit."

The woman kept talking, but Carla's head was in a fog. Somewhere in that fog, her parents were out there, trying to tell her something, but she couldn't make out what they were saying.

"Talk louder," she blurted.

"Miss Parnell?" The fat lady waved a hand in front of her face like a windshield wiper. "Are you following me?"

"What am I going to do?" She came back in focus. Her parents' faces faded away, exposing reality.

"Like I said, you can see a private doctor, or enroll in the HIV/AIDS clinic we run here. Remember, you're not the first person to get HIV. I suggest you join a support group. Learn from other people's experiences."

Carla didn't respond. The woman continued, "You'll have to make some tough choices. About whom to tell."

"What?" Carla's eyes filled with tears as she considered. Bunky? Did Bunky have it too?

The counselor fidgeted, shuffled some papers, and looked up at the wall clock.

Carla realized that she was taking up too much fucking time. Starting to cry, she groped inside her purse for a tissue and blew her nose.

"Oh shit." Carla stared at the bright red spot on the tissue. The matronly woman reached into a drawer and handed her a fresh wad, not offering to take the bloody one. Carla knew her nose was all fucked up from cocaine.

"You must tell your sex partners and anybody you've shared a needle with."

She had to be kidding.

"They need to know," the woman droned, "so they don't go infect others and so they can get treatment themselves if they're positive."

"How long have I had this?" Carla asked, but her question was ignored.

"Regular medical care is a must." The woman's voice made Carla want to put a stranglehold on her pudgy neck. "Modern drugs can keep the HIV virus under control. The drugs are complicated. You need to find a doctor with experience." The woman let her gaze linger on Carla's emerald and diamond ring, the one her dad had given her when she'd turned twenty-one. "Or sign in at the Health Department Clinic. I have a packet of information for you. But my advice is to tell others. Those who you think will support you. This is something you'll have to live with the rest of your life. It'll be your responsibility to take care of yourself and the more people who know of your illness, the easier your problem will be."

Carla sat there, unable to move. *Tell people? Support?*

"You think about it. Read the information in this package." The woman got up and handed her a manila envelope. Still, Carla couldn't move.

"I have to see my next client now," the woman finally said. "Here, take this." She reached for a sheet of paper from a pile on her desk. "The ten most important questions to ask your doctor."

As Carla headed out into the noisy, crowded streets of midtown Manhattan, she let herself be jostled by pedestrians, aimless, afraid to be alone. She ended up at the crack house where she used to hang out before she got the million from her dad's estate. She did a line of coke. It helped, but when she came down, she still had HIV. She came off the high slowly, not crashing like she sometimes did. Through the lone dingy window, she could see that it was dark, and she decided to go home. She would tell Bunky. Maybe he had it, too, and had never told her. Wouldn't that be sweet? Anyway, that counselor was right. Bunky did have a right to know. But no one else.

The residence on Park Avenue seemed empty when she stepped off the elevator into the elegance of the apartment's seventeen rooms. Sara would have left for home, but where was Bunky? She searched for a note. Not finding one, she headed for her bedroom. Weary and scared, she sank onto the down comforter, and without premeditation, called the number that she had memorized when she was in kindergarten.

"Hello?" A deep male voice.

"May I speak to Ashley?"

"She can't come to the phone right now," the man said. "I'll be happy to take a message."

Must be the guy that Rory had told her about — the doctor, twice Ashley's age. How she'd met this guy right after Dad died. How he'd fucking moved in with her. How totally un-Ashley. Carla had been intending to call Ashley and get it straight from her, but, well, she hadn't.

"This is Carla, her sister, may I speak with her, please?"

"Can she call you in the morning. We're running late."

"No, she can't fucking call me in the morning." Not caring if she sounded hysterical, Carla screamed. "I need to talk to her now."

"Very well," the voice said.

"Ashley, my love, you have a phone call," Carla could hear in the background, "your sister — No, Carla."

"Carla!" Ashley picked up in an instant. "Hi, honey. You just caught us. Conrad's taking me to dinner at Le Bec Fin. Very posh, but it is Valentine's Day. Remember Dad used to take Mom there on special occasions?"

"Ashley —" The words would not come out, that she had HIV. Suddenly Carla cared what Ashley thought. She'd always lived in her big sister's shadow. How could she now tell her how far down into the muck she'd sunk.

"What is it, Carla?" Ashley's tone changed to serious. "Is something wrong?"

"No," Carla said, stemming the flow of tears that needed to be un-leashed. "I just wanted to say Happy Valentine's Day and make sure that you were all right." Shit, it was Valentine's Day?

Ashley lowered her voice. "I am better than all right," she confided. "You know, all these years, I've never had a 'Valentine' — unlike my gor-geous little sister who had more than her share. Right?"

True, Ashley had been too busy studying. No time for fun. Too busy for dates. Too busy to get HIV.

"I'm happy for you," Carla managed, disheartened. She couldn't tell Ashley, not tonight.

"Hey, I've gotta run. You can't believe how many strings Conrad had to pull to get a reservation tonight." After a pause, Ashley's voice soft-ened, "Carla, we do have to get together. Sometime soon. Okay?"

"Sure," Carla mumbled, recognizing the threatening undertone. *We all know how bad you've fucked up your life.*

Hanging up the phone, Carla lay back and wept. Wept for her mother whom she still missed desperately. The rest of the family, Frank and Meredith, to be exact, thought her too indulgent with Carla, but they were wrong. When Mom was alive, Carla had someone to talk to. Mom always understood. Carla knew that if her mother were alive, she would never have let her sink so far.

Carla dialed Rory's number. Rory had been thirteen when Carla was born, a second mom to her. But Carla figured if she told Rory, Rory'd tell Chan. Chan was a doctor. He'd know what to do. But would they tell the others? No, she couldn't face the shame.

"Hello?" A bright young voice. "Stevens' residence."

"Becky? Or Emily?" Carla asked, trying to sound normal.

"It's Em. Hey, Aunt Carla?"

"Yes," Carla said, desperate to hear Rory's voice, so much like Mom's. "Em, can I speak to your mom?"

"She's not here," Emily said. "Dad took her out. Somewhere in Doylestown. 'Cause he's on call. Nobody wanted to trade on Valentine's Day. You gotta hot date tonight, Aunt Carla?" Both Rory's older girls liked to swap gossip with Carla about the fashion scene in New York. Styles, hot models, teen stuff, but Carla let the phone slip into her lap.

Next thing she heard was that annoying beeping. As she reached to hang up the phone, she saw the scribbled note on her pillow. Her engraved personal stationery, Bunky's hand.

Meet me at the Buzz Club, Valentine. Let's party.
Love ya, babe,
Bunk

With a sinking emptiness, Carla crossed the room to her desk. Her hands shaking, she fondled the bottle of sleeping pills she used to take her down from the highs. Then she cursed. Only two left. Had there been a full bottle? She didn't remember, but she knew she would have taken them all, then and there.

She was shaking now. Making her way to her closet, she stumbled face first into a hanging rack of dresses. Still standing, grasping a handful of garments, she selected one, a slinky red sequined number, and yanked it off the hanger. She had to find Bunky. She needed something now and Bunky would take care of her. Carla's cravings surged as she wriggled into the dress and groped for a pair of spike heels. She needed to get fucked up. That's all she could think, I need to get fucked up.

CHAPTER SIX

"Senator, Mr. Schiller's here." Matt Cleveland plunked a thick dossier on Frank's desk in the Senate Russell Office Building and started to unwrap a Snickers bar. "Right on time. Six o'clock."

"I'm beat. Two straight days of closed hearings on intelligence matters. Scary stuff coming on the heels of the Armed Forces Committee. All I need right now is that old man." Frank looked up and ran his fingers through his hair. "And get that candy bar out of my sight. Here I am trying to stick to the Atkins diet, living on cheese and no-sugar Jello."

"Don't forget you're meeting with Senator McCain. Seven in the Dirksen Building." No sympathy from Matt.

"Let's hope this does the trick." Frank patted the dossier, then reached into a drawer for his stash of cashews.

He was crunching a few when Matt ushered Carl into his office. Frank offered the usual amenities. Did he want coffee? Tea? He held out the jar of cashews. Carl politely declined all as he settled into the client chair opposite Frank's polished mahogany desk. Frank assessed Carl's tremor and judged it to be no worse than two months earlier, but nevertheless he felt a certain guilt in making the old man travel to D.C., when he could have seen him in Philadelphia the next day.

Frank asked about Phyllis. Carl asked about Frank's congressional agenda. To get off on the right track, Frank indulged the lawyer by confiding that he was worried about national security. That there needed to be a loop connecting intelligence with technology, with the armed forces, with immigration. Carl told Frank that Phyllis was just getting over bronchitis.

Then Frank got down to business.

"I have retained the law firm of Stewart and Stewart to create a challenge to Dad's will," he began. "I think it's in the best interest of the family. I assume you knew I'd go ahead and do this, but I wanted to let you know in person before I filed, out of courtesy. You'll find the arguments well presented." Frank pushed the brief across his desk as if he expected Carl to pick it up. Carl didn't. He just wrinkled his face, smoothed back his dyed hair, and stared back across the desk.

"You'll see the premises. That Dad suffered from dementia. Disabled by the cancer. Metastases all over."

"Except the brain." Frank felt Carl's eyes bore into his. "I'm sure you've checked the medical records."

"Yes," he admitted, "but —"

"I told you before. A challenge will not prevail. Your father took precautions. I assure you, Frank, that this course of action will ruin you politically."

"What is this, Carl, a threat?" Frank's voice rose. "Because there's more. No question that Dad was under the undue influence of an avaricious stepdaughter with no legal rights to his estate."

"Stop right there, Frank," Carl said, taking out a white starched handkerchief and mopping his brow. "I must be coming down with that virus Phyllis had."

Now came the tricky part. Frank had decided to disclose his challenge to Carl's competence, and the conflict of interest inherent in the financial gain he'd enjoy as executor of such an unorthodox trust. Frank had researched Parkinson's disease, and his experts had assured him that dementia is common. In fact, Carl wasn't talking as if he were demented, but Frank's experts promised to make a good case that the old man's competence could be questioned based on statistics. A tricky maneuver as Carl was managing partner of Donnor and Schiller. Meredith was a senior partner at the firm, but Frank figured that he had no choice, and his wife wholeheartedly agreed.

"No, Carl, I won't stop. There is the matter of your integrity, I mean how can you be capable of unbiased judgment? Then there's your health."

Carl stared across the desk. His black eyes did not flicker as they focused on Frank, and his tremor seemed to have disappeared.

"It's all in here," Frank said, pushing the dossier toward him. "Stewart and Stewart, firm here in D.C."

"Listen carefully, Frank," Carl steeled his voice. "I advise you to reread the letter that Paul left for you. Read it very carefully."

"What?" Frank had almost forgotten that rambling note.

"Read it," Carl repeated firmly. "Your father's will has been reviewed not only by my firm, but by specialty firms in Washington and New York City. I repeat, a challenge will not be successful and the process will be a nightmare for you and the family."

"As far as I'm concerned, I don't have a family, except for my wife and child. I'm doing this so I can launch a successful presidential campaign. Just as my father wanted. I would have expected to have your help and the help of my family. No, I'm not standing by —"

"Try to understand. Your father did what he thought was right. Now put this aside." Carl pushed the dossier back toward Frank, unopened. "Reread your father's message to you and prepare to excel along the lines he laid out. The four tenets of his credo, his legacy to you. If you want that money, this is what you must do. It's the only way. Frank, I have never lied to you, never misled you."

"You've got to be kidding! You set this thing up so you could be in control. Control of the family you never had. You always were jealous of my father. You, with no kids of your own — coercing a dying old man?"

"Frank, you can't afford a political mistake."

A jolt of acid hit Frank's stomach and he reached inside his shirt pocket for the roll of Pepcid Complete. What right did this old man have, preaching to him?

Carl rose and headed for the door in his shuffling gait. "I'm sure you're busy," he said. Frank did not rise, and Carl turned. "Frank, things that are said in the heat of passion are best forgotten. I understand your frustration. For my part I intend to go on as if this conversation never took place. But there is one thing —"

Frank stood, dumbfounded, refusing to let the lawyer get the best of him.

"Carla," Schiller said. "I'm afraid that she's gone downhill. Peggy Putnam has a running list of complaints, but yesterday I received a frantic call from Sara Waring. You know how levelheaded Sara is and how loyal."

"We all know Carla's using drugs," Frank said coldly.

"Today the apartment manager called to tell me they're starting eviction proceedings. He claims she's bringing in 'undesirables.' Using the service elevator, and —"

"And what?" Frank demanded. His impatience escalated. First the threat to his career and now Carla tarnishing the Parnell name.

"Allegations that she had been providing sex in exchange for letting her friends up. The night guard got fired. It's a mess."

"For crying out loud, I can't afford this type of behavior."

"That's why I'm telling you, Frank. Best that you take care of this. Maybe that psychiatrist that Ashley has been seeing can give us some advice. Carla needs help."

"I'll have Meredith look into it," he said.

Carl left without another word, closing the door behind him. Immediately, Frank called Meredith. "Get her out of the meeting," he demanded of her secretary.

"Frank, what's wrong?"

"I didn't give him the brief. He scared the hell out of me. A threat. *Political ruin* was his terminology."

"Don't you think he's just reacting to the veiled, or not so veiled, allegations of his ineptitude?"

"No, I think that it was a real threat. That they anticipated us doing something like this and they got a shitload of lawyers to make it ironclad."

"Shitload?" Meredith remarked and Frank imagined her eyebrow shooting up. No obscenities. No coarse language. Something his dad said on the exact day Frank told him he wanted to run for office. Not even in private, he said. Keep it out of your vocabulary. Otherwise it'll slip out when you least expect. And Meredith usually called Frank on it when he slipped.

"Sorry. I'm telling you, he put it out as a threat. He said to read Dad's letter again. Follow the guidance and we get the money. This was a threat, a warning."

"I'll fly in tonight, Frank," she promised. "We'll figure out what to do next."

"Will you bring a copy of Dad's absurd note? We need to read it again together. And when you get here, I'll fill you in on what the old man said about Carla. More problems."

"'Dear Frank,'" Meredith read. Her short dark hair was wet from the torrents of rain that enveloped the East Coast. She'd taken the Amtrak Acela from Philadelphia rather than wait for weather clearance for the Gulfstream. Changing out of her dusky blue business suit, she threw on a terry bathrobe and accepted a snifter of brandy, as she and Frank situated themselves on twin oversized ottomans in front of the fireplace. Rain continued to pelt the front window, and she hesitated as thunder shook the room.

> You have made me so proud. A United States senator. If only your mother and your grandparents could have been here to share such a grand accomplishment. I can only believe that you will use your tremendous influence to promote peace and prosperity for our country and the world.
>
> I reflect on your childhood with feelings of inadequacy. If only I had spent more time with you when you were a young boy. If only I had spent more time with your mother. Maybe she would not have taken that fateful trip to Bermuda, leaving you without a mother and with a father overly absorbed in his career. When we became a real family with Vivian, you were already a young man.

"A real family?" Frank sneered. "A new family, yes."
Meredith put her arm on Frank's shoulder and read on,

> If you focus on these values, you will strengthen your appeal to the American people. Just think, my son, president of the United States. A dream that you and I and Meredith have shared. To accomplish this, I am confident that you will take this legacy seriously.

This is what I want for you: ethics and compassion as a senator; dedication to family; commitment to the community, both personal and financial; celebration of your faith, Catholicism, and for Meredith, Judaism. I understand you may prefer that your inheritance be immediately available, but I don't think that would be to your advantage. Carl understands my motivations, so please respect his advice and counsel. He has handled all aspects of the estate with extensive legal consultation. The trust that I have established is innovative, perhaps controversial, but it is absolutely legal.

"I read that as a threat," Meredith said. "Especially after your meeting with Carl today. He must have something set to go, should you contest. Maybe it's a public-relations campaign. Like headlines: Senator Parnell contests will — charges that old man was incompetent, crazy, or whatever sensational sound bites those vultures can dream up. Make you look avaricious — ungrateful. Politically, I don't think we'd survive it."

"So what are we going to do?" Frank sounded petulant and he knew it. "We had Stewart and Stewart prepare the basis for contest."

"But, honey, they weren't predicting success," she reminded him. "Said they'd do their best, but —"

"Carl refused to accept it, even to read it. If only someone else in the family would jump on this. But no, they respect Daddy's wishes. For crying out loud, the rest of them don't need the money."

"So we'll do it his way." Meredith reached over to smooth his hair. "Go through the motions. Pass the sham test."

"Like I'm not busy enough. Now I've got to play a high-stakes charade. Family patriarch. Pillar of the community. Lay leader of the church. Might as well sign me up for canonization."

Meredith shrugged. "Nice to know I have permission to be Jewish. Carl must have thrown that in. Your dad never resented me, but your uncle never approved of our marriage."

"The family's a mess," Frank said, changing the subject to Carla's apartment crisis. "We need to get her into a rehab clinic."

"Yes. Somewhere very discreet."

"Maybe she'll just kill herself," Frank said, resenting the family's dysfunction interrupting his quest. "She overdoses. We suppress the cause of death. We have one less contender."

Meredith stared at him. "Frank, I can't believe you said that."

"Yeah, yeah. Back to our situation. So we do all the goody-goody stuff like we're the champions of Dad's insane credo? Pass that test with flying colors? Heck, we can do anything for one year. We may even get to like our new lifestyle."

"I think it's the only way to get the lion's share," Meredith said.

"So we'll put together a plan to ace the test. May have to take acting lessons to pull it off."

"There's something else I've been thinking about, Frank," Meredith said, screwing up her face as she did when something important was on her mind.

"What?"

"The Parnell Foundation."

"What about it?" Frank's mind raced to plan the tactics of their new strategy. He needed Meredith to stay focused.

"What if I left my position at Donnor and Schiller and became the chairman of the board?"

"What?" Frank was incredulous. Meredith was a tough lawyer, through and through. She couldn't just walk away from an equity partnership.

"Think about it," she said. "The foundation assets exceed two billion. Think of the political clout that goes with allocation of all that money. Your dad never bothered to leverage the foundation, not even during your senatorial race."

Clearly, Meredith had given this some thought. Frank was impressed. What a lush playing field for Meredith to marshal her superior manipulative skills.

"Who could be better than I?" Meredith was on a roll. "I'm an attorney — a plus. I'm the daughter-in-law of the beloved founder — how perfect. I will step down from my day job to concentrate totally on the foundation — a statement of dedication. We make the case that Carl is so busy managing Paul's estate that he's overextended."

"You're going to walk away from the million plus you're pulling in at the firm? After how hard you've worked?" Half jokingly, Frank added, "Remember my salary's capped at a hundred-fifty grand."

"I'll take a leave of absence. It'll be an investment for the future. If we control the foundation and you ace that test, we'll be where we want to be. Think two thousand eight. Two terms — that's two thousand sixteen. We'll only be sixty then, and who knows what we'll do next?"

"Yeah," Frank could feel the mania build. "Let's set our goals: get Carla cleaned up, you get the chairwoman thing with the foundation, I prepare to take the test. First, we kiss up to 'Uncle' Carl and even Cardinal Sean. Try to figure how that blasted test will be scored. Meredith, what would I do without you?"

CHAPTER SEVEN

Ashley forced herself to chew slowly as she tackled the veal cutlet, the third course of their evening meal. She and Conrad sat across from one another at the family dining room table, a table that had seen little use since the formal dinner parties that her parents used to host before her mother's illness.

She wanted to bolt down the food and get back to her studies. She'd pulled just a mediocre grade in cardiology and worried that she'd never ever understand all the blips and bleeps on electrocardiograms. She had no ear at all for the *lub-dubs* of the heart tones, and realized now that she was not cut out for cardiology. What Ashley did love was pediatrics, neonatology to be specific. Whenever she had an extra moment at the medical center, she'd find herself peering through the glass barrier into the neonatal unit, wishing that she was still a part of the team, making rounds with the attending and the residents.

"Conrad, I've been thinking," she said, setting down her fork. "Maybe I'll apply for a pediatric residency."

"You have to be joking, my love. Dealing with snotty noses, disgruntled parents. Believe me, that's not for you."

"How about neonatology? When I did my rotation at Children's Hospital, I felt really intense. Like everything was life and death. Such small babies. So vulnerable. So fragile. Like I could really make a difference."

"Little brain stems. So premature, most of them are better off if they don't make it. Those who do have serious neurological problems. Now that's one specialty you don't want. And just think about the hours, the night call. No, not for you. As a matter of fact, once things are settled next year, there's no reason for you to even finish a residency."

Ashley felt her face flush. Whenever she spoke to Conrad about her career, he made her feel so inferior, so incompetent, like she shouldn't even be in medical school. Was that last remark trying to tell her that she was too stupid to practice medicine?

Her best friend, Ruthie Campbell, her only friend who knew about Conrad — how he'd moved in with her, become her lover, her confidant, her soul mate — had warned her that Conrad was making too many of her decisions. Was this an example? Or was she truly not competent enough?

Ashley remembered her last conversation with Ruthie. A tense conversation over a cafeteria lunch. Ruthie complained that Conrad was a control freak. "He tells you what to wear, who to see, who you can study with, how to spend every minute of your time." What Ruthie had not said, but what she had implied, was that Conrad was after her money. But naturally Ruthie would think this. Ruthie struggled financially and didn't trust anyone.

"Now I know you're kidding, Conrad," Ashley finally said. "I've wanted to be a doctor all my life, I'm just rethinking what kind."

"My love, once you graduate we can be out in the open with our relationship. Then we'll see. But for now, your father did want you to follow your mother's footsteps."

Ashley took a sip of wine, taking care not to drink more than half a glass or she'd be too sleepy to study. Deciding to change the subject, she said, "I can't wait to tell everybody about us."

And that was true. Once she graduated, there would be no need to keep their relationship a secret. They could be out in the open and — she had to hold her breath every time she wished this — they could get married.

Ashley had always known that she wasn't the smartest among her fellow students. She had to work hard for good grades, harder than her colleagues. And she had always known that she was not attractive. Not beautiful, like Carla. Not outgoing, like Rory. And to make things worse, she had that stuttering problem, not as bad as when she was a kid, but enough to embarrass her.

But now she had Conrad, so protective. He made her feel attractive and special, leaving Ruthie's concerns unfounded. Conrad cared enough about her to be concerned about any decisions she had to make. But there was one thing about Conrad that she could not share with anyone, not even Ruthie. Ashley suspected that Conrad had Peyronie's disease, a penile curvature that should make sexual intercourse painful for him, but apparently did not. She'd read about this condition, but had never seen a case. And what did she know, anyway? She'd been a virgin before him. What she did know was that sex with him left her satisfied and fulfilled. But, she did have this weird inability to recall the actual details and sensations. Too embarrassed to mention it to Conrad, she'd self-diagnosed herself with unclassified sexual dysfunction syndrome. Surely that would correct itself after they were married.

Ashley's thoughts were interrupted by Mrs. Mendoza. "Mrs. Parnell calling, Miss Ashley," she announced, handing her the phone.

She looked up at Conrad before accepting it.

"Meredith?"

Ashley listened as Meredith made it clear that she expected her help with Carla. And Meredith intended to bring in an addiction specialist. She insisted that Ashley bring Conrad, too, reasoning that as a psychiatrist, he'd know how these interventions worked.

Ashley felt the surge of inferiority hit as it always did when dealing with her imperious sister-in-law. The perfect political wife. The brilliant lawyer. A woman who did not take "no" for an answer.

As Meredith stated her demands, Mrs. Mendoza returned with a pear tart, setting it down in front of Conrad. Ashley watched as he picked up his fork then set it down while he waited for her to hang up. What if he refused to take part? Her attention drifted from Meredith until she heard her say, "Unfortunately, Rory won't be there. They're going to Disney World. Seems selfish to me, but bottom line, she and Chan won't be participating."

"Oh no." Rory always knew the right thing to say at the right time.

When Ashley hung up, Conrad cut her a slice of tart as she tried to explain that Carla had a drug problem and the family needed to get involved.

"Don't kid yourself, there's no quick fix for drug addiction," Conrad said, twirling his wine glass. "Your sister's too deep into the culture. But sure, we'll show up if that's what your brother's wife wants."

Ashley let out a sigh of relief. She wouldn't have to deny her sister-in-law, but she did wonder why Rory, always so unselfish, had not made helping Carla a priority.

CHAPTER EIGHT

APRIL 2001

Carla took Ashley's call in bed. As soon as she hung up, she reached for the Vicodin, took out three and swallowed them without water. Her head throbbed with each breath. She had no memory of the night before except crawling out of bed to vomit. That must have disgusted Bunky because he'd left their bed. Not that he'd been better off. He'd gotten fucked up too: crack, pills, alcohol.

What was it that Ashley had said? That she'd be dropping by the Manhattan apartment today. Sure, like right in the middle of her school shit. How likely was that? And on April Fool's Day?

When Carla was a kid, this had been Dad's special day. She and Ashley used to scheme to get the best of him, but he had always one-upped them. Carla remembered when she was seventeen, Ashley had dared her to "borrow" Dad's Porsche for a trip to the mall. Dad and Ashley had followed her there and moved the car. She'd gone berserk at the empty parking space and she could still hear their crazed laughing when they jumped out and yelled, "April Fool's!" Carla decided to simply blow off Ashley's call as an April Fool's joke.

Then Carla heard the knock on her bedroom door. "Miss Carla?"

Carla massaged her forehead. Wasn't this Sunday? Sara's day off? Why was she here checking up on her? Ever since that ugly eviction threat, Carla had been afraid that the family — Frank, in particular — might press Sara to betray the family code of privacy that Dad had required of the household staff.

"Are you okay?" Sara raised her voice.

"I'm okay." Carla wiped specks of dried green vomit off her face.

"Miss Ashley's coming over soon, so you'd better get dressed. I'm going to fix a luncheon. Lobster salad, her favorite."

The thought of lobster made more bile rise in her throat. So Ashley's little joke had gotten to Sara.

"April Fool's," Carla called, not getting out of bed. "Sara, will you send Bunky in?" She needed a hit.

Sara did not respond, and Carla knew she'd have to get the stuff herself. Just the effort of climbing out of bed made her heart race. She felt wobbly, but she stumbled to the bathroom and splashed water on her face. Brushing her teeth made her woozy so she set the toothbrush down and sat on the toilet to run a brush though her tangled hair. Shit, her hair needed styling and highlights. She looked down at her nails, broken, the red polish chipped. She looked like hell, and she felt like crap.

"You got the shit?" Carla pushed off the toilet as Bunky shuffled into the bedroom suite. A vision of a Calvin Klein model in a silk robe, he'd showered but not shaved, orange-red stubble peppering his chin and curls tumbling across hazel eyes.

"Yeah, babe, but your sister's coming. Sara's out there getting ready for a feast. Can you eat anything yet? I had rye toast. Settled my stomach."

"Just get me the rocks. I gotta get fucked."

"Seriously, babe, I'm gonna split. No way I'm mixing it up with your family."

"I can't face her like this. Look at me. And Ashley, with that dressed-for-success look."

"All you gotta do is act normal, babe. Say whatever the fuck she wants to hear."

"So she's really coming?" Carla sank onto the dressing room bench.

Bunky sauntered into her closet and returned with pressed wool slacks in gold tones and a matching silk long-sleeved blouse. "Wear this and put on some makeup. Here, let me pull your hair back." He reached for a jeweled clasp and pulled her lank hair off her neck.

"That's better, and remember, babe, don't get into the AIDS thing. You do, they'll grab you right out of here. You know what I mean?"

Carla did know. She and Bunky had gone back and forth. Should she ask her family for help? Or tough it out herself? To her huge relief, when she'd gotten up the guts to tell Bunky about her HIV test, he said he didn't give a fuck. Refused to get tested. Refused to wear a condom. After all, they had drugs that cured the virus. He knew all about drugs. He'd been off and on them since he turned fifteen. Mental drugs, he'd explained. For schizophrenia. But he was cured now. Same thing would happen with AIDS, he said. Carla knew better, but what good would it do to argue? Bunky's confidence was infectious and they'd dialed up their lives, getting stoned every night, using more and more of the white powder to the point that their life together was a blur. So this is what it had come to, Bunky and her, their brains fucked up. Her body infected. She tried to recall what Bunky had told her about her money getting low.

"I'm not going to tell anyone," she said. "But what about money? Should I ask Ashley for more?"

"Find out how to get that inheritance, babe."

Bunky went over to the drawer where they kept their stash — same place she kept Dad's letter. He picked up the letter. "Says here that you used to be daddy's pride and joy."

"That's crap. My whole fucking family always thought I was a spoiled brat. All the shit I got into at that prison of a girls' school. Booze, pot, sex in the backseat, sneaking into motels. Rory and Ashley, perfect little ladies. Carla, the fuck-up, the nuns kept telling me, but not in those words."

"Hey, it says, 'Imagine how proud we were of you when you became a fashion model. You had so much talent, so much beauty.'"

You wouldn't be proud of me now, Dad. Good thing you and Mom aren't here, Carla thought.

She didn't need to rehash the rest of the letter. Complaints about her mood swings, her inability to focus, not meeting her fucking commitments.

"Come on, Bunky, quit reading that crap. I'll never be what he wants. So why keep going over this? Just fire up the pipe."

Bunky ignored her and read on, "Carla, I feel I must bring this up. Are you taking drugs?"

Yes, Dad, I am, she wanted to scream. Remember those parties you and Mom threw? I was ten when I started helping myself to those bottles in the liquor cabinet. Dope in high school, right under the nuns' noses. Getting high, drunk, both. Cocaine after that. Some pills, but mostly coke. Then crack, and that I could never stop. So forget it, it's too late.

"All that blah, blah, but he never comes out and says what the fuck do you have to do to get the inheritance money." Bunky put the sheet of paper down. "Find out what your sister is doing. She got a letter too. Then we'll have to put together a plan."

"I can't stop this shit and neither can you. So there's not going to be a plan."

"Babe, we gotta find a way through this."

She knew that passing Dad's test was hopeless. There was no *way*. "Right now just get me that pipe."

"No. You're gonna have to tough this out. You take a hit now, you'll freak out. Just stay calm. Take one of these." He handed Carla a Xanax and two Motrins. "We'll get fucked soon as your sister splits."

Bunky left, and Carla rang for a piece of toast.

"Miss Carla," Sara said as she carried in a tray laden with bagels, toast, muffins, jellies, and a coffee service. "You need more than one piece of toast." Carla felt the appraisal of her eyes. "You going to shower? They — Ashley'll be here soon."

Carla took a bite of a bran muffin, feeling that it was going to stay down, but remembering that she'd not brushed her teeth, that she hadn't washed her hair in days. "Yes, I am."

The hot water felt good, and she stood in the shower until her heart started beating so fast she thought she would pass out. So she got out, toweled off, and dressed in the clothes that Bunky had laid out. She clasped her wet hair on top of her head, feeling much better, a bit back in control. Good enough to take on Ashley. Good enough to take on the whole family. Well, maybe not that good. When she heard the door chime, she started to rush out, but stopped abruptly. The voice greeting Sara was not Ashley's. It was Meredith's, the sister-in-law from hell. She had to open the door a crack to hear Sara. "Ashley hasn't arrived yet. Nor Mr. Schiller."

Uncle Carl? Two weeks ago Uncle Carl and Aunt Phyllis had dropped by without warning. A Sunday afternoon. The place was fucked up. Shit all over the place. Stoners — friends she hardly knew — passed out on the sofas. Obviously, she couldn't let the Schillers up, so she'd suggested coffee at a nearby Starbucks, a place too noisy for private conversation, which she didn't want to have. She knew that the Schillers meant well, but she did not need their interference. That's what she'd told them, only not in those exact words. Wasn't she a legal adult with the right to her privacy? So had the Schillers talked to Meredith? And Ashley? Were they all here to fucking mess with her?

They must have moved into the library or the living room, and Carla had to inch her way down the hall to catch what they were saying. Meredith's voice. "So that's what precipitated my call. Ongoing complaints from the building manager and, finally, the threat of eviction."

Carla assumed that Meredith was talking about one of her clients.

A man's voice. "So she used to be a model. Her drug habit is out of control. Her parents are deceased."

"Yes, Dr. Adair. Here, let me show you a picture of Carla from about two years ago. We don't know if she was taking drugs back then, but here she is representing Sensation Cosmetics. You'll see the difference."

Shit, Meredith was talking about her? To a doctor? She must know about the HIV? That was supposed to be confidential.

"What a shame," she heard a male voice say. "Any family history of substance abuse?"

"None whatsoever," Meredith said, just as her cell phone rang. "Excuse me. Frank? We're here with Dr. Adair. Carla's home, but Ashley's not here yet, or Carl."

Carla stayed put.

"No, I'll call," Meredith said after a pause. "You need to stay out of this. Did the Justice Committee finish with Microsoft?"

A more lengthy pause. Carla's brain screamed, *Get the fuck out of my apartment.*

"Of course Microsoft's lawyers want to drag it out." Carla heard Meredith chuckle as the doorbell chimed. "Someone's arrived. Must be them. Love you too."

Carla inched out to peek around a marble column. Here she could see Sara usher the so-called doctor to the library through the door connecting the living room and dining room. Would she be able to slip by the library and leave by the rear elevator that opened into the pantry off the kitchen?

Meredith headed toward the foyer and Carla slipped back into the hallway. Run, her instincts screamed, but she stood rooted, not able to figure a way to escape.

"Ashley, Conrad," Meredith said. "Thank God you're here."

"Took the helicopter," the Conrad voice said, the same one who'd answered Valentine's night when she'd called Ashley.

"Ashley, we're going to need you." Meredith was definitely taking charge. "Since Rory couldn't be bothered."

Carla felt her heart sink. If shit was going down, she could count on Rory to cut her a break. Ashley would try, but wouldn't have the guts to go up against Meredith. Ashley had never faced a fucking problem in her entire over-protected life. Super student, Pollyanna Ashley. And what the fuck was this Conrad doing here? She'd told Ashley she wanted to meet him, but she'd never gotten her shit together. And now he was here?

"I hope that you find Dr. Adair satisfactory," the Conrad voice said. "Of course you know I'm acting chair of psychiatry at Penn, but substance abuse is not my field. However I have used hypnosis —"

"We appreciate your being here," Meredith said, cutting him off.

"Meredith?" Ashley's voice sounded tiny and Carla remembered how quiet she'd been as a kid. Maybe because she stuttered. "W-where's Carla?"

Carla wanted to run out and hug Ashley, tell the others to get the fuck out. Now, not later. She backed up in the hall, planning to duck back into her room for a blast of rock. Then split.

"Mr. Schiller is here, Mrs. Parnell," Sara announced before Carla made it back to her room.

"Send him in here," Meredith called. The bossy bitch. Carla had always wondered what it was like for her and Frank. In bed. Like who did what to whom?

"Meredith, sorry I'm late." Uncle Carl's voice.

Carla fought the overwhelming impulse to rush out. If only she could sit in his lap as she had when she was a little girl. Carl and Phyllis had never had a child, and Carla was named after "Uncle Carl," always his special one. Until lately, when they had drifted apart. Carla still felt horrible about the way she'd blown them off the last time they came to see her. It hadn't been a good time for her that day. Today was not a good time for her either. The HIV thing curdled in her stomach. Could she confide in Uncle Carl? Crazy thought. What she had to do was get out of the apartment.

"Ashley and Conrad are in the living room. Dr. Adair is waiting in the library."

"The psychiatrist?"

"An addiction specialist," Meredith said. "Ph.D. psychologist. I met with him last week. Told him about Carla. How she'd become withdrawn, unpredictable, careless about her appearance, slovenly even. Lying about her whereabouts and her friends. Druggie friends sleeping at the apartment. Trouble with the building management. How could this happen, I asked him? Carla had so much going for her."

Carla had to clamp her hand over her mouth to keep from screaming. These people had no right fucking up her life. Especially now that she was going to die from AIDS.

Meredith kept on lecturing. "Dr. Adair explained how drug addiction was an illness, a disease like diabetes or kidney failure. Believe me, when I tried to explain that to Frank, he wasn't buying. Self-indulgence, he says. He's always complained that Vivian and Paul spoiled Carla."

"What drugs is she hooked on?" Carl asked, his voice shaking as if it too had palsy.

"Dr. Adair thinks cocaine. Maybe crack cocaine. Ecstasy. Maybe even heroin. Based on what I told him, he thinks she's sinking fast. That if her addiction is left untreated, it could be fatal. Ashley wanted to wait for Rory to get back from her vacation, but Frank agrees that we should do it now as you recommended."

"Frank's not here?" Carl asked.

"Oh, no. Drug abuse is the kiss of death in a politician's family despite all that talk about it being 'just an illness.' He needs to distance himself. Let's hope this intervention works. Did you read that book I sent you?"

"I looked it over," Uncle Carl said.

"No time for all that prework and practice sessions," Meredith said. "We have to make the best of this."

Carla knew she was fucked. She'd heard about interventions. Everybody showing up to throw all your shit in your face. Then force you off to detox.

"You're doing a good thing, Meredith," Carl said. "You're just what this family needs right now."

"I had expected Rory to take the lead," Meredith said, as Carla stood grounded, needing to hear what they had planned for her. "What a complicated family. No way Frank and I are having more than one child."

And I'll never have a kid either, Carla thought. The concept came as a shock. Not like she'd wanted kids, but with AIDS — she'd be dead.

Then they started talking about Rory. How she refused to postpone her trip, claiming that they'd promised the kids. How tough it was for Chan to get another doctor to cover his practice. So Rory couldn't be bothered about her, Carla surmised, as she rushed to the safe in her dressing room where she kept the bag of rocks and the pipe. When she jerked open the door, she discovered the safe was empty. She slumped back against the racks of clothes. Where the fuck had she put the stuff? She crawled to her purse, ripped through it. Pills, only pills. She needed rocks. She threw the purse across the room, scrambled up, rifled through her drawers, her bathroom cabinet. Nothing. She scrambled back to her purse, yanked out her cell phone, called Bunky. No answer.

"Miss Carla?" It was Sara. Carla had told Sara to drop the "miss." It sounded too Gone with the Windish. But all the Parnell housekeepers called the kids "Miss" or "Missus" or "Mister." And they were supposed to do the same, only Carla didn't. "Mrs. Waring" was "Sara."

Carla cracked open the door. She could smell coffee, but caffeine wasn't going to help. "Sara, I have to go find Bunky." She tried to tone down her desperation. "He's probably hanging out near the park. Just be a few minutes."

"Mrs. Parnell sent me to get you," Sara's voice faltered and her hands trembled. "They're here to see you. Mrs. Parnell and Mr. Schiller is here too. And Miss Ashley with Dr. Welton."

Right. To put me in fucking prison. Carla felt like a trapped animal.

Her heart raced, her voice shook. "I don't know what kind of game you're playing, Sara, but I don't like it."

She slammed the door in Sara's face. She would not stay and listen to any more. If she couldn't find Bunky, she'd need cash to buy on the street. She ripped open the secret drawer beneath her dressing table, pulled out a pouch and checked her cash: $500 in fifties. She grabbed it, stuffed it into her purse, and bolted toward the door, halting abruptly when the door did not budge.

"What the fuck?" She banged on the door and yelled, "Sara, get me out!"

No response. She pounded with her sandal, feeling a rush of paranoia. As a user, she lived paranoia.

"Carla." Meredith's voice, not Sara's, and she was right outside the door. Carla heard the insertion of a key.

"Carla, it's me, Ashley. Come on out. Okay?" This was "April Fool's" all right and she was the fool.

She heard the key turn, and the door opened. She was trapped. She ran to the window. Could she just jump? Nineteen floors onto Park Avenue? She felt an arm on hers. Uncle Carl's.

"Let's talk, Carla," he said. Carla turned to face him. Meredith was at his side, a look of horror on her angular face, like she thought Carla would really jump. And maybe she would have. Carla couldn't be sure. Then she saw Ashley standing at the door, a man next to her, his arm encircling her waist.

Just stay calm and act normal, Carla told herself. Don't fall into their trap. You've always talked your way out of shit. Smart talk. You can't let them put you away.

"What are you all doing here?" She needed to stall for time.

"Carla, there's somebody I want you to meet," Ashley said. "Conrad Welton. He's a doctor."

Carla stared, not bothering to hide her hostility.

Welton held out his hand. "Charmed to meet you, Carla."

"Better not," Carla mumbled. "I'm coming down with the flu." She needed to keep them all at a distance. The taste of vomit lingered in her mouth, making her stomach queasy. She needed a drink.

Welton withdrew his hand, but Ashley pulled away from him and threw her arms around Carla.

"And, this is Dr. Adair," Meredith interrupted, gesturing toward a trim man with curly brown hair and matching moustache. He was maybe ten years older than Carla, mid-thirties. He had a twitch in his eye, making him seem nervous and shifty. Not someone Carla could trust, she knew that.

"Miss Parnell, I'm happy to meet you." He squeezed through the door, extending a puffy white hand.

Carla cringed at the voice she'd heard discussing her with Meredith. She kept her hands behind her back. "It's really not a good time," she said. "I do have plans." She glanced around. "I guess no one called me to check. Sorry."

"Let's go into the living room." Meredith, used to issuing orders, herded the group out of the bedroom and ushered Carla to the sofa. She sat Carla next to her, too close. Uncle Carl settled himself on her other side. She was trapped.

"Dr. Adair is an addiction specialist," Meredith began.

"And Conrad is a psychiatrist," Ashley added, too smug.

"We're all here to help you." Meredith again.

"I don't need help."

"Why don't you just hear us out, Miss Parnell," the shifty doctor said. "May I call you Carla?"

"I don't care what the fuck you call me," Carla shot back, losing control easily. "I don't know what you're doing here anyway. I'm sorry, everybody, I have to go." She tried to get up, but Uncle Carl's frail arm held her back. Anyone else and she would have bolted, but she couldn't push Uncle Carl away.

"I promised your father that I would take care of you," he said. "Now let's talk."

Carla sat silently between Carl and Meredith, then Carl put his arm around her as he had when she'd been a child. He always said that he was her godfather, even though he was Jewish. Her Catholic godfather, a cardiologist that her mom knew, had died when Carla was two, and she didn't even remember his name.

"Carla," Meredith began, "we know you're in trouble — that you have been using drugs."

"What are you talking about?"

"It's been going on for a long time," Ashley said. "We're here to help you."

"What right —?"

Uncle Carl interrupted. "Talk to us about it so we can get you some help."

"Look, maybe I've made some mistakes. Sure, even used some drugs." She shrugged, casting her eyes downward. *And I have AIDS,* she almost said aloud. "Look, everybody does a little pot. Clinton. George W. Anybody who says they don't is a liar."

No one said anything.

Still looking down, Carla mumbled, "My life hasn't been so good lately, and once in a while I take something to help me feel better. Nothing serious. Nothing I can't handle."

The addiction doctor said, "You feel in control of your life?"

"Yes. You're blowing this all out of proportion. Really now, I have to get going." Carla looked at her wrist, and remembered that she had lost her diamond Piaget watch.

"Carla, Ashley has been very worried," Ashley's boyfriend said. "Very concerned."

Mister, it's me who has problems, Carla wanted to scream. Instead, she kept silent, eyes cast downward. How was she going to put a stop to this?

"Look, I'm an adult. Nobody has to tell me how to live my life." Carla stared at Meredith. "And that includes Frank. He's the one who sent you here, right, Meredith? My lifestyle doesn't fit his political agenda, the illusion of a perfect Parnell family."

"Carla," the addiction doctor broke in, blinking as he spoke. "We're here to talk about reality. First, we know from the paraphernalia that you keep in the apartment and the drugs found here over time that you are a heavy user. We also know that the people that come and go here are known addicts."

Stay calm, under control, throw them off, Carla tried to tell herself. Don't lose it.

"Did you know that addiction is a chronic disease?" Ashley's boyfriend sounded like one of those voice-over commercials. "If you have it, you have to deal with it. If you don't, it can be fatal."

"We want to get you into a treatment program," Ashley said. "Fortunately, this disease can be treated."

"A disease? Like HIV is a disease? A treatable disease?" Had these words slipped out of her mouth?

"Yes," the doctor said. "Like —"

Carla cut him off. "Uncle Carl, help me out here. Who's been feeding you all these lies? I just admitted that I use drugs sometimes. Okay? But that doesn't make me an addict. I can't believe that you all would accuse me of that." She did not miss the sideways glance from Carl to Sara.

"We're not with you every day," Meredith said. "That's why Mrs. Waring is here."

Carla gasped and spun toward her faithful companion and protector. Sara knew way too much.

"I'm sorry, Miss Carla," Sara's voice trembled, "but Mrs. Parnell convinced me that we all had to get together to help you. Otherwise bad things will happen. I just know they will."

"How could you turn on me? I trusted you."

Tears welled in Sara's kind, dark eyes, and Carla wanted to apologize immediately, but the doctor interrupted. "Carla. I know this is difficult for you. For us too. We want you to face reality. We'll be going over some specific examples that we have prepared. All we ask is that you listen. Okay?"

Carla felt so bad about yelling at Sara that she nodded her head. She was in a trap and the only way out was to listen to their bullshit. She felt like hell — shaky, sweaty, heart racing, head raging.

Meredith pulled out what looked like a printed agenda. "Mrs. Waring will start off." she announced as if she were on Court TV.

Sara started to read from a yellow lined pad of handwritten notes. She began by staring at them, but as she went along, she began to look up at Carla with eyes that pleaded for understanding.

"Miss Carla, when they explained what they wanted me to do, I sat at the desk in your father's office. I wanted to remember everything important, everything that might help you. I started four years ago when you moved here from Philadelphia. Before you met Bunky. Just about the time your mama got diagnosed with melanoma. You were going to Parsons. You weren't happy there."

Carla shrugged. Damn right. Her grades had been too rotten for an academic college, so Dad bought her way into Parsons School of Design. She'd flunked out the first semester. But she met people who got her into modeling – and into heavier drugs. For a couple of years she'd had a good run. Mostly catalogues until she got to be the "face" for Sensation Cosmetics.

Carla, mute, nodded.

"You were very thin back then. Still are, skin and bones. Anyway, I started to think that you were drinking too much, like in the morning. And I noticed suspicious medicine bottles back then. I thought they were diet pills."

Yeah, back then it was amphetamines.

"Since they had a doctor's name and all, I didn't bother you about them, Miss Carla." Sara had turned toward Carla and spoke to her as if no one else was in the room. "About then I started to smell that sweetish marijuana. I didn't like it, but I let it go. Then after your mama died, I knew that you were slipping bad. I don't know much about drugs, but I did try to talk to you about it. Remember?"

"Yes," Carla said.

"I wish I'd tried harder. You begged me not to tell Mr. Paul, and then he got the cancer and he was at Sloan-Kettering and Fox Chase and Baylor and Mayo Clinic that first year. And things got worse and worse."

She was right there.

"Do you remember when you got fired from the modeling agency after you didn't show up for your shoots? And nobody knew where you were? That was when things started to get really bad. And after that Bunky moved in here? All our arguments about how he was taking advantage of you?"

"Mrs. Waring," the doctor prompted. "Why don't you get back to the list"

Carla felt like screaming. *Hadn't enough been said?*

"Yes, doctor." Sara picked up the yellow pad and started reading an endless list of Carla's abuses. Wild parties. Damages. Blackouts. And the final straw, prompting the eviction process.

Carla listened as if the person Sara was discussing was someone else, a disgusting slut. Not herself at all, but a fucking loser, one with no self-respect, no redeeming qualities. Then Sara finished by saying she hoped it wasn't too late.

"Too late?" Carla asked aloud. Too late for her was AIDS.

"Thank you, Mrs. Waring," the shrink said. He kept up his repulsive blinking habit. "Now, Mrs. Parnell?"

Carla buried her head in her hands. She'd never liked her sister-in-law and had always tried to avoid her, never imagining that someday she'd be presiding over her life. Now Carla felt trapped, like in a tornado where everything was sucking her into a vortex of confusion. Maybe she did hate what she'd become. Sometimes she did think about just ending it all.

"Carla, deep down, you must know that you need help," Meredith started out. "Your habit and your friends have taken all of your money. A million dollars in six months. Your junkie friends are taking advantage of you."

"What do you know about my friends?" Carla forced a civil tone.

"You're right. This is about *you*. About giving *you* the help you need. We've made arrangements for a treatment program," Meredith concluded.

"I'll think about it," Carla said, trying to focus on getting out. "Maybe you're right, but I need time to think about it. Anyway I appreciate your concern. I really do."

"The Roberts Clinic," said Uncle Carl, taking Carla's hand in his and pulling her so close to him that she could feel the random tremors. "It's the best. It's in upstate New York. In the Catskills. Quiet, comfortable, and experienced."

"No. I know people who have been to places like that. Horrible. All kinds of ugly drunks and junkies. No, I don't think so."

"You need inpatient care," the jerk said. "You're fortunate that your family can afford it."

"Fucking fortunate," Carla mumbled, not caring if they heard.

"Mrs. Waring, why don't you pack her things," Meredith said. "Nothing formal. But enough warm clothing for the cool mountain evenings."

Carla thought of the one AA — or was it NA — meeting she'd gone to with her friend, Jan. Jan was clean now. Did the Twelve Steps. But Carla had spoken up at the meeting. "I'm Carla," she said. "I'm an alcoholic and an addict." She could still hear the chorus ring out, "Hi, Carla."

"You just get well," Uncle Carl said, reaching for Carla's hand. "Your health, that's all that matters. Dr. Adair will accompany you. Everything is set up there."

Carla knew she was being railroaded. Everyone had turned against her. What choice did she have? She had to go. If she didn't, they'd kick her out of the apartment, and she didn't have money for another place. She figured she could get her hands on drugs inside. Maybe somebody in there could give her advice on how to face AIDS. After she got back, she and Bunky would still be together. Bunky. She'd have to let him know where she was, but first she had to get her hands on that stash. Where the fuck was it? Sara was right. She didn't remember shit.

Sara was packing sweaters into her duffel bag when Carla returned to her bedroom. A suitcase was open on the bed, full of shoes, slacks, shirts, nightgowns, bras, panties. Her travel kit lay beside it, already zipped up. Sara looked up as Carla approached, dropping the clothes in her hands and opening her arms.

"I'm sorry I yelled at you," Carla said. "I was in shock. I still am."

"Miss Carla, I am so sorry. Mr. Schiller convinced me that I just had to help. You know how much he cares about you. Then Mrs. Parnell told me exactly what I had to do. I worked hard on that list. You know, everything on it is true."

"I know you meant to help me, Sara," Carla said, going to the woman, taking her hands and squeezing them, "but I need your help right now." Sara slipped her hands out of Carla's grasp and started to pack underwear into the overnight bag. "Please, you have to tell Bunky where I am." Sara started to shake her head, back and forth. "Tell him I need him and let him stay here, please, Sara."

"I can't do that, Miss Carla. I promised Mrs. Parnell. Besides that doctor said that you can't have contact with people who still use drugs."

"Come on, Sara, you've got to do this for me."

"I'm not going to lie to you. Dr. Adair says that I've been an 'enabler,' that by protecting you, I've allowed things to get worse. I'm not going to lie to anyone anymore. No more drugs. You can't get back with those users."

"I won't. Just Bunky."

"No," Sara said, this time looking directly at Carla. "I've packed his things. And I'm changing the locks. He's trouble, Miss Carla, real trouble."

Carla figured she could get word to Bunky somehow. Sara would get over this high moral ground, and become her supporter again. If only her mother were here, *she'd* make them all go away. Or Rory, who'd always rescued her.

"Sara, one more thing" Carla said. "And this is important. It'll take hours to get to this place upstate. I need my stuff. Just to get by. I need it real bad. I thought I had some, but I can't find it. Did you see it? Please Sara. After today, I'll be in treatment. This will all stop, but I'm desperate, just for tonight."

Sara shook her head.

"Please, Sara. I'm begging you."

"Nothing's left, Miss Carla. I flushed it all down the toilet."

"No." Carla reached out to strike her, but when Sara lifted her thin arm to shield her face, Carla dropped her hand. "You flushed my fucking life."

CHAPTER NINE

Dan Parnell set down the twenty-pound bag of dog food and punched the blinking message button.

"Hi Dan, this is Gina." Her voice in his kitchen? He must be delirious from a day pruning royal palms in the unseasonable heat.

"I'd like to invite you to my house for Easter dinner. I know it's last minute, but Monica is going to be there too. Of course, if you have plans, I'd surely understand. But it would be great if you can make it. Three o'clock." She went on to provide directions, but Dan knew exactly where she lived. In a Spanish stucco, cream-colored, one-story house with a red-tiled roof. In Fort Myers, not far from Lee Memorial Hospital where she worked.

Taking only enough time to fill the dogs' water bowl, he reached for the wall-mounted phone. His hand trembled as he dialed the call-back number. He needed to react before he lost his nerve.

"Hello." He recognized the male voice.

"Terry? It's . . . " Dan hesitated, not knowing what he should say, "It's your dad?" Too presumptuous. He decided on, "It's Dan Parnell. Is your mother there?"

"Nope. She and Carrie are out shopping. So are you coming tomorrow?"

"Yes," Dan said. "Will you let her know?"

"Sure thing. That's cool 'cause I've got a couple things to talk to you about."

As Dan drove across Alligator Alley on Easter morning, he could still see it in his mind's eye, their tiny two-room apartment in Miami. How he and Gina had to rearrange the cheap living room furniture to allow for the two cribs. How the walls were so thin, and how worried they were that the babies would keep their neighbors awake. How it had all come to an end. The air conditioner in his Tundra was blasting, but Dan started to sweat. Would Gina give him a second chance? He reached up to loosen his tie. Maybe he shouldn't have worn one, but he wanted to look respectful. He cranked the air-conditioning up even more. He calculated carefully when to take his last smoke, so that Gina wouldn't smell stale tobacco on him.

Dan had returned to Lantana in January after his father's funeral, mortified by the scene he'd made. For days, he'd simply roamed his property, talking to no one. His foreman stepped in and took over all the decisions about the trees. His only company was Lucy, his yellow lab, and Lucky, his black one. In the end, he decided to write to Gina. In that first letter, he groped to find the right words to express all the pent-up guilt, all the years of loneliness. He apologized for his embarrassing tears in Pennsylvania. He wrote of his pride, totally undeserved, in the children. About what a magnificent job she had done. He'd never been much of a writer, but the words that he'd never been able to speak poured out.

He had not expected a reply, but within a week, a thank-you note arrived. That opened the door. He wrote to Gina again, and she wrote back. And now he was on his way to her house for Easter dinner.

As Dan parked the truck outside Gina's house, he checked the mirror on the visor, combed his floppy hair, stuck a cinnamon-flavored Eclipse into his mouth, and straightened his tie. In his anxiety, he didn't notice the white stretch limo parked across the street. He grabbed the pot of Easter lilies off the floor of the truck and almost dropped it as he stumbled on a crack in the sidewalk.

Dan rang the bell, hearing chimes from within. The jasmine growing among the gardenias and azalea beds on both sides of the entrance sent out a powerful fragrance. He felt profound fright and intense serenity. Both at once. Both overpowering. Then Gina appeared, held the door open for him, and he stepped into a space loaded with flowers and plants. He couldn't help but gasp. Gina looked beautiful in a lavender dress with matching sandals, her hair pulled back and held by a clip.

"Dan," she said, "it's good to see you."

He pushed the oversized pot of lilies toward her and felt relieved that she took them.

"How thoughtful. Why don't we put them in the living room? I know just the spot."

He followed her across polished oak floors.

"Terry, Carrie, your father's here." Said so naturally, as if it were part of a routine.

Both of his kids appeared. Both had a curious expression. Dan wondered if they expected him to release a dam of tears.

"Hello." Dan said, sticking close to Gina as she placed the lilies on a small round table.

"Welcome." Carrie gave him a friendly grin. "How was the drive from Lantana?"

"Uh, fine," Dan said, at a loss as to how to strike up a conversation.

"And," Gina said, "our guests are in the kitchen."

"Oh," was all Dan could think to say. He'd forgotten about his celebrity half sister, Monica Monroe.

"Monica's in the kitchen." Gina took his arm. "Can you believe it? She had a concert last night in Miami and invited Terry and Carrie as her guests, as well as her niece who lives in Tampa. So I asked them all to Easter dinner, and they flew in from Miami on her private plane."

Gina stood so close that Dan could smell her hair. Her touch on his arm made his heart hammer. Could she hear it?

"And Monica brought her fiancé. Somebody a sports nut like you will recognize. They gave me the most beautiful bouquet."

"Oh?" Again, this was all Dan could think of to say. He was a jazz fan, but didn't have a clue about Monica's kind of music.

"Dan," Monica had been arranging flowers in a crystal vase, "I'm so happy you're here." She wiped her hands on a towel, and stepped forward for one of those social hugs. Dan forced himself not to pull back and to be gracious when she put her arms around him and leaned in to peck his cheek. "This family is still a mystery to me. I do want to get to know everybody."

"Of course, you recognize this guy?" Gina announced.

"Uh, nice to meet you," Dan said to the stranger who stepped up to shake his hand. Only he wasn't a stranger. Dan knew him. But from where? Good-looking, casual clothes, hazel eyes, brown hair in a crew cut. Tall, with an athletic build. Why was Gina saying that he'd recognize him? Dan wasn't into movie stars or popular singers.

Gina must have noticed Dan's puzzled look and came to his rescue. "Or maybe you don't? ESPN Sports?" She tossed out one more prompt. "Thursday nights?"

"Every guy's not a sports fan," Monica said with a wink to her guy.

"Pat Nelson?" Dan finally sputtered. "Geez, man, I'll be damned. Yeah, I just didn't expect I'd be meeting the modern-day Jim McKay."

"Glad to meet you," the sports announcer grabbed Dan's hand. "Caught out of context, huh?"

"Right," Dan said, slapping his forehead with the palm of his hand. "*Pat Nelson, Sports in Review.* Just last week, you interviewed Tiger Woods — the 'Tiger Slam.' Geez, I'm sorry."

"And my niece, Jenna," Monica interrupted. "She's hanging out with me and Patrick this weekend."

Dan held out his hand to a young woman with large hazel eyes and shoulder-length dark hair. He figured her to be about the same age as his twins.

"She's a real sports fan," Nelson said. "Ask her anything. Any sports trivia."

Monica chuckled. "Jenna, meet Dan Parnell, Terry and Carrie's father."

Indeed Jenna was a sports fanatic and Dan detected a spark of mutual interest between her and Terry. But what would he know about kids that young and romance?

The meal provided both a leg of lamb with all the trimmings and a thorough analysis of professional sports, thankfully playing to one of Dan's limited conversational strengths. It wasn't until Monica and her retinue had left that Dan, for the first time since Gina had walked out on him, was alone with her and the twins. As Boney James played in the background, Dan sat on the sofa next to Gina, their bodies close, but not touching. Terry paced back and forth between the kitchen and living room, and Carrie sat comfortably by her mom.

"What's with all the pacing?" Gina asked. "Trying to work off the dinner?"

"It was great, Mom," Terry said.

"Couldn't have done it without you two. Dan, did you know that the kids are fine cooks? Chefs, I should say, as in gourmet."

"Mom, you exaggerate." Carrie patted Gina's knee.

"We learned to fend for ourselves while Mom worked." Terry's tone made Dan squirm. The kid had a chip on his shoulder. Who could blame him?

"Well, Terr, what do you think?" Carrie asked with a wide grin.

"About what?" Terry turned to give her a withering look.

"The gorgeous Jenna? Don't forget that I'm your twin. I can read your mind."

"What's the deal? Are we related or not? Monica is my biological aunt." He stopped and faced Dan. "But Jenna is the daughter of her adoptive brother. So there's not blood relationship. Right?"

"I guess, but remember she doesn't know about the Parnell-Monroe relationship," Gina said. "So keep it hush-hush. Dan, when do you think the news that she's a Parnell will become public?"

"Don't know," Dan said. "I don't deal in family politics."

Terry shrugged, then he and Carrie chatted about Monica's concert and Nelson's television show until Carrie finally excused herself. Dan took that as his cue to say good night and stood up to leave. Immediately, he felt the void as the warmth from Gina's body next to his dissipated. But he couldn't change his mind and sit back down, so he thanked her again and headed out into the light drizzle toward his truck. Terry was waiting for him there, half hidden by a clump of palmettos.

"Can I talk to you a minute?" Terry asked.

"Uh — Sure." Dan shoved a pack of cigarettes back into his pocket. "Hop in." He went around to open the passenger door for Terry.

"Let me get the air cranked up." Dan turned on the ignition, adjusted the fan, and turned off the Kenny G CD.

"What did you want to talk about?" Dan was the first to break a long silence between them.

Dan hadn't realized it, but Terry had two cans of beer in his hands — Coors.

"I don't know much about you," Terry said, flipping off the lid of one can and handing the other to Dan. "You didn't say much in there."

"I'm not much good at social stuff." Dan shrugged, accepting the cold beer. "I pretty much stick to myself on my palm farm."

"That's what you do?"

"Yup. Started the business in Lantana nine years ago. I grow the trees from seedlings, harvest them, sell them, plant them, the works."

"I never knew. Mom never told us much about you. Just that she left — or you left — she was never clear."

"I'm sorry."

"Yeah, well, it was tough. Carrie and I were okay. Never knew you. Never missed you. But it was hard on Mom, raising two kids on her own."

"How is she doing?" Dan knew this sounded stupid, but he had no idea how to communicate with his own son. What did Terry want to know about his past? About the Parnells? How much did he resent him for what happened twenty-two years ago?

"She's the reason I need to talk to you," Terry said. "She's been through too much. You hurt her again —"

"Terry, I won't. I swear it."

"Hey man, calm down. It's cool." Terry took a slug of beer. "I just want to know what you're going to do?"

"What do you mean?" *What was Terry talking about?*

"I mean, about my mother. Why do you think she invited you here today?"

"I guess because of —" Dan had asked himself this a million times. Curiosity? Did she pity him? Did she want the kids to get to know their old man? Or, could it be that she actually wanted to see him? After all these years? "I don't know." Dan lowered his head and began shifting the unopened Coors from hand to hand.

"Mom wants to see you," Terry said. "Though I don't know why. You never gave her one iota of support. You come from one of the wealthiest families in the world, and you offered her nothing. Us, nothing. Obviously you never gave a damn about us."

"That's not true. She wouldn't accept anything."

"Sounds like Mom," Terry interrupted. "But what about Carrie and me? Never a word. Nothing. Sure, our last name. But never a hint that our biological father was one of *those* Parnells."

What was Dan's excuse? The truth: he hadn't wanted to screw up their lives.

"Then mom gets a call," Terry went on. "That attorney of yours, Schiller. Wants us all up north for the will. She says, no way. Then Schiller calls again. Sends down a goddamn private jet."

"I didn't know."

"Then we finally get a look at you and the grand Parnell family. The family that was too good for us. Too good for my mother. Isn't that it? Isn't that what happened?"

"All my fault." Dan began to squirm. Of course, Terry must hate him. But what could he do to make amends? "What do you want me to do? How can I ever make it up to you and Carrie? Your mother?"

"You can never make it up." Terry said, jiggling the empty Coors can. "Mom's forty-five years old. No way you can give her back those years. No way Carrie and I can ever have a real father. You know what? Mom never even had a boyfriend. You know what I mean?"

Dan nodded, all at once feeling elated — and guilty.

"And now she can't wait to hear from you. I know about those letters you've been sending her. What's that all about?"

Dan felt like a child being scolded by an adult. "Look, Terry, the truth is I don't know what to do. Yes, I want to see her and you and Carrie."

"I have some ideas," Terry said, reaching over, taking Dan's un-opened beer can, flipping off the tab, and handing it back.

"What are you thinking?" Dan asked.

"About your old man's estate," Terry said. "What's going on?"

"When Dad died, he left most of his money to a trust. You heard that when the will was read," Dan answered.

"I caught that much. Can you get that money?"

"Truth is, I don't want it," Dan said, uneasily, turning to face Terry. "I live very simply."

"How about us?"

Where was his son going with this? "Uh, your mother — I mean, she never wanted anything. You heard what she said."

"How about us?" Terry leaned in toward Dan and waved his hand in front of him. "Carrie and me?"

Dan gasped at the appalling truth: he had never even once thought about passing his inheritance to his children. He felt a sudden sense of horror. Why had he assumed that they would feel the same as Gina? Why hadn't he reached out to them? They're twenty-three years old now, he realized.

"So Mom's Mom," Terry went on. "Can you believe it? All that money Paul Parnell gives her? She gives it all to charity. Wouldn't even use it to pay off our college loans. "Mom's a stubborn and proud woman."

"Yes," Dan said. "My father tried to get her to take money over the years. She sent everything back."

"Carrie and I each got a million from your old man. That's all well and good, but what about the rest? There's supposed to be almost two billion. So, what do you have to do to get it?"

"Be the person my father wanted me to be." For the first time Dan seriously considered Dad's bizarre challenge. "Do the things he said in the letter."

"The letter?"

"Before he died, my father wrote a personal letter to each of us."

"What did it say?" Terry prodded.

Dan was not sentimental, but these last words of his father had etched themselves on his brain.

Dan clutched the steering wheel and recited, eyes staring ahead. "The letter said that he and my mother were so happy when I was born. How after my mother was killed, he felt that he had neglected me and Frank. That he let my Parnell grandparents practically raise us. That when he met Vivian, he was happy again, but that was too late for me since I was getting ready to leave for college."

"Neglected you? Those were his words?" Terry asked, wide-eyed.

"Yes, and he said that he was sorry."

"Neglect must run in the family. So, how does it relate to your inheritance?"

"He developed a code of values that he wants us all to endorse."

"What are they, specifically?"

"First, family. He wanted me to reconcile with you and your mother and your sister. He said, 'Gina's integrity humbles me.' His exact words." Dan felt his voice start to tremble and tears prick his eyes.

"Ho-l-y shit." Terry let out a long breath.

Dan continued, wanting to get this all out. "He's big into religion. Into family. And he wants us to be generous."

"Be generous?" Terry reflected. "Yeah, I remember the part about the four points. God, family, community. What was the fourth?"

"Professional responsibility," Dan answered.

"That all?" Terry asked, settling back, crunching the Coors can between his hands.

"Just that he hopes I endorse his credo, have success and happiness, that he's sorry he missed so much of my life."

"Just like me," Terry breathed. "Your old man wasn't around much?"

"Honestly, Terry, it was so long ago."

"You think the old man meant this shit?"

"I'm convinced he meant it."

"Any problem if I share this with Carrie?"

"Of course not." Dan wondered bitterly why he hadn't taken the initiative himself. Again he'd let his selfishness overwhelm his responsibilities.

"Are you going with it?" Terry asked. "Going to — shall we say — comply?"

Dan turned to face his son. "Terry, I hadn't intended to do anything about it. But if you feel that I should —"

"Yes, definitely, you should."

"I just hadn't considered it. I mean, with my simple life." As Dan sat with Terry in the chilly air of the truck, reality struck. Terry was right. Of course he had to go after the inheritance. For the first time, maybe he could do something for his family.

"Believe me, for someone who's never had any, money's important," Terry said, pointing to the garage out back. "I bought myself a Beemer with Granddad's money — cherry red. Pretty cool, huh?"

"Pretty cool," Dan said, turning to face him. "Terry, I'll do whatever I can."

"Sounds like the right thing," Terry paused. "Should I start calling you Dad? Like, isn't that what your old man wanted?"

"Yes," Dan said, his eyes now leaking tears. "That would be good."

"Sounds weird. Dad." Terry paused. "Yes, I can do it. Wait 'til I tell

Carrie. You know, she likes you. Must have been that weepy scene in New York."

"Now, that was embarrassing," Dan said, feeling the flush rising up his neck. The kids needed a man for a father, not a crying baby.

"Dad, you want to make everything up to us? Pass this test. Become Mister Family Man, Mister Religious Leader, Mister Community, Mister Financial Genius. I mean, say there's a couple billion that's going to be divided up. Right? Six siblings divided into that." Terry slammed his fist on the dashboard. "Boggles my mind. You know Mom makes about forty grand a year. Let's see, to make that much, she'd have to work for five thousand years. And you act like it's chicken shit."

"It's just that I like living simply."

"And you could be living like a king." Terry took Dan's untouched beer can. "I don't get it."

"I should have reached out to you and to Carissa." Dan said, sputtering out the words. "I was just too scared. I don't know, of rejection, I guess."

"No worries." Terry drank a slug of beer and reached over to squeeze Dan's shoulder.

"I'm glad we had this talk," Dan said, sensing the beginnings of a new relationship.

"We got a plan then?" Terry started to open the truck door. "About the inheritance stuff?"

Dan nodded an affirmative.

"Just one more thing," Terry said, glancing at the overflowing ashtray. "Mom is so antismoking. Never forget how she freaked out that time she caught me and Carrie out behind the palmettos with a pack of Marlboros. Must come with being a nurse."

"Yeah," Dan said, knowing this to be true, swearing right then that he'd stop. And swearing that he'd find a way to get what Terry wanted. But how? The very thought of opportunism was so alien to him.

CHAPTER TEN

Chan kept one eye on Rory and one eye on the kids as they boarded the Parnell Gulfstream. "You gonna be okay, honey?" he asked for the third time.

"I'm good." Rory forced a smile. They were standing on the tarmac outside the private terminal at Orlando International Airport. Chan and the kids were heading home to Doylestown. "Eight kids, a week in Disney World, I'm exhausted. This'll be a reprieve."

"I still think you're crazy." Chan scrutinized Rory so closely that she had to squint to hold back the tears. "I mean, why you? Dan lives in Florida, for heaven's sake. Why do you have to personally check out the property?"

"I wanted to make sure the house will handle all the kids when we come down for vacation, but I will miss all of you. You sure you'll be okay?"

She knew he would. Mrs. Owen, their supernanny-housekeeper could manage just fine.

"Yeah, yeah. A break from us. Alone on a sunny beach?"

"Ready, Dad?" Emily shouted from the doorway of the aircraft. "We got everything on the plane."

"We'll miss you, Mom." Misty had deplaned and run over to hug Rory one more time. "Don't be gone too long."

"I'll be home next weekend. Now, you two better get on that plane before the pilot leaves without you," Rory called, desperate that they leave before she fell to pieces.

"With all those kids on board? He's not leaving without me." Chan leaned in for one last kiss and one last searching look before taking Misty's hand and leading her onto the jet.

Two years earlier, Rory and Chan had adopted the three children of their best friends and neighbors, who'd perished in a car crash — Karen, ten; Misty, eight; and Tyler, seven. With both sets of grandparents in nursing homes, no other family, no will, no provisions of any kind for the children, they'd intervened so that the county would not separate them. Ever since, they'd done the best they could to integrate the kids into their chaotic household, but there was still the occasional emotional crisis. They had five biological kids: Emily, 14; Becky, 13; ten-year old twins, Chip and Charlie; Ricky, seven, the same age as Tyler. Three plus five made eight noisy, active kids.

The kids had had a fantastic week at Disney, one that had been promised ever since the family merger. One that had been put off twice. Two years earlier when Vivian Parnell died, and the past November because of Paul's imminent death. When Meredith had called insisting that Rory put the trip off again to help Carla, Rory had refused. However, her reason had nothing to do with the children's trip.

Rory lingered until the plane became a tiny dot in the sky. Now, she was alone for the first time since she had made a crucial decision. It was important to her that she not cry in front of Chan or the kids. But now, alone in that parking lot in a rental car, pent-up fear unleashed wracking sobs.

Five years earlier, just months before her mother was diagnosed with malignant melanoma, her father had started construction on the compound in Longboat Key, Florida. He'd envisioned a winter retreat big enough for the whole family. A ten-bedroom main house, a guesthouse with two full suites, a gym, spa, tennis courts, pool, and pool house. But when her mother became ill, he'd lost interest, and delegated the completion to the builder and a local designer and hired a couple, the Tallys, to manage the property. No one in the family had actually stayed in the place except Frank during his political travels.

Now as Rory headed for Sarasota, she couldn't stop thinking about her parents. The bone metastases that made her mother's last two years so painful. And her father's pancreatic cancer diagnosis came just three months after her mother had died. Try as he might to fight the cancer with radiation and chemo, the disease marched relentlessly, invasively forward. He tried alternative medicine, nutritional cocktails, magnet therapy, acupuncture, even Laetrile from Mexico before denial progressed to acceptance and he'd put together that perplexing will.

As for her biological father, Rory rarely thought of him, but when she did, it was with an ambiguous mix of resentment for leaving her and relief that he had, so that her mother could go on to marry Paul Parnell. Where was Tony Barricelli now? What type of illnesses ran in his family?

"Mrs. Stevens, I'm Leo Tally." A tall black man with a military crew cut whom she judged to be about forty met Rory at the rental return in Sarasota and ushered her into the waiting Mercedes. Leo wore a simple white golf shirt and pressed tan slacks that made him look efficient and competent and his bright smile signaled confidence. "So glad to meet you, ma'am."

"Thank you, Mr. Tally," Rory said in a voice hoarse from crying. "I'm glad to be here."

"The missus has been getting ready all week."

Rory knew immediately that she liked this man. His dialogue kept her distracted as he proudly filled her in on the Longboat Key property affairs. As they proceeded through the second of two security gates, Tally suggested, "Once we get there, Mrs. Tally will get you settled and then we can tour the property. Make sure everything's to your specifications."

"Sounds good, but there's somewhere I have to go first," she said. "Could I use one of the cars?"

"Why you could drive this one or the Land Rover or the Porsche?"

"The Rover will be fine," Rory said, not in the mood for a sports car.

"No, I've never seen Dr. March." An overweight woman with brassy hair guarded the entrance to the inner sanctum. So far, she had not looked at Rory. "No one in particular referred me."

"Insurance?"

"Yes, I have United Healthcare, but I want to pay in cash."

"Well, that's not necessary, ma'am." The woman looked up at her for the first time. "We'll send in the paperwork."

"Still, I want to pay in cash."

"As you wish, but the doctor may want tests."

"That's okay," Rory said with finality. She needed to see the doctor quickly before she lost her nerve.

"Wait over there." The receptionist pointed toward a row of vinyl chairs by a fish tank. "The doctor will see you soon."

Rory knew it was stupid, just finding a doctor in the yellow pages. The guy could be a real idiot. But this was how she'd chosen to do it. She had refused Meredith's insistent demand that she be in Manhattan to help Carla, and had come to Sarasota alone so that Chan, a very skilled, very busy, and very popular family doctor would not know.

"Mrs. Stevens?"

The man calling her name was thin, balding, with a sparse handle-bar moustache. His white coat was wrinkled and a stethoscope dangled around his scrawny neck. Rory judged him to be in his early forties. That was good. Not too young. Not too old.

"Hope we didn't keep you waiting too long," he said, ushering her into a cubicle with just enough space for an examining table and a chair. "April's still busy in Florida. I'm a solo practitioner. Not many of us left, I'm afraid. My wife is always after me to take a partner."

Rory had cautioned Chan to do the same thing. Maybe this guy was okay.

"What can I do for you?" he asked, glancing at her chart. "All I know so far is that you're thirty-eight years old; your temperature, ninety-nine point eight degrees, borderline high; pulse one twenty, too high, but not unusual for a first visit; and blood pressure one ten over seventy, excellent. So, you'll have to take it from here."

"I don't think it's anything," Rory said as he motioned her up on the examining table. "I'm probably wasting my time and yours."

"Let me be the judge."

"I've never been a hypochondriac," she continued, "But lately I have been abnormally tired."

"How long have you felt this way?"

"My father died recently. I took care of him during the last weeks of his life. I guess it's been four months."

"Were you close to your father?"

"Yes, very close. I miss him terribly."

"Must have been exhausting, caring for him at the end."

"Yes, it was. He died of pancreatic cancer. You know how horrible that can be. He had hospice care and they were wonderful, but still. Then the funeral. I must be just run down."

"Tell me more about how you feel."

"Just tired, very tired. My energy level is so low."

"How about sadness?" he asked. "Are you very sad?"

"Yes, about my father, but I have so much to live for, I need to get on with my life. I don't think that's what's making me tired, but I know that depression certainly makes people feel like I do."

"Feelings of hopelessness?"

"No, I feel guilty that I'm not myself, but not hopeless. Worried, maybe. Certainly not hopeless."

"Feelings of worthlessness?"

"I feel I'm not doing as much as I should for my family. I mean, feeling like this, so tired." *When was he going to stop these useless questions?*

"Mrs. Stevens, have you ever thought about ending your life?"

"What?" Rory clutched the edge of the examining table. *He was asking her about suicide?* "No, Dr. March. Quite the opposite, I'm worried that I may have something seriously and physically wrong with me."

"Ever think about whether life is worth living?"

"Of course not."

Suddenly, tears tumbled down Rory's cheeks.

Dr. March pulled out a tissue and handed it to her. "I'm really not depressed," she said, dabbing away the tears. "Worried, yes."

"Okay, Mrs. Stevens," the doctor said, reaching for more tissues. "Let's do a physical exam."

Without even asking her to undress, Dr. March listened to her heart and lungs. He had her lie down and he palpated her abdomen.

"Rapid heart rate," he pronounced. "Otherwise healthy, physically."

Rory was about to ask him about the purplish bruises on her arms and legs and the red spots on her arms. When Chan had asked about the bruises, she'd told him she'd tripped over a skateboard in the back yard. Dr. March hadn't asked.

"I think that you have a touch of depression," he diagnosed. "I'm going to give you a prescription for an antidepressant. It's called Paxil. I'd like to see you back in a week to make sure you aren't having any side effects, and to see if I need to increase the dose. What you have is called situational depression. Depression triggered by the recent death of your father. It's very common, but we should treat it before it becomes severe. Okay?"

Rory blew her nose on fresh tissues.

"Okay," she said to placate him. She did not intend to fill the Paxil prescription. "But, Dr. March, I'd like you to do a complete blood count including a platelet count. And a chemistry panel and thyroid test." Please, let it be low thyroid, she thought. But deep in her nurse's mind, she knew there was some other, more serious, cause for her symptoms.

His eyes narrowed as he looked up from writing the prescription. "I'm not sure that's indicated. I like to do my part to keep medical costs down by not ordering unnecessary tests."

"If you would just humor me, doctor. Maybe I'm just paranoid. I'll pay for the tests so there's no insurance impact." *Just do* it, she wanted to scream. *This is my life.*

"If you insist." He frowned, but did reach for her chart and began to write.

"How soon will you have the results?" Rory asked. He was obviously rushing to terminate the fifteen-minute visit he'd allocated.

"Call me next week," he said.

"But I have to go out of the country," she lied. "Could you make it STAT? Can I call you tomorrow for the results? It's really important to me."

"STAT?" He pivoted to face her. "Yes, if you're leaving the country. You can call late in the day."

Rory wondered if he was having second thoughts about his diagnosis. Depressed people don't usually take international trips. She also thought about her husband with a surge of appreciation. Chan would never slap somebody with her complaints on an antidepressant without a comprehensive evaluation.

Rory headed directly to Sarasota Memorial Hospital to have her blood drawn. The skies had turned dark and rain fell in sheets as she darted between the parking garage and the entrance. Wet, chilled by the blast of air-conditioning, Rory's body started to shake. Always surrounded by family and friends, she felt totally alone. At home, she knew all the lab techs at Doylestown Hospital. She was "Dr. Stevens's wife?" Most people there didn't realize that she was a nurse since she hadn't worked after Emily was born.

As Rory held out her arm, a thin young black man stretched the rubber tubing around her upper arm. "Ouch," she said as he tightened it securely, squeezing her arm. She wasn't worried about the pain, just the bruise it would leave.

"Make a fist," the technician said with a reassuring smile. "I'm good, so it's not going to hurt."

"Okay," she said trying, unsuccessfully, to return the smile.

Rory thought about her days in the hospital. Where she'd met Chan on the pediatric floor of Jefferson when he was a resident. They'd often laughed at how prophetic it was — now that they have eight kids. Maybe someday she would go back.

"Done." She hardly felt the prick as the needle went in. With a swift move, the tech released the tourniquet. When the tubes were filled, he slipped out the needle and slapped on a gauze pad. "Your job is to hold this on that hole I made."

Then he stared at her forearm. Looking up, he seemed to pause before speaking. "Mrs. Stevens, you see these red marks?" He pointed to the bright red spots, the size of a pinprick, scattered all over the surface of her forearm. "Make sure you check on your lab results right away. Your doctor ordered them STAT."

"I will," Rory said. So the young tech had noticed. Dr. March had not. These were *petechiae*, signs of easy bleeding. Rory had noticed them on various parts of her body over the past few weeks. She had reddish hair and fair skin with freckles, but she'd never had spots like this before, and they seemed to appear after any kind of pressure. She felt that something was really wrong, and was grateful that she'd hidden the marks from Chan with long sleeves and full-length nightgowns.

❦

Rory spent the rest of the afternoon and the next morning with the Tallys. Anything to keep distracted, to stave off her fears. She tried to concentrate on the details the couple reviewed about the 16,000-square-foot house, the ancillary buildings and the two and one-half acres of lush greenery. She was sure the Tallys thought her a dimwit.

But she immediately liked Ann Tally. She reminded Rory of Sara Waring in Manhattan. Both exuded energy. Ann took voluminous notes, as she pressed for details on the personal likes and dislikes of each family member. Rory did her best on the Parnell family rundown: Frank and Meredith and how demanding they could be; Dan, not a participant in family affairs, but his former wife lived in Fort Myers, only two hours away; Carla, inferring that her lifestyle and friends might be problematic; Ashley, how sweet she was and in a new relationship; and Monica, the megacelebrity. The Tallys, like the caretakers of the other Parnell properties, knew that their jobs depended on airtight confidentiality. So they were privy to Monica's Parnell relationship, which was still undetected by the media.

Ann seemed genuinely excited about Rory's eight kids, a rare reaction. Lots of people considered her and Chan politically incorrect. But when the housekeeper asked about each of the kids, Rory found that she could not go on. She choked back tears and announced that she was going to walk the beach, even though it was raining.

The day after seeing Dr. March, Rory ate lunch on the terrace trying to savor the cloudless blue sky. It was much warmer than the day before and she decided to walk again on the beach. The heat of the sand felt so good between her toes. She planned to call Dr. March's office at three thirty to get her test results, but as she stood at the edge of the lapping waves, she felt sweaty, short of breath, and her heart pounded. She had always had so much energy and now just walking a few steps made her legs feel like clubs. Making her way to a nearby beach chair, she sat rehearsing the worst-case scenario. If her premonition was right, what about Chan? That's why she'd had to do this by herself. If everything turned out okay, she would not have upset him unnecessarily. And what about the children? The three adopted ones were just starting to feel secure in their boisterous household.

She had not been sitting long when Leo Tally approached. "Mrs. Stevens, I'm so glad I found you out here," he said, a deep frown signaling concern. "There's a doctor's office in Sarasota that called twice. They want you to come in right away. Any time, they said. They'd take you any time. Just come on in."

"Thank you, Mr. Tally," Rory said, no longer doubting her suspicions. "Could you drive me there now?"

"Becky," Rory tried not to choke on tears when her second oldest daughter answered the phone. "Is Dad there?"

She had waited until she was sure Chan would be home and the younger children in bed.

"Yeah, he's here, Mom, helping Emily with her algebra. But I got to talk to you. Dad said it's up to you. There's this party at Samantha's. The first part is at the ice skating rink, the one in Warrington. I can never remember the name. Boys and girls. Then an overnight at her house. Only girls. Please, Mom, say yes. Dad thinks that Samantha is too into boys, but they're not coming to her house. Just to the ice skating."

How many decisions like this would Chan have to face? "Whatever Dad says."

"But he said whatever you said," Becky pleaded.

"Let me talk to him, honey," Rory said. "Shouldn't you be off to bed?"

"I'm thirteen. It's only ten o'clock!"

"Run along now. And good night, Becky. I miss you."

"I miss you too, Mom." Then, "Dad!" Rory heard her yell.

"Chan," she didn't know how she would find the words.

"Hi, honey, I was wondering when you'd call. I would have called you, but I'm stumped. I used to get all As in math, but I can't figure out Emily's algebra."

"Chan, I don't know how to tell you this, but I'm ill." Rory stopped. There was a long silence. "Chan, I have leukemia."

"Come on, Rory. What's this all about?" Rory's heart broke as she heard terror shatter his voice.

"I didn't want to tell you. I didn't want to scare you. But I'm quite certain. Not positive without a bone marrow, but —"

"Bone marrow?" Chan echoed. "Just who's the doctor here? What's this about bone marrow?"

"I didn't want to bother you. We've had so much going on. So I made an appointment with a doctor down here. Nobody we know. Just someone from the phone book. I just wanted to get some blood tests without you getting distressed and all of Doylestown knowing. His name is Dr. March. He's here in Sarasota. I told him I was unusually tired, and he thought I was depressed, so I asked him to do a CBC. Today he called me in. My white count is very high with lots of blasts. Platelets low and hemoglobin eight point four."

"Honey, please let this all be wrong. This cannot be true."

"He'd already scheduled me for admission at Sarasota Memorial. Wants to do a bone marrow, and start me on chemotherapy. Chan, I'm so sorry. I don't want to put you through this."

"Rory. Stay there," Chan said, a peculiar shakiness in his voice. "I'm flying down tonight. We'll have you back here by tomorrow morning and straight to the University of Pennsylvania."

"The children, Chan," Rory tried to hold back the tears, but failed miserably.

"Rory, everything will be okay. First, we don't know what we're dealing with. *If*, and I say, *if*, you do have leukemia, that's a curable condition. And I want you started on therapy by this time tomorrow night."

"Okay," she sobbed. "Please hurry. I am so very scared."

"I'll be there. Try to stay calm — get some rest. Tomorrow will be very demanding. And give me the number of that doctor. Honey, I promise, everything will be okay."

"I'm so sorry," Rory groped for Dr. March's phone number. "I don't want to be a burden on you and the kids."

"I love you, Rory. You're all I care about. Goddamn it, how did I miss this? So anemic. Those bruises. How could I have missed the signs? I'll make it up to you, I promise."

CHAPTER ELEVEN

MAY 2001

The late May sun was bright, the sky clear, the air warm, and the mood jubilant as the University of Pennsylvania Medical School Class of 2001 marched up to receive their diplomas. But once they'd returned to the tent to turn in their black gowns, the bittersweet reality of leaving behind so many friends and so many memories cast a melancholic spell. Under that spell were two graduates — one with pale skin, honey-brown eyes, and hair the color of cinnamon, the other with skin as dark as mahogany, glossy black hair, and deep brown eyes. Best friends for four years, Ashley Parnell from Main Line Philadelphia and Ruth Campbell from inner-city Baltimore had much in common as women, despite the vast difference in their socioeconomic backgrounds.

"I am so sorry, Ruthie," Ashley was saying. "My brother, Frank, arranged a graduation party at the house. For the family only. I had hoped that Conrad and I and you and your mother could have an early dinner before you headed back to Baltimore."

"Hey, no worries," Ruthie said. "Now that I'm out of my apartment, I'm anxious to get back home. I only have two weeks before I go to Albuquerque. But I will miss you, girl."

They hugged for a long time before Ashley heard a cough behind her. She didn't have to turn. She knew it was Conrad. He wouldn't approach her directly because they'd had to keep their relationship a secret at the med school. But not for any longer. Anyway, Ruthie, Ashley's only confidante, knew all about Conrad. She didn't approve of him. Neither had Conrad approved of Ruthie. Ashley realized now the sad truth that the girls hadn't spent any free time together for over two months.

"And I'm even more sorry," Ashley said, "that we'll not be able to take that break in Anguilla this year. We had such fun last year, didn't we?"

"That we did, but hey, I'd better go find my mom, and you'd better get back to Conrad. He's lurking over there. Not too patiently." Ruthie leaned in closer. "Now you remember what I said about him. Don't let him pressure you to into anything you do not want. I told you before, Ashley, that man's a chameleon. Charismatic, yes. But I've seen him go from hostile belligerence to disarming neediness right in front of my eyes."

Ashley said nothing, but her heart began to race. She should defend Conrad, but she couldn't.

"You hear me?"

"Yes, Doctor Ruth, I hear you." Ashley tried for a smile.

"I'm serious. There's something wrong here. You've changed, Ashley. I want you to be happy, for sure, but, well, we've been over this before. Take care, girl, and keep in touch."

The women embraced and parted. Immediately, Ashley felt as if a lifeline had been cut. When Conrad tried to lead her away, she stood her ground until Ruthie disappeared from sight.

True, Conrad had not approved of Ruthie. It wasn't so much the color of her skin, but that she bought her clothes at Wal-Mart. Conrad loved the trappings of wealth: the clothes, cars, the house, the staff, the airplane. For Ashley, none of that mattered, maybe because she had been born with everything that money could buy. But at what cost? When she met someone, what did they see? Did they see her as a person? Or as a recipient of her family's money? As a result, Ashley had few friends, and losing Ruthie left her feeling desolate.

Before she'd met Conrad, she'd hoped that Ruthie would take a local residency and they could live together in the Devon house. But Ruthie had taken a pediatric residency at the University of New Mexico, and Ashley would do cardiology in Philadelphia at Jefferson Hospital. Watching Ruthie walk away made Ashley want to run after her, but Conrad kept a firm hold on her arm.

"Let her go," he told her. "Today's the beginning of the next phase of our life together, my love."

"Dad, let's go." Elise tugged at Frank's suit jacket. Med school graduates milled about with families and guests, but Frank needed to press the flesh with the president of the University of Pennsylvania and other Penn dignitaries as he waited for Meredith, a trustee of Penn, to return from the procession of dignitaries. A simple rule: every vote counts. Elise would have to wait.

"In a minute," Frank snapped, straightening his tie and glancing down to check his daughter. She looked like a little angel in her white pinafore fringed in ribbons of lavender, and white patent leather shoes. He wanted her with him, hand in hand. The proud, doting father of a fairy princess, a magnet for the media.

After the disastrous meeting with Carl Schiller, Frank and Meredith resolved to paint a perfect picture. Frank made amends with Schiller, telling the old lawyer that he understood, accepted, etcetera, etcetera, everything he wanted to hear. To expedite the process of model son, Frank put his aide Matt Cleveland in charge, reminding him to do whatever it took to make sure Frank passed his father's "test" with flying colors. Matt understood how critical this money would be to Frank's political future and, by association, Matt's.

Two years earlier, Frank had agreed to interview Matt as a courtesy to his powerful Philadelphia Republican family. The kid had just graduated from the University of Pennsylvania with a Ph.D. in clinical psychology. Little did Frank know that a psych major would come in handy, but it turned out that Matt had an uncanny insight into the minefield of politics. It also didn't hurt that he was attractive, impeccably dressed, and articulate. And despite his polished demeanor, Matt had a down-to-earth personality that clicked across the wide social spectrum of his constituents. Matt had become Frank and Meredith's closest confidant, their right-hand man.

In the meantime, Frank had solidified his position in the Senate with appointments on the Judicial Committee as well as Armed Services and Intelligence. With the presidential election going to George W. Bush, he had powerful allies in the administration. Paul Parnell and George, Senior, had been buddies, and Frank had cut his political teeth rubbing elbows with George W. and Jeb. And now with Cheney getting that defibrillator implanted in his chest, George W. might be looking for a running mate in 2004.

On the occasion of Ashley's graduation, Matt had organized a family celebration. Assuming that the inheritance test would require some sort of audit, he wanted to chalk up family events like points on the scoreboard. So Matt set it up at the house in Devon, where all the Parnell kids had grown up, and which now belonged to the trust even though Ashley still lived there.

"Come on. We gotta get to Aunt Ashley's," Elise continued to nag as Frank shook the proper hands.

"Dad talked to a million people," Elise complained when Meredith joined them.

"You know what it's like when your dad's a senator. Remember the election? How hard we had to work for Daddy to get this job?"

Elise smiled as they were escorted to the waiting limo. "Yeah, that was fun. I got to stay up late at the parties."

"So, Frank, you're finally going to meet Doctor Welton," Meredith said as the car moved onto the ramp leading to the Schuylkill Expressway.

"'Doctor Impressed With Himself' according to your description."

"You have to admit that I'm a pretty good judge of character. That's why the less talented attorneys take me to court for voir dire. You wait and see, this guy's a classic narcissistic personality."

"What does that mean?" Elise never let a big word go. She was a champ at interrupting.

"Narcissistic." Meredith catered to the child's every question. "It means that you think you're such a big deal. Have to be the center of attention."

"Who's like that?"

"That man Aunt Ashley's been seeing. But don't go repeating it. Remember what I told you about keeping confidences?"

"I remember," said Elise, picking up Harry Potter.

"More than seeing," Frank said. "More like living with."

"Did Matt uncover anything on that background check?" Meredith asked hastily, glancing at Elise.

"The guy's acting chairman of psychiatry at Penn. Does a lot of consulting. Specialty is hypnosis. Owns a condo on Locust."

"Pricey address. Good credentials."

"For crying out loud, Meredith, he's fifty years old."

"Hmm. Twice her age. Well, Ashley's always been on the mature side," Meredith considered. "A father complex, perhaps? Never had a serious boyfriend, and all of a sudden — sound Freudian?"

Frank reached into his valise and pulled out a thin folder. "Here, read the bio Matt pulled off the Internet. University of Cincinnati Medical School. Staff shrink at the Menninger Clinic in Kansas City."

"Hypnosis," Meredith remarked. "Don't you find that a bit spooky?"

"Hypnosis is used a lot in medicine. Nothing spooky about it. Look at the bright side. Between the demands of medical training and being preoccupied with romance, Ashley will be too busy to worry about other things."

"Still, Ashley's Little Miss Perfect. She's certainly guaranteed a nice piece of the pie."

As they drove up the long, circular drive lined by massive trees, Frank thought that the stately Georgian mansion looked the same as it had thirty-five years ago, except that the gardens were now even more splendid. Rhododendrons, roses with fancy names, riotous blooms of flowers he could not identify flourished. Gardening was Mr. Mendoza's passion and Dad had given him carte blanche. He still remembered the day the three of them moved in. He'd been five, Dan seven. He and Dan learned every nook and cranny. Frank's memory flashed back to one of the few arguments between his father and his new wife, Vivian. Vivian had wanted to build a house in one of the Bucks County suburbs. Frank cheered when Dad put his foot down. "No, Vivian," he'd said, "this is where Dan and Frank grew up. We're staying. You can redecorate all you want, but we're not moving."

Ashley greeted them at the door with a tepid hug as a couple of kids flew out, shouting something to Elise. Frank felt a stab of pride at how picture-perfect Elise looked, compared to the Stevens hooligans. Why the hell Rory and Chan had adopted those three extra kids was beyond him. And Ashley looked stunning in a black sheath that clung to her slender form. Her auburn hair hung in waves to her shoulders, a style that made her look much more attractive than that old-fashioned bun she usually wore at the nape of her neck.

"Congratulations, doctor." Meredith's smile looked genuine. "We're all so proud."

"Aunt Ashley," Elise joined in. "I'm gonna be a doctor too!"

"Hey, that's great, honey," Ashley said, bending down to kiss her cheek.

Elise ran off and Frank looked up to face a man who so resembled his father ten, maybe twenty years ago, that he blinked. What had Meredith said about an Oedipal complex?

"Conrad," Ashley stepped aside, "this is my brother, Frank. Of course, you remember Meredith."

Frank tried not to stare as he shook the guy's hand. Politics forces handshakes, and Frank mentally classified this type of greeting on a scale of one to five. Very limp, this one, barely a score of one.

"Welcome," Conrad said, with a smile. "Happy to meet you."

"Likewise," Frank said, offering his Bobby Kennedy toothy grin as if this were a smiling contest.

Right away, Frank knew he was not going to like this guy. Limp handshake. Damp hand. The familiar, protective way he ushered Ashley inside. The audacity of welcoming him into his own house.

"Chan's here with the kids," Ashley said. "I guessed you noticed all the commotion. I'm devastated that Rory's still in the hospital, and I'd so hoped that Carla would be out of the clinic, but —"

"Carla's made good progress." Welton sounded supercilious, as if he were a member of the Parnell inner sanctum. "But I recommended that they keep her there another couple of weeks."

Who in the heck was this guy to be making recommendations about his sister?

"Conrad and I went up to see her last week," Ashley said. "She's really changed, Frank. She wants to use her money to help others. You'll never guess her new cause?"

"Money?" Meredith's eyebrows shot up. "Can't be much left."

"What cause?" Frank had counted on Carla being too impaired to be a contender for the trust. "Starving models?"

"AIDS," Ashley said. "She learned a lot in rehab from HIV-positive patients. Anyway, she's really serious. As serious as I've ever seen her. She looked better too. Put on a few pounds. Got her hair fixed. Remember, Meredith, how bad she looked?"

"I do," Meredith said.

"Uncle Frank?" a male voice interrupted.

Frank turned to face Dan's kid, Terry.

"Mind me calling you 'uncle'?" The kid had a crooked grin. "I'm trying to practice family togetherness, and all that."

"I didn't realize you'd be here." Frank didn't care if his tone betrayed annoyance.

"Dan — I mean, Dad — couldn't make it, but since I'm now located in D.C., I could. Going for family teamwork. You know? I mean, with so much at stake."

"At stake?" Frank echoed.

"Right." Terry gestured around the room. "You know, my sister and I grew up not even knowing that we were grandchildren of a billionaire. Imagine that."

"Interesting," said Meredith, glancing at Frank with her practiced smile.

"Frank," Ashley said to diffuse the uncomfortable silence, "did you know that Terry is the new assistant manager of government affairs at Keystone Pharma?"

"Yeah, and I used you as a reference," Terry said. "Being a senator and all, I figured it couldn't hurt. Hope you don't mind."

Before Frank could say whether or not he minded, and he had minded, they were interrupted by Mrs. M. announcing lunch.

The adults, including the two older Stevens girls, settled at the dining room table. Then Frank stood to make the congratulatory toast. "To Doctor Ashley."

Champagne glasses clinked. For a moment it looked as if Chan would not raise his glass, but eventually he did and took a small sip. Frank wondered how he could even be here. If Meredith was in the hospital, he could never leave her side.

"Thanks," Ashley said, blushing. "It means so much to Conrad and me to have you with us. If only Rory and Carla were here."

"And your mother and father. They would be so proud," Welton said, patting Ashley's hand.

Who the hell did this jerk think he was, the family spokesperson? Frank felt himself clutching the edge of the table in frustration.

Ashley turned to Conrad with a shy smile as Frank watched Dr. Welton rise, champagne glass in hand.

"Ashley and I have another wonderful reason to celebrate," he announced.

Frank had not seen this coming. He glanced at Meredith. She was giving him the look: "I told you so."

"Ashley and I are to be married." Welton had a melodious masculine tone, as if he should be doing voice-over commercials. A voice that politicians, himself included, tried to emulate.

Shyly, Ashley held out her hand. On her left ring finger was a wide gold band with a single ruby embedded in the center. She twisted the ring proudly. The ring belonged to Conrad's mother. It's an heirloom."

Chan was the first with congratulations. Then Welton sat back down, pulled Ashley toward him, and kissed her on the lips. She blushed a deeper shade of red, and Frank did have to admit that she looked radiant. A beautiful woman had bloomed beneath that bookish personality. But was she in love with this guy?

Conrad seemed to manipulate the conversation after that. The people he knew. The text books he'd written. Frank frowned at Meredith. She had been right. This guy had an insatiable need to be admired by others. He didn't seem to give a darn about anybody else at the table, including his fiancée. Frank considered himself a master of dinner talk, but this guy was putting him to shame.

As lobster cocktails were served in martini glasses, Conrad explained that he and Ashley wanted to marry soon. Why wait? They'd waited for each other too long.

"Big wedding?" asked Terry.

"Aunt Ashley, how many bridesmaids?" asked Emily or Becky, Frank wasn't sure which.

"Quiet wedding," said Ashley. "So soon after Dad's death, and with me just starting my residency program."

As the entrees were served — rack of lamb, asparagus risotto — Conrad steered the conversation dangerously close to family financial matters.

"Frank, how are things going with your father's, shall we say, unconventional, plan to distribute the estate?"

"Conrad knows a lot about finance," Ashley said, innocently.

Meredith's eyebrows almost lifted off her face as she awaited Frank's response.

"Yeah, I've been wondering about that, too," Terry said, suspending a forkful of risotto.

"Tonight's a celebration," Frank said. "Not a business discussion." Meredith shot him one of her "good job" looks and he couldn't help a sheepish grin.

"One thing we do know is that Monica has renounced her part of the money," Conrad said, ignoring Frank's remark.

"Monica's a cool number," said Terry. "But I still can't believe she doesn't want the money."

Conrad's inquiry into the money? Terry getting interested? Carla chasing a cause? Frank thought he would be lucky to get one-sixth of the total, following all the rules as he was. How could his dad have created such a crazy scheme?

Frank was deep in thought when Chan mercifully changed the subject. " Frank, you talk to your buddy, Jeb, lately? Is he going to fix those Florida voting machines?"

"That idiot? Oh, oh." Terry dramatically covered his mouth with his hand. "Oops. I forgot. I'm on Republican turf."

Through the rest of the meal, Conrad took over the conversation again. Before dessert was served, Meredith and Frank excused themselves. Frank was giving a morning speech at the Washington Press Club, "Protecting our Homeland against Terror," and he needed to review his notes. But once in the car, Frank vented harshly. What he'd learned at the family get-together had him worried. Had he and Meredith underestimated the competition?

CHAPTER TWELVE

Conrad Welton paced the patio of his new home, the Parnell family's place in Devon. Face twisted in annoyance, his mood sour, he fumed. His sanctuary, overlooking the rose garden, shaded by stately trees, the centerpiece of tranquility, invaded by Ashley's raucous relatives and their bratty offspring. And to make matters worse, Ashley was late getting home. Her excuse? "Three late-morning admissions, a bone marrow aspiration, a central catheter placement." On ordinary days her chronic lateness annoyed him, but on this day, it infuriated him. And why such dedication? She'd be dropping out of medicine in January anyway. She didn't have to knock herself out, pretending to be the perfect medical resident.

Conrad had feigned graciousness to Frank Parnell and his wife and Parnell's aide when they'd arrived in Ashley's absence. A month earlier, Frank's aide informed Ashley that Frank was throwing a family Fourth of July barbeque. She had blindly acquiesced, but for the last time. Conrad tried to keep his fury under control as Parnells now swarmed all over his new home, splashing in the pool, chasing each other all over the perfect lawn, the thunk-thunk of tennis balls from the court giving him a headache.

He was about to head inside for a painkiller when he saw Ashley's car pull up the driveway. He waved to her from the patio and waited while she rushed inside to change.

Five minutes later, she emerged from the house wearing a red-and-blue sundress that she was too flat chested to fill out properly. The dark circles under her eyes made her look haggard, and her auburn hair was frizzy and unruly.

"Conrad, who all's here?" Ashley asked, stepping out to join him.

"Frank and Meredith, that guy who puppets for Frank, all the Stevens except Rory, Dan and his offspring, and Monica and Patrick. He's some kind of television personality, not a bad guy. But I can't tell you how much hell those kids are raising. They were playing kickball in the rhododendrons until —"

"Poor Rory," Ashley interrupted. "I talked to her last night. She's started her third round of chemo, and her platelets and white count are still way too low. I just hope she doesn't need a bone marrow transplant. But what about Carla?"

"You know about addicts," Welton answered. "Your sister is going to relapse. I don't want you getting your hopes up."

"I think you're wrong, Conrad. Carla's changed. She was anxious to be here so we could bounce around some ideas she has for HIV. She's even thinking of going to Africa to see for herself how bad it is. Meantime, she wants me to pick the best research institutes for her to help. Believe me, this is a new agenda for my little sister."

"Look, you better get out there and make nice-nice with your family. That's what today's all about. Frank is trying to score family points."

"Conrad, you shouldn't talk that way," Ashley admonished.

Ashley had told Welton about Frank's outburst when the will was read. Obviously, he planned to be the one to pass the test and receive the inheritance. Then there was Dan. Everyone said that he lived simply, but now he had an opportunistic son. Rory was ill, but still a big risk. Carla would be no problem. Bunky would take care of her. And Monica had renounced the money, loud and clear. As for Ashley, Welton planned to make sure she was a contender even though she didn't give a damn about her inheritance.

Welton took Ashley's hand and led her out to the party now in full swing on the deck surrounding the infinity pool. The entire property from the guesthouse to the tennis courts was decorated in patriotic red, white, and blue. Big flags. Little flags. The hammocks and tabletops draped in stars and stripes. Balloons everywhere. The day was perfect, with cerulean skies and wispy clouds randomly distributing the warmth of the sun. Ashley took all this wealth for granted, even the weather. Welton thought how similar she was to Crissy, his late wife.

So far he hadn't told Ashley about Crissy. She had been nineteen when he'd married her; twenty-two years old when he'd divorced her; twenty-four when she died thirteen years ago. Soon he'd have to tell Ashley, before her family started digging.

"Imagine that kind of energy," Ashley said as she led Welton toward chaotic screams in the pool. "Marco", followed by the chorus of "Polo," repeated over and over with giggles, screams, and splashes. Welton tried not to cringe. He didn't like children. Messy, whiny, demanding, he'd seen them suck every iota of attention and energy out of well-meaning parents. No child of his would compel such a sacrifice. They'd hire a nanny and never have to bother. Paul's note to Ashley had said for her to "be like her mother, to balance a personal and professional life." Ideally, Ashley should have a baby, too. He realized that if Crissy had gotten pregnant, things may have turned out differently.

The Marco Polos stopped as Welton and Ashley stopped at the edge of the pool. One of the older girls yelled, "Aunt Ashley, get your bathing suit on."

"Later," Ashley called, waving and smiling.

Welton nudged Ashley over to join Meredith, who was stretched out on a chaise near the edge of the pool. He'd done a double-take when he'd seen her earlier — the iron lady in a two-piece turquoise bathing suit. Not bad. Her blunt-cut brown hair styled, her nails perfectly manicured. He glanced at Ashley's nails. After years of nervous chewing, they were ragged, but better now that he was coaching her.

"Hi, Ashley." Meredith started to get up.

"Don't get up," Welton said, reaching to touch her shoulder.

Meredith leaned back, relaxing. "What's up with our rehab patient?" she asked. "She'll be here. Right?"

"Supposed to be," Ashley said.

"Hey, slow down!" Meredith held out an arm to catch one of the Stevens kids before the child tripped onto the concrete. Dripping wet, she and her brother ran shrieking toward the house.

"Ricky's got my floatie!" the little girl yelled. "Dad got it for me. Ricky has his own."

"I'm sure he'll bring it back," Meredith said. "Look, Elise is waiting for you over by the slide."

"Okay, Aunt Meredith," said the little girl; then, "Aunt Ashley, when are you comin' into the pool?"

"Maybe later, Misty," Ashley said, patting the child on her wet head.

"Where's everybody else?" Ashley asked.

"Monica and Patrick are on the tennis court with Terry and Carrie," Meredith reported. "Gina didn't come. Couldn't get off work. Can you believe it? Anyway, Frank and Dan and Chan are setting up the volley-ball net on the other side of the courts, and I'm the designated pool mon-itor, a job I would gladly relinquish. One kid's enough to make me crazy and there are nine in there."

Welton put his arm around Ashley's waist to urge her away from the turmoil in the pool, but Meredith went on, "Oh, and Matt Cleveland, Frank's aide, has a crush on Carrie."

"Carrie?" Welton asked.

"Carissa, one of Dan's twins," Meredith clarified.

"We'll be glad to take over with the kids," Ashley volunteered, "but first I'd better check out the barbeque operation. Oops, looks like I may be too late."

"You kids hungry?" yelled Matt as he pushed a cart heaped with hot dogs and hamburgers from the barbeque pit.

Amid louder squeals of delight, Meredith hopped off her deck chair. Tossing a pile of beach towels over to Ashley and Conrad, she ordered, "Let's get these kids dried off. I'll round up the adults. Everybody ac-counted for but Carla."

Welton stood, hands on hips, while Ashley started chasing children with towels.

"Kids, sit over by the picnic tables," Meredith shouted. "Adults, take the umbrella tables up on the terrace. Mrs. Mendoza's orders. She's lay-ing out a buffet."

Frank came jogging toward them and took his place beside his aide at the helm of the barbeque operation. Both donned chef hats and red, white, and blue aprons. From first glance, Welton had disliked Cleve-land, a pretty boy, with a distinguished streak of white highlighting his dark hair. Today, he was all smiles, laughing and joking with the kids.

"Who does he think he is?" he whispered to Ashley, but her answer was obliterated as a brass band appeared on the scene and started up "Yankee Doodle."

Frank seemed to have gone all out to make this a festive affair. He even appeared to be getting a kick out of it. His usually serious demeanor gave way to a frivolity that Welton had not expected and did not trust. Meredith also looked different, relaxed, and comfortable with the family.

Disgruntled, Welton stood by Ashley as she dutifully doled out the towels to one child after another. She called to two older girls. "Cool bathing suits!"

Both voices rang out, "Aunt Meredith took us shopping."

"Watch out, Conrad," Ashley warned as two children plowed into his legs, almost knocking him into the pool.

"What the —" he hollered. "Can't somebody get these kids under control?"

"They're just having a good time." Ashley forced a smile, and Welton had to remind himself not to lose his cool.

"Almost got you, didn't they?" As Welton recovered his balance, Monica Monroe strolled to his side and met his gaze with a wide smile. Her body in short shorts almost made him gasp.

"Ashley," Monica said, "Meet Patrick Nelson, my fiancé."

Welton watched Ashley as she held out her hand to the man by Monica's side.

"Honey, this is Ashley. She's the doctor, the one who lives here." Monica gestured around the grounds. "It's was tough preparing him for all of you, when I'm mostly clueless myself."

Welton noticed how Ashley stared at the buff guy's chest, which was marred by a tortuous scar running from the base of his neck to his umbilicus. The guy must have had some major health problem. Hadn't Patrick Nelson been an athlete before he got into sportscasting?

"We were just on our way to the buffet table," Ashley said. "The adult one, over there." She pointed to the red, white, and blue extravaganza now laden with food. "Want to join us?"

"Love to," Monica said.

Wealth was one thing, Welton thought, but did this lady have so much that she'd renounced the Parnell money? "Ashley and I are en-gaged," he said as they walked toward the buffet. "So you and I have something in common, and I'm new to the family myself."

"Patrick, good meeting you." Ashley had stopped staring. "I'm not a sports fanatic, but I did read an article about your new show in *People* magazine. I wanted to watch it, but since I'm on-call most of the time — How's it going?"

"Super. Keeps me hopping." Patrick said, with an easy television smile.

"So super that I don't see much of him," Monica said. "But today worked out great. We were staying at Patrick's mom's place in the Hamptons. Just a short plane ride away."

"Pat," a male voice called.

Welton turned and couldn't suppress a groan.

Dan's kid, Terry, was lifting up a can of beer. "Rematch after the eats?"

"You're on," Patrick flashed his television smile again.

"Only if you make it doubles," Monica said. "Get Carrie. Or Ashley, do you play?"

"Yes, but not that well," Ashley said. "Plus I was on call last night —"

"Some other time," Welton said. "Now let's get something to eat."

"Maybe I should wait for Carla," Ashley said, glancing around. "She should be here by now."

Waiting for Carla — how long would that take?

CHAPTER THIRTEEN

Carla had been looking forward to today's family gathering. She was proud of her progress in rehab, and had tried hard to shake the shame of what had sent her there. She was anxious to see Ashley and Rory. Would she confide in them about having HIV? She didn't know, but she would ask Ashley's advice about signing up to be a volunteer at an AIDS clinic for kids.

Toying with the idea of competing for a share of her dad's inheritance, Carla had decided that with all that money, she could do a lot of good. She'd even thought about nursing school. Unless they didn't take HIV-positive students. But would they have to know? HIV was supposed to be confidential. Or maybe she could do more good as a social worker? Her immediate plan: get Ashley's advice and then talk to Bunky about it. He'd always been after her to try for the money, and now that she was clean, maybe she'd have a chance.

That morning she'd been up early to attend an NA meeting. The nice thing about Manhattan was that meetings went on almost around the clock and so far she hadn't missed a day. When she got home, she'd made a pot of coffee and toasted a bagel. Then she changed into a flowered sundress with a matching shawl. With her new hairstyle and yesterday's manicure and pedicure, she knew she looked good. She smiled, confident that the family would be pleasantly surprised.

Then she picked up where she'd left off in a biography of Eleanor Roosevelt. She'd started on biographies of powerful women when she was in the Roberts Clinic. So far she'd read about Queen Elizabeth I, Katherine Graham, and Florence Nightingale. Learning about all of these women, she'd come away awed and inspired. She now felt that she, too, could make a difference. And wouldn't Ashley be impressed. Other than her medical texts, Ashley read only thrillers. Rather superficial, Carla thought. She smiled, anticipating the look of surprise on Ashley's face later that night when she pulled out her Eleanor Roosevelt tome.

When the doorman rang up to announce Bunky, Carla checked her watch. Nine fifteen. He was early. The car to take them to Pennsylvania wasn't due until ten. She had promised Sara that she would not let Bunky into the apartment, but she couldn't leave him in the lobby for forty-five minutes. Since she'd been released from Roberts Clinic, Sara had not left her side, but today Carla had convinced the maid to go home to her husband since she was going home to Pennsylvania.

Not that her family would be happy to see Bunky, but Bunky was a part of her life. She'd walked away from everything and everybody else, but she could not walk away from Bunky. When it came right down to it, Bunky was the one human on the face of the earth who really cared about her because he wanted to, not because he was paid to or because they were related. But to honor her family's wishes, she hadn't let Bunky move back into the apartment.

She knew that he needed to get clean before she could live with him. She realized how vulnerable she was, how easy it would be to slip. She'd heard so many horror stories in those meetings. As for Bunky, he still used — too heavily — but not in her apartment. Her plan was to save enough money to get him into the Roberts Clinic. Amazing as it seemed, Carla was now a huge fan of the Roberts Clinic. She'd be eternally grateful that her family cared enough to send her there, and she would tell them so today. And she'd also tell Ashley that she thought her boyfriend was a real prick. Ashley and Welton had visited her in rehab, and he hadn't shown her one iota of empathy. After weeks in group therapy, Carla felt pretty damn sure that she could pick up on personality disorders. Welton's was narcissistic and manipulative. The type of guy who's into control and domination. The type who hides behind charm and social niceties.

Carla had learned a lot. During that awful ride up to the clinic, she'd warmed up to Dr. Adair and now she saw him every week in his Manhattan office. He'd hooked her up with a doctor who specialized in HIV. She now knew that her virus level was quite low and her CD4 count fairly high, which was good news. In general, the CD4 count goes down as HIV progresses. And the best news of all: Bunky had been tested. He was HIV negative, and he now used a condom.

"You look great, babe," Bunky said, as she did a twirl when he stepped off the elevator. He had shaved, but his reddish curls flopped over his eyes and hung over his ears almost onto his shoulders. Meredith and Frank would not be pleased. According to them, worthiness was related to the clean-shaven, short haired, preppy look.

"Where's your watchdog?" Bunky glanced nervously about as they stepped into the living room.

"Sara's not here right now," Ashley said. She felt a pang of guilt, but they'd be leaving soon. Carla had promised herself no more lies, but this seemed so minor, so temporary.

She saw Bunky glance down the hall leading to her bedroom, but she shook her head, so he headed for the door again. "I gotta meet a guy," he said, "before we go. He's downstairs. Just be a second, babe."

"Okay, but we're supposed to leave at ten."

"You nervous?"

"A little, but mostly I'm anxious to see everybody, to show them that I'm okay." Carla brushed her lips against his cheek as he stepped into the elevator. "And, you know what? I really am okay."

"That's cool, babe."

Bunky was gone for five minutes. She waited for him in the living room, leafing through *Self* magazine. Yesterday, at a meeting, a girl she'd seen on some soap asked her if she was going back to modeling. She'd told her no. That lifestyle was just too high-risk.

"Got a little something for us, babe. This you're gonna love." Bunky was back and lifting the glossy magazine from her hands, replacing it with a white plastic bag. "This is some special shit."

"You got me drugs?" Carla gasped, and yanked her hands behind her back. The bag fell to the floor. She pulled her legs up into her abdomen and pushed back into the plush padding of the sofa. She needed to disappear into some kind of safety zone. She needed the image of that bag to evaporate. But it didn't. Bunky picked it up and swung it in front of her face, taunting her, tantalizing her.

"Just for us. Just for today," he was saying.

Carla straightened out, and struggled to sit up. Finally, words formed in her mind and she spat them out as vehemently as she could. "After the hell I went through getting clean! You're bringing me shit! Get rid of it! Get rid of it now!"

Bunky, still holding the bag, gently settled her back on the cushions, taking care the pillows in back of her were aligned. Carla felt her heart heaving, pounding so loud that Bunky must hear it too. She saw a bright white flash and instantaneously she knew that she wanted what was in that bag. Really wanted it. No, she *had to have* what was in that bag. Every nerve, every muscle in her body demanded it. She started to writhe.

"Bunky. Give it to me." Her voice sounded like the growl of a dog.

"Hey, hold on, this isn't ordinary shit." Bunky pulled the package just out of her reach. "This is ex — quisite."

From somewhere in Carla's head came a contrary order. "You gotta flush it down the toilet." After she'd uttered those words, her body started to shake. "Or you get the fuck out of here."

Still dangling the bag out of her reach, Bunky drew Carla up against his chest and kissed her. Stroking her hair, he pressed her body close to him, murmuring into her ear. "Come on, babe. It's the Fourth of July, Independence Day, and we're gonna celebrate by getting fucked. Just this one time. Just to get through family day."

Carla began to moan as she fell into the circle of Bunky's arms. He rocked her like a baby, reassuring her, "Without the shit, babe, we're gonna be too shaky. Face it, you want it, don't you, babe?"

Did she want it? *Yes. Yes. Yes.* Every pore in her body craved the cocaine high. When Bunky loosened his grasp on her, she felt she was having a convulsion. She wanted it so fucking bad. She *had* to have it.

He set the bag down momentarily to make her comfortable among the array of pillows. Her teeth chattered when he took the pipe from the bag. She went to reach for it, then pulled back her hand. And as Bunky took out the rocks, Carla fought to remember the Serenity Prayer. She tried to call up the moment in time, the breakthrough moment with her counselor, the exact moment she knew she had to stop. Stop or die, he'd said.

Bunky brought out the cigarette lighter. "Guy I got this from said this is the best, babe, a gift."

Carla shrank back, leaned forward to grasp the pipe, then pushed back again. She needed to get the fuck out of here. She needed to take a hit. She couldn't move.

"No, Bunky, I can't. I promised . . . to . . . help . . . the children . . . I need to."

"Trust me, babe, this is what you need."

He offered her the pipe. Carla locked onto his eyes. "Trust me, babe," he repeated.

She felt herself slipping away into a place so fragile that a whisper could knock her over. Even her heart beat seemed to falter as the last vestige of her resolve evaporated. She reached for the pipe and Bunky guided it toward her quivering mouth. She inhaled, deeply, greedily. The rush was immediate. She felt her heart flutter in that intense, immensely pleasurable way. Oh yes, she could get through this day. Face her family, Bunky by her side. She would be just fine.

Carla sank back into the comfort of the pillows, closed her eyes and floated. She felt a certain pounding sensation in her chest, but it dissipated as her mother appeared and started walking toward her. Mom's beautiful smile, warm, so inviting. And Daddy followed, looking proud, as he had that day when he had the front-row runway seat at her St. John's show.

CHAPTER FOURTEEN

Frank and Matt wore Uncle Sam costumes as they flipped burgers and roasted corn on the huge brick grill at poolside.

Matt grinned. "Must be doin' something right. Kids're all coming back for seconds. When do we get our chance to eat? I know you can't have the corn, but those cheeseburgers, no bun, are on that crazy low-carb diet."

"Today we're here to serve, buddy." Frank nudged Matt as Dan's pretty, dark-haired daughter headed toward them. "Carrie, give this young man some help while I get more corn."

How strange, Frank thought. For twenty-two years, Carrie and Terry were off the family radar screen. Now here they were at the Fourth of July barbecue as competitors for Dad's money. But for today, he and Meredith had made a pact. No politics. No strategizing. Just the family patriarch putting on the perfect picnic. Scoring points.

Frank was surprised that he was having such a good time as master of the grill. There were moments when he even thought that maybe he didn't hate kids so much, until one of the Stevens twins plowed into him and the platter he was carrying crashed to the ground. Luckily, it was plastic and empty.

"Slow down, you guys," he yelled.

"Sorry, Uncle Frank." The guilty kid braked momentarily. At least the Stevens' kids were having a good time. Odd, after all those years resenting Rory, Frank's feelings were now mixed. Rory had been just a child when Dad married her mother, and he realized now that he had been a jealous teen with an attitude. He'd always blamed Dad for defiling the memory of his mother by marrying Vivian. But now, after hearing the story of Monica, Frank was beginning to appreciate how lonely his father must have been. Frank knew how much he depended on

Meredith. If anything happened to her, Frank concluded he *wouldn't* be able to go on.

"Elise," he yelled at his daughter, "get your cousins and tell them to sit down."

"Okay, Daddy," she shouted. "Chip! Charlie! Misty!"

Elise was a good kid and Frank knew that he should start doing more with her. He'd promised Meredith that he would be a better father as soon as he got appropriations for Justice and Commerce though Congress. There was always something. Too many speeches. Too many fund-raisers. Too many political favors. As he headed for the house, Mr. M. met him with a cart of steaming, yellow ears of corn. "You wanta roll these in, Senator? I'm boiling more, so just send someone in if you run out again. I hope you know how wonderful it is to have all of you out here. Just wish Mrs. Stevens weren't so ill."

"Senator!" Mrs. M.'s voice intruded, shrill and urgent. "Telephone, Senator Frank."

"No business today," Frank called back. "The Fourth of July. Government's not in session."

But the ashen look on Mrs. M.'s face made Frank blink as she shoved the phone into his hand. "A detective. New York City. 'Urgent,' she said."

"For crying out loud," Frank responded. "Okay, okay, if you take this corn over to Matt."

"Frank Parnell here." Not caring if he sounded annoyed.

"Senator Parnell?"

"Yes, what is it?" Some political disaster? Tomorrow was a big day. Mueller's nomination as Director of the FBI. Intelligence and Armed Services had Frank so steeped in terrorism that he feared the worst. But from a detective?

"This is Detective Francine Harris from the NYPD, sir. I'm at the Parnell apartment on Park Ave. I'm afraid I have some tragic news. It's your sister. Carla Parnell. She's dead, sir."

The words hit like a blow to the stomach. Frank found that he couldn't breathe.

"Are you there, sir?" A sweet voice for an NYPD detective.

"No! I mean, yes. Carla? Dead?" Frank started to reached for the corn cart next to him, but Mrs. M. had taken it away. He lurched, righted himself, and dropped the phone.

In slow motion he bent and picked up the instrument, amazed that it hadn't shattered on the brick path. "Senator, are you okay?"

"What happened?"

"Here's all we know. The housekeeper, Mrs. Waring, came back to check on your sister. Said she had a funny feeling. When she let herself in, she found Miss Parnell sprawled out on the sofa in the living room. She tried to shake her. Got no response. Called nine-one-one. When the paramedics arrived, they estimated that based on body temperature, Miss Parnell had been dead for at least an hour."

Had Carla overdosed? If so, it'd be imperative to keep it quiet. "Does anyone else know?"

"We called you first. We're still here at the scene. Does your sister have any illness which might explain — ?"

"I don't know. How did she die? I mean, can you tell?"

"No evidence of foul play. Earlier in the day she'd had a visitor. A young man. Building security says he goes by the name Bunky. Real name, Rodney Lester."

Oh, yes, the junkie who screwed her out of all her money. That ridiculous name. She'd wanted to bring him with her today.

"Bunky?" Frank was at a loss. The last thing he wanted was to raise any suspicions about drugs.

"We're trying to find him. Strange, his driver's license lists this address. Does he live here, Senator?"

"No. He most certainly does not live there. Detective Harris, this is all such a shock. We were expecting Carla here in Pennsylvania today. I was starting to get worried, but with holiday traffic — My God, I can't believe this. Of course, my wife and I will come to the city directly."

"We won't know the cause of death until the autopsy. We'd like access to medical records."

Frank did not respond. He couldn't let the police trace Carla to the Roberts Clinic.

"We'll take her to the city morgue. It's protocol."

"Detective, I can't have my sister's body taken there." Carla's modeling portfolio flashed through his mind — long blonde hair, incredible violet eyes, a perfect, if too thin, body. "I want her taken to Cornell Medical. If that's a problem, have the commissioner call me." Frank gave her his cell phone number. "I'll be there as soon as possible."

What had happened? Frank needed Meredith to think this through. Shock and bitter anger intertwined in his heart. Carla had been such a cute little girl, but Dad and Vivian had spoiled her shamelessly. Now he was left to deal with the cover-up of her drug abuse. The political spin would be critical. The wrong spin could ruin his chances for the presidency, forever. *Paul Parnell's daughter, sister of Senator Frank Parnell, dies of a drug overdose* the headlines would scream. Frank remembered the Jeb Bush fiasco with his daughter. Together, he and Meredith needed to finesse their way out of this mess, create sympathy for the Parnell family.

Frank thought of the inheritance; now there would be one less contender. He put the shameful idea away and threaded his way across the pool deck where Meredith had been. Kids were all over the place. He had to swerve to avoid Monica and Patrick as they headed purposely toward him, hand in hand.

"Frank, do you think we can talk a little later, after the mob scene?" Monica called out.

"Not now," he said. "Have you seen Meredith?"

"Is something wrong?" Monica asked, staring at Frank.

"No. I mean, yes."

"Meredith is over there," Patrick, said pointing to Rory's two oldest girls.

"Excuse me," Frank mumbled as he rushed across the lawn to her. "Meredith, we have to talk. Not here."

Frank led Meredith into the paneled library across from the formal living room. "What's going on?" she asked as he sank down into his father's favorite chair.

"Carla's dead."

"What?" Meredith gasped, hand clutching her chest as she lowered herself onto the matching sofa. Frank explained the little he knew.

"Drugs," she said.

"Same conclusion as mine." Frank leaned forward in the chair, cradling his head in his hands.

"Okay," Meredith began, "I'm trying to remember what I read getting ready for that intervention. Crack cocaine is involved. Crack can damage the heart. Cause actual damage to the tissue and cause fatal arrhythmias. Okay, what do we know about arrhythmias?"

Frank shook his head.

"Electrolyte imbalance. Anorexia nervosa. Something about potassium, I don't know. Anyway, models and entertainers often suffer from eating disorders. They die from it. Yes, sudden cardiac death. Let's think this through. We've got to get this right."

Then Frank knew what she meant and took solace. Her mind was so quick.

"We have to get to Manhattan. Quickly build medical consensus on cause of death. There can be no mention of her stay at Roberts or her drug abuse. We spin this as a rare, catastrophic medical event."

"We're going to need political clout," Frank said.

"And we have it," Meredith said with determination. "For now we paint a picture of a model's preoccupation with weight. Carla was so very thin. Anorexia, an obsession with weight, is plausible. Focus on damage control. Brief Matt. Get our public relations people on it. Develop the medical talking points and stick with them."

"Can Ashley help?" Frank wondered aloud.

"Maybe," Meredith said, getting up. "She's a doctor. We'll need her on board to lend credibility."

"What about Welton?" They were both standing now, and Frank felt a chill go down his spine, suddenly realizing that not a tear had been shed over his sister.

"We're stuck with him for now," Meredith grimaced. "But I don't trust that creep for a nanosecond. But we have to get moving. What to do first?" She answered her own question. "Get Matt."

"Should he stay here and keep things under control, or go into the city with us?" Frank asked.

"For now he should stay here," Meredith decided. "We can't have any loose cannons going off." Meredith paused and put her arms around Frank. "You know this will be tough on Rory. She already feels terrible that she couldn't make the intervention."

"We can't worry about her right now." Frank squeezed Meredith's hand. "I'm going to get Matt."

When Frank rushed outside, a momentary silence interrupted the clamor of kids and the banter of adults.

"Matt, I need you inside. Right away."

"Duty calls. Carrie, you're in charge of burgers." Matt stripped off his apron. "Can't believe they keep coming back for more." Without another word, Frank hustled Matt into the library to brief him on the Carla situation.

Having spent the last three months as the designated family orchestrator, Matt had no problem grasping the urgency of the tragedy. Before Frank could suggest that he take over operations, he grabbed his cell phone. "First call, Senator, our PR firm. Then I'll get started on a priority list of next steps. Mrs. Parnell, you and the senator will have to tell the rest of the family soon. How much do you want to say?"

"Just that there's been an accident," Meredith said. "At least for now."

"Yeah, I'm worried about saying more because of Dr. Welton and the senator's nephew, Terry. The less we say right now, the better. Then there's Patrick Nelson. Too many outsiders."

"I'll gather everybody," Meredith agreed. Then she paused. "I guess Chan will have to tell Rory. With her immune system knocked, she doesn't need this stress." Frank recognized Meredith's genuine concern for his stepsister and was comforted that his own emerging sympathy was matched by hers.

Frank's cell phone rang. The deputy police commissioner. Of course, New York-Presbyterian Hospital, a Cornell affiliate, would be fine. There'd have to be an autopsy. Did Frank need a police escort? Anything else the police could do? Paul Parnell, personally, and the Parnell Foundation had deep ties to Cornell, the most recent being a $2,000,000 dollar grant to fund training in palliative medicine. Frank hoped that Parnell philanthropy had been adequate to ensure the confidentiality that would keep Carla's cause of death out of the media.

"Okay, Frank," Meredith stepped toward him, notebook in hand. "We'll leave in the helicopter right after we brief the others. Include the Mendozas. They're like family and were close to Carla. We'll just have to stress confidentiality."

"And shouldn't we call Carl Schiller?"

"Matt has him on the list of communication priorities. He put together this." Meredith handed Frank a sheet of paper with a list of bullet points in bold caps — **TALKING POINTS FOR FAMILY.** "Then as things unfold, we'll update and spoon-feed the press."

Frank glanced over the four simple statements: Carla is dead; we don't know what happened; doctors think it might have been her heart; Meredith and Frank are on their way to Manhattan.

"This looks fine." Frank handed the paper back to her. "Oh, for crying out loud, what about Cardinal Sean?"

"Tell him there's been an accident," Meredith instructed. "Carla is dead. Very unexpected. We need more details before we make any public statement." And Meredith could not help but add, "Tell him to keep his mouth shut. Fight the urge to pontificate."

"Yeah. Now, let's get everybody together. Meredith, can you tell them?"

"Matt's assembling them in the living room," Meredith said, patting Frank on the back. "And no, Frank, you have to do this."

"The media, I can handle. But the family? What will I say?"

"You'll say the right thing," Meredith said, grabbing Frank's hand and leading him into the living room.

Dan was sitting on the long sofa between his offspring. Chan had gathered all the kids at the foot of the circular staircase. For once, they sat soberly among the pile of pillows he'd tossed to them. Ashley sat with Conrad Welton in the closest wingback chair, he carefully scrutinizing her. Monica and Patrick sat on the edge of the matching loveseat hand in hand. Standing off to the side, no doubt fretting about so many damp bathing suits sitting on the expensive furniture, were the Mendozas. Frank noted how much gray had crept into their hair since Dad and Vivian hired them eighteen years earlier. He watched as Matt maneuvered himself over to the side of the sofa nearest Carrie.

The room went completely quiet as Frank faced the quizzical faces. Even the children were silent. As those nine sets of inquisitive eyes converged on him, he realized that he was no good with kids. Could they handle the concept of death?

"I have something very tragic to tell you," he began.

Frank could feel the ripple effect as the family shifted ever so slightly, all eyes riveted on him. "I don't know how to go about this, especially with the children . . ." He started to falter and could see Ashley and Chan exchange a worried glance across the array of kids. "But we got a call a few minutes ago. A call with shocking, terrible news. Something has happened to Carla."

Ashley gasped. "What happened? Was she in an accident?"

"She's dead. Mrs. Waring found her. That's all we know."

"My God, Frank, that can't be true," Chan leaned forward, fists clenched.

"Dead? Carla dead?" Ashley echoed trance-like. "No, there must be some mistake. She was supposed to be *here*."

Frank shook his head as Meredith came to stand by him. He put his arm around her.

After a long silence, tears now trickling down her cheeks, Ashley asked, "Do we know what happened?"

"We don't," Frank answered. "Perhaps something to do with her heart."

"Then it wasn't an accident? It wasn't," Ashley glanced across at the kids, "self-inflicted?"

"Heart? In somebody so young?" interrupted Monica as she glanced pointedly at Patrick.

Dan extended an arm around both of his children, and Frank could guess what he was thinking. They were the same age as Carla.

"Is Aunt Carla dead?" asked the youngest Stevens boy in a squeaky voice.

"Yes, honey," said Meredith. "She's gone to be with God in heaven."

"Like Grandpa," said one of the twins matter-of-factly.

"Frank, what are we going to do?" Ashley was sobbing openly now.

Welton drew her closer to him, encircling her in his arms. At that protective maneuver, Frank flashed back to his father. That same serious look, the same wrinkling of the brow, the set of ice-blue eyes. The two of them involved in what Meredith called an Oedipal complex.

"We'll figure out what's happened and do what has to be done once we get to Manhattan," Frank said. "Meanwhile, Dan, you and Carrie and Terry should stay here with Matt. At least until tomorrow." Frank flinched at the glazed, teary eyes of his stunned family. "And, of course, absolutely no media leaks. Tomorrow, we'll issue our own press statement."

"Here?" Welton gestured around the room. "Ashley's too upset for houseguests."

"Conrad, if only we'd picked her up and driven her in." Ashley moaned, ignoring her fiancé's question.

"There's nothing we can do for your sister now, my love. I told you before that she'd go back on drugs."

Meredith winced at Welton's insensitive remark. And Ashley tried to wriggle out of his arms.

Meredith spoke for the first time. "As for the logistics, Chan, you and the kids should wait this out at home." Her voice softened to a near whisper. "And you'll have to tell Rory. Monica, you and Patrick should probably go back to the Hamptons. With all the media attention, it's best that you're not here. Ignoring Welton's remark, Meredith said, Dan, I assume you and Terry and Carrie will stay here?"

All three nodded their assent.

"And Matt will stay here and keep the communication loop open. But nothing, absolutely nothing, to the media. Everybody understand?"

Frank looked to each for their response. All nodded, even Welton who was still clutching Ashley.

"Car's waiting," Mrs. M. announced, as heads still nodded. "Senator, we're so sorry, Peter and me. We will be here to do whatever you need."

"You were always among Carla's favorite people," Meredith said to the distressed couple. "Thank you for taking on the burden of unexpected houseguests." Frank again reminded himself how lucky he was to have Meredith by his side.

As Frank and Meredith turned to go, Chan spoke in a hoarse voice. "Ashley," he pleaded, "will you help me with the kids?"

Fuck your kids, Welton wanted to scream. *Fuck the entire Parnell family*. He tightened his hold on Ashley, but she managed to pull out of his grasp and go to Chan. Welton let his eyes travel the room, and he nodded his head almost imperceptibly as he inspected each target. They would fall, one by arrogant one. Carla was simply the first.

CHAPTER FIFTEEN

"— now and at the hour of my death. Amen." Rory fingered the beads of her mother's coral rosary, but her mind wandered. A recurrent theme with her right now. Was her illness a type of payback for all the good things that had been her life, until now? She could never remember being unhappy. True, her father left when she'd been a toddler, but she had no memory of him. Her mother got through medical school on a small inheritance and made ends meet. To Rory, her mom had been no less than perfect.

Rory had been eleven when Vivian Baricelli met Paul Parnell. He'd told her that she looked just like her mom — freckles, wavy auburn hair, and lilac-colored eyes. And he told her how he had always wanted a little girl. After they married, Mom explained that Paul wanted to legally adopt her and change her name from Barricelli to Parnell, but that they did not know the whereabouts of Tony Barricelli. Rory loved Paul and was in awe of her new brothers. Dan had just left for college, but Frank was still in high school — class president, varsity sports, honor student.

From then on her life got even better. Paul became CEO of Keystone Pharma. Mom was a successful doctor. Even though her teen friends didn't think having a pregnant mom was cool, Rory adored her little sisters. She was like a second mother to Ashley, taking her everywhere in that fold-up stroller. Carla, crankier and naughtier, had always looked up to her, relying too often on Rory to bail her out of trouble.

Then Rory met Chan at the University of Pennsylvania when she was a nursing student, and he a family medicine resident. They fell instantly in love, had a perfect wedding, and beautiful children. Now her Mom and Dad were dead. Carla was dead. And she was into her third round of chemo.

Chan had brought in all the specialists. Hematologists, oncologists.

All speaking in euphemisms, all chasing that elusive remission. And Chan, even though he pledged to tell her the truth, still sugarcoated her prognosis. Right now she was still on induction therapy to get rid of the leukemia cells in her bone marrow. Since there are always residual cells, she'd need to go on post-remission therapy, and that meant at least four more courses of chemo. Endless, it seemed. But she wouldn't give up. There was a knock on her partially open door. The family knew that she couldn't stand to be totally isolated, that she needed to stay connected.

"Mom? Are you awake?"

"Yes, come on in, sweetie." She sat up in bed and tucked the rosary under her pillow as Becky tiptoed in.

"I brought you some tea and a muffin." As she set down the tray, Becky brushed Rory's arm.

"Oh, Mom, I'm so sorry. Is it okay?" Becky inspected the gauze patch that covered the catheter in Rory's left forearm.

"It's fine." Rory hoped that to be the truth. Her veins had become impossible. The doctor had threatened a surgical insertion if this intravenous got disconnected.

"Good. Dad said to tell you that Tyler can't come in today because he may be getting a cold."

"I just can't wait to get better so you guys don't have to worry about every little sniffle."

"I know. Us, too." Becky leaned down to kiss Rory's cheek. "I gotta go help Dad find stuff for the kids to wear to Aunt Carla's funeral."

"Bye, sweetheart. You cheer me up."

Alone again, Rory thought of Carla. Had her beauty been her downfall? That sexy walk she managed in four-inch heels. The formfitting pants and sweaters, the very short skirts. The long blonde hair she flipped this way and that and those distinctive eyes. As far as Rory was concerned, the only physical attribute she had in common with Carla was her lilac-colored eyes. Rory had always been a few pounds overweight, but Carla made her feel obese with her ultrathin glamour look. And now Rory herself was as thin as Carla had been.

A knock interrupted. Ashley, properly businesslike in a black pants suit, hair pulled up off her neck, stood at the door. Rory had asked that she stop by.

Rory motioned her to the bedside chair. "Thanks for coming. I need to talk to you about Carla's funeral. Chan means well, but his protectiveness sometimes keeps me in the dark."

"Frank and Meredith have pretty much arranged everything," Ashley said, nibbling the cuticle of her thumb. "Naturally, we didn't want to bother you after that spinal tap yesterday."

Rory did not have energy to waste so she cut straight to her objective. "This is our last chance to do something for Carla. Frank and Meredith don't know her that well."

"I'm sure they've worked it all out with Cardinal Sean."

"Carla and Cardinal Sean never saw eye to eye. Thus my concern."

"But the service is t-tomorrow. I'm sure everything will be okay." The hint of a stutter. Rare now, only when Ashley was very stressed.

"Let's get Meredith on the phone." Rory was adamant.

When her sister-in-law came on, Rory slowly adjusted her position in bed. She still had spurts of vertigo, but not the horrible nausea and vomiting she had experienced earlier.

"Meredith, I know you're busy, so I'll get right to the point," Rory said, eliminating all small talk. "I want to make sure that tomorrow's ceremony reflects Carla's taste."

"You needn't worry," Meredith said. "Ashley, I tried to consult with you, but Conrad said to do whatever Frank and I thought best."

How could Ashley have left this judgment up to Conrad? Rory thought. "Ashley and I want to write a brief eulogy," Rory announced.

Two gasps followed. "Rory, I can't." Ashley's face twisted and she paled. Rory knew how much she feared public speaking.

"*I* would do it, but I can't." Rory gestured toward her head, draped in an ivory-colored scarf.

"That's a nice idea," Meredith blurted, "but Frank will take care of the eulogy."

"I'm sure he will do a fine job." Rory didn't add, *In support of his political future*. "But I want something more personal. Our tribute to our sister."

"Frank may not think — I mean, the funeral is tomorrow."

"Frank will do as you ask." It was no secret to Rory that Meredith was both the brains and the power behind the successful Frank Parnell story. "Now, let's go over the music."

Cardinal Sean had chosen a Gregorian chant motif for the parts of the Burial Mass. Carla thought Latin was exotic, and she'd be pleased with the full choir along with a soprano and a tenor soloist. Meredith recited the hymns.

"Take out 'Amazing Grace.'" Rory mustered as much vehemence as she could. "Carla hated that song. Have Monica sing "Ave Maria," as she did at Dad's funeral. Carla had commented how beautiful it sounded in the cathedral."

"Sure," Meredith said. "Okay."

"'Gentle Shepherd, Psalm twenty-three' is okay," Rory went on. But, 'Like a Child Rests'? I've never heard of, and I'll bet Carla hadn't either. Get rid of it and add 'Panis Angelicus' — in Latin." Rory spelled out the Latin hymn. "Ashley, any ideas?"

She shook her head.

Then Rory asked about pallbearers and Meredith ticked them off. Only two were acceptable to Rory. Carl Schiller and Matt Cleveland. The others were political cronies of Frank's. Rory figured that since she didn't know them, neither would have Carla.

"We need men who really cared for Carla when she was alive."

Ashley said, "Peter Mendoza and Sara Waring's husband. They were devoted to Carla."

"Ah, that's a nice thought," said Meredith, "but since Frank has already asked the others —"

"That leaves two more," Rory interrupted. "Patrick Nelson — she was looking forward to meeting him. And what about Bunky? Wouldn't Carla want him to —"

"Uh . . . Frank had a call from the New York Police. He's dead."

"What?" Ashley gasped.

"You're kidding?" For a moment Rory thought Meredith made this up as an excuse to avoid an undesirable pallbearer.

"They found his body in an alley, outside a crack house by the East River. You can imagine the public relations nightmare if this gets out."

While Ashley gasped, Rory said, "Then substitute Leo Tally from Longboat Key. Carla didn't know him, but she would have liked him. He was so wonderful to me."

Rory fell back, exhausted. It had been a long time, if ever, since she'd made any request of Frank. Meredith was stubborn and strong willed, but Rory felt she'd agree. Out of respect or pity, she didn't know which. "So will you get Frank to go along with these changes?"

"Yes," Meredith finally said. "And thank you, Rory. You're right, of course. I'll talk to Frank and the cardinal now. And that priest who oversees every detail of the cardinal's ceremonies," Meredith chuckled. "This Latin liturgical stuff is out of my league." The compassion in Meredith's voice was unmistakable, and Rory vowed to defend Meredith the next time anyone called her a bitch. "And Ashley, you'll do just fine."

After the call, Rory said, "I want to show you the poem I wrote. All you have to do is read it."

Ashley seemed nervous, checking her watch frequently.

"Rory, there's something else. Let me come right out and say it: a bone marrow transplant. Our compatibility match turned out good, not perfect since we have different fathers, but good enough."

"Well if this round of chemo works okay, I won't need it. Right?"

"Well, maybe, right," Ashley replied with that grave expression Rory knew so well. "But your cytogenic tests came back. The results were — were not favorable."

"Meaning?" Ashley's a doctor. Rory needed to hear her point of view. Suddenly, Carla and the eulogy were forgotten.

"Meaning that treatment will be difficult."

"Tell me, Ashley. Chan tried to explain, but I'm not sure I understand what it means, 'not favorable.'"

"Acute myelogenous leukemia is classified into subtypes. It has to do with your chromosomes. It's called cytogenic analysis and it's used to —"

"Go on," Rory said, steeling herself with a few gulps of air.

"Has to do with prognosis. There are favorable profiles and unfavorable."

"And mine is unfavorable. I still don't know what that means, but I know it isn't good."

"It's likely you will need a bone marrow transplant, and I'm the best bet for an HLA tissue match, meaning there's a better chance for compatibility. Even if Conrad —"

"What about Conrad? Is he making your decisions?"

"No." Ashley looked away. "You know what, Rory? I've never been in love. I never knew what it felt like. I feel afraid when I'm not with him."

"Afraid?" Rory asked.

"I don't know." Ashley spoke so softly that Rory had trouble hearing. "Once we get married —"

Rory didn't know what to say. She felt that this relationship was all wrong, but how to get that across to Ashley who seemed mesmerized by the hypnotist?

"He wants me to drop out of my residency next year and —"

"What?" Rory struggled to pull herself up straighter in bed. "You've worked so hard. Being a doctor has always been your dream."

"I know. But he thinks —"

"Too many things are happening, too fast." It seemed crazy to be having this conversation in the middle of Carla's funeral — her not favorable leukemia prognosis, Bunky's death, Ashley's love.

"I'm just so scared of losing him." Ashley had that faraway look. "I need him. Without Dad. With Carla dead."

"Don't drop out of your residency," Rory managed. She sank back onto the pillow, feeling her eyes almost rolling into the back of her head. "Give it some time."

"Aunt Ashley," Karen's shrill voice interrupted from downstairs. "Your car is here."

Ashley jumped up and kissed Rory's cheek. "I have to go," she said.

"But, the poem," Rory protested.

Ashley held out her hand and Rory tore a handwritten sheet from a notebook. "I'll do my best, I really will. But I have to go."

Something is wrong, Rory thought.

Please God, I failed Carla, don't let me fail Ashley, too.

CHAPTER SIXTEEN

Ashley huddled against her fiancé in the backseat of the limo as it made its way down the Schuylkill Expressway to the Vine Street exit. In her hand she clutched the poem that Rory had composed. A beautiful poem, touching in its simplicity. Three sisters, one now with the angels.

"Lean on me, my love," Welton said as the black stretch pulled up to the curb of the Cathedral of Saints Peter and Paul. Its Palladian façade and copper dome was hosting the second Parnell funeral in 2001. For a fraction of a second, Ashley was a little girl and it was her dad, not Conrad, helping her out of the car. The memory dialed back to second grade.

It was 1980, the year a middle eastern terrorist group planned to release a deadly virus that would infect thousands. Military intelligence had evidence that the terrorist cell had infiltrated the United States Army Medical Research Institute for Infectious Diseases laboratory in Fort Detrick, Maryland, and stolen classified biotechnology. Enabling technology that would allow the terrorists to infect a common adenovirus with fragments of DNA, resulting in a mutant that would cause a fatal hemorrhagic fever. Something like the Ebola virus.

Paul Parnell's pharmaceutical company, Keystone Pharma, had the technology to create an antidote for this fatal infection — at least in theory. The technology, a kind of genetic engineering, had never been developed. But Keystone held the patent and the virology know-how.

The chief of staff of the Armed Forces came to visit Paul at the Devon house one evening. No one knew who he was, the visit was so secretive, but years later Paul told Ashley. Immediately after the clandestine visit, Paul summarily assigned key scientists to develop the antidote without telling them why they were being taken off their other high-priority projects. His scientists worked hand in hand with the

USAMRIID scientists to make the vaccine and get it approved through the FDA. Since the project took six months of total dedication, word leaked out to the financial world that Keystone Pharma's blockbuster projects were seriously delayed. The timing of the annual shareholders meeting couldn't have been worse. Angry stockholders rushed to the microphones to lodge complaints about the incompetency of the chairman of Keystone. The board of directors knew that national security was involved, but nothing more. They were divided as to whether to fire him.

Four weeks later, terrorists infiltrated a U.S. military base in the Philippines. They'd transported the deadly virus via an abandoned tunnel and scaled the huge tank that provided water for the troops. More than one hundred military personnel fell ill, and twenty-nine died before the mutated virus was discovered. Within hours the FDA, in emergency session, approved the Keystone vaccine for immediate shipment. The entire base was vaccinated, including individuals who already had symptoms. There were no further deaths.

Paul Parnell became a national hero, awarded the Presidential Medal of Honor and later the Nobel Prize. Instantly, Keystone Pharma became *the* premier global pharmaceutical company. The stockholders now adored him. That had been a long time ago when Ashley was seven, Carla only five.

"You look beautiful in black, my love." Welton tucked her arm in his and she returned to the here and now.

"It's the only black dress I have, but it's too short and I don't like that it's sleeveless." She pulled a lacy black shawl tighter around her shoulders. Carla would have laughed at her modesty, Ashley realized, not bothering to dab the fresh tears trickling down her cheeks.

As she and Conrad entered the imposing cathedral, Welton pointed out Frank and Meredith across the vestibule. "Stay right by my side," he murmured.

Naturally, Meredith looked elegant in a black dress and a black lace veil draping down from her hat. *Why hadn't she thought to wear a veil?* Ashley thought as Frank turned from his entourage to greet them.

"I've got to hand it to you," Welton said immediately as he and Frank shook hands. "Your finesse worked. 'These tragedies can happen in young women on extremely low-calorie diets. Electrolyte imbalance, erratic heart rhythm.' Pure bullshit, but politically acceptable." Conrad didn't look angry or embarrassed to be talking to Frank like that. But Ashley cringed. She knew that Conrad didn't like Frank, but he'd never been rude to him.

"Carla did have old heart tissue damage." Ashley felt she should come to Frank's defense. "Anorexia in models is not uncommon."

"And HIV positive. Now that was quite a shock."

Yes, Ashley thought, but should it have been? HIV is part of that lifestyle.

Frank glared at Welton, who raised his hands. "My lips are sealed," he stage-whispered. "Now if you will excuse us, Ashley has to concentrate on her poem."

Two strong men. The term alpha male lingered in Ashley's head as Frank went back to join his cronies.

"I think Carla planned to tell me about the HIV, but now I'll never know." Ashley fingered the paper she held tightly in one hand, willing herself not to stutter when she was at the lectern. Carla would be so embarrassed. When they were kids, Carla used to tease Ashley about her speech impediment. But she stopped when they'd grown older, and Ashley had never held a grudge.

Ashley and her fiancé made their way slowly through endless bouquets of flowers toward the casket. Flowers of all types, but mostly white — maybe lilies, maybe orchids, Ashley wasn't sure, but she did thank God that someone, probably Rory, had remembered that Carla was crazy for flowers.

Ashley had seen many dead bodies, but nothing could have prepared her for the sight of her little sister, looking so peaceful and innocent, lying in the satin-lined box as if she'd decided to crawl in for a nap. Meredith had chosen well, an ivory silk suit. No blouse, but a single strand of ivory-colored pearls that had belonged to their mother. Carla's hair was styled the way she'd worn it as a teenager, parted on one side with a casual sweep across her forehead. But her beautiful violet eyes were closed forever.

Ashley felt her knees buckle as she reached the kneeling bench. She fell to the bench, silently repeating the Hail Mary over and over. Finally, Conrad on her right and Cardinal Sean, who'd appeared on her left, helped her down the aisle to the front of the cathedral. When they each held out a monogrammed handkerchief, she took them both.

"Ashley, I'm so sorry," her uncle whispered. He kept speaking in a low tone, but she had zoned out.

"She'll be okay," Welton said, pulling her close. "I'm sure you must get back for the service."

With a flush of shame, Ashley realized that she needed to pull herself together. She had to help the family get through this horrible day.

"Cardinal Sean, I'm sorry." She choked back tears. "I just wish that I'd been there for her."

"We all wish that we had," he said, sounding so human.

Then she realized that her uncle had never even met Conrad. She hadn't told him about their engagement. Did he know that they were living together? Naturally, he wouldn't approve.

"Cardinal Sean, this is Dr. Conrad Welton," she said. How foolish to be making such trivial polite talk as if it were a party, not a funeral. She and Carla would never giggle together again. Never share secrets. Never have kids who'd be cousins.

"Dr. Welton." As Cardinal Sean reached for Conrad's hand, a priest in a long black cassock tapped him on the shoulder and pointed to his watch.

"You have to go, I'll take care of your niece, sir," Conrad said, the intended handshake foregone.

"Thank you, my son," said Cardinal Sean as he followed his priest escort. As the cardinal headed toward the sacristy, Ashley thought of the trip the family made to Rome when he was installed as a cardinal by the pope. Quite an extravaganza. Carla had been her irreverent self, but for months afterwards, Ashley had wanted to be a nun.

"No wheelchair, Chan," Rory said as their chauffeur pulled to the curb at Eighteenth and the Benjamin Franklin Parkway. "I'll be okay."

"Sure, honey. We'll go in the side door and sit in the front pew."

Chan had wanted Rory to stay home. Too much exertion; too many germs. But in the end she prevailed. Still, she was too weak to get out of the car on her own. And too thin, with sparse hair under the wide-brimmed hat.

As soon as she was settled into the front pew, Chan went back to join the family. In a moment, Uncle Carl slipped into the polished wooden pew beside her. Rory tried not to flinch when he reached to touch her arm, the one that was covered with bruises from infiltrated IVs. But his touch was so gentle she needn't have worried.

"Rory, I can't believe your kids," he whispered. "They are so well behaved. What a credit to you and Chan." It was warm and sunny, but Rory shivered under layers of black crepe.

"Remember how much Carla loved flowers?" Carl commented.

Rory nodded. Even though the family requested that in lieu of flowers, contributions be made to the Parnell Foundation in support of AIDS victims, surprisingly, a Meredith decision, the cathedral was full of blooms in muted colors. *Carla would be pleased*, Rory thought.

The pallbearers she had selected had assembled, and the procession began as the organ filled the cathedral with the music she had chosen. Fresh tears came to Rory's eyes as her children started to file into her pew. First Tyler, her youngest, adopted, still insecure after the death of his parents, still wheezing from last night's asthmatic attack. Ricky, older than Tyler by one month, followed. Close behind were Misty and Karen, looking so much like their biological mother in midnight blue, floor-length dresses and matching hats. Her twin ruffians, Charlie and Chip, were next, as somber as Rory had ever seen them, wearing the same navy blue jackets and gray slacks that they had worn at her dad's funeral. Chan, Becky on one arm and Emily on the other, completed her clan. As Chan took his place at the opposite end of the pew from her, he leaned forward and caught her eye. They exchanged the crooked smile that they always did when all the kids were accounted for.

Meanwhile, the rest of the Parnell family were taking their seats. Frank, straight backed and somber, Meredith, elegant in a black sheath, Elise showcased between them. They sat in the first row directly across the aisle from Chan. Next to them were Ashley and Conrad Welton.

Ashley, wrapped in a lacy black shawl, looked more vulnerable than usual as she clung to that strange man. Immediately in back of them, Dan sat with his reunited family. They were a ray of sunshine.

Family seated, the procession commenced. Rory knew that she did not want all this pomp and ceremony. She made a mental addition to her list of topics she needed to talk to Chan about.

"Grant her eternal rest, O Lord, and let perpetual life shine upon her." Cardinal Sean's prayer resonated through the cavernous cathedral.

CHAPTER SEVENTEEN

Conrad Welton was a patient man. Two months had passed, and Ashley was still fixated on Carla. With Carla's high-risk lifestyle, the sisters hadn't even been that close, a fact Ashley chose to ignore. She actually believed that Carla had turned her life around. Save the world. Cure AIDS. That would have endeared her to Paul Parnell and his test. Except that her druggie friend, Bunky, had been only too eager to deliver crack to Carla.

His years playing shrink to prisoners had again paid off. A simple phone call. A face-to-face meeting with his former patient. So convenient, his chosen specialty. Conrad had never abused his skills. He used them only when necessary, and only when there was zero chance of being discovered. Soon he'd terminate his career, leave the University of Pennsylvania, and take control of the Parnell family and its inheritance.

When he'd first researched the Parnell family assets, Welton had not realized the extent of Paul Parnell's wealth. He'd figured that at least one billion dollars would be split among five siblings — Dan, Frank, Rory, Ashley, and Carla. That would have meant $200,000,000 — plus or minus — for him and Ashley. But as the scenario played out, that estimate had escalated. Monica had appeared, but had rejected her share. Carla had died, and Rory would surely succumb to leukemia before the January test date — one way or another. Only Dan and Frank stood in the way of Ashley inheriting the whole sum. Dan could be eliminated fairly easily, but Frank, as a U.S. senator, would be more of a challenge. Nevertheless, with four months left to work out the details, Welton felt well positioned to accomplish his ultimate goal.

Conrad checked his watch — 2:45. Ashley was supposed to be home by three. He'd told her it was important, a surprise. Of course she'd given him the "I just can't leave during rounds" speech. But he'd prevailed and she'd promised. Now he fingered the papers in his hands. His birth certificate. His marriage certificate. A stamped copy of the divorce. And for good measure, Crissy Moore Welton's death certificate. He knew that Ashley kept her birth certificate in the safe in the library. A minute or two for her to retrieve it and they'd be off to the Chester County Courthouse.

The day was bright and sunny and Conrad had instructed the Mendozas to pick copious bouquets of flowers from around the property to fill the house. Personally, he hated the smell of flowers, but this was Ashley's special day. Then he told the couple to take the afternoon off. Another glance at his Rolex before he heard the purr of the Mercedes engine coming up the driveway.

When Ashley came through the door, she looked so disheveled that Welton spoke harshly.

"Go fix your hair and put on some lipstick," he said, arms on hips, a look of disapproval on his face.

She bolted in through the door, a panicky look in her eyes.

"I'm not late," she stated, groping in her bag for her comb and lipstick.

"No, you're not." Welton knew she'd show up on time.

"I had to lie, to tell them that I was sick. I feel so bad, but it was the only way I could g-get out since I'm in the ICU this w-week." How he hated that disgusting stutter. "So what's so important?"

"Come in here, my love." Welton led her through the flower-laden foyer to the library, waiting for her to appreciate the bouquets of flowers arranged along the path.

"Why is the safe open?" She stepped back, a quizzical look on her face.

"Reach in, my love," he said.

"Okay." When Ashley's hand landed on a document, she picked up and inspected it.

"My birth certificate?"

"Yes, my dear, and mine." Welton took the paper out of her hand and matched it up with his. "We're going to the courthouse this afternoon. Now you know why you had to get home early. It closes at five."

"Courthouse?"

Cut the echo machine, he wanted to say. Instead, he took her hand and fondled the gold ring with the ruby she wore on her ring finger, left hand, as he'd instructed. "My love, you didn't even notice the flowers I had set up in here to celebrate our marriage license day."

"Oh, Conrad, I don't think I'm ready yet. No, I'm not." She paused as she looked around, showing no appreciation of his efforts. Then, "I need to finish out this year at the hospital. Not yet, please, can't we wait?"

"My love, we've waited so long. This is a very special day. There is something I want to tell you today; we can do that in the car on the way."

Ashley stood mute.

The stench of the flowers made Welton nauseous. He had sacrificed his own comfort to make this special day beautiful for her, and she had ignored it. Spoiled, overprivileged, little rich girl. "Come, Ashley," he said, patiently. "Pick up your purse, and we'll be on our way."

Welton wasn't sure why he'd waited so long to tell Ashley that he'd been married already. Now about to mount the courthouse steps, he couldn't put if off any longer. In Pennsylvania, for a marriage license, one must show evidence of any previous marriage and the outcome. In Welton's case, it had been both divorce and subsequent death.

He placed the documents in a leather portfolio and led Ashley outside to his waiting Porsche. The top was down, the day sunny and bright, and Ashley's hair already a wreck. Perhaps the noises of the outside world would dampen the story he'd have to tell her.

"Are you happy, my love, one step closer to our perfect life?"

Ashley buckled her seat belt and leaned back into the leather. "Are you sure we're doing the right thing?" she asked. "So soon after Carla's death?"

"Why wait? And don't you want to have a child?"

"Naturally, some day, but not yet. I'm too overwhelmed right now. My residency, trying to be there for you."

"Let me tell you something, Ashley, life is too short to wait. I was married once, and I'm sorry I waited until now to tell you."

As Welton had predicted, Ashley's jaw fell and she stared at him wide-eyed. "You were — you never told me. I mean, I didn't know. I mean, why didn't you —?"

"My love, it's a very sad story. Still so painful that it hurts to talk about it. She was very young, and, as I came to learn, very mentally unstable. I guess I thought I could help her, as a psychiatrist, but I was wrong. Then one day she ran away."

He pulled the sports car off the road into a small park so he could face Ashley, gauge her reaction.

"Ran away — Like —"

"I'll explain everything, my love." Welton adjusted his voice an octave lower.

"Did you get a divorce?" Ashley interrupted. Her eyes were focused on her lap, avoiding his face. She started to twist the ring, tugging it off her knuckle.

"Yes," Welton said, drawing out the drama as he reached to still her hands. "I didn't want to, but I thought it best . . ." He hesitated and his voice broke.

"What, Conrad?" Ashley had turned to face him, a trusting look in her eyes.

"She died." He cast his eyes downward. "I thought that I'd never fall in love again. And then after all those years, by some miracle last January you walked into my office. Ashley, because of you, my life has meaning again."

Ashley turned toward Conrad in her bucket seat and reached for his hand. "Why didn't you tell me? I didn't know you'd been through such hurt."

"So now you know why I'm so anxious to marry you. I've lived too much of my life without you. You are everything to me, my love. Will you marry me? Very soon?"

"Yes," she said, leaning in to kiss him. Ashley could demonstrate empathy without resorting to either chemical or hypnotic suggestion.

"We're on our way to get our license now, my love." Conrad extricated his hands and put the car in gear. "Let's get there before the courthouse closes. Afterwards we'll go home and change, and then I'm taking you to Le Bec Fin for a romantic dinner. We can set our plans amidst candlelight. I hope we'll be married by this time next week."

Welton received a glowing smile. His disclosure had gone down better than he'd dared to hope. But he could not become complacent. The Parnell family would start digging into his background. And with that digging would come a distortion of the facts.

CHAPTER EIGHTEEN

Three days later Ashley and Meredith sat in the backseat of Meredith's Town Car. They were on the New Jersey Turnpike, heading to the Waldorf-Astoria Hotel in Manhattan. En route, Ashley hadn't said much, and Meredith finally stopped trying to make conversation. She'd reached into her attaché case, pulled out a brief, and started to mark it up. Riding in silence, Ashley had already chewed one thumbnail down to the quick and was starting on the second. Her stomach felt queasy, and she wished she'd taken the time to nibble the dry toast that Mrs. Menendez had set out for her. There'd been a scene the night before, Ashley knew that, but she had to squeeze her eyes shut to remember.

She and Conrad had been so happy Friday night as they'd made plans to marry on Saturday morning, September 15. Just the two of them and a judge at City Hall in Philadelphia. They'd notify family and friends after the brief civil ceremony. Cardinal Sean would be outraged, but Conrad said that they could have a church wedding later if her family insisted. She'd consented. That was not the focus of last night's horrible disagreement. Conrad's rage was focused on the Parnell Foundation, the board meeting in Manhattan, where she was now heading. The argument was coming back in fragments.

Conrad saying, "You cannot go into Manhattan with that woman. I forbid it. She refused my offer to join the foundation board of directors. An offer I made in good faith, wanting to do the right thing, wanting to give back to society. And she outright refused."

"Maybe after we're married." Ashley's conciliatory attempt had not tempered his anger.

"If they don't accept me, I don't want you catering to them. Face the facts, you're family is arrogant. They don't care about you. They just drag you out when it fits their needs."

"It's for Dad. He wanted me to play a role in his foundation," Ashley had countered.

"You will not go into New York for that Parnell Foundation board meeting. They have humiliated me. You don't need your family. They don't need you. I am your family now."

Ashley had nodded a silent assent.

"I have to go out of town early, my love. You call Meredith and make any excuse you want, but tell her you're not going."

"Yes, Conrad," she'd said. He'd taken her in his arms, but what happened next she simply could not remember.

And that's what concerned Ashley the most. She had these complete blackouts. Always after she and Conrad had sex and sometimes for no reason she could figure out. What could be wrong with her? Why was her mind blanking out? Each time she woke up in Conrad's arms, she felt special and loved and cherished. And he, too, seemed satisfied. And because he did, she'd never mentioned her memory gaps, not wanting to upset him.

Another concern, she was quite sure that Conrad suffered from Peyronie's disease, a medical condition caused by plaques or scar tissue on the penis. With an erection, his penis was bent, and the first time she'd tried to touch it, he'd flinched and gently removed her hand. She'd never discussed that with him either. And because her memory was such a blank, she couldn't say whether sex for Conrad was painful as it often is with Peyronie's. Now that they were to be married, shouldn't they be discussing this?

Suddenly, the chauffeur jerked to a stop at the Verrazano Bridge tollbooth to avoid an aggressive lane changer. "Sorry ladies," he said, sliding the partition just a crack.

"How are we doing for time?" Meredith looked up from her paperwork. "Ashley, are you okay?"

No, I think I'm crazy. Ashley opened her eyes, letting the image of penises fade.

"Traffic's congested." The chauffer slipped the Plexiglas barrier open to make this announcement.

Meredith checked her diamond-studded Piaget. Ashley recalled that the Christmas before her mother died, her parents had given the identical watch to her and Carla too. Ashley kept hers in a safe, since everyday scrubbing at the hospital and expensive watches did not mix. She wondered what had happened to Carla's.

"We can't be late." Meredith glared at Ashley as if it were her fault.

"I'm sorry I wasn't ready," Ashley said sheepishly. "I had to wait until Conrad left."

"Now why's that?" Meredith asked, resuming her edits.

Ashley merely shrugged.

Because I defied him, she wanted to say, but didn't. Here she was in the car with Meredith, deliberately disobeying her future husband's explicit order.

By the time Ashley awoke that morning, Conrad had already left for the airport for an early flight. He'd left the airline confirmation on her bedside table. Round trip, first class to Cincinnati, returning the same day, arriving at ten fifty p.m. Why Cincinnati? she'd wondered. At Conrad's insistence, she'd taken the week off her residency program. A request that did not sit well with her chief resident. To get ready for the wedding, Conrad said. But what was there to do besides chose a dress? Then the call from Meredith, insisting that she accompany her to Manhattan for a special meeting of the Parnell Foundation Board. Meredith reminded her that it had been her father's dream that all his children participate on the board. How could she deny her father who had given them all so much? With Conrad out of town until late that night, plenty of time to shop for a dress later in the week, and yet another reason she needed to go to New York City, she'd made her decision. With any luck she'd be home before Conrad that evening.

Meredith and Ashley did arrive at the Waldorf on time. Frank greeted them at the registration desk and immediately pulled Meredith close.

"Today's the big day," he said, nodding toward Ashley. "I'm glad you got her here."

"Family solidarity," Meredith said. "The whole team's here except Rory."

Frank kept his arm around Meredith's slim waist. "Do I tell you enough about how much I appreciate you? How I could never live a day without you?"

Ashley watched with a twinge of envy as Meredith placed a light kiss on Frank's lips. Funny how controlling she'd always thought Frank, but compared to Conrad, he now seemed so spontaneous. She moved closer to Meredith and Frank, listening halfheartedly as Frank briefed his wife on congressional issues, specifically, the Mexican illegal immigrant situation. Vincente Fox was pushing Bush hard for resolution.

How could they be chatting about world affairs when in half an hour, they'd both be facing the cameras of a big press conference, Ashley thought. Thank God she didn't have to say anything. She just had to sit through the press conference before the board meeting. But afterward, Ashley had an agenda. She'd needed this excuse to get to New York City, but she had to be back home by eleven p.m.

Meredith, as chair of the Parnell Foundation, had called the press conference to announce the new members of the board of trustees, of which Ashley was one. Conrad had lobbied to take her place, but Meredith had refused. Conrad was irate. Understandably so, Ashley thought. But unknown to the media attendees, the real story to be unveiled today was the acknowledgment of Monica Monroe as a Parnell. And Monica's and Patrick's secret wedding. How romantic, Ashley thought, I wonder if my marriage to Conrad will attract publicity. She hoped not.

Despite Matt Cleveland's hard work, Frank knew that the day could well turn into a disaster. The truth about the relationship between Paul Parnell and Monica Monroe, both household names, would leak soon enough. The tabloids were already making outrageous speculations. Could Monica have been Frank's mistress? Had Monica been the late Carla's lesbian lover? Pure sleaze, but the only way to counter it was to come out with the truth. The Parnell-Monroe spin on the truth: Paul Parnell's long-ago sexual indiscretion paled compared with his determination to protect his daughter's life and ensure that she was raised in a loving family and later brought into the Parnell family.

Matt had had to negotiate every nuance of the media talking points with Monica's aggressive manager. Matt's goal was to position Frank as the son of an American hero. Not a saint, but still a hero. The story of Monica's idyllic life should play well with the antiabortion crowd without overtly alienating the right-to-choosers whom Frank had tried so hard to dance around.

And thank God for small — or not so small — blessings. In Vegas the past week, undetected by the paparazzi, Monica and Patrick had been married. On that alone, the media would have a feast. Outing a Parnell family secret and a celebrity marriage in one swoop. The media didn't know yet that today's boring press conference would turn so juicy. As for his political future, with Monica representing hip, young swingers and Patrick's popularity with jocks around the country, Frank could feel his political base broaden. So today might be a smashing success. Or not.

"Ready, darling?" Frank checked his Patek Phillipe and straightened his tie. "Showtime."

Meredith nodded and they strode out onto the Waldorf ballroom's platform hand in hand, parting in the center for their assigned podium. Meredith as the chairperson of the Parnell Foundation would open with introductions. Frank would follow, then Monica, and finally, Patrick Nelson. All had prepared statements. Afterward, they'd take questions at Matt's discretion.

In the foundation meeting to follow, Ashley, Terry, at Dan's request, and Monica, as well as Rory in absentia would be elected to the board of the Parnell Foundation. That would fulfill Paul Parnell's wish. If all of them stayed out of Meredith's hair, the plan could work out.

Frank stole a look at Ashley in the front row. He hadn't seen her since Carla's funeral, two months earlier. That morning when Meredith had called to set a time to pick her up, she'd said she was too ill to go into New York. But Meredith did not take no for an answer and when she arrived at the Devon house, Ashley was almost dressed and ready to go. Meredith did not tolerate insults to her meticulous schedule without major unpleasantness, but today she seemed sympathetic, surmising that Ashley might actually be ill.

Meredith now took her place at the podium, looking glamorous but professional in a canary yellow suit and matching heels that drew attention to her shapely legs. She exuded self-confidence as she pushed her blunt bangs off her forehead and began to introduce the board of directors. The list read like a Who's Who of the mid-Atlantic, and included the former governor of Pennsylvania, the former CEO of Keystone Pharma, Philadelphia's favorite entertainment star, a New York City author-rabbi, and Cardinal Sean.

"But we're here today to announce an extension of this dedicated board," Meredith's voice rang out.

Watching boredom replace curiosity on the reporters' faces, Frank could read their minds: why are we wasting our time on a self-serving tribute to the Parnells?

"My father-in-law created this foundation with a dream, and today that dream has come to closure. Paul's dream was to make the Parnell Foundation the core of the family's philanthropy."

Frank suppressed a smirk when a middle-aged female reporter stifled a yawn, gathered her notebook and left. She'd be sorry.

Meredith was loving her role in the limelight. She'd often said to Frank that maybe someday she'd do the Hillary Clinton thing and go for the Senate. "As you know, I am privileged to represent the Frank Parnell branch of the family, and have served as chairperson since Carl Schiller stepped down. We are all so thankful for the leadership Carl has brought to the foundation, and we are grateful that he has agreed to remain as a trustee."

What a lie, Frank knew, but beautifully delivered. Meredith despised Carl, and, although the old man was too much of a gentleman to admit it, the feeling was mutual. He had stayed on the board to look over her shoulder. He was already giving her a hard time about her revised portfolio of contributions, which leaned heavily toward those causes that would enhance Frank's political future. For crying out loud, Frank thought, the foundation owed its very existence to Dad's money, so why not use it to his advantage? Control of annual distributions of half a billion dollars could only help with his constituents.

"Today I am proud to announce four new Parnell family board members. Paul's daughters, Dr. Ashley Parnell, Mrs. Rory Stevens, and Ms. Monica Monroe, and his grandson, Mr. Terrence Parnell."

There was a rumble of voices before Meredith called for a dramatic moment of silence in memory of Carla. The buzz hushed as the reporters respectfully bowed their heads until Meredith uttered a throaty "Thank you," dabbed at her eyes, and continued. "Now, I'd like to introduce my husband, Senator Frank Parnell."

Frank walked out to the second podium. "I want to tell you a story of a courageous man," he began as he laid out the story of his father's affair with a young woman and the story of Monica, as the videocams began to whir, the cameras to flash, and furious scribbling to appear on notebooks. When he finished, he thanked the media and was about to introduce Monica, when, to his surprise, the audience started to applaud. That was a first at any press conference he had ever participated in, and Frank could imagine Matt backstage, patting himself on the shoulder or more likely, sneaking a kiss from Frank's pretty niece.

"Now," he announced as the applause dwindled and the throng settled back to think up questions. "Here's Monica Monroe with an announcement of her own."

Cameras jockeyed for position and flashes went off from every direction. Soon Frank thought they'd start chanting, "Monica! Monica!" like her concert fans.

Monica approached the third podium with a flourish. After significant discussion had been held, she wore what she called her working clothes. Her manager had out argued Matt, who still remained appalled. Skintight black pants, a formfitting top that scooped almost to her navel, stiletto heels, long black hair flowing wild and reckless. Hardly the symbol of a philanthropic board of directors. "Image is all in this business," her manager had preached. "Every appearance has to enhance the image of the glamorous entertainer. Business is business and she's a brand. Just like Tide or Tylenol. That's why she pays me. I gotta constantly promote her persona."

Privately Monica might be a sweet, serene lady. Beautiful, ravishingly so, but unimposing in her personal demeanor. Publicly, she had to be a sensation — a star performer. Frank had seen her dynamite videos. But he'd never seen her do a live performance until now. The girl had real presence. Knew how to work a crowd. Well, why not? She'd been center stage at concert productions throughout the world. He could only salivate at the prospect of her at political rallies.

There was a new gush of applause and a few whistles.

"This is a very important moment for me," Monica began and cameras flashed. "I'd like to tell you my story."

In her crystal voice, Monica recounted her perfect life with her "real" parents, the Monroes. She directed the cameras to where her father sat in the front row, beaming with pride. Monica explained how she'd been adopted. How she had four older brothers. How her mom had died when Monica was fifteen of breast cancer. How she'd only recently discovered that Paul Parnell was her biological father. How he'd protected her life. She ended with a touching prayer she'd composed for her adopted mother, Denise Monroe, for Paul Parnell, and for her deceased biological mother, Abby Ames. There was not a sound in the room, other than the whir of camcorders.

A moment of silence. Then Monica switched to pure professional as she extolled the virtues of the Parnell Foundation, ticking off her favorite charities — breast cancer research, access to health care, shelters for abused women, teen mothers, hospice care for end of life. To these causes she vowed her personal attention. She appealed for volunteerism, financial support, altruism in general.

The media pack didn't know how to react. Was Monica going to walk out among them and pass the hat or circulate a sign-up sheet? Then a dramatic shift of gears as Monica flipped back her raven hair, pivoted to face backstage, and flung out her arm.

"And now that I've shared my past," she announced. "I want to tell you about my future."

There was a rustle and jousting for position.

Patrick strolled out like a guest on *Larry King Live*. Tanned, fit, brown hair trimmed to a longish crew cut, the familiar sports personality joined Monica at the podium. They embraced, and once more Frank was reminded of how perfect they looked together. What these two could do for his campaign!

"Everybody's been wondering why I've become such a sports fanatic. Now you know! My new husband, Patrick Nelson!"

Questions were shouted from every angle, but Matt stepped up to the fourth podium. Frank breathed a sigh of relief. His aide had pulled off quite a coup. This whole production had been his idea. So far so good.

Matt fielded the questions. All directed to Monica. Funny scene, hard-core business reporters begging for juicy tidbits about Monica's secret wedding.

After the press conference broke up, Frank and Meredith and Monica and Patrick were all high-fiving each other when Carl approached Ashley.

"Went well, didn't it?" Carl said.

"Yes." Ashley planted an affectionate kiss on the old man's cheek. "Now for the board meeting. How long do they usually go?"

"Meredith runs a tight ship. Two and a half hours, I'd say. When I was chairman, they went longer, but Meredith sticks to her agenda, then moves for adjournment. She's not big on board input."

"So you think we'll be out of here by three o'clock?"

Carl nodded. "I think so. Board members have flights to catch. But, Ashley, I need to talk to you. Can you stay for a while afterward? It's important."

"Not today, Uncle Carl, I have an appointment in the city. Then I'm going home."

"It's important. How about dinner tonight? Just the two of us? You can get a room here and leave first thing in the morning."

Ashley remembered that she'd made no arrangement to get back to Pennsylvania and that Conrad would be home before midnight. But it would be so wonderful to spend time with Uncle Carl. Of all the people in the whole world, she trusted him the most. Perhaps he could give her some guidance. She'd taken the week off from the hospital. And if she was successful later this afternoon, she'd be better off staying in New York. With a queasy feeling, she decided to leave a message for Conrad that she'd stayed overnight in Manhattan. He'd be angry, but she'd worry about that later. "Okay, Uncle Carl, that would be nice. I'll get a room here at the Waldorf and meet you for dinner. When and where?"

"I'll make the arrangements. Do what you have to do in the city. I already have a restaurant in mind, and I'll leave a message about time and place."

Later, she considered that room service at the hotel would have been a better dining choice.

CHAPTER NINETEEN

"Dr. Parnell, I've consulted with your sister's oncologist, and spoken directly to Dr. Stevens, your brother-in-law." The tall, balding hematologist sounded miffed. "I don't know why this is such a rush job, but as you are a Parnell, we'll make a policy exception."

"Thank you," Ashley said. Doctors could be so rude. She'd never talk to a patient like that.

"We'll need routine blood and urine tests. Then we'll take you to the procedure room."

Ashley, having rushed out of the board meeting, gladly accepted the plastic specimen cup, headed for the rest room, then returned for the technician to draw her blood. As she rolled up her sleeve, she wondered why she hadn't arranged this sooner. Why had Conrad been so insistent that she not do this? She was a healthy twenty-five-year-old woman. The procedure might not be pleasant, but it was not difficult or dangerous. Even though she and Rory were only half sisters, they had an unusually close match for a bone marrow transplant. Why had Conrad tried to prevent her from doing whatever she could to save Rory's life?

She felt as if she'd regained some sense of direction, some clarity of self, as if a layer of fog had lifted inside her head. She couldn't explain why she had drifted so far from Rory and Chan and the kids. They used to be so close. What kind of sister was she to let that happen?

"Will you come with me?" The rude doctor jerked his head for her to follow him down a corridor to a small alcove. Without inviting her to sit, he announced, "Your pregnancy test is positive. That complicates things."

"What?" Complicates things? Pregnant? She struggled to assess the implications. Grasping the edge of the square conference table she squeezed her eyes shut, forcing a prioritization. First, she must have the bone marrow procedure. Second, she'd have to absorb the shock of her pregnancy. And that meant telling Conrad.

The doctor just stood there, hand on hips. "You are pregnant."

"But I want to go through with it," she said.

"Go through with it?" the doctor echoed. "The pregnancy?"

"No. The bone marrow, I meant. Today."

"Oh no, we won't be doing that bone marrow today."

"But my sister needs it. Certainly a bone marrow under a local will not —"

"Dr. Parnell, we can't move forward without an obstetrical consult. Maybe after you have seen your obstetrician — they don't like any procedures done in the first trimester."

"Obstetrician?" Ashley slumped forward, leaning heavily on the table. "How can this be?" But she *had* let Conrad convince her not to take birth control pills.

The doctor shrugged off her stupid question.

"Can I see an OB here? Now?"

"I know how anxious you are to help your sister. But now that you're pregnant, it'll be up to you and your —"

"I have to do it today," Ashley interrupted. This doctor had no idea that she'd had to sneak off from Conrad to do this, the second explicit act of defiance that she'd risked that day.

"Can I get you something?" The doctor inched out the door. "If not, I do have to get back to other patients."

When Ashley got back to the Waldorf, she had just enough time to check into her suite, freshen up, and check her voicemail. There had been one from Carl with details on dinner and four from Conrad. All the same. Call him immediately to let him know she'd gotten home from wherever she had gone. She'd turned off her cell phone, disconnected the phone in the room. She was not ready to share her stunning news. Not even with Conrad. She needed time alone to think. A baby would change everything, but how, she didn't know. She thought of her mother. What would her mother do? But she couldn't imagine her mother in a circumstance like this.

Ashley found Carl seated at a table near the center of Le Bernadin, a magnificent seafood restaurant, her dad's favorite. As he rose to greet her, she couldn't help but notice that his tremors were more pronounced and that he looked even more frail than at Carla's funeral. Would it be fair to add to his burdens by sharing her problems with him?

"How about a Kir Royale?" he asked as soon as she was settled. "I still remember when I brought you your first."

"That would be nice," Ashley said before catching herself. Then, "No. I mean, I think I'll have Perrier."

"Okay, mind if I have a martini?"

"Of course not. Or will it interfere with your medication?"

"One drink's okay, but I thought you might have something against alcoholic beverages judging from your reaction to the Kir."

"I'm pregnant, Uncle Carl." The words flew out, unintended. "I just found out. Today when I went to Sloan-Kettering for Rory's bone marrow."

"Pregnant?" Carl looked stunned. "Bone marrow? Does Conrad know?"

"He didn't want me to do the bone marrow, and no, I haven't told him about either," she said, her voice trembling now.

They were both silent as the waiter solicited drink orders.

"Naturally, I need to figure out what to do," she said when the server left. "Conrad does want a child. At least he says he does, but I don't think he really likes kids. What he wants is hard for me to understand."

Carl frowned. "Ashley, I realize this is not a propitious time, but there are things I have to tell you about Conrad. I don't know how much you know."

"Uncle Carl, I know some things. I know he was married before. Is that what you mean?"

Carl reached across the table for her hand. "But do you know any of the details?"

"That she was mentally ill and she left him. They were divorced, and then she died. He feels terrible to this day. Guilty that he wasn't able to help her."

"Anything more?"

"No, he seemed so broken up when he talked about it. I didn't want to pry. Maybe after we're married, he'll open up."

"Promise me you'll not marry him right away," Carl said.

"We have the license, Uncle Carl." Ashley could feel his hand tremble as he held hers. "Saturday. That's five days away. At City Hall."

"That would be a big mistake. Let me tell you the story of Crissy Moore. Her name was Cristina, but everybody called her Crissy."

"Crissy," Ashley echoed.

"I'll tell you what I know. Maybe that'll put your feelings in perspective."

Ashley took a sip of her sparkling water.

"Conrad married Crissy in nineteen eighty-three."

Ashley calculated: eighteen years earlier.

"He was thirty-three; she nineteen. She —"

"How do you know all this?" Ashley interrupted.

"Dan and Frank asked me to engage a private investigator."

Why would they do that? she wondered. Frank's obsession to protect the Parnell name, synonymous with his political career. And Dan? When did Dan ever care about her?

The waiter stepped in to check on their drinks, but Carl pressed on. "Crissy was the sole heir to her father's estate. He died in nineteen eighty-two, leaving her close to a billion dollars."

Ashley's jaw dropped.

"The money was held in trust until she reached twenty-three. Her cousin, a psychiatrist in her forties, was trustee."

"Conrad didn't tell me that," Ashley whispered. "Just that she was insane."

"There is no evidence that Crissy had any sort of mental illness, but once they married, she withdrew from her friends. Hardly ever went out."

Ashley's mind immediately fixed on her own situation. How Conrad had insisted that she stop seeing her friends. Especially Ruthie. And to her shame, she had.

"Then Crissy left him. Quite suddenly. Not only did she leave him, but she left the country. For a time she lived in Paris with her trustee cousin who took a leave of absence from the Menninger Clinic where, by the way, her cousin and Welton were both staff psychiatrists."

"Yes, I knew that he was at Menninger before U of Penn." Ashley started to chew the cuticle of her thumb, remembered how Conrad despised that habit, then placed both hands on her lap and stared at the ruby in her ring.

"Crissy's lawyers arranged the divorce, which became final just months before she came into her inheritance."

Ashley tried to reconcile Conrad's story with this. Conrad had told the truth that he'd been married and divorced. But had Crissy been mentally ill? If she were that rich, maybe there'd be no records. Anything unpleasant in wealthy families could simply be covered up. How well she knew about that.

"The divorce had stipulations," Carl continued. "For an undisclosed sum of money, Welton agreed never to contact her. To walk away, making no further claims. But still, whenever Crissy came to the United States, she'd get a protective order. That was before her death."

"Her death?" Yes, Conrad had said she'd died.

"Here's what happened. Veronica Moore, the cousin, stayed with Crissy in Paris for eighteen months before returning to Kansas City. Before she could settle back into her practice, she was killed. Hit and run, not far from the clinic. The driver was never apprehended."

"Uncle Carl, certainly you're not saying that Conrad had anything to do with this?"

"Crissy came back for the funeral. Protective order in place. Her limousine exploded as she climbed in to leave the cemetery. She and her driver were killed outright. That's it. The police made inquires."

"Conrad?" Ashley whispered.

"In Philadelphia applying for a psychiatry position. They never found her killer. They never found the hit-and-run driver."

"That's just too bizarre. Crazy, really."

"Ashley, I've told you this so that you would take care, not rush into anything," Carl said, gently taking back her hand. "But now with the baby—"

Ashley was white faced and shivering. "Do Frank and Dan know this?"

"Yes. They're concerned. They want to find out more." Then why hadn't Frank said anything to her today? But, of course, Frank had much more important things to do than worry about her.

Carl said no more until the menus were presented. "What has Conrad told you about his past?"

"His parents are dead. No brothers or sisters. He grew up in Cincinnati. Went to Ohio State. University of Cincinnati for med school. Cleveland Clinic residency and fellowship. I've seen all the diplomas. Then Menninger Clinic. Then University of Pennsylvania." She searched her memory for more.

Uncle Carl's frown deepened. "He does have a brother. Stanley Welton. Lives in Cincinnati. Wife, two teenage sons. Second wife."

"He does?" Ashley hoped she wouldn't faint.

"The brothers are estranged. Did Welton ever mention that he was sent to a military school when he was twelve?"

"No," Ashley admitted, her breaths coming in short gulps.

"Middle school and high school," Carl said.

"Are his parents still alive?" *How much of what he'd told her had been a lie?*

"His father died on a gurney in a hospital elevator. On the way from the ER to the coronary care unit. Heart attack. Welton was alone with him on that elevator. As it turned out, Conrad, Sr. left everything to brother Stanley. Ultimately, his mother convinced Stanley to share the estate, and Stanley agreed to a fifty-fifty split until his wife stepped in to negate her husband's generosity. Not long after that their mother committed suicide."

"So much tragedy," Ashley said, hurt and angry, but mostly she was frightened. Why had Conrad lied to her? And why had he gone to Cincinnati today?

The waiter appeared again. "Are you ready to order?" he asked, bowing slightly.

"Not quite ready," Carl attempted a social smile. "Ashley, let's take a look at the menu."

The menu featured three lists of seafood and instructed diners to pick one item from each list. Knowing she'd be unable to eat, Ashley's hands started to shake and she had to set the menu down.

"Uncle Carl, I'm not that hungry. Can you order for me?"

When the waiter returned, Carl ordered for both of them. She doubted whether she could eat a morsel, but didn't want to make a scene.

A waiter appeared with bread choices, and when he left, Carl met her eyes. "Honey, I need to ask you this. Please don't take offense. Has Welton ever hurt you? Threatened you?"

"No, it's not that." This would be a struggle to explain. "But I've been having, like, blackouts."

"Blackouts?" Carl prompted.

"I know it sounds absurd. It's like parts of my life are blanked out. I can't remember things." She shook her head. "It's like what Alzheimer patients must go through."

A searing suspicion then flashed through her head, jolting her. She grasped the table with both hands to stabilize herself. *Could Conrad be drugging her?* As a psychiatrist he had access to every type of antipsychotic and sedative medication. As a hypnotist, he would routinely use drugs to alter his patient's state of consciousness. What if he had been giving her something like midazolam, a sedative used in surgical procedures, or propofol, an anesthetic that induced memory gaps? How easy it would be for him. And it would explain the blackouts. But why would he do that? All he had to do was ask, and she'd do anything to please him. Wasn't that what love was all about?

She couldn't share these paranoid suspicions with Uncle Carl. What she would do as soon as she got home was search the house for any trace of drugs or needles. Across the table, Uncle Carl kept his gaze on her and she felt compelled to explain. "Like sometimes when I wake up, I seem to be in a fog that covers my memory."

As the waiter presented their first course, Ashley fiddled with her napkin. As soon as he left the table, she pushed her food away.

"I don't know what's going on," Carl said, leaning toward her, "but you need help dealing with this. Come stay for a while with Phyllis and me."

"I'm so s-scared, Uncle Carl," she managed to stutter.

Carl's expression reflected deep concern. "And you're going to marry him? You can't do that until you get to the bottom of these memory lapses."

Ashley twisted her engagement ring inscribed with their initials intertwined. Maybe Carl was right. Maybe she wouldn't go through with the marriage this week. But what about her pregnancy?

Carl looked at her neglected plate and said apologetically, "Maybe a seafood restaurant was not the best choice tonight. Let me be honest with you, Ashley. I set up a meeting tomorrow morning with a law firm that specializes in marital-property law. Things like prenuptial agreements, but much more. I had wanted them to explain to you your options."

"No prenuptials," she said, her jaws clamping together.

"It's not just about money," Carl said, scrutinizing her. "It's much more fundamental, but you need to hear from these experts. You'll be surprised as to how many different ways there are to deal with such a situation."

"No prenuptials." she repeated. She started to grind her teeth. Once she'd mentioned something about whether she needed one to Conrad. He had erupted in anger. That's all she could remember, but the mere mention of the word drove a pulse of fear though her body.

"Mam'selle? Did you not care for the food?" The waiter looked disapprovingly at her untouched plate.

"The lady is a little unwell," Carl offered. "Mine was delicious." He looked back to Ashley. "So, let's agree to meet with these attorneys in the morning. The timing is perfect since you're staying in the city overnight. They can explain everything to you. Then I'll take you back to Philadelphia tomorrow. In the meantime, let's move to a more pleasant topic."

After a feeble attempt to recap the foundation board meeting, Carl called for the waiter. "I think we'll skip the next two courses," he said, turning to Ashley, "unless you think you can eat something."

Ashley nodded her assent, but then her eyes settled on the cheese cart, being presented at the next table.

"Maybe some cheese," Carl said, and Ashley chose a simple cheddar. She had a child to consider now and she needed nourishment.

By the time they left the restaurant, Ashley felt more settled, and when Carl's driver dropped her off at the Waldorf, she assured him that she'd be okay. Alone in the luxurious suite, Ashley tried to analyze what she had learned. She accepted that what Uncle Carl had told her was fact. But the vague accusations? That Conrad somehow had something to do with his wife's death? And that of the woman's cousin? And his own father? As the night wore on, a sense of panic began to build. Her heart started to race and she heard Conrad's voice in her ears, very melodious, but she couldn't make out the words. She began to admit to herself that she was afraid of Conrad. And that thought made her heart race even faster. What if only a bit of what Uncle Carl had implied was true?

Sitting up in bed, she turned on the bedside light. Picking up a notebook, she began to think more clearly and list her most urgent concerns on the page.

No. 1: Was she in love with Conrad? Or had he come into her life when she'd been just too vulnerable? Did he have some kind of sinister control over her? Was she afraid of him? Had he been giving her drugs?

No 2: Had Conrad had anything to do with the death of those other people? If so, her life and her baby's life were in danger.

No 3: What about the baby? Would she have to marry Conrad for the baby's sake? An ice pick jabbed at her heart. Or was it quite the opposite — she needed to protect her baby from him?

Her thoughts raced back and forth while she tried to find a solution. Finally, she got up and paced until light started to filter through the curtains. Exhausted, she heard Conrad's voice. Faint at first, then loud enough for her to make out the words: "You will never leave me; if you try to leave me, I will find you; I will find you no matter where you go."

As she watched the dawn of a beautiful morn, she began to feel a sense of clarity, a clarity that had eluded her for so many months. Standing at the window, drenched in a cold sweat, Ashley realized that she had let herself be controlled by Conrad Welton. Not a superficial or frivolous control, but a profound control, imprisoning her.

Ashley dressed slowly, wearing the same cranberry silk suit that she had worn the day before. She packed the few cosmetics she'd purchased and put them in her purse. The meeting with the lawyers was scheduled for nine a.m., and she had made up her mind to listen carefully to what they had to say. She wasn't hungry, but she left early enough so that she could pick up a muffin and coffee in the financial district. And fruit and milk, too, she reminded herself, still in awe that she was pregnant.

In the cab from the Waldorf to lower Manhattan, she decided she would go home with Uncle Carl as he'd suggested. Maybe ask him to help her get away from Conrad. But she had to stay in Philadelphia because of her residency. Could Uncle Carl deal with Conrad so she'd never have to face him again? Maybe.

"Here we are, ma'am." The driver grunted as Ashley reached into her purse to pay the fare.

"Thanks," she mumbled, considering herself lucky that she didn't have to deal with the chaos of New York City on a regular basis. As she climbed out of the cab, she looked around for Tower One, World Trade Center. She needed the fifty-second floor, but she was twenty minutes early. Plenty of time to find a café, maybe a Starbucks. As she walked among the massive concrete flowerpots that lined the perimeter of the huge complex, she wasn't even sure which building was Tower One and which was Tower Two. Uncle Carl would know once she met up with him.

The day had turned bright and sunny, and Ashley envied the energy and optimism on the faces surrounding her. Everybody walked with purpose as if they knew who they were and where they were going. But where to go for coffee? She checked her watch to see if she still had time. Fifteen minutes. Naturally, a law firm would have coffee, bagels, fruit for a nine o'clock meeting. Then her cell phone rang. Conrad? She almost had not turned it back on. She checked the number. Not Conrad, so she answered.

"Ashley? Uncle Carl here. Just called to tell you that I'm running a few minutes late so why don't you go on up?"

"Okay — if I can find the right place. So far I haven't figured out which building is which."

"You're there? Right?"

"Yes, but I don't want to get started without you."

"Tell the receptionist that I'll be there by nine fifteen. The more I think of our discussion last night, the more important this morning is," he said. "So have an extra cup of coffee and have them wait for me."

"I didn't sleep all night. Thinking about everything. Maybe I will stay with you and Aunt Phyllis."

No response. Must have lost the signal. Ashley walked toward one of the tall towers, intending to go inside and ask security whether she was in the right place. People were converging from all directions. "Is this Tower One?" she asked a stranger.

Her answer was an affirmative nod so Ashley continued into the lobby. Now all she had to do was find the right bank of elevators.

She approached a security guard at his kiosk. "Excuse me, sir, could you tell me where —"

A deafening explosion and a tremor rocked the building. Lurching forward, Ashley grasped the edge of the kiosk to stay upright.

"A bomb! Holy shit! Ma'am, you better get the hell outta here." The security guard shoved her aside in his rush for the door.

At first Ashley just stood there, stunned. The building kept shaking, glass and clumps of debris falling from the lobby ceiling. Then she saw flames pouring out of an elevator shaft. People streamed toward the doors. Some were screaming, many in languages she did not understand. Still, she hadn't moved. For a second she wondered whether her mind was playing tricks on her? A nightmare? Is this what it was like to be going insane?

Then more blasts from above and people running. Wild-eyed, frightened. More explosions, not as loud as the first, and more glass breaking. Chunks of ceiling coming down like rain. She wondered if it could be an earthquake, not a bomb. The East Coast didn't pay much attention to earthquake precautions. Get under a ledge or beam? She wasn't sure. Whatever, she had to do something in case the whole building collapsed. She heard alarms inside and outside as she joined the throng of humanity pouring out the doors.

Outside, a crowd stared upward. Ashley half expected to see King Kong thumping his breast at the top of Tower One. What she saw was a huge hole in the upper part of the building. Bright orange flames and heavy plumes of black smoke poured out of the gash, rapidly contaminating the bright blue skies. She heard, "Hit by a plane. There's a plane inside there. I saw it hit. Everybody get out of here."

For the next several yards, she didn't know how many, Ashley moved with the crowd. Away from the building, in short, halting steps. Periodically the crowd turned to gaze, everyone mesmerized by the gaping, pulsating hole. Sirens now screamed from all directions and firemen were starting to rush in, bisecting the crowd, pushing her and her fellow gapers to the fringe.

All Ashley could hope was that those trapped inside would be rescued. So many firemen rushing in, but what about those who had been in that awful burning gash? Her knees buckled, realizing that five minutes later she could have been in that exact place. Then she heard a thud, close to where she stood. Then another. She looked back up at the inferno at the most horrifying sights, people jumping from the high floors, free-falling. Men in suits. A woman with long dark hair. A man in jeans. Ashley started to head toward them, as if she could help, but a man pulled her back.

"Get out of here, lady," he yelled. "Nothing any of us can do. They got thousands trapped up there."

As her interceptor held her back with one hand, his other pointed upward at the focus of the crowd on the ground. Rather than screams, a collective breath was held as a jet plane slammed into the second building at a height a little lower than the first. Another fireball, another inferno. Air now more dense with smoke. Sirens everywhere. Firemen and police pouring in. Escorting victims out. Some stumbling, some on stretchers. While she stood, chunks of concrete and aluminum and glass burst out from the second building. Now everyone was running, covered with white ash like Halloween ghouls.

Ashley felt a shove from behind and lunged forward until a strong hand reached out and grabbed her arm, pulling her in the direction of the others, away from the buildings. In the midst of explosions and flying debris, a car close by blew up, igniting in a fiery blast. An image seared Ashley's brain of a girl — Crissy — blown up in a car at the cemetery. So that's what it had been like.

In a violent motion, Ashley twisted the ring off her left finger. With a jerk she flung it as far as she could toward Tower One. Then, like everyone else, she ran.

"Chinatown, Brooklyn Bridge, Fulton Street Ferry," the police shouted. "Get out. Move. Evacuate."

Ashley fell in with the crush of people. By now she was covered all over in ash. Her heels were too high and she discarded her shoes. She struggled to keep up in her slim skirt, sure that she'd be trampled if she fell. But she needn't have worried. The crowd was in control. Grim, stunned, but helping one another. She watched as two young men took an elderly gentleman by the arms and urged him along. All along the street, storefronts had opened up and were handing out bottles of water. A shoe store owner offered footwear, and she accepted a pair of sandals, the soles of her bare feet bloody from the shards of glass.

The ground shook. She was sure that this time all of New York City was under attack. For a moment the crowd halted and, as one, turned to stare. A collective gasp. A burning tower imploded in front of them. Thousands of people were dying at that very instant.

The cadre of marchers remained remarkably calm, grimly resuming their retreat in near silence. Ashley kept moving with the mass westward, toward the Hudson River until, amid a thunderous roll, the entire throng turned around again. The remaining tower, the first one hit, the one Ashley had stood in, collapsed into billows of smoke and debris. Lower Manhattan's skyline was being erased, leaving in its place a mass grave.

Too much death to fathom. When the throng reached the river, Ashley took her place in the line waiting for a boat to New Jersey. After only a half hour, she climbed aboard a Circle Line tourist boat. The boat was jammed, but she found space on a bench by the outside rail. Still sirens, still billows of smoke, and now overhead, fighter jets circled Manhattan.

"Blood. Red Cross needs blood." Ashley looked to a matronly woman with a clipboard. "Will you donate?" she asked the thin young girl who had squeezed in beside Ashley.

"I can't," the girl said. Ashley noticed how violently she was trembling. When she looked up her eyes were red and puffy, and there were tear tracks down her sooty cheeks. "I would, but I'm pregnant. Oh, God, I think Craig's dead."

"Sorry, miss," said the woman as she moved to Ashley.

"I can't," Ashley said, unwilling to disclose her pregnancy, but wanting an excuse. "I'm sorry, but I've had hepatitis. I can't donate blood," she lied.

Ashley turned toward the girl next to her who looked no older than eighteen. She had long hair, but Ashley couldn't guess the color underneath the soot. Her slacks and short-sleeved shirt were concrete gray, as was the skin on her arms.

"Are you okay?" Ashley asked.

"He doesn't even know." Fresh tears started to enlarge the sooty tracks.

"Your husband?" Ashley asked.

"No, my boyfriend. We always said that if I got pregnant, we'd get married. But Craig worked for Cantor Fitzgerald. He was in there. The North Tower — the one hundred third floor. What if —"

"I'm sure he got out," Ashley said.

"We were going to meet for lunch. I was going to tell him today about the baby," she said through bouts of sobs. "What am I going to do?"

"I don't know," Ashley said, answering both the girl's question and her own.

For a moment they both looked up as a jet fighter swooped in closer.

"Where do you live?" Ashley asked once the roaring noise dissipated.

"New Brunswick. With my Aunt Bea."

"I'm pregnant too," Ashley blurted out. "I'm not married either."

The girl grabbed Ashley's hand. "My name is Julie Janinski. Why don't you come home with me? Just for now."

"But your aunt —"

"Aunt Bea? No problem. Honestly, she has a heart that won't stop."

Ashley considered her options. When she'd pulled off that ring, she'd set her course.

"Please. I could use some companionship. At least until the shock wears off. Please come home with me." Julie began to tear up again. For a minute they both looked across the waterfront at a sky darkened by smoke and clouds of billowing debris.

She knows, Ashley thought. She knows that her Craig is dead. Maybe Ashley could help her in some way. "Hey, I don't even know your name." Julie said, sniffing back the tears.

"Ruthie." Ashley grabbed her best friend's first name, but needed a surname. "Ruthie Hester." Her mother's maiden name.

CHAPTER TWENTY

Judging the media briefing a wild success, Frank and Meredith headed back to Pennsylvania. Early the next morning, they settled into their respective offices in Philadelphia. As was their habit, they each read the *Washington Post*, the *New York Times*, the *Philadelphia Inquirer*, the *Pittsburg Post-Gazette*, Harrisburg's *Patriot-News*, and the *Wall Street Journal*. At eight forty-five, one of them would call the other. Each would have a list of priority issues culled from the news of the day, the focus being how the news impacted their long-term strategy. September eleventh was one of those rare days that this discussion did not take place.

Instead, they watched the day erupt on television, frantically clicking on CNN, then Fox, then the others, back and forth. At first, the sketchy story about a plane hitting New York's World Trade Center. Then, Frank's hotline rang. It was Matt from his Washington office. All hell was breaking loose in D.C., but nobody knew what had actually happened. Matt suggested that Frank hunker down in his office. Keep phone lines open. Cancel all appointments. The president was in Sarasota, reading to school kids. Matt promised to call Frank back with the latest at first word.

Frank stared at the TV coverage mutely as the second plane struck the second tower. It was three minutes after nine. He was riveted in horror. One minute later, Matt was on the line. "We're at war, but we don't know who with."

"What's Congress doing? Will there be a special session?" Frank was too numb to think. Would they be coming together? Or going into hiding?

"Setting up a safe place in case an emergency session's called. You'd better get to D.C., boss. FAA's shutting down all air traffic, so the fastest way is by car. The corridor from Philly to D.C. should be okay. Wouldn't want to be stuck in Manhattan. They're closing down all the tunnels and bridges."

"I'm on my way." Frank started throwing random papers into his briefcase.

He was in his limo focusing on the small TV as the American Airlines flight crashed into the Pentagon. His cell phone rang just minutes after.

"Where are you, boss?" Matt asked. "The Pentagon. Have you heard?"

"Yes. I'm approaching Wilmington."

"Okay, call me when you get close to Baltimore. I'll line up an escort so you can get into D.C. —" The signal faded and the conversation ended. Frank tried to get him back on the line with no luck. Only then did he call Meredith to tell her that he was on his way to D.C.

TV reception for the next half hour was erratic, but for the most part Frank was able to monitor the disaster. Matt had called back and arranged to have the Maryland State Police pick him up on the proximate side of the Baltimore Tunnel. Security was heightened everywhere, and with a police escort from the tunnel to the Russell Building, by noon he'd be joining his fellow senators — unless, like the White House, the Senate Building had been evacuated.

His driver was searching for a local radio station when the phone rang.

"Frank, it's Tom Ridge."

The governor of Pennsylvania. Frank's first thought was that the governor wanted him in Harrisburg. Certainly, he'd realize that a senator's place was in Washington at a time like this. The governor came right to the point. A fourth plane had been hijacked. It had crashed in Somerset County. United flight 93. Newark to San Francisco. Terrorists suspected. Did Frank want to join him at the sight?

He instructed his driver to head west, to Somerset County. He called Matt, who had just heard. Halfway through Pennsylvania, his car was intercepted by a state trooper and escorted to the crash site. Standing on scorched ground as close as he was allowed on the brink of the huge crater, Frank learned of the heroes on Flight 93. In a three-way call with Matt and Meredith, he discussed whether he should join the other senators in D.C., or stay at the Pennsylvania crash site. They decided he should stay in Pennsylvania to assist the families of the victims. Meredith had just asked whether she should join him at the site, when the governor and his aide rushed toward Frank.

"Darling, I have to go," he said. "And no, there's so much chaos here, you'd better stay in Philadelphia."

Frank broke the connection just as Governor Ridge approached. Frank did not like the look on his face, or on the face of his aide. Something else must have happened. The country was under siege.

"Frank, you have an urgent call." The governor had to raise his voice to be heard over the commotion surrounding the command center. Frank didn't hide a look of annoyance. He'd asked Matt to hold his calls.

"The call's from a Mr. Carl Schiller." the aide explained. "He assured me you needed to take it."

"Carl Schiller?" Why would he call in the middle of a crisis of these proportions? Then Frank remembered. Carl had stayed in Manhattan last night. He was having dinner with Ashley to tell her what they'd learned about Welton.

"I'll talk to him." Frank guessed that the old man wanted to report his eye-witness experience.

"Hello, Carl? I'm at the crash site right now. Don't have time to talk."

"Frank, thank God I reached you. I scheduled a meeting with a law firm this morning. Their offices are in the World Trade Center. The meeting was with Ashley."

"What time?" Frank felt his stomach churn. Timing had been critical this morning in Lower Manhattan.

"Nine o'clock. I got held up in traffic. Didn't make the meeting, but she did. I talked to her only minutes before the first plane hit. I was several blocks away."

"Ashley? In one of those buildings?" Frank felt a numbness creep through his body.

Frank checked his watch. It was now one thirty p.m. "What about Welton? Has she contacted him? Rory?"

"No, no one's heard from her."

Frank struggled to think, as fear replaced reason.

"I'm okay." He must have started to wobble because the governor reached out to steady him.

"Carl, I don't know what to think." Frank could hear the tremor in his own voice. What if Ashley had been trapped in one of the towers? "Wouldn't she have called Welton?"

"After what I told her last night, I'm not sure. But Welton's beside himself—keeps calling. And there's something else. Not even he knows. Ashley's pregnant. She just found out yesterday." Frank could hear Carl sniffle. "I'm really afraid she was in the tower. If not, we should have heard something. The city's a war zone, but—"

Ashley could be dead? His sister buried under tons of rubble? Frank stared into the gaping hole in the Pennsylvania field.

"Carl, keep trying to locate her. And you'd better call Dan, just so he knows."

"Sure," Carl said, then hesitated. "Frank, you are going home?"

"Right now I'm going to call Meredith. She'll contact you."

As soon as Frank terminated the call, the governor asked, "National security?"

"No, a family matter," Frank said. "It's my sister. She's missing. She was at the World Trade Center. I need to call my wife."

"Frank, I'm so sorry." Ridge pointed to a white van. "Please. Use the makeshift communication center. Do what you must to find your sister."

Once he'd gotten though to Meredith, she'd already had several calls from Welton. "He's frantic. Carl told him that she'd been at the Trade Center. I assured him that we'd pull every string. Matt's putting out an alert to NYPD, but they're so overwhelmed. Frank, this is awful."

"Meredith, you know what really surprises me? I care. I truly care about Ashley."

"I know you do, darling, but right now, let me take care of the family affairs. And you know what? I'll bet Ashley is okay. Just shocked or something. You know how weird she's been lately."

They agreed that Frank would stay at the crash site to participate in the two o'clock news conference. Then he'd head back to Philadelphia.

It was after eight by the time Frank arrived at his country house in Bucks County. He let himself in with his key, finding the house dark except for the foyer lights set to dim. No surprise. Rory and Chan had insisted on taking Elise to their home in nearby Doylestown, leaving her parents free to deal with the day's public and personal tragedies. There had still been no word of Ashley. He had suggested that he have his driver pick Meredith up in Philadelphia, but Meredith had insisted that he go straight home. She still had to follow up on a few hospitals where Ashley might be. She'd have one of the firm's cars take her home.

Frank poured himself a glass of Chardonnay before turning on the big screen TV, switching among the news channels. Over and over. The twin towers imploding. Was Ashley buried there? Or one of those who had jumped to her death? How long would it be before they knew?

At eight thirty, Frank glanced at his suit pants, stained and flecked with debris, which reminded him that he needed to shower and change his clothes. The phone rang when he was drying his hair. He wrapped the towel around his waist and ran into the bedroom. Please, God, let it be that Ashley's safe.

"Chan here, Frank, sorry to bother you. What a hellish day. Meredith said you were at the Pennsylvania crash site. I can't even imagine, but that's not why I'm calling —"

"Ashley?" Frank preempted.

"No, we haven't heard a thing. I finally had to give Rory a sedative. Something she hates, but with the kids — That's why I'm calling. Meredith decided to pick up Elise tonight. We expected her by now."

Frank's shoulders sagged. He'd craved a night alone with Meredith. Just the two of them, no Elise. "I'll call her on her cell," he said. "If she's tied up, I'll run over and get Elise if that's what Meredith wants."

"I've tried her cell," Chan said. "No answer. I left a message."

It was then that Frank heard the chime of the door bell, followed by a loud, rapid pounding at the front door. For crying out loud, what was going on out there? Why would Meredith use the front door? And why would she be trying to knock the door down?

"Got to go, Chan, I think she's home now."

Before heading down the step, Frank glanced out the window. He drew in a sharp breath. A state police car, red and blue lights flashing. Had to be news about Ashley.

"Senator, sir," stammered the rosy-cheeked, strapping state trooper, "Will you come with me, sir? There's been an accident, sir. I've been ordered to take you immediately — I mean as soon as you're dressed, sir. I'm to take you to Jefferson Hospital emergency room."

Jefferson was where Ashley was doing her residency. "What kind of accident?"

"I don't have all the details, sir. Just that they need you there. I can wait right here while you —" Blushing, he gestured toward Frank, where the towel wrap was starting to unravel.

Frank turned toward the stairs. Should he go with this polite young man? Was there any security risk? After what happened today, nothing could be taken for granted. But this trooper was clearly not a terrorist. He hastily ran his hand though the rack of slacks. What to wear? A stupid issue after a day like today, but an issue a politician is programmed to consider. He snatched up a pair of dark gray slacks and a short-sleeved shirt. The loafers he grabbed were mismatched, one brown, one black.

The officer was clearly nervous as he shifted from foot to foot as Frank came back down the stairs.

"Car's ready," he said, already halfway through the door.

"Front or back?" Frank asked, blinking at the flickering red and blue lights against the night sky.

"Uh, sit up front, sir," he said with a glance to the back seat manacle restraints. As the trooper navigated the property's long drive, Frank took out his cell phone to try Meredith again. She'd be concerned, finding an empty house, lights on, wet towel.

"Can you tell me about Ashley's condition?" Frank asked as soon as the cruiser had made it to Route 611, heading toward Street Road and I-95 into the city.

"Sir?"

"My sister, Ashley Parnell?"

"Sir, this is not about your sister. The accident victim is your wife, sir. Mrs. Meredith Parnell. So sorry, sir."

Frank stopped breathing. How could he? There was no air in the cruiser. Grasping the dash with both hands, trying to steady himself, he finally spoke, "Is my wife —" He couldn't say the word.

"We'll be at the hospital in fifteen minutes," the trooper said, swerving to pass the vehicles signaled to the shoulder by the siren and flashing lights. "Light traffic tonight, we'll be there right away."

Frank was numb with panic, but not numb enough to realize that an evasive answer portended the worst. His twelve years of Catholic education, mostly neglected now, came back in a flash and he began to recite the Hail Mary nonstop.

CHAPTER TWENTY-ONE

Conrad turned on every light, the Parnell estate a beacon to guide Ashley home. In a circular motion, he paced the first floor. Foyer, living room, library, dining room, den, kitchen, conservatory. Around and around at a steady pace. The red-hot anger that had kept him up all night was now an icy fear.

He went over the facts. Ashley had lied to him. Having given her word, she had gone into Manhattan with Meredith. She'd attended the press conference and the foundation board meeting. According to Terry, the only Parnell who returned his calls, she hadn't made a peep during the meeting, and had left within minutes of adjournment. The next thing anyone knew was that she had dinner at Le Bernardin with Schiller. The old man admitted it, adding that he and Ashley were to meet with lawyers in the morning. The law firm was located in the World Trade Center, North Tower, Tower One. The first to be hit, the second to collapse. Schiller had been running late, Ashley early.

For the fifth time that day, Conrad called Schiller at the Parnell apartment in Manhattan. Each time Schiller picked up himself. Each time the conversation went, "Carl, you must know something. With all the Parnell connections. I've been trying to get the senator, but I can't get through to him."

"The country's in a national emergency. We've got investigators in Manhattan looking for Ashley. Meredith herself is leading the effort to find her, and that woman does not take no for an answer," Carl Schiller had answered.

How well Welton knew that. "We have to find her. She must be hurt or lost or suffering from posttraumatic shock. She's never been on her own before, now to be thrown into this mayhem. She just won't know what to do. Tell me, what can I do? There must be something."

"I'll stay here in the city until we find her," Carl promised, but Welton could hear the defeat in his tone.

"I'll join you as soon as they open the tunnels," Welton said.

"Suit yourself."

Welton said to himself, *How fucking ironic that terrorists attack Manhattan at that very moment that Ashley is heading to see lawyers, just three days before they were to be married.*

Heading to see lawyers. Welton had been explicit with Ashley: no prenuptial agreement. That she was seeing a lawyer behind his back convinced him that Ashley had relapsed. Relapsed just at the crucial point. Welton knew that Ashley was alive. There was no doubt in his mind, and he would find her. He would get her back to the Esdaile state, a difficult hypnotic depth to manage, but not for someone with his skills.

By ten o'clock, Welton's knees throbbed and he settled into Paul's deep leather chair in the library. He picked up the remote, awaiting anything new on the TV, trying to piece together what he'd learned about the location of the law firm where Ashley was to meet, relating its location to the worst of the damage reported in the North Tower before it collapsed. Massaging his temples to ward off a tension headache, he wrestled with facts. Crissy, now Ashley. What if Ashley had *not* escaped?

Welton had gone to Cincinnati to put an ugly plan into effect. Next week, he and Ashley were to be married. In January, just four months away, he'd have the Parnell money.

Conrad Welton was a successful, respected psychiatrist with a distinguished medical background, but in truth, he was a madman. And he had waited a long time to find a solution to the obsessive hatred he held for his brother, the equally distinguished Dr. Stanley Welton, a Cincinnati plastic surgeon. Welton held a searing grudge against his brother, who he believed had alienated him from his parents, causing his father to turn on him and his mother to abandon him. What Welton was planning, in his insanity, was first to see that Stanley's two sons met a tragic death. Then he would make it seem as if Stanley's wife, the mother of the two boys, had committed suicide. Next, Welton planned to buy out Stanley's partners in his company, Surgi-Center, so that he could bring about an avalanche of lawsuits: malpractice, negligence, sexual harassment, misappropriation of funds. Welton would settle for nothing less than total humiliation. Then, at the moment of his choosing, Welton would watch Stanley take his last muffled breath, just as he had their father.

But he needed money and for that he needed Ashley alive.

At eleven Welton was about to click off Philadelphia's channel ten and turn to Fox News when a photo of Meredith Parnell filled the screen. "Our hearts go out to the Parnell family, especially Senator Parnell who spent this tragic day consoling the families of Flight 93 in Pennsylvania," intoned the news reporter.

Frantically, Welton clicked around various channels, but the news was dominated by the day's devastation and speculation as to what evil forces had perpetrated the atrocities. At the computer he immediately found the sketchy facts. Meredith Parnell had died in a fatal car accident on I-95 near Woodhaven Road when her chauffeur-driven limousine struck the rear of a tractor trailer that had swerved to avoid an out-of-control Jeep. The impact of the crash threw her across the passenger compartment, breaking her neck on impact. She was pronounced dead on arrival at Jefferson Memorial Hospital. The driver of her vehicle was treated for minor injuries and the driver of the truck was unharmed.

"Aha!" Welton smiled for the first time that day. Ashley had always said that Meredith was the brains behind Frank Parnell.

CHAPTER TWENTY-TWO

Ashley sat with her new friend, Julie, in Aunt Bea's kitchen. Both were too numb to eat, but with Aunt Bea's clucking and hovering they'd forced down a little baked chicken. They'd showered off layers of soot, and Ashley had put to use the package of L'Oreal sable brown dye she picked up during her march out of Lower Manhattan. Now her cinnamon hair was darker and chopped from shoulder length to just below her chin. Both women sat wrapped in fluffy bathrobes, unable to shake the chill despite the cozy room temperature and the comfort food.

"Two mothers to be," Aunt Bea kept repeating, urging them to finish the twelve-ounce glass of milk she'd poured for each. Aunt Bea had known that Julie was expecting, and she accepted Ashley's pregnancy without judgment, never asking why she did not have her own place to go.

"Aunt Bea, I've checked with everyone. Craig's mother — anybody I could think of who works with him. I know Craig's dead, Aunt Bea. His office was —"

"Julie, my dear. There are a lot of people missing. Just wait."

"But the baby. What am I going to do?"

"Oh, Julie, dear." Aunt Bea hugged Julie, comforting her, promising her she could have her house, making Julie promise that she and the baby live with her. "And of course, Ruthie, my dear, you can stay here with your baby, too."

Aunt Bea's generosity stunned Ashley. How willingly she'd squeeze two mothers and two babies into her tiny two-bedroom home. She'd never met such a big-hearted person before. Aunt Bea, a spinster, short and plump, with white hair permed into curls, welcomed Ashley into her home, no questions asked. It was clear that Aunt Bea had two passions, feeding people and nonstop, daytime television. Her eyesight was failing and her hearing had deteriorated, so she kept the volume on loud and sat directly in front of the set. In the aftermath of September eleven, she couldn't get enough news. Over and over, she played the flames raging out of the towers, the people jumping, the soot-covered survivors. As these images kept pouring out, Ashley remembered the sound as that car had exploded so very close to her. That was how Crissy, Conrad's wife, had died.

And it was through Aunt Bea's TV that Ashley learned of Meredith's death. Shaken, she'd absorbed the news silently, agonizing as to whether to attend the funeral. Maybe by disguising herself? But the services were to be private. The location not even disclosed. Meredith had been Jewish, so she'd have to be buried, Ashley couldn't remember the exact requirement, something about before sundown of the following day. With what had been happening to the country, naturally, Frank would opt for something quiet.

Facing the finality of Meredith's death, Ashley felt her own resolve turn steadfast. She would do all in her power to protect her child. When her father's inheritance was settled, she could confront Conrad. He'd so easily dominated her before, and she couldn't risk losing control to him again. This time it could mean her life and that of her baby.

With the television still blaring in the background, Ashley gently massaged her abdomen, thinking of Frank and Meredith. They had one of those symbiotic relationships, feeding off one another, supporting one another, seemingly communicating without words, always on the same wavelength. Meredith had been the perfect wife for Frank. And Ashley would never forget her sister-in-law's efforts to help Carla.

The day of Meredith's funeral, Ashley busied herself by helping around the house. She dusted Aunt Bea's furniture, vacuumed the rugs, and mopped the kitchen floor, chores that she was doing for the first time. That evening she announced she'd be leaving the next day. Aunt Bea tried to talk her out of it, but Ashley knew she couldn't stay. New Jersey was too close to Philadelphia, Conrad's epicenter. He would find her.

"You're sure you'll be all right, Ruthie?" Aunt Bea asked over and over as she kept stuffing food into a thermal bag. "You know that you can always come back here."

"I know, Aunt Bea," Ashley said. "Naturally, after talking to my aunt in Toronto, I think I should be with family. My uncle is a lawyer. I can do secretarial work, and my aunt can help out with the baby."

A blatant lie, but Ashley felt no guilt. If this fib made Julie and Aunt Bea feel better, why not? Her life from now on would be nothing but lies.

"I understand. You just better send pictures of the baby." Aunt Bea predicted that Ashley would have a boy and Julie, a girl. So she and her lady friends had shopped accordingly at a garage sale. As Ashley said her good-byes, the old lady pressed a bundle of tiny powder blue garments into her hands.

"Thank you." Tears filled Ashley's eyes as she kissed Aunt Bea's downy face. "You'll never know how much I treasure your friendship."

At the train station, Julie reached over and patted Ashley's abdomen. It was still flat whereas hers already had a small mound. "You know, Ruthie, you never did tell me who the father is. I didn't want to pry. You seem so — secretive. Do you want to tell me?"

In just a few short days, Julie had become like a sister to Ashley, the little sister that she'd lost in Carla. "Yes," Ashley said, "I do want to tell you, but I can't. But as soon as I'm able, I will pay you and Aunt Bea back for your kindnesses."

Ashley had formulated a plan: take the train from New Brunswick to Trenton, from Trenton to Washington D.C., from D.C. to as far west as she could get on her money. She had more than a million dollars, but she had no idea how to get at it. Uncle Carl's firm took care of her financial matters. Until now, she'd never given it a second thought. Just charged what she wanted and wrote checks with abandon.

On the train, Ashley peeked into the plastic bag containing the baby clothes. On top was an envelope. "Baby Boy Hester" was scrawled in shaky letters. Inside was a wad of twenty dollar bills. "God bless you, Aunt Bea."

Now, she would learn about living on her own. She would not be there when her father's wealth was distributed. She wouldn't need all that money, anyway. She had her medical training. Ultimately she'd be fine, supporting herself and a child on a doctor's income, just as her mother had. Thanks, Mom, for giving me the self-confidence to do this.

But as the train jostled along, she started to cry. "Ma'am?" A balding man in a suit stood in the aisle. "Could you move over one?"

The voice scared her, and Ashley shrank closer to the window, trying without success to stifle her tears. Tears for herself, for Julie, for Rory, for Meredith, and for all those strangers who'd lost their lives in front of her eyes.

CHAPTER TWENTY-THREE

The second contact listed in Meredith Parnell's wallet, "call in case of emergency" was Carl Schiller. Mr. Schiller wasn't home, but his wife directed the police to an exchange in Manhattan. The man on the line sounded elderly and devastated. They hated to have to break the news so bluntly, but what could they do?

The first contact had been the dead woman's husband, a U.S. Senator from a wealthy Philadelphia family. They chose to send the closest state trooper to escort him to Jefferson Hospital. On arrival, the husband had bolted through the emergency room door, shouting out his wife's name. When the ER doctor told him his wife was dead, the guy screamed, moaned, was inconsolable. They finally had to admit him, just to be on the safe side. Everybody mumbled that all that money couldn't save Frank Parnell's loved one.

The first call that Carl made was to Dan in Florida.

Gina answered, assumed the worst about Ashley, calling out to Dan. "It's Carl, about Ashley!"

"Carl?" Dan picked up. "Ashley?" How many times had he and Gina spoken of Ashley, her ambition to be a doctor, and her very bizarre fiancé. And now it didn't matter. She was dead.

"Dan, it's not Ashley. We don't know anything. Haven't heard anything. Nothing."

"Okay. Is there anything we can do? Should I come up?"

"It's Meredith."

Dan took in a sharp breath as Carl sobbed in the background.

"Meredith is dead. She was killed tonight in a car crash. And, Dan, yes. Please come home now. I don't think the Gulfstream can fly —"

"Frank?" Dan asked. "Elise?"

"Frank had to be sedated. They kept him overnight at the hospital. Elise is with Rory. Please, come home, Dan. I need you. The family needs you."

"Of course, Uncle Carl. Gina and I will leave right away."

"Meredith's funeral will have to be the day after tomorrow. If you wish I can make the arrangements. Frank's in no condition, and Meredith and I belong to the same synagogue."

"Yes, Uncle Carl. We'll drive straight through." Dan checked his watch. "It's about a twenty-two hour drive. I'll call Terry and Carrie. They're both in Washington, and can be there within hours. Carrie's close to Matt," Dan said, leaving out how close she really was, like in his bed close. "And Terry's assigned to the Washington office of Keystone Pharma."

"Yes," Carl seemed to catch himself. "I'm still in Manhattan. The bridges and tunnels are still closed, and I'm hoping for news about Ashley. But it was Meredith leading that effort."

Dan and Gina hastily packed and within the hour were on the road in Dan's new cherry red Toyota Tundra. Dan marveled at how effortlessly he and Gina had restarted their lives together. When he had offered to leave his palm plantation in Lantana to move to Fort Myers to be with her, Gina had laughed it off. "Easier for me to change hospitals than for you to transplant all those trees," she'd said. And that was it. She switched from Lee Memorial Hospital in Fort Myers to the pediatric unit at St. Mary's Medical Center in West Palm Beach. They'd set a remarriage date, a private ceremony, just them and the twins, between Christmas and New Year's. Dan could no longer comprehend life without Gina, and he was sure that his brother had felt the same way about Meredith.

Gina, accustomed to night-shift nursing, drove the first seven hours until Dan, the "early to bed early to rise" farmer, took over at five a.m. Reclining in the passenger's seat, Gina was in a chatty, reminiscent mood. "Tell me again about how you fell in love with those palm trees," she said. Dan smiled, as that story had become their shared secret.

"Well," Dan began, "ever since my lovely wife left me because I was such a jerk —"

"Not that part," Gina said, reaching over to ruffle his hair.

"After kicking around the world for twelve years, pining for my beautiful woman, living off the inheritance from my mother's ill-fated trust fund, never finishing college, ending up in Key West, down to my last dime."

"Not really a dime," Gina said.

"Money low, emotions rock bottom from such a worthless life, I got up the nerve to drive to my beloved wife's place where she was hiding my beautiful twins. All I planned to do was park across the street. I just wanted a glimpse of them."

"Aren't you sorry you didn't just knock on the door?" Gina said, arranging a pillow behind her head.

"I was too scared. So I'm driving up from the Keys to Fort Myers. I get stuck behind several of those flatbed trucks hauling stacks of palm trees piled one on top of the other. The roots of each tree looked like huge balls wrapped in burlap. Something about those trees, neatly stacked piles of trunks and balls, hypnotized me. Idiotic as it sounds, I followed one of the flatbeds as it turned off the main drag. When the driver pulled up to a new condo site, I got out of the car and struck up a conversation with the driver and crew. I started helping them hoist the palms and situate them according to the landscape architect's drawings. This was not normal behavior for me or any sane person. But those trees were so majestic. I felt a unique bond to those trees, like they were a magnet. The guys told me that they worked out of Lantana, Florida, voted nine years in a row Tree City, USA."

"Did you see your twins that day?" Gina asked. Dan smiled sadly, remembering when he'd first told her that he used to drive over to Fort Myers just for a glimpse of them. He'd been such a coward, had wasted so many years.

"Terry off to baseball; giggling girls arriving with overnight bags."

"Carrie's first sleepover," Gina murmured.

"Once I'd done my stalking, I drove over to this Lantana place, stopped in a coffee shop, and again struck up a conversation with the locals. They told me about a parcel of land for sale. Planted with maturing coconut palms and young carpentaria. It had a small house, and a storage shed with tools and my favorite toy, a John Deere tractor."

"And you, of all people, became a farmer."

"I did and it was the only time I ever asked Dad for anything. He cosigned a loan, and I never missed a payment. Of course, I have Bill Jeffers, the best foreman in the world. And the best part now? I don't have to drive across the state to sneak a glimpse of my beautiful wife."

Dan turned to Gina as her eyes fluttered closed.

Yes, Dan loved his trees and he also loved the swelter of South Florida summers. Despite gallons of sweat, bugs, and poisonous snakes, he was content working outdoors, his men and dogs at his side. More than once he'd used a pistol to dispose of a cottonmouth.

And now he had Gina. And he was building a relationship with his children. But he would need to pay more attention to getting them their inheritance. He'd already deprived them of too much. He worried that he'd become too distracted by all the family tragedy to make any plans. Added to that, he didn't have a clue as to how to go about making happen those things his father had stipulated.

Dan and Gina arrived in Center City, Philadelphia at eleven p.m. They checked into the Four Seasons, confirmed the place and time of Meredith's funeral with Carl, and inquired about Frank.

"Frank is not good," Carl reported. "The doctor released him from the hospital this morning into the care of Matt, his aide, and Carrie. Your daughter is incredible, Dan. Don't think they would have let him go if she hadn't been there."

"Frank? Like —?"

"Can't stop sobbing. Can't say anything coherent. Won't sit, just paces."

"Gina's a nurse, maybe she can —"

"Not tonight. Carrie got Frank to take a sedative. But could you go out there in the morning? The services are at two o'clock. Private, but you know the media will be swarming."

"Of course," Dan promised, scratching his head. What could he ever think of to help his brother?

At seven the next morning, Dan and Gina headed for Frank's. A slight chill was in the air, and rain was forecast for the afternoon. The Four Seasons had sent them off with umbrellas.

Gina had spoken with Carrie. Frank had slept fitfully on the couch in the library for only an hour. Matt had left for Frank's Philadelphia office to run interference with Washington in what was now the second day after the attack on America. Then he'd join the family at the synagogue for the services.

As Dan turned into the long driveway leading to the house, he heard Gina sigh. She still hadn't gotten used to Parnell opulence. The French country house with its stables and various outbuildings dominated acres of rolling hills and autumn flowers and green pastures dotted with grazing horses belonged in a magazine.

"Quite the hacienda," she said softly.

"Meredith loved her horses."

"Wish I'd gotten to know her," Gina murmured, as they parked in the circle in front of the main door.

Actually, Dan couldn't imagine Meredith and Gina hitting it off, but no use going there. "She had her good points and bad points," he said.

Carrie met them at the door. "Mom, thank God you're here. Uncle Frank is inconsolable."

In the conservatory, Frank sat, bent over, head in hands. Dan tried not to stare. Frank might be his younger brother, but it was Frank who the world looked up to. Frank who Dad had always depended on. Gina went to her brother-in-law, put her arms around him, and whispered in his ear.

"Carrie, could you get us some tea? And some biscuits or toast."

Dan had never felt so inadequate. What should he do? What should he say?

"Dan, let's get Frank up to the table where we can talk," Gina said.

"I'm so sorry." Dan's voice was hoarse as he and Gina each took an elbow and maneuvered Frank to the round table by the bay window. Frank moved like a limp puppet, his shoulders hunched, his face puffy and unshaven. As Dan eased him into the chair, he felt a flood of compassion that was immediate and intense. He wanted to pour out the flood to his brother, but no words came. This is what it must be like for mutes, he thought, automatically patting his pocket for cigarettes, remembering they weren't there.

"I can't go on without her," Frank finally said, tears rolling down his cheeks. "She was my life." He looked around the tastefully decorated room. "Everything here is Meredith. I just can't . . . go . . . on . . ."

"You must," Dan had found his voice at last. "Keep thinking: what would Meredith want? What would she want you to do? You can't let her down now just because she's not with you." Dan had no idea where all this advice was coming from. But when he glanced at Gina, there was approval on her face.

"So Frank, let's talk about Meredith. About what she would expect from you today? It's her funeral, man, she'd want you there. Wouldn't she?"

"I . . . never had a chance to say good-bye. It could have been my call that made her unbuckle her belt to get at her phone. By the time I got to the hospital, she was gone." Frank drooped forward again.

"She knew you loved her, Frank," Gina said, as Carrie came in with the tea service. "Anyone who saw you two together could tell. Now, let's have our tea, and then we'll get you ready. The service will be private and beautiful. Meredith would expect that."

Frank lifted his head to stare at Gina. Then he grabbed the wad of Kleenex that she held out to him and blew his nose. "Look at me. For crying out loud, I can't face anybody. "I can't even face my daughter. My little girl doesn't have a mother."

"Think about Meredith," Dan said again. "Meredith is counting on you when it comes to Elise. You know that, man."

Frank said staring ahead into nothingness. "Yes, Meredith adored our little girl."

"Then you need to be there for her," Dan said, amazed that he sounded like a coach. Not like someone who'd fucked up his own life for so many years.

"Frank, Dan's right," Gina said. "Meredith believed in you. Just ask yourself, 'what would she want me to do?' Let that guide you." Gina paused and held Frank's eyes. "Okay?"

There was a long silence. Then Frank rose and went to a side table. For a long time, he stared at a watercolor portrait of Meredith and Elise. "I'll try," he said, wiping the dwindling tears.

"Gina and I will be there for you," Dan vowed. "First, we'll get through today."

Again, Dan thought about his brother. Dad's favorite. Straight As. Varsity sports. Attorney. Senator. Dan shivered at his newfound ability to console and direct the icon.

CHAPTER TWENTY-FOUR

Rory was too ill to attend Meredith's burial service. She had no pain, but she had zero energy. She needed IVs for nutrition and fluids. She had a catheter in her bladder. Although she tried to stay awake, she found herself sleeping more and more. And that terrified her. She was afraid that she might slip away before she could say what she had to say to those she loved. Now that Ashley was dead, she'd lost hope of a bone marrow match. She knew she was dying and she needed Chan to help her through it. Her worst fear: that Chan wouldn't be able to bring himself to talk to her about this last phase of her life.

She'd passed through the Kübler-Ross phases — denial, anger, bargaining, depression. She was now into acceptance. She was not afraid of death per se, but she was desperate to share her emotions with Chan. She'd tried, but each time he'd changed the subject. Before her leukemia diagnosis, she and Chan used to talk about his patients facing death. Analyze the dying process. Agree about how important it was to face reality. To communicate about what really counted. But when *your* life is involved, theory goes by the wayside.

She and Chan had to talk, about the children, how to help them cope. Their older daughters were adolescents. And the younger ones? And the three who had already lost two parents? Together she and Chan had to decide what to say. They had to give the kids a framework that would allow them to move forward.

"Let's see if she's awake."

Chan's hushed voice came from the hallway outside her bedroom. The door opened a crack. From the sun that streamed through the window, Rory guessed it must be midmorning. She was not expecting company. Chan had discouraged well-meaners from the church and neighborhood from stopping by.

"Rory, is it okay to come in?" A familiar male voice, but she couldn't place it.

"Who is it?" she asked.

"It's Dan."

"Dan?" She should have anticipated his visit. Of course, he'd be in town for Meredith's funeral, but Dan had never visited their home. He strode into the room, and she thought of how much both her brothers looked like Dad's political rivals, the Kennedys .

"Sit down," she invited, hoping for the strength to make him feel welcome. "I'm glad you're here, Dan. I really am. I'm sorry I couldn't be there for Frank yesterday. How is he?"

"Devastated," Dan said. "Just hope he can get himself together. They need him in Washington these days. The country's in such trouble."

"Is there any word on Ashley?" Rory asked, her voice listless, holding out little hope.

"No," Dan said. "I think we have to accept that she was killed outright. But with Meredith — and Frank the way he is —"

"Dan," Rory interrupted, "did Gina come with you?"

"Yes," he said.

"Chan, could you ask her to come up?"

When Chan left the room to find Gina. Rory said, "Dan, I know we've never been close, but in the time left —"

"What do you mean?" Dan started to cross and uncross his legs. "You'll beat this, Rory."

"No, Dan, not without Ashley," Rory lowered her voice. "I know it, and Chan knows it, but he won't let us talk about it. I don't want to die until I can talk to him. About the children mainly, but also about him. I want him to have a life."

"Here she is," Chan stepped aside to let Gina through the door.

Rory couldn't help but notice how Gina glowed with health and happiness as she entered the sick room and headed immediately to her bedside. "How are you?" she murmured as she bent to kiss Rory's bony cheek. When she took her hand, Rory could feel an immediate warmth.

"So, Rory," Gina asked, "is there anything I can do?" She had been told about a new leukemia study, but would Rory live long enough to go on it?

"There's a new drug —" Chan started.

"You've been on so many treatments already," Gina said softly.

"But this is different drug class," Chan blurted.

Gina's dark eyes fixed on Rory's. After a moment, Rory said, "Do you know what I really want?"

"Why don't you tell us?" Dan murmured.

Rory looked at Chan, saw the raw fear in his eyes, but, with Dan's opening, decided to press on before Chan came back with some cheerful response that would steer them out of dangerous territory.

"I want to talk about what's going to happen," she said, holding Chan's gaze. "I don't want to pretend that I'm going to come through this. Don't you understand, Chan? I need your help."

"For God's sake, honey, I have tried. I've tried to do everything I could think of." Chan began to wring his hands, but he did not take his eyes off of hers. "That new study. I know it's the answer. I talked to Keystone Pharma today. You'll be the first one on the study as soon as the FDA clears the Investigational New Drug application. It's your dad's own company. They'll do everything in their power to get you that drug."

"Chan," Gina said gently, "you've been an incredible husband. You've given Rory so much. Love, friendship, constant support. The best that medicine has to offer. Peace of mind that the children are happy and healthy and well balanced. No one could have done more than you have."

Chan turned to stare at Gina. Then he lowered his head into his hands and his whole body started to shake. "I didn't do enough," he said.

Gina went to him and said firmly, "Chan, Rory needs to talk to you. She needs to know that it's okay to let go. She needs you and the kids to help her do this one last thing."

Chan looked up. "Rory?" he whispered.

"Yes, what I'm most afraid of is that I'm going to die, and that we will never have talked about our situation. That's the only thing that really frightens me. Dying while the whole family is pretending that I'm going to make it. There's so much we have to talk about. And maybe not much time."

"What are we going to tell the children?" he moaned

"They already know, I'm sure. They're starting to withdraw more and more. I want to be able to say good-bye to each of them. To tell them how much I love them. To tell them that they'll be okay. To tell them to help you, and to help one another. To tell them that we'll all be together in heaven. I need to do that, Chan."

"I'm so sorry," Chan said, moving to sit on the edge of the bed, planting a kiss on her forehead. "I tried to pretend. I didn't know how scared you were —"

Dan shut the door behind them.

Dan and Gina headed for the Devon house. They decided to stay in Philadelphia for a few more days until Frank's and Rory's situations stabilized, and until the search and rescue effort at the World Trade Center had come to some semblance of closure.

"So sad," Gina said after a prolonged silence. "How is Chan going to handle all those kids?"

"He's a prince of a guy," Dan said, "but it's gotta be tough."

"He was in complete denial, of course. I've been a nurse too long not to recognize it. I'm glad we could help Rory get through to him."

"Chan didn't say how long he thought she had," Dan said, making the turn onto Lancaster. "With all that's going on in the family, I just can't help thinking that I'm such a lucky man. To have you back and the kids. They're happy that we're together. Don't you think?"

"Yes, and now Terry has his dream job in Washington, and Carrie's madly in love with Matt."

"I agree," Dan said, but he had to remind himself not to let Terry down. In the midst of so much tragedy, he'd still have to deal with Dad's "test."

"Are we getting close?" Gina asked, craning her neck to admire the classic architecture.

"Still a few more blocks. I wonder what we're going to find? An empty house, I guess."

"Won't your father's housekeepers be there?" Gina asked.

"It's Sunday," he said. "I do have a key."

"What about Welton?" Gina raised her eyebrows.

"I hope he's out, but we'll see."

Dan pulled into the long, circular driveway and Gina sucked in her breath. "Just look at these gardens." Autumn foliage surrounded the stone homestead with its attached carriage house and the original stone barn in back. "Hey, are those tennis courts out by the pool? I missed them the last time I was here. My goodness, I still can't believe you grew up here!"

"Guess I took all this for granted when I was a kid," Dan replied. "But you know what? I can't wait to get back to our place in Florida."

"At least it's not snowing this time. Brrr, it was cold last January. Looks like somebody's here."

The front door was not locked so they didn't ring the bell, but simply walked in. The door opened into a foyer dominated by a huge chandelier of Venetian glass. On the far wall was an original *Water Lily* by Monet, the most prized piece of family artwork as far as Dan knew. He led Gina past the library and solarium on the right, the living room on the left, and the stately dining room. That room still made Dan cringe as he recalled having to sit through stiff, formal dinners. Back then, as now, he liked simple, fast meals.

They came to a stop at a closed door with music coming from inside.

"Music room," Dan said, opening the door.

"Dan, Gina?" Welton's eyebrows shot up in surprise. With both hands, he swept back silver-tinged hair. Then he rose out of a lounge chair, set down a hefty biography of Winston Churchill, and using the remote, lowered the volume of Bach's violin concerto.

"I'm so glad you're here." He approached, but stood at the door as if to block their entrance. "We need to talk. I tried to talk to Frank yesterday, but he was too anguished about his wife. Still, you'd think that he'd have more concern for his own sister."

"We have to come to grips with reality," Dan said. "Ashley was at the wrong place at the wrong time. She's gone."

"Ashley is alive!" Conrad stated emphatically. "She's alive and I have proof."

CHAPTER TWENTY-FIVE

Truth be told, Welton relished having the house and property to himself. Ashley had been gone five nights now, and although he needed her back, he appreciated the serenity and the undivided attention of the servants. He'd not gone back to the University of Pennsylvania. He needed to concentrate on finding Ashley. He was now sure that she had not been killed last Tuesday. He'd carefully crossed checked the timing of her last contact with Schiller, and he'd hired an investigator, C. R. Crane, to check the location of the law office where she'd been headed that day. Stewart and Stewart's New York City office in the World Trade Center had been on the opposite side of the initial explosion and on the fifty-second floor. Crane had reported that all occupants and visitors in the proximity of Stewart and Stewart had been accounted for. And now, Conrad had definitive proof that Ashley had not died last Tuesday.

He had commissioned his investigator to keep looking for Ashley. She was out there, either in shock, or possibly defying him. But Crane's fee was daunting, and Welton intended to approach Frank Parnell to help defray the cost. But the arrogant senator did not return his calls. And now he faced the most ignorant Parnell of them all, Dan, the tree farmer, and Gina, his meddlesome wife.

They'd barged into his home, interrupting his solitude.

Now he had to repeat himself.

"Ashley is alive. I have proof, and I would hope that you would care enough to help me find her."

"I'm sure you're distressed," Gina said. Had she comprehended what he said?

"Yes. Of course, I'm distraught. My fiancée is out there somewhere, stunned, confused, maybe injured. We must find her. Now that there's proof. That's why you're here. Correct?"

"Proof?" Dan asked.

This fool didn't even know. "Schiller told me that they found her ring. Her engagement ring."

"That can't be good," Dan began.

"They found the ring not buried in rubble, but close to the surface of the plaza. You do realize what that means?"

Both of them just stood there shaking their heads. Welton noticed that Dan was carrying an overnight bag.

"It means that she was on the outside, not inside the tower. It means that she must have escaped. It means that she's alive. Hurt, confused, suffering from posttraumatic shock, but alive."

Gina asked, "But where is she?"

"We don't know." Conrad wanted to scream. "But she's alive. Your family has to help me find her."

"I'll speak to Carl." Dan turned and Gina followed. "I'll use the phone in the library."

They returned to the music room in ten minutes. Conrad again turned down the volume on the stereo. Music was the only thing that soothed him and the Parnell collection and equipment was phenomenal.

"There's been no sign of Ashley. NYPD has come to no conclusion. But they did find her ring as you said, relatively close to the surface.

Welton realized that Dan Parnell and Carl Schiller believed Ashley was dead. They would influence the rest of the family. Welton needed Ashley to be found.

"Gina and I plan to stay here in the house," Dan said. "Frankly, we hadn't expected you'd still be here."

Conrad started to say, "It's my fucking house." But grasping the edge of his chair, he breathed deeply. "Ashley and I live here together. We were to be married this week. We plan to make this our home."

"That no longer seems sensible," Dan said. "We'd rather you move out. *Today. Now.*"

Conrad's face turned hot. "Ashley wants me here. She knows I'll be waiting for her *here*. I'm sure that's understandable to you. What we have to do is find her." *I know she's not dead. I can feel it.* "I'm begging you, bring Ashley home. When you do, I'll be waiting here for her."

Dan shook his head. "When I talked to Carl Schiller — as executor of the estate — he said to tell you to leave."

Bach played at very low volume in the background as Welton hesitated, shifting his weight from side to side.

Dan said, "I will wait here until you pack your belongings."

With that, Dan Parnell pronounced his own death sentence. In Welton's mind, Dan had previously been beneath contempt. Now, he had become another enemy who needed to be eliminated. With a sneer of disgust, Welton stomped off to collect his clothes.

"Dan," Welton tried once again as he carried out his last load to the Parnell Mercedes in the driveway, "how can I convince Schiller and your brother to launch a search for Ashley? She's alive. Doesn't finding her ring prove it? How else could it have gotten there, so close to the surface? Just think about it, and do the right thing."

All Dan said was, "There'll be a memorial service next month — we'll let you know the details."

"Fuck you. Fuck the Parnell family," Conrad said as he drove off in the Parnell Mercedes.

CHAPTER TWENTY-SIX

"I'll finish the laundry, Sandra," Ashley shouted up from the basement. "You run along to the gallery. Then I'll take the boys to the library."

"I still can't believe you have them reading books," the other woman said on the way out. "Hey, Marcy, when you're out, will you pick up some laundry detergent?"

Two kids generate a ton of dirty clothes, Ashley thought, as she checked the time — five o'clock — plenty of time to put this load away and get to downtown Santa Fe before the library closed. She was feeling safe in New Mexico, safe enough to hang out in the library to check the *Philadelphia Inquirer* for mentions of her family.

She was living with a family in Santa Fe — Sandra Becker, a single mom, and her two children. Sandra was an art dealer with her own gallery in the heart of Santa Fe's art district. She and her former husband had been co-owners, but Sandra had bought him out after a nasty divorce. On the train leaving New Jersey, Ashley had decided to head for New Mexico to be near her dear friend Ruthie who was doing a pediatric residency at the University of New Mexico in Albuquerque. Ashley had vowed not to contact Ruthie, but she felt heartened just knowing that she'd be close by.

Arriving in Santa Fe on a Friday night, her money running low, she'd stayed in a hotel near the train station, and first thing the next morning she examined the want ads for a job. She tried to be realistic. She was an unlicensed physician, not having finished the year of post-graduate training necessary to practice medicine. Even if she had, any attempt to apply for a license would trigger an investigation. Her current goal was to stay out of Conrad's reach until the inheritance was settled. That was only three months away now. As much as she missed her family, especially Rory, she knew that Conrad would find her, and use his horrifying manipulative skills to get what he wanted, her inheritance. Was he insane? A cold-blooded murderer? She didn't know, but she could not take a chance with her life and the growing life of her baby.

She had circled several possibilities, and started making calls. The first was a nanny for a lady doctor — no good, she wanted three references. The second, a companion for an elderly man. Again, references were needed, and the man's son was a lawyer. The third, had led her to Sandra Becker, who made no mention of needing references. Ashley had liked Sandra immediately and she felt a welcome bond as they fell into easy, comfortable conversation. Her new boss was maybe ten years older than Ashley, very pretty, with blue eyes, curly black hair, and tons of energy. She had two little boys, age four and seven, for whom Ashley would be a combination nanny and housekeeper. She'd have Saturdays off when Sandra's mom was free to watch the kids.

The Beckers lived in a four-bedroom house on the edge of town. Ashley was given the master suite as her apartment, bathroom, closet, sitting area, and bedroom. She would have the use of Sandra's Taurus during the day for errands, and Sandra would take the van. Ashley had identified herself as Marcy Powers and no proof of identity was requested. How soon could she start?

"Naturally, I'd like to see your home and meet the children." Ashley struggled not to sound overly anxious, but she'd wanted to shout, *Now, I can start now.*

Sandra had locked up the art gallery, and they drove to her house, an adobe-style, on a cul-de-sac in a pleasant looking neighborhood.

"Bart, Justin, meet Miss Powers," Sandra ushered two redheads into the cluttered kitchen. "Sorry, didn't have time to put the breakfast things away."

The little one, Justin, held up his hand for a high five and waited for Ashley's response. She brought up her palm to slap against his. The older one trailed behind, engrossed in a handheld videogame. Ashley stuck out her hand, and he took it with a shy smile.

"It is 'Miss,' isn't it?" Sandra asked as they walked into the littered living room. "You can see why I need you." Sandra gestured to the floor cluttered with toys. Ashley noticed how hassled she seemed and real-ized how lucky her mother had been to have the Mendozas. But before Paul, Vivian, too, had been a single mom back when Rory was a little kid.

"Yes, Miss," she said.

"Now, tell me," Sandra asked when Ashley had settled into a chair in the living room. "Why are you looking for a nanny job?"

"Mrs. Becker, I'll be honest with you. I'm pregnant. It was a mistake. My family feels I've dishonored them. So I can't go back to them. But I'll be an excellent nanny. I'm a hard worker. And dependable."

"What about after the baby?"

"I don't know."

"Well, let's worry about that later. I'm offering you the job for now. It doesn't pay much, but you'll have a home, food, a car to use."

"What is the salary?" Ashley asked, wondering how she would judge it. Before September eleven she'd never really cared what anything cost. Since then she'd survived on the $680 she had in her wallet that morn-ing, $500 worth of traveler's checks she'd cashed as she left the Waldorf, and the money from Aunt Bea. As for the rest of her money, in a bank somewhere, it was useless. She couldn't get at it without leaving a fi-nancial trail.

"One hundred twenty dollars a week. Of course that assumes six days and all the housework."

"Okay, Mrs. Becker," Ashley held out her hand. "When can I start?"

"Call me Sandra. As far as I'm concerned, you can move your things in tonight."

That had been four weeks earlier.

Now with the two boys in tow, she headed for the library. She sent Bart to the children's room and kept Justin at her side. She logged onto the computer, going straight to the *Philadelphia Inquirer* site. She searched for any Parnell reference. What she found made her heart stop. On the front page of the local section, she read that her own memorial service was scheduled in two weeks. Hands shaking, she turned off the com-puter. Should she call someone in the family to stop the public mourn-ing?. She slumped back into the chair, trying to envision the service at

Saints Peter and Paul. Who would say what? Would Conrad have a role? She felt sure that he would insist, but would Frank allow him to speak? Or maybe now that she was dead, nobody cared. She wondered who knew that she was pregnant? Did Conrad know? She willed that he did not. Protecting her child from him was now her life. Staying *dead* was the surest way to do that.

During her previous trips to the library, Ashley had checked out books on hypnosis. She had learned how effortlessly Conrad, with his expertise, had manipulated her, systematically isolating her from her family and friends. And she could not stop thinking about Crissy. He must have controlled her, too. Then he'd killed her, or had her killed. When she heard or read about the attacks on September eleven she re-lived the explosion of that car, so close to her that day, and imagined her body, like Crissy's, blown into a million pieces.

Ashley had also checked online for medical articles about pregnancy and bone marrow donation. Rory's leukemia haunted her. In running away from Conrad, she had abandoned the sister who'd been like a sec-ond mother to her. But she was sure that Rory was still alive. If not, there would have been a story in the *Philadelphia Inquirer*. That is, unless Frank had successfully excised Rory from the Parnell public relations circuit.

Based on the medical literature, Ashley had formulated a tentative plan. After she reached her second trimester, when procedures were less risky to the fetus, she would approach Ruthie for help in arranging an anonymous marrow donation. She wasn't sure about the medical and legal implications, but she was determined to try. Nonetheless, the tiny weight of the baby would not allow her to jeopardize that life.

"Marcy, can I get a book?" Justin tugged at her jeans.

"I have one for you." She reached into her bag and pulled out a Dr. Seuss, about red dogs and blue dogs, Justin's favorite. Then bending down, she tied his shoes.

"Marcy, why are your hands shaking like that?" he asked. Then, "I have to pee."

Ashley took Justin's hand and headed to the children's reading room to collect Bart. As the Becker kids trotted into the bathroom, Ashley pic-tured little Ricky and Tyler, all of the Stevens kids, without a mother — unless she did something before it was too late.

CHAPTER TWENTY-SEVEN

Ashley's memorial service took place at the same time as thousands of others around the country. Cardinal Sean officiated at the Cathedral of Saints Peter and Paul, his third service in less than a year for a family member. After the services Frank, Dan, and Gina assembled at Devon where they were to meet with Jack Preston, private investigator.

Since Meredith's death, Frank had returned to his office in the Russell Building in Washington. The problems of terrorism and anthrax consumed his days, and his nights were haunted by his impossible loss. Functional, but not at the top of his game, he knew he was no longer presidential material.

The Parnell extended family had settled back into a sad, but steady routine, only to be disrupted by a visit from Welton to Frank's Philadelphia office. Welton, still insisting that Ashley was alive, had hired his own private investigator to find her. The man claimed that he had located a witness who'd identified Ashley on a train headed for Chicago six weeks earlier.

"I keep telling you that I know, I feel, she's alive," Welton kept repeating with aggression and passion. "They found her ring in the surface rubble. Now you tell me, if she was buried at Ground Zero, wouldn't she *and* the ring be *under* the mess? Ashley's suffering posttraumatic shock, I tell you. And now, that she's been seen alive, you Parnells have to admit you're wrong."

Frank had been skeptical, but he had asked Matt to call in Jack Preston, the private investigator whom Carl Schiller had tapped for the original Welton investigation, the same one who'd dug up the information about the Welton/Moore marriage, Welton's estranged brother, and the shady rumors about Welton's past.

Now as Frank waited with Dan and Gina and Matt and Carrie for Preston to arrive, he remembered that just before getting into the limo on that dreadful day, Meredith had urged him to dig deeper into Welton's background.

"I have everything set up in the library," Mrs. M. announced. "Peter has a fire going there since you Floridians aren't used to this chilly weather."

"Guess I can take this off then." Dan slipped out of his coat. "I had to buy it in the airport. I'm always forgettin' how blasted cold it gets up here."

On the way into the library, Gina lingered to admire the artwork hanging in the hall. Frank overheard Carrie reminding her mother of being dragged to museums as a little girl to study the American Impressionists. Frank made a mental note to ship the entire collection to Gina. He'd been thinking about moving into the Devon home. If he did, he'd replace the Impressionists with Meredith's collection of modern art.

"Seems weird to be back in our childhood house," Dan said.

"Yeah, lots of memories." But for Frank, none of his mother. He'd been four when she died and no matter how hard he tried, he couldn't conjure up a single memory. He vowed not to let Meredith's memory slip away from Elise.

"How's Elise?" Carrie asked as if reading his thoughts.

"Good. But with Ashley gone, I'm thinking about making a change and moving here. Meredith wanted Elise around horses and all, but the truth is that Elise doesn't share Meredith's passion," Frank said. "Elise would rather be with other children. There are kids in this neighborhood."

"You can always enroll her in a riding academy," Dan suggested.

"I'll keep the horses in Bucks County so she can ride on weekends. I'm doing my best, but I've never been worth a damn as a father."

"Don't be so tough on yourself," Dan said.

And Frank replied, sounding sad, but sincere, "Elise is my life now."

The resulting silence was interrupted by the door chimes.

"Must be that private investigator," Dan said, and trying to lighten the mood, "*Spencer for Hire*. I love that Robert Parker. Matter of fact, Jack Preston's picture reminds me of Hawk. Shaved head, two hundred and fifty pounds and all muscle. Ex-FBI. Has a law degree."

Mrs. M. returned with a hunk of a man who did look like Hawk. Introductions followed as Mrs. M. served coffee and cakes.

"Ladies and gentlemen," Preston bowed dramatically to Gina and Carrie. His voice was booming yet articulate. "I'm happy to be back on the Conrad Welton case because I believe that doctor's a very bad actor. As for Miss Ashley Parnell, excuse me, Dr. Parnell, let me say first off, that I do not know whether she is alive. But what I have found out is that Welton hired a P.I. to look for her. He tracked down a witness who claimed to have seen Ashley on that train headed for Chicago."

"None of us believed him," Dan said. "Welton's a pathological liar. Right?"

"About this, he was accurate," Preston said. "But now it may be a moot point."

"What?" All four responded in chorus.

"C. W. Crane, the P.I. for Welton, ran a lookout on credit cards, routine in cases like this. We now know that a telephone call, charged to Ashley's ATT card, was made in Santa Fe, New Mexico."

The family members stared at each other in disbelief.

"Now it could be a fluke—like somebody got access to her card. But a call in Santa Fe was charged to it. Just one, a local call. C.W. flew to New Mexico last night."

"New Mexico?" Dan repeated.

"Good friend from med school's doing a residency in Albuquerque," Preston said. "Name's Ruth Campbell, but she's heard nothing from Ashley. Either she's telling the truth, or she's putting on a good act. But I want to question her in person. Immediately. Can I use your plane?"

"So perhaps Ashley *is* alive?" Frank raked the fingers of both hands through his hair. "Welton was right all along?"

"We have to get out there. If she's as far away as New Mexico, she's hiding." Dan said. "Hiding from Welton. He must have done something to really spook her."

"You got it," Preston responded. "That guy's got a bad history, but no time for all that now. About the airplane, a Lear, if I'm not mistaken?"

"Mr. Preston, are no secrets safe from you?" Carrie asked.

"Not if I'm doing my job, and please, call me Jack. My hunch is that we're going to get to know each other quite well as we peel the onion on this case."

"Just remember," Matt said, as he punched in the number of the private terminal. "We can't have any leaks, even in the family. Just the five of us. Okay?"

"Not even Rory?" Gina asked. "Finding Ashley would mean so much to her."

Frank made the decision. So far only he and Carl knew about Ashley's pregnancy. "There's something else," Frank said. All eyes focused on him. "Jack, you need to know this too. Ashley is pregnant. She told Carl the night before she was killed — or disappeared. It's why she could not give the bone marrow for Rory that day. She went to the clinic, but they wouldn't proceed."

"Rory and Chan don't know?" Gina clarified. "Or Welton?"

"No, just Carl and us," Frank said. "I don't see any reason to tell anyone else at this point."

"Keep it tight," Preston said. "Too many involved and we'll lose control. We don't want to tip our hand to Welton. Sure he doesn't know that she's pregnant?"

"We don't think she contacted him after she found out," Frank said, "and he hasn't mentioned it."

"I got the plane," Matt announced. "It can leave within the hour."

"Got room for me?" asked Dan with a goofy look. "I've never been on the family plane," he explained. "I hate flying, but to find Ashley —"

Carrie interrupted, "What do we think Ashley's doing for money?"

"She can't have much," Preston said, tucking his small notebook inside his jacket. "She left with a few hundred dollars and hasn't tried to access any accounts. That's why Crane was keeping a watch on her credit cards. Friends, perhaps?"

CHAPTER TWENTY-EIGHT

"Marcy," Justin jumped up as Ashley walked in the front door. "Wanta play Power Rangers?""

"After dinner." She tousled his hair as he hugged her legs. She gave her older charge a friendly tickle, knowing that he couldn't tear his eyes from the Nintendo screen for even a nanosecond.

Sandra called from the kitchen, "Glad you're home for dinner, although it's only Hamburger Helper. That's one more thing we have in common. We're marginal cooks."

"Things my mother never taught me. But I think I'm getting better."

"If you consider pizza and Chinese take-out getting better."

Ashley laughed. "Can I help you with anything? Salad, maybe?"

With time, Ashley had come to consider Sandra Becker more a friend than an employer. Sandra trusted her to run the household, and the women had become best buddies. Ashley had Saturdays off, and usually she just hung out at the house, but that day she'd driven to Albuquerque. She'd planned to look up Ruthie at the University of New Mexico Medical Center. She longed to apologize to her for dropping out of her life when she'd met Conrad. Ruthie had been the closest friend she had ever had. She'd also wanted to ask Ruthie's advice about pregnant bone marrow donors, but now she had another problem too. That morning she'd noticed splotches of blood in her panties. Spotting was a scary sign at three months gestation. Ruthie, always so practical and such a good doctor, would help her figure out whether anything was wrong. After she got over the shock of seeing her alive.

She walked into the lobby to ask if Ruthie was on call. Like all children's hospitals, the lobby made a valiant attempt at cheeriness, at attempt overshadowed by reality. This was a place for very ill children.

This was a place where Ashley wanted to be. After much thought and research, she had decided that she wanted to be a pediatrician, a neonatologist to be specific. Being in a hospital again opened up a compartment in her mind that she'd slammed firmly shut. Her future as a doctor had been put on hold, but it would soon change.

At the information desk, surrounded by concerned parents, she asked whether Dr. Campbell was on call. The answer was yes; did she want Dr. Campbell paged in the neonatal unit? Again a yes. They handed her the phone, but the unit announced that Dr. Campbell was doing a procedure. "Would she like to leave a message?"

Ashley hung up. Her good idea now seemed dubious. She thought, *I abandoned you and now I'm asking for your help?* Ashley left the hospital and debated with herself during the drive from Albuquerque to Santa Fe whether she should try to call her friend later that day.

"Hungry?" Sandra asked, interrupting Ashley's renewed debate as to whether she would call Ruthie.

"Yes. Tired *and* hungry," Ashley admitted.

She'd skipped lunch as she'd wandered about the University of New Mexico medical complex, refusing to part with even a dollar of her cash. Reluctantly, Sandra had agreed to pay her in cash, even though her employer existed on plastic and had to make a special trip every week to the ATM.

Ashley pulled out a head of lettuce, a tomato, and a cucumber with one hand and, and with the other, she retrieved three slices of American cheese. "Just going to wash up," she called. "Be back in minute."

On the way to her room, she hastily unpeeled the plastic wrappers and stuffed the cheese slices into her mouth. Back in the kitchen, she poured a twelve-ounce glass of milk. "For the baby," she said, dabbing at the white moustache. "Amazing how much better a little food can make you feel."

"You haven't gained much weight," Sandra remarked. "You should have seen me when I was pregnant. Especially with Justin."

"I'm just at three months," Ashley said, patting her abdomen, which showed just the touch of a curvature.

"You'd better get to an OB," Sandra said for the hundredth time.

"Prenatal care is very important. Mine was very good. All you have to do is make the call."

Right, and pay the bill. Ashley had planned to put off seeing a doctor for a few more months. Of course, she was a doctor herself, but that was in another life, a life where she had medical insurance. But Sandra was right. With the spotting, she'd have to make an appointment soon.

Sandra had the radio on in the kitchen and was humming along with the music. "I like that song," Ashley said, to change the subject.

"Monica Monroe," Sandra said. "Voice of an angel. And what a life story. Did you read how she was adopted? Her biological father was some filthy rich guy. Paid the mother megabucks not to have an abortion. It was all in the news a couple of months ago. Did you know she married that TV sports guy?"

"No, I didn't know," Ashley lied. Wherever this conversation was going, she needed to steer it away from the Parnells.

"Her biological family has had a string of trouble. Can't remember the name. One of the brothers is a senator or governor or something back east. Anyway, one woman was killed in a car crash and another had some bizarre heart disease, and one was killed on September eleven. Read it in *People* magazine at the dentist."

Ashley made a mental note to get that magazine as Sandra hummed along with Monica.

"By the way, some guy rang the doorbell today," Sandra said as she stirred the box of Hamburger Helper into the ground meat. "Asking about you."

"What?" Almost dropping the wooden salad bowl, Ashley braced herself against the countertop. "L-looking for me?"

"Yeah, a smooth talking guy, in his forties, I'd guess. Short, stocky, wiry brown hair. Said he knew I had a new nanny. I asked him what business it was of his, and he asked me if I had checked your references." Sandra was staring at her now.

"Sit down, Marcy. You look so pale. What is it?"

"Did you find out who this m-man was?" Ashley was shaking, gasping for air. "Who sent him?"

"No. He didn't introduce himself. Matter of fact he never mentioned *you* by name. Just kept calling you 'the new nanny.'"

"Did you give him my name?"

"No. I asked him again what business this was of his."

" 'Woman like you, alone, should be more careful about who you trust your children to,' was all he said. It shook me up for a minute. Then I figured that he was just a neighborhood busybody. What do you think?"

Ashley leaned back against the cabinets. "I don't know. Maybe somebody in my family," was all she could think of to say. *I have to get out of here* was screaming in her head as she forced herself to finish setting the table.

"Marcy, you haven't told me much about yourself." Sandra wrinkled her brow in worry. "I didn't want to probe. You've been the perfect nanny to the boys. I'm just so appreciative. But if there's going to be trouble, I can't risk the safety of my boys. They're all I have."

Ashley stood frozen to the tile floor. How had Conrad found her? And where could she hide from him?

"I'm sorry," she said to Sandra. "I don't mean to cause you trouble."

Sandra came to Ashley and started to put her arm around her shoulder, but Ashley pulled back.

"I'm not feeling well," she said, massaging her forehead. "A migraine. I just need to lie down."

She had made that one mistake. Otherwise, she'd been so careful. She had a platinum American Express, a Visa, a Saks card, and a First Union Bank card. She had her passport and driver's license. But she had never used any of these for any reason. She still had her cell phone, but hadn't dared to keep it charged lest she be tempted. The only mistake she had made, and it was a stupid one, was to make one call from the road to Sandra's gallery. Last week, she had taken the boys to the pediatrician's office because Bart had an ear infection. On the way home the transmission in the Taurus went out. They were not far from a strip mall, so she took the boys in hand and trudged to a pay phone. Bart was moaning about the pain in his ear and Justin was crying. On impulse, she'd reached into her purse, pulled out her ATT calling card, and called Sandra at the gallery. That was probably how Conrad located her.

She waited until she was sure that Sandra and the kids were asleep. She'd packed her few belongings, and at one a.m. she crept into the kitchen, heading for the refrigerator. She selected a carton of milk, an entire packet of cheese slices, a leftover chicken breast, and several apples and oranges. She moved to the cupboards and as quietly as possible removed cans of tuna, packets of drinks, Pop-Tarts, two muffins, and a loaf of white bread. She stuffed them all in a plastic kitchen bag, remembered that she'd need a can opener, and lifted one out of the silverware drawer. She decided to leave the note in that drawer. It read:

Sandra, I am sorry. I have never taken anything in my life. I promise I will repay you as soon as I can. I loved working for you. Please say good-bye to the boys. I will miss them.
Thank you. Marcy.

It was the same drawer where Sandra left the grocery money. With relief, Ashley found that Sandra had replenished the funds for the next week, $220. Mentally she added up her money. $220 here; the $120 that Julie's aunt handed to her; $30 from her original amount; and nearly $450 from her weekly wages. That came to $850. And Sandra's credit card was in the drawer, too. She would take it, and use it for gasoline, but only for tonight.

Getting the car out of the garage without waking Sandra would be risky. But that risk paled compared to the chance that Conrad, or whomever he had hired, might be watching the house. In the dark, she searched up and down the street. She saw no cars lurking out there, so she carried her two bags — one canvas, with her clothes, the other plastic, with her food — into the car. Then gingerly, Ashley pressed the garage door opener. Holding her breath, she started the Taurus and backed it out onto the street. Heart pounding, she jerked it into drive and took off toward the Interstate. She was too scared to look back.

She would drive as far away as one tank of fuel would take her. First, she had to get out of Santa Fe, but to where? Colorado to the north? Texas, if she headed due south? Oklahoma to the east? Arizona to the west? As the Taurus sped forward, she still hadn't decided. Her focus was fixed on the rearview mirror. At one fifteen in the morning she met few cars as she zigzagged her way to I-25, disturbed by the occasional set of headlights appearing, then disappearing behind her. But should she take the Interstate north or south? She figured she'd have about four hours, five at the most, before the cops caught her. Less if Sandra woke up early, found her car and money missing, and called the police. But her gallery didn't open until one on Sundays, and since there was no school Bart would sleep 'til noon if you let him. Still, the little one would be up at seven, toddling around until he woke up an adult. Realistically, she told herself, Sandra would call the cops around seven thirty or so. By then, she'd need to abandon the car.

Before pulling onto I-25, Ashley stopped at a 24-hour gas convenience station. Using Sandra's Visa card, she gassed up, purchased trail mix, beef jerky, assorted breakfast bars, packets of cheese, boxes of that sterilized milk, and a New Mexico map. It was one thirty a.m.

Returning to the car, she flipped on the overhead light and unfolded the map when a sheriff cruiser pulled up beside her. She jerked off the light and stuffed the map under the seat. The lone officer got out of his car and glanced suspiciously at the Taurus. Giving Ashley the briefest of nods, he headed into the store. She breathed a huge sigh. She had her Ashley Parnell driver's license, but would she have shown it?

She drove slowly, fighting the urge to get as far away from the sheriff as fast as possible. When she reached the first Interstate entrance, she took it. No more debate. She found herself retracing her path of the trip to Albuquerque on I-25 South the day before, passing the Santa Fe County Municipal Airport and through native American reservations. She kept scrupulously to the speed limit, resisting the urge to stare into the rearview mirror. If only she could drive into Albuquerque, find Ruthie, and hide out with her, but she knew she could never do that now. She drove past Las Cruces, New Mexico, and started to come up with a plan. She'd drive as far as El Paso, Texas, a city she judged would be big enough to have an airport and a bus and a train terminal.

Crossing the New Mexico–Texas state line at five thirty a.m., Ashley strained to locate a sign pointing out a bus or train station. Her stomach had started to rumble and she felt dangerously faint. Other than the three pieces of cheese she'd snatched at Sandra's and a glass of milk, she hadn't eaten since the previous morning's breakfast. Once she got to the airport, she'd be okay. But suddenly she questioned her plan. Since September eleven, IDs were being checked and double-checked at airports. So when she saw a sign for a bus depot, she headed for it. She parked the Taurus in the long-term parking lot, and headed to the lone cab keeping vigil at the terminal's entrance.

"Train station." She'd tossed her bags into the backseat and climbed in.

"'Lil lady, you're up early in the mornin'," the bulky driver drawled. "Change your mind?"

"What?" she asked.

"You show up at the bus depot and wantin' to go to the train. Now what's that all about?"

"Somebody dropped me off at the wrong place," she said. "The jerk."

"A Yankee lady," the driver said turning around to get a better look. "Figures."

Ashley said nothing during the rest of the ride. The driver stopped his commentary, and flipped from one radio station to another. When he dropped her off at the train station, she paid him ten of her precious dollars, gathered up her motley bags, and approached the terminal. She planned to take the first train heading somewhere. Later, she'd consider the possibility that the man who showed up at Sandra's might not have been from Conrad, but from her family. The thought of her family, especially Rory, tore at her resolve. But she couldn't take the chance of calling her family. She had to stick to her plan. She could not allow Conrad to force himself back into her life with his powerful mind control, probably enhanced by drugs. He wanted her inheritance, she was sure of that now. After that she'd be of no use to him. She'd have to stay missing until the money was disbursed. Even if it meant letting Rory down, perhaps killing her. She'd risk anything for Rory, except her child. Her unborn baby had to be protected from Conrad.

Departures were posted on the board in the center of the terminal. The Sunset Limited would depart for Orlando, with multiple stops in between, in thirty-five minutes. As Ashley stood trembling in the ticket line, she saw that the train made a stop in New Orleans. She'd been there with her parents when she was a teenager and had loved the offbeat characters, the unique culture, the fabulous food. Once in New Orleans, she knew she could blend in with the tourists until she figured out her next move. For now she'd purchase a ticket to Beaumont, Texas, which was half way to New Orleans. With any luck she'd manage to stay on the train all the way to New Orleans. Once she got there, if she felt safe enough, she'd rethink her approach to Rory. She'd be in the second trimester of her pregnancy, a safer stage for a donor procedure.

Still thinking about Rory, Ashley boarded the train. As she searched out a seat, she became aware of the kneading sensation in her abdomen.

CHAPTER TWENTY-NINE

Dan had not expected such opulence as he stepped for the first time into the family's Learjet. As he and Preston settled into plush seats, he felt the strongest urge to smoke since he'd quit cold turkey right after the previous Easter. The cabin felt manly, like cigars and whisky. Dad and Frank must have entertained plenty of political cronies in the skies.

"Mind if I smoke?" Preston asked, pulling out a pack of Marlboros. "Now you know why I leaned on the senator to get the plane. You don't wanta be anywhere near me if I don't get my fix."

Dan didn't object even though he was moving into a holier-than-thou attitude toward smokers. When Preston held out the pack toward him, he shook his head to decline. He did want one, but instead he reached inside his jacket pocket for the Nicorette gum he kept on hand for emergencies. Chan had given him some of that nicotine nasal spray for the tough urges, but it made his eyes burn and tear so badly he'd used it only once.

He must have drifted off to sleep right after the steward served a full-course meal. The plane had already landed when Preston's big hand squeezed his shoulder. "Time to rock and roll, sleeping beauty."

Dan jerked his arm back, for a moment wide-eyed and confused.

"Sorry if I scared you." Preston's deep baritone sounded reassuring. "Hey, anybody ever say how much you and your brother look like Bobby Kennedy?"

"That's what people say," Dan said, rubbing his eyes. "Remarks like that used to piss off Dad. He was so Republican that the notion of his sons looking like the Kennedys irritated him. As for me, I don't like the Kennedy dynasty any better or worse than the Bush dynasty."

"Read something about your brother takin' on old man Teddy in the Senate. Forget the issue."

Dan stood to retrieve his jacket and the small duffel bag that Gina had packed. "Yeah, maybe. Me, I'm not political. Hell, I don't even have a voter's registration card."

The year before, right after Florida's insane presidential election, he'd made the mistake of mentioning this to his father. Dan thought he'd have a stroke right there. The old man was dying of pancreatic cancer. He didn't need that kind of blatant disrespect. Paul and Frank were personal friends of the Bush family, staunch supporters of both George W. and Jeb in Florida. Dad was too far down cancer's path after last November's elections, but Frank was beside himself with politics as the Florida debacle tilted back and forth between George W. and Al Gore.

The air was still cool when they deplaned. "I love the West," said Preston as they headed for the private terminal. "Wouldn't mind living out here. Get a ranch, a few horses, peaceful. How about you?"

"I have a ranch of sorts in Florida," Dan said.

"Horses?" Preston asked as he adjusted what Dan guessed was a lapel microphone. "My kids would love horses."

"No horses. No livestock. Just palm trees. I call it a plantation. Sounds better than a farm."

"Cool, man. When I retire, I wanna go west. Maybe New Mexico. Maybe Arizona. Not as far as California."

"Me, I'm never leaving the Sunshine State."

"Let's grab coffee and some breakfast and review the plan," Preston said as they climbed into their rented Land Cruiser. He sounded in charge. Good, Dan thought, because he didn't know what the hell they were supposed to do now. They found an isolated table in a diner not far from the airport. The sky was becoming pinkish in the east and Dan pulled off his watch to set it to Mountain time.

"As I see it, Ashley ran away to escape Welton and he's hell-bent on finding her," Preston said, dialing his booming voice down. "Gotta be the money. He marries her. Then what?"

"He gets it," Dan said.

"Yes. But is he satisfied with that?"

"What?" Dan looked perplexed.

"Call me paranoid. Call me clairvoyant. But people like Welton are psychopaths. Their sense of ego and entitlement has no bounds. They have no conscience. In this case, I wouldn't put it past him to try to annihilate the entire panel of Parnell siblings. After all, he believes he *deserves* their money. He's *entitled* to it. And nobody is going to screw him out of it."

"You're kidding. Right?" Dan stared at Jack Preston, a forkful of scrambled eggs poised midair. "You're saying he intends to kill us all?"

Preston took a second before answering. "First, let's consider his father. From what we know, they had a disastrous relationship. Started out okay. But something went wrong, and Conrad was sent to military school. There he had a few scrapes, like stealing money, bullying, but nothing that got him thrown out. But that two-bit trouble must have pissed the old man off and he effectively downgrades his son. He supported him but in a second-rate way. Conrad goes to Ohio State, brother Stanley gets Princeton."

"What about the brother?" Dan asked, familiar with the overachieving brother scenario.

"Five years younger. A plastic surgeon. Owns one of those fancy cosmetic centers. Married, two sons, a player in Cincinnati social circles."

"Both physicians," Dan commented.

"Yes, and Conrad, Sr., too, an orthopedic surgeon." Preston continued. "Eventually, our boy gets into the University of Cincinnati Medical School on a scholarship and does a psychiatric residency there."

"And his concentration is hypnosis?"

"It is. But let me tell you about a suspicious incident that happened in Cincinnati. Picture this: Conrad, Jr.'s a resident when Conrad, Sr. shows up in the ER complaining of chest pain. With a diagnosis of a *mild* heart attack, he gets sent to the coronary care unit with his son. Elevator stalls. Finally opens. Picture this: our boy's pumping away on a dead dad."

Preston took a slug of coffee and resumed. "As for the will, our boy's totally cut out. Everything goes to Brother Stanley. An annuity for their mother, which reverts to Stanley at her death."

"Rather harsh." Dan was reminded of his own father's strange last will and testament.

"Then I learn there are rumors of a paternity issue. Remember, this was pre-DNA." Preston paused as the waitress freshened their coffee.

"I dug up an attorney who said Conrad's mother had made inquiries about challenging her husband's will on our boy's behalf, but nothing came of it. Several months later, she overdoses on sleeping pills. From that point on, Welton's been estranged from his brother. Couple years later, brother Stanley's wife, Lenore, is killed in a hit-and-run." Preston stopped long enough for a gulp of coffee. "Same year Lenore dies, our boy marries a nineteen-year-old heiress." Preston went on to explain the tragic story of Crissy Moore. "Nobody's gonna tell me that's coincidence. But proof? Nada."

Dan pushed his empty plate aside. "Jack," he asked. "What's your theory on Meredith's death?"

"I've investigated all the angles. I don't see it being anything but an accident. A car collision, simple as that. But Carla, another story, maybe."

"Carla?" Dan jerked back in his chair. "She was a drug addict. She relapsed. Overdosed. Frank sugarcoated all that shit to make it sound like anorexia, but we all know the truth. Don't we?"

"My guys are still checking in New York, so I won't say more. But you do recall her boyfriend was found dead too? Coincidence? I don't believe so, Dan."

"Holy shit, you're saying that —"

"I'm only saying that our first priority is to find Ashley. Find her before Welton does." The waitress appeared with the check and Jack Preston reached for it. "Parnell expense account," he said. Then he switched to a whisper. "As long as Welton thinks your sister is alive, he'll track her down. His endgame? Get what he thinks he deserves. How? Coerce her into marrying him. Keep her alive. Eliminate the competition. Wallow in the entire Parnell inheritance."

"You really believe this?" Dan asked, wondering who was the craziest, Conrad Welton or Jack Preston.

Preston scratched his smooth, black head. "Tell you the truth. I don't know. I have guys checking all the angles, and we'll see what happens here in New Mexico. Man, who would believe this scenario? That's what you're thinkin', right?"

"Yeah, that's what I'm thinking," Dan agreed.

When they'd climbed back into the Land Cruiser, Jack explained to

Dan how Welton's private investigator had made it easy to pick up his trail. C. W. Crane had used his own name for a rental car and hotel. How that made things easy, Dan did not comprehend, but he assumed rightly that Preston was good at what he did. Earlier, Preston's man had followed the Crane guy to a small art gallery on the plaza, the center of the Santa Fe art scene. Crane was inside the gallery only five minutes, before he headed to a residential address on the outskirts of town. Preston's agent watched as Crane rang the doorbell and then stood talking to a slim, dark-haired woman. Preston showed Dan a digital image of the two chatting. After the woman closed the door, Preston's agent followed Crane back to his hotel and made arrangements for around-the-clock surveillance. Since then Crane had not left his hotel room.

"Okay, this is the place." Jack pointed to a modest-sized adobe house situated in a cul-de-sac — a kid-friendly place, Dan judged, noticing the swing sets and basketball hoops. "Perhaps I shoulda had my guy talk to the woman yesterday, but I didn't want to spook her. So Dan, you're gonna ring the bell and play the caring-family card. If your sister's in there, she's running from her identity. She needs to be convinced that you'll protect her. I'm gonna wait in the car — for now."

Dan felt awkward, inadequate. He'd never been close to Ashley. Would she trust him? He approached the door and rang the bell. The woman in Preston's photo with a look of annoyance, more like a scowl, confronted him. A little boy with red hair tugged on her checkered robe. He was whining.

"Look, I'm busy," the woman said, defiantly. "This is not a good time."

Why had Jack sent him in? Social skills were not among his credentials.

"Uh, ma'am, I'm not selling anything," he said. "I'm Dan Parnell. I've come to look for my sister. Please help me."

She stopped just short of slamming the door. "And who is your sister?"

Dan pulled out a pocket-sized album that showed photos of Ashley from childhood with Dad and Vivian. With Rory and Carla. With Frank and Meredith. A recent photo from her medical school graduation. And one from the Fourth of July party — Ashley and Monica, arm in arm, poolside, with Dan in the background. The woman opened her eyes wide at that one. Dan also had with him a packet of newsclips reporting Ashley missing at the World Trade Center and announcing the memorial in Philadelphia, but he held off on these.

As the woman hesitated, Dan used a trick he'd seen in the movies. He stuck his foot into the crack at the door. He heard a kid's voice from the back, "Mom, is Marcy back? Can she take us to the park?"

"No, Bart," the woman called. "Finish your breakfast."

"Mrs. Becker, could I come in and talk? It's important."

The woman looked deliberately from Dan to Dan in the photo. Then she stared at the one of Ashley in front of the Devon house, a young professional in a baby blue suit with a white silk blouse and an expensive-looking scarf. Her hair was pulled up, the way she always wore it.

"Marcy?" the woman murmured. Then she looked up at him. "Who did you say you were?"

"Dan Parnell, ma'am." She had flipped over to the next photo, this one of Ashley with Rory's kids around the pool. Dan pointed to Ashley in a red, two-piece suit with a matching sarong. "That's Ashley, my sister."

"Marcy never — Was that Monica Monroe with her in that other picture?"

The little kid had settled around the woman's feet to race his Matchbox cars. Then a kid about seven or eight careened around the corner, stopping short. "You a cop?" He scrutinized Dan closer. "How come you're not wearing a uniform?"

"No, Bart, he's not a policeman."

"But you said you were gonna call the police 'cause our car's missing. I don't like to ride in your van. You got too much junk in there."

"Bart, go get dressed. I'm going to have to take you to work with me. Now go."

"Are you Marcy's friend?" The kid ignored his mother and directed another question to Dan. "Do you know where she went? She was supposed to take care of us today."

"Ma'am, if 'Marcy' is my sister Ashley, I'm afraid that she's in danger."

"She's in trouble, all right," said the woman. She stepped aside and motioned Dan into her living room. "Go ahead," she said. "Sit down."

"Thank you, ma'am," Dan said, more hopeful now that this wasn't a wild-goose chase.

"I can't believe your family. All that money. Just because she's pregnant. Banished by her family or too scared to even tell them, she never exactly said. And now you all come chasing after her." The woman started shaking a finger at Dan as if he were a naughty child. "She's afraid of you. I can't understand why a family can't be more supportive. A lovely young woman forced to clean someone's house and take care of her kids. You some kind of Puritans? Planning to brand her with a scarlet letter?"

"I do know that Ashley's pregnant, ma'am. But that's not the reason she came out here. She's running away from an abusive relationship with a man."

"The man who came here yesterday? Asking questions about my nanny, Marcy Powers?" She sank down into one of the living room chairs. "She seemed so sweet, so sincere, and she was so good with the boys. Now it's back to the drawing board. Finding a nanny is no easy feat. I should have known that something too good to be true is —"

"Is she still here?" Dan asked, struggling with the role of amateur detective. What goddamned question should he ask next? He'd found out —almost— that Ashley was here. "My sister is in serious trouble," he said. "We need to help her. Okay?"

"Your sister stole my car," the woman said. Dan couldn't tell if she was more concerned about 'Marcy,' her car, or her need to find a new nanny.

"I can help," he offered. "But most important, we have to find Ashley. Before someone else does."

"The guy who was here yesterday?"

"Yes, he was sent by the man who wants to hurt her. Trust me, as her brother, we just want her home safely." Dan didn't think the woman recognized the Parnell name. But this was New Mexico, not exactly mainstream USA. "Ma'am, I know you are busy, but I have a colleague outside in the car. He's a friend and a private investigator. Would it be all right if I asked him in so we can talk about this together?"

She walked over to the window, pulled back the curtain, and peered outside. Then she flipped through the family photos one more time.

"I guess," she said, biting her lip. "By the way, I'm Sandra Becker. Wait here, I need to go check on Bart."

From the door, Dan motioned Preston to come inside. They waited in the living room until Sandra returned, wearing a creamy silk robe instead of the faded checkered one.

After Dan introduced Jack, Sandra seemed less suspicious. Dan wasn't sure how Frank would prefer Ashley's Parnell identity handled, but he decided not to equivocate. "Mrs. Becker," he said, "there are things that we want to tell you. But we need you to keep all this confidential until the time that it's safe to divulge them?" Jack Preston gave him a nod of approval.

"Yes." She sounded breathless with curiosity. "You can trust me."

Jack took over, "The Parnell family is a very wealthy and influential family. Dan and Ashley's father was Paul Parnell —"

"As in the Parnell Foundation?" Sandra asked in disbelief. "My sister just received a grant from them for her work with Native Americans. That Parnell?"

"Yes," Dan said, "my father."

"Monica Monroe? I read all about her adoption. That Parnell?"

"Yes," said Preston, sounding impatient.

"Marcy Powers, the woman who worked as my nanny, is a multi-millionaire?" Sandra took a deep breath and slowly exhaled. "She saved every penny. Here," She got up, went into the kitchen and came back with a scrap of paper, "this the note she left."

"What did she take, ma'am?" Jack asked. His deep voice was authoritative.

"This week's grocery money. Two hundred dollars. I can't find my Visa card. And my Taurus is missing. I was about to call the police to report the car and the credit card. I kept rereading her note. If it had only been the credit card, I would have just have reported it as lost, but I need my car."

"You haven't reported this?" Jack clarified.

"No." She grimaced. "I didn't know what to do. Marcy had the day off yesterday. She drove to Albuquerque to do some sightseeing. She seemed fine when she returned right before dinner. Then when I told her about the guy who was asking about her, she said she had a migraine. I figured that being pregnant, on her feet, walking around all day, she was just worn down. Then this morning, she's gone."

Jack pulled out five $100 bills. "Take these. We will track down your car. If we can't locate it, we'll make sure you get a new one within the week. We will also cover any charges to your credit card."

"Thank you," she said. "God, I hope Marcy, I mean, Ashley, is okay."

"Mrs. Becker," Jack moved in close. "It is critical that we find her as soon as possible. She's running from a very dangerous man. Can I ask you to keep your credit card active and give us access to your account? And most important, you must not tell anyone about this. There is no need or obligation to inform the police as the Parnells will reimburse you generously. If that man comes back, or anybody else, simply say that your nanny left, that she gave no reason, and no forwarding address. Can you do this, Mrs. Becker?"

"Of course," she said, stepping back from the big man's intimidating glare.

"Thank you," Dan said, breathing more easily. "We will keep in touch."

"Mrs. Becker, for your own safety, just tell any inquirer what I said." Preston reached into his pocket and pulled out a business card. "If you hear anything related to Marcy, as you know her, or Dr. Ashley Parnell, please call this number immediately. Anything from her or anyone who purports to be looking for her. Mr. Parnell is the only member of the family you should talk with. Anyone else saying they are from the family will be frauds. Understand?"

"That man yesterday asked if Marcy was in touch with somebody in Albuquerque. A lady doctor. I can't remember the name. I told him no, she never mentioned knowing a doctor," she said, bending to pick up her small son as he started whining again. "Did you say doctor? Marcy? A doctor?"

"Yes," Dan said. "Graduated from medical school last June."

"No wonder she was so good with Justin and Bart when they were sick. She knew just what to do."

CHAPTER THIRTY

Ashley found a seat near the rear of the car, the only unoccupied row and just a few steps from the toilet. That was bad news, good news. Close enough to smell the odors of human waste and chemicals, but not far in case she needed to use the facility. She'd purchased a ticket to Beaumont, Texas, paying less than she would for New Orleans. If she'd been tracked from El Paso, they'd look for her in Beaumont. But she would not disembark there. Between Beaumont and New Orleans, she would move from car to car along the train, trying to look as honest as possible, not daring to take a seat. Once in New Orleans, she would lose herself in the crowd of tourists. By now Sandra would have reported "Marcy Powers" to the police. How she'd longed to tell Sandra the truth, and how sad it was to leave New Mexico without seeing Ruthie.

The train left the station in El Paso with a jerk that sent a stooped elderly woman sprawling into the aisle. As Ashley jumped up to assist her, she felt a surge of liquid warmth saturate her panties. Next, a cramping pain in her lower abdomen and another gush of warm fluid. Hastily, she shoved the woman's bag of belongings into her hands. She needed to get to the restroom.

"Can you put it up there?" The woman pointed to the bin above Ashley's seat. "I think I'll sit right here. That fall's gonna kick up my arthritis, that's for sure."

But Ashley had already latched the door behind her in the small, odorous space marked "toilet." When she pulled down her jeans, she saw the blood that had soaked though her panties. The train lurched and she fell backward onto the open circle of the toilet. Panic blanked out any rational thought process. What should she do? What were her options? Her meager obstetrical experience failed her completely.

"Anybody in there?" a male voice, loud and annoyed. "You been in there fifteen minutes."

Ashley shifted on the toilet, waiting for the next cramp to resolve. The blood on her underwear was brownish, not bright red. She couldn't remember. Was that good or bad? She did have a sanitary pad in her purse that she stuck against the soaked panties. What else could she do? She needed to get out of the tiny room.

"Hey, I gotta use the toilet!" Another round of knocking on the door.

Ashley stood up. Pivoting, she faced the toilet, bent forward and vomited. The pounding on the door grew, so she wiped her mouth with a paper towel and hastily washed her hands, not taking time to dry them. Sacrificing any dignity, she unlatched the door and walked past a disheveled middle-aged man.

"About time," he muttered, "women."

The old woman had taken the window seat so Ashley sat on the aisle. She tried to think clinically. That abdominal twitching, insignificant at first, was stronger now and coming in waves. Vaginal bleeding and cramping pain were catastrophic symptoms at three months gestation. The old woman next to her was peeling a ripe banana. The smell intensified Ashley's nausea and she turned her head away.

"Would you like one?" The woman poked her arm. "They're not going to last much longer."

"No thank you," Ashley said. "I'm not feeling that well."

"You do look pale, my dear." The woman reached into her bag and pulled out a packet of saltines. "Here, nibble on these. They'll help settle your stomach."

Ashley took the small pack that looked like it came from a restaurant. Maybe the crackers would settle her stomach. And maybe if she accepted them, the woman would leave her alone. She reclined her seat and closed her eyes. Trying not to make a sound, but with silent tears soaking her pack of tissues, she endured what seemed like endless hours of a jostling ride. Twice she got up to check the bleeding. The flow had increased to that of a heavy period and it was now a fresh red. She bought more pads from the dispenser and supplemented them with wadded paper towels. Increased bleeding and intensifying pains. She was losing her baby. There was nothing she or anyone could do. She'd treated enough first semester spontaneous abortions to understand the situation. And, the one reason she had to stay alive and safe was dying.

Sobbing openly now, Ashley turned to the woman next to her who had tried on several occasions to make conversation.

"My dear, something must be terribly wrong," she said, patting Ashley's arm. "Who hurt you like this? It has to be a man."

At this moment, Ashley felt something break loose inside. She pushed the woman's arm aside, and bolted for the rest room.

CHAPTER THIRTY-ONE

Conrad Welton paced the confines of his townhouse on Rittenhouse Square. The property he'd once thought spacious now felt claustrophobic. But soon he'd be back in the Parnell mansion. He'd just got off the phone with C. W. Crane. Ashley had been confirmed alive, in New Mexico. A car was now on its way to take Welton to the airport, and he'd be with Ashley by late that afternoon. All he had to do now was contain his excitement and postpone the wrath he'd focus later on Crane.

"Take her out of that house, by force, now," he'd ordered his investigator.

But Crane had balked. "No way, doc," he'd said. "I'll keep her under surveillance. Once you get here you can do whatever you want, but I'm not risking my license on an abduction charge."

When the phone rang, Welton grabbed it, picking up his overnight bag. "Be right down."

"Dr. Welton, it's Crane. I have bad news for you. The Parnell woman is missing."

"Missing? Missing, like where?"

"I can't answer that, doc. She must have left during the night. I arranged for surveillance starting at five in the morning. Everything was quiet. Then around eight thirty there's company at the place. One of the Parnell brothers arrives with a P.I. from Philly. Name's Jack Preston. Guy with a good rep."

"I don't give a fuck about anybody's reputation but yours," replied Welton. "I'm paying top dollar. You're supposed to be the best. Right? You tell me you have Ashley under surveillance. Now you tell me she's missing? You better explain that. Better than that, find her!" Conrad was shouting. His body started to shake and he felt a surge of pain starting in his neck and spreading to his left temple.

"Only a matter of time. I just wanted you to know so you wouldn't rush down here. Could be she's left the area. I talked to the woman where she was staying. She's pretty shaken. Won't say much. But does admit that it was Ashley, her nanny, that is."

"Nanny?" Welton yelled. "Find her." He tossed the phone onto the couch. With one hand he massaged his neck. This stress was not help-ing his already elevated blood pressure. His racing heart meant he had to get into a relaxation space.

When he reached the bedroom, Conrad put a cool compress on his forehead and began the self-hypnotic routine. After a minute, the phone rang. He let it ring and tried to deepen his trance until he could no longer ignore the pounding on his front door.

"Dr. Welton, your limousine is waiting, sir," the doorman reported. "I tried calling up, but —"

"Dismiss it," Welton ordered. He needed time to think, but first he had to concentrate on getting rid of the throbbing pain in his neck. He returned to the softness of his bed and attempted to reenter his trance. He checked the time: eleven a.m.

It was one p.m. when Conrad awoke, comfortable and pain-free. His heart rate was slow and steady. Calmer now, he showered and changed from his dress slacks and sports jacket to jeans. He checked his pulse. Again, he reminded himself that he must control his rage. Rage trig-gered symptoms. Physical or psychological, he wasn't sure. He'd seen a cardiologist who'd ordered more tests.

Taking a deep breath, he called Crane. "What do we know?"

"She took off in her boss's car." Crane's voice sounded confident. "She bought gas and food at a convenience store. We don't know where she's headed."

"What do the Parnells know?"

"Not more than I do, doc," Crane said.

"Have you talked with them? Their investigator?"

"No. Do you want me to?"

"Why not? We all want to find her, don't we?"

Welton didn't care who found Ashley. All he wanted was to get her in close proximity to him. He'd implanted enough threatening sugges-tions that once she was back with him, it would be easy to enforce those messages. This time there'd be no excuses, no delays. They'd head im-mediately to Nevada, where they wouldn't have to wait for a license. His plan for the rest of the greedy Parnell family was ready to activate. With Ashley so unreliable, he couldn't afford to rely on her performance on the test. He had no choice but to eliminate her competitors.

"It would help, doc, if you suggest to the Parnells that we team up."

"I'd call the senator, but you said he's already down there."

"No, doc, it's the other brother, the one from Florida, Dan Parnell."

"What?" Welton did not think that Dan had the commitment to get involved. Wasn't he a recluse? Then he remembered his aggressive son. And how Dan had forced Conrad out of his home.

"I'll call the senator. You find Ashley. Lean on Ruth Campbell," Con-rad instructed. "Ashley would trust her, more than her family." She must have gone to New Mexico to be near her friend. When Conrad put the call into Frank's office, he was put on hold, then told that the senator was in Florida.

"At the Parnell home?" he'd asked.

"Um, sorry, sir, can't say."

Welton called Crane back to tell him to verify whether or not Frank was staying at the family compound. If so, his job just became that much easier.

CHAPTER THIRTY-TWO

"So much for healthcare reform." Two of Frank's aides and their boss packed up after a briefing session on the Healthcare Task Force. Frank was a member, but like his other responsibilities, he'd let his participation lapse and was now catching up. "Not a surprise with the focus on security and intelligence."

The aides nodded in agreement as their briefcases snapped shut.

"We have to push for drugs for seniors," Frank said, reaching for a handful of cashews. Once he had emerged from the deepest valley of depression, he'd started to gain weight. So back on Atkins. "The Clintons could have had this thing wrapped eight years ago. Healthcare was the focal point of their campaign, for crying out loud."

"Right, Senator," the young man said. "Dropped that ball like a hot potato."

"I'd better stop my tirade. Judicial Committee's in forty-five minutes." Frank rose to usher the pair out of his office. He'd been on the phone much of the morning about homeland security. He felt behind the curve since September eleven, but he was determined to catch up and earn his $150,000 annual salary.

His intercom buzzed. "Matt's here," his secretary announced. "With lunch. If you can call what he's got for you lunch."

Matt balanced a tray with a club sandwich surrounded by chips for him; a huge bowl of lettuce, a small plate of crisp bacon strips and slices of yellow cheese for his boss; a plate of dill pickles and two cans of Diet Coke. "I've got some stuff you ought to see." Matt laid out the food on the conference table. As Frank doused his salad with blue cheese dressing, he guessed the "stuff" was family, not congressional.

"Your sister. You know that Preston tracked her to a train headed for

Beaumont, Texas. She bought a ticket in El Paso with cash, but she left the train in Sanderson, Texas. Then he lost her trail. Dan stayed in New Mexico, and Preston went to Sanderson, but —"

"Beaumont? There's nothing there but oil rigs. And Sanderson? What's going on there?"

"Beats me," said Matt. "Dan had no clue, either. But we have some new info. Jack talked to a woman who sat next to Ashley on the train. Identified her from a photo. Old woman — the busybody type — said Ashley cried the whole way. And she seemed sick, looked pale, and spent so much time in the bathroom that passengers complained. Woman said she was not very friendly. But the woman was quite sure that Ashley did not return after the stop in Sanderson."

Frank felt a twinge of queasiness. Guilt, or low blood sugar thanks to the Atkins diet? The thought of Ashley with no money and pregnant? Were they doing all they could to find her? How he missed Meredith; she'd know what to do.

"Jack's checking rental cars, airports, trains, buses. Twenty-four hours, she could be anywhere."

"How tough is it to get a new identity?" Frank asked, reaching for one of Matt's chips. "Passport? Driver's license?"

"Costs money and you gotta have connections. She can't have much money. We know she hasn't tried to access hers."

"She won't be able to get far. I still can't believe it — having to take care of somebody's house and kids?"

"Carrie and I were talking last night," Matt said, crunching a potato chip. "Try to think like you're on the run, I told her."

"And?"

"'If I were that scared and if I had no money and if I were pregnant, I'd contact someone in the family,' she told me. 'Pick the one I thought I could trust the most. Either that or show up at the Salvation Army or St. Vincent de Paul's.' We checked them out, too. No trace."

"If it were family, we'd know," Frank said.

"Maybe," Matt said. "Unless 'family' swore to keep a secret? Remember, not everyone in your family knows what's going on."

"I keep thinking about Rory and Chan." Frank paused to make

up his mind before making the commitment. "When Elise and I were having dinner last night, I had an idea. You're not going to like it. Means I'll be out of D.C. for a while."

"Let's hear it, boss."

"I'm considering taking Elise down to Longboat Key to be with her cousins for Thanksgiving. I could brief Chan there. And he could decide whether to tell Rory."

"Yeah," agreed Matt. "Just in case Ashley does contact them."

"Getting through the holidays is going to be tough for Elise." Frank found it hard to believe that he was planning to spend a family holiday with the Stevens family. He'd spent so many years resenting them.

"Sounds good, Senator. Chandler Stevens is a good man."

"Besides, we'll be in recess."

"Let's hope there's not another attack," Matt said. "I don't like those threats that Intelligence is bringing to the committee. Can I have that last pickle?"

"No. If it's zero calories, it's mine," Frank grabbed it up. "My substitute for a Hershey bar. Osama bin Laden and the Taliban have Congress tied up in knots, but I think I can get away for a few days, even though I'm swamped."

"Meantime let me fill you in on Preston's information about Welton." Matt pulled a small pad out of his jacket pocket and recapped for Frank what they knew of Welton's past.

My dad wasn't the only one with a weird last testament, Frank thought, and he asked, "What the heck happened to make him disinherit his oldest son?"

"Jack Preston found a high school friend of Jessica Long, Welton's mother. She claimed that Jessica got pregnant right out of nursing school. Married Welton, Sr., whom she'd dated the summer before. Speculation is that she was pregnant by somebody else. At some point Conrad Sr. gets wise."

"Quite the soap opera. So who was the supposed father?"

"Not a clue," Matt said, "but you have to get to that Intelligence hearing."

Frank reached for his suit jacket and straightened his tie. "Things are heating up on Iraq. But, know what? I *will* take Elise to Florida. Why don't you come down, bring Carrie?"

CHAPTER THIRTY-THREE

Welton's only vestige of the Parnell largesse was the Mercedes he had appropriated. Peggy Putnam, guard dog of the Parnell assets, hadn't come for it. But the car only sat in the garage, eating up parking fees. Welton considered his finances: The $1,000,000 settlement from the Moore estate that had been spent long ago. His professor salary was barely enough to pay the condo fees and taxes. He'd borrowed against the condo equity to pay C. R. Crane $500 a day plus expenses. The dismal situation of his financial affairs made his heart skip a beat.

He reassured himself that he had taken his Cardizem. The day before, his cardiologist told him he had a serious arrhythmia. That he might need a pacemaker. That he'd need electrophysiologic tests to be sure. There was no time for that now. He needed to stay calm, steady, and cool to implement his plan. Either Crane or the Parnell investigator would find Ashley soon.

The phone on his desk rang.

"Doc, I've got news. The Parnell woman is still in New Mexico. What do you want me to do?"

"Where is she?"

"At that woman doctor's you told me about. Parnell showed up at her apartment a few minutes ago in a cab."

"Do you think you can keep her under surveillance this time? I've got a plane reserved. Just keep her under wraps until I get there."

CHAPTER THIRTY- FOUR

From the balcony off her bedroom, Rory watched dolphins frolic in the Gulf of Mexico. She needed to limit her time outside to five minutes. Her head was completely bald, and even though the sun warmed her aching bones, she had to protect her delicate skin. All the cells in her body had taken a beating, especially the white blood cells that protected against infection. When the kids came in to see her, they had to wear masks. But they came more frequently now that she and Chan had talked to them — each individually — about her possible death, about how together they'd be okay. She'd be in heaven watching over them. Even Emily seemed to accept that her mother would not be there to see her grow up.

The decision to move the family to Florida had been impetuous. She'd simply mentioned to Chan that the cool weather gave her chills, and the next day he'd made arrangements to move into the Longboat Key compound. Chan had taken an indefinite leave of absence from his practice, and arranged for the kids to be home schooled. What he would do after her death, she didn't know.

"Time to come in, Mrs. Stevens," Mrs. Tally announced. "Your doctor will be here any minute."

Rory rose from the chaise lounge, pleased that she could make the short trip to her bed on her own. Today she'd find out the results of her last bone marrow test. In her heart, she felt that the news would not be good. She remembered Ashley explaining to her that she had the *not-favorable* type of leukemia. A tear made its way down Rory's cheek. Ashley had been her last hope for a cure.

"Here's our patient," Chan announced to the stately gentleman who presided over hematologic cancers at the Moffitt Institute in Tampa. In deference to Rory and the substantial Parnell support of their research, the chief had made a house call.

Rory dabbed at her eyes, grabbed a scarf, and had it halfway tied around her head when they walked in.

"Rory, my dear," the doctor said, "no need to get fancied up for me. How are you feeling?"

"Not bad except for the lesions in my mouth. I'm using that ointment you gave me, but my mouth is sore. And yes, I know, that's a side effect of the chemo."

CHAPTER THIRTY-FIVE

Ashley's muffled cries were heard by no one as, in the confines of the train toilet, she expelled the fetus. She sat on the toilet until the worst of the pains had subsided, and she judged that all the tissue was out of her uterus. She did not flush the toilet. Closing her eyes, she groped with her bare hand in the bloody water. Feeling solid tissue, she extracted it, wrapped it in a protective wad of paper towels, and gently placed the bundle in the bottom of the trash bin beneath a blanket of discarded towels. At three months gestation, the fetus was only three inches long, an ounce or two, with little organs and a heartbeat. But, no hope of viability. This she knew from her embryology course. Without even knowing whether it was a boy or a girl, she said good-bye to her baby in that unsanitary, inhospitable cell.

Rude, incessant pounding on the door finally urged her to clean herself up and emerge from the cubicle of horror. She ignored staring eyes, and did not return to her seat. Her nosy companion was snoring loudly when Ashley reached into the overhead bin and retrieved her belongings. She lugged them into the next car, and as the train rumbled into Sanderson, she got off. She felt as if a layer of terror had been peeled off her body, and that her protective instincts for her child could be organized for herself. She knew her that her blood type was Rh-negative. If her baby had been Rh-positive, she'd need to have an injection of RhoGam within the next seventy-two hours to prevent antibody formation and hemolytic anemia in any future child that may be Rh-positive, too.

She considered her options. Shouldn't she contact her family? But who? They all thought she was dead. They'd had a memorial service for her. Or could it have been the family who'd sent someone to look for her at Sandra's? She had assumed Conrad was behind it, but could it have been Frank?

At the Sanderson station, she counted her money. She'd saved all her salary and with what she'd taken from Sandra, she could afford to go to a hospital here. But hospital charges were so erratic, she was afraid there wouldn't be much left. Even if she could afford to stay a few days while she figured out what to do next, she had to make a longer-term plan. Without the baby at the heart of her every concern, her priorities needed to change. And there was Rory. Ashley had pushed her into the background. Now Rory was front and center, but was it too late?

She needed to deal with first things first. Right now, she needed medical attention. The train whistle blew, followed by the announcement that the train from Del Rio, Texas was arriving, westbound for Alpine, Texas, and El Paso. Ashley made a decision. She'd take this train to El Paso, transfer to Albuquerque, and find Ruthie. Ruthie could order the blood test she needed, and get her the RhoGam if she needed it. Once that was accomplished, she'd figure out what to do next.

"Ashley!" Ruthie flung herself at her friend, hugging her, then holding her out at arm's length. "I've been out of my mind with worry. Everybody's looking for you. Your family hired a private investigator. And so did Conrad, to find you. They both left their cards. I swore I'd call them if I heard anything."

Ruthie stopped talking and gasped as Ashley started to slide downward against the closed door. "I need your help," Ashley managed.

"Over here." Ruthie moved the pile of papers covering the sofa. "Tell me, what is it? Oh, you look terrible."

"I had a miscarriage. On a train. By myself."

"You were pregnant? My God, Ashley, what an awful situation. What can I do?"

"Right now will you help me clean up?" Ashley responded. She felt like she was a million years old. "Then I need some medical help. You see, I'm Rh-negative."

"I'll get you into the ER tonight." Ruthie picked up the phone.

"But I don't want to use my name."

"Don't worry, we'll make up a name. And all will be fine."

Two men in rental cars followed Ashley and Ruthie to the hospital, lurked in the ER, and reported back by cell phone. Duly noted by each other, they made no contact.

CHAPTER THIRTY-SIX

Dan had been on the phone with Gina when his beeper went off.

"We've got her, Dan," Jack Preston's message boomed. He reported that Ashley was in the ER at the University of New Mexico Hospital, under an assumed name. She was being treated for a miscarriage.

"Poor kid," Dan said.

"I hear you," said Preston. "She's with that med school friend and my guy there says she seems okay. Stable, not hysterical or anything."

"How long will she be in the hospital?"

"Not long. Come to Albuquerque right away. It's an hour drive from Santa Fe. If she's discharged before you get there, my man will follow her, stay with her, but not apprehend." Preston gave Dan the contact information. "Get briefed and make contact with Ashley. Tell her whatever you think will work to get her to come back to Florida. Just remember that the P.I. Welton hired is aping everything that we do, so be on the lookout for interference."

"What if Ashley doesn't want to see me?"

"Convince her," Preston said. "Meantime, I'm on my way. Can't get out of Texas fast enough."

Ashley and Ruthie sat at the kitchen table sipping green tea and munching cheese and crackers. Ashley's miscarriage would not prevent her from having more children. A blood test confirmed that the fetus had indeed been Rh-positive, and Ashley had been given the injection. She hadn't needed a D&C, but she'd lost a lot of blood and the doctor recommended a transfusion. Ashley decided against it. Her red cells would regenerate. Ruthie agreed.

The women discussed their residencies, one aborted, one prospering. Their thoughts and plans were interrupted by the doorbell.

Ashley cringed. "I don't want anyone to know I'm here." She hadn't yet broached the subject of Conrad, or why she had fled New York City.

"Okay," said Ruthie. "I'll get rid of whoever it is."

The sliding chain engaged, Ruthie opened her door just a crack.

"Dr. Campbell, I'm Dan Parnell, Ashley's brother. Can I come in?"

"Uh, no, I don't think so," Ruthie said, keeping her voice low. "I'm kind of busy now, and I'm not feeling well. I had to take the day off."

"I know that my sister is here," Dan said. "Will you tell her that it's important? You see, she may be in danger."

"Dan?" Ashley joined Ruthie and peeked through the crack in the opening. Her hand raked her dark, short hair. Would he even recognize her?

"Ashley, can I come in?" he repeated. He stepped inside, quickly closing the door behind him. Glancing around the small studio apartment, he headed for the windows, drawing the curtains closed. Then, tears glistening in his eyes, he opened his arms and pulled Ashley into a tight embrace.

"I'm sorry about the baby," Dan said as they drew apart. "But I'm so glad that you're alive."

Ashley clung to Dan. Her brother, always so remote, now a lifeline to her family. She remembered how sensitive he'd been the day of their father's funeral, and here he was tearful, yet so strong against her body. Dan drew her onto the sofa that would later convert to Ruthie's bed. They sat for a moment, silent, as he stroked her short, boyish hair.

Ruthie excused herself to make more tea. Something terrible was happening in this iconic family; she still did not know what.

"I am mortified about what I did," Ashley said. "I was so scared of Conrad. What he might do to the baby. That's why I ran when I got the chance. But now that I miscarried, I don't know what to do."

"I'm here to help you, Ashley. The family knows about Welton, about his background. You were right to be frightened. Everyone will be overjoyed that you're alive."

"Rory," Ashley said, "what about Rory? I abandoned her. Selfishly abandoned her by running away."

"No, no, that's not true," Dan said, holding her hands in his. "You were pregnant. You were very brave. Of all people, Rory will understand."

"How is she?" There is was, the awful question.

"Not doing well. There's been resistance to the chemo. I can't give you all the medical details, but I know from talking to Chan that the situation is dire."

Ashley sat up straight. "She needs that bone marrow transplant. I've got to get to Philadelphia now."

"She's not in Philly; she's on Longboat Key. Chan moved the family there. I was going to suggest that we go there tomorrow morning. It's Thanksgiving and what more could we be thankful for than finding you alive?"

"Could we go tonight?" Ashley asked, reaching to pick up her purse. "Now?"

"Logistics," Dan said, pulling out a cell phone. "Jack Preston, a private investigator, is flying in on the family plane. I'll coordinate with him. I'm thinking that first thing tomorrow is more feasible. In the meantime, we're arranging for round-the-clock security here."

Ruthie returned with a tray of steaming mugs.

"Ruthie, is it okay if I stay here with you tonight?" Ashley asked. "I have so much to tell you."

CHAPTER THIRTY-SEVEN

Frank grinned at Elise's excitement as she dove into her luggage, searching for her bathing suit, anxious to join the Stevens kids in the pool. The weather was Florida perfect. Sunny skies. Eighty degrees.

Why would anyone want to live up north, Frank considered, as he changed into shorts and a golf shirt. Leo Tally's voice came over the intercom. "Senator, will you pick up? It's Mr. Dan. Says it's important."

"Frank, we've found Ashley." Frank listened as Dan described the circumstances and suggested that he and Jack Preston leave with her for Longboat Key. That Gina and Terry join them there. Then the whole family would be together.

"She's okay?"

"She really wanted that baby. But now she's dedicated to helping Rory."

"Can't get here too soon. Rory looks deathly ill. Sorry for the word choice there."

Frank thought of Elise, of how he would have to bring her up with no mother. The memory of his dad, when his mother died, how remote his father had been. Frank wondered whether Dan had felt the same sting of neglect. His own future was Elise, and he resolved to be a concerned father and to make sure she stayed close to her noisy cousins since that gave her great comfort. For the first time ever, he thought smugly, he had all their names straight. Elise had rehearsed him.

"Whoops, I've got a call coming in," Frank said, glancing at the number.

"Probably George W., calling for advice. I'll see you tomorrow in Florida."

Dan disconnected and Frank picked up the other line, recognizing the Detroit area code. His uncle had looked so frail at Meredith's funeral. But the caller was Carl Schiller, not the cardinal.

"I'm in Detroit on business, Frank, and I'm having dinner with your uncle tonight. He's going to ask me about the family so I thought I'd call you. Surprised, I must say, that you're in Florida."

The old man must think I'm down here earning points for Dad's test. The thought made Frank grin. Nothing could be further from the truth. Since Meredith's death, he had wasted not one iota of time fantasizing about his political future. That dream had died with Meredith. Whoever got Dad's millions, so be it.

"Carl, we have wonderful news. You'll find it hard to believe."

"You have my attention."

"Ashley's alive. I just got off the phone with Dan, who's with her. She's okay, but she lost the baby — miscarriage."

Frank briefed Carl. He plumped up the pillows on the bed and re-layed the whole story of Conrad's background, including the suspicions that swirled around his family and his former wife. Much of it Carl knew.

"How can I get in touch with Ashley?" Carl asked. "And how do you plan to handle the media once they find out she's alive. Will there be any political backlash?"

Frank wanted to say, "who gives a fuck?" Without Meredith, he didn't care about the media or even about publicity. But he would honor her stance on obscenity. "As for the media, I haven't even thought about it. I just want Ashley back here safe and sound." Ready to end the conversation, he said, "When you see Cardinal Sean tonight, give him my best."

When Frank hung up, he did a mental inventory. Ashley had just been located. Who had to be informed? Uncle Carl and Cardinal Sean were covered. Dan and Gina, ditto. He'd let Matt and Carrie know as soon as they arrived from Washington. That left Terry, Elise, and the Stevens, all ten of them. Was he missing anyone? Yes, Monica Monroe.

CHAPTER THIRTY-EIGHT

Ashley and Ruthie woke early on Thanksgiving morning despite having slept little. They'd talked all night about their lives, and what would happen next. Ruthie from inner-city Baltimore, a neighborhood where not even the police ventured. Ashley from the exclusive Philadelphia Main Line. Ruthie listened to Ashley's account of how she was determined to help Rory before, like Carla, it was too late. When Ashley got around to telling Ruthie about Conrad, she did not hold back; she poured out all her fears and suspicions. Ruthie said nothing to dissuade her of her concerns.

Jack and Dan had arranged to pick Ashley up at nine a.m. The family plane would then fly them directly to Sarasota. By afternoon, Ashley would be reunited with her family. One minute she felt elation; the next, a surge of guilt. She hadn't breached the implications of her disappearance. Had she broken the law by running away? And would she do it again if it meant escape from Conrad? The hardest question: what would happen if she had to face Conrad alone?

When Preston and Dan arrived, Preston handed Ashley a shopping bag. "Here's something to wear."

Ashley pulled out a large-brimmed black hat and a pair of oversized dark glasses.

"Camouflage," he said, "just in case we have followers."

"Conrad?" Ashley felt herself start to sweat.

"Not to worry, we'll be on the lookout. Once we get you into your family's compound, you'll be safe. Never seen security like that place."

When Ashley and Ruthie hugged good-bye, Preston's eyes kept sweeping the outside perimeter.

Welton flipped open his cell phone. He'd been pacing, awaiting the call from his investigator.

"Crane here," the voice confirmed. "Something's going down, doc. They've got the girl. Preston and Dan Parnell. They're heading for the airport."

"Stay with them. Find out where they're headed."

Welton took a deep breath. He had to control his breathing. Hyperventilation made his heart beat more wildly. His hand was steady when he picked up the phone and placed a call to Terry Parnell's cell phone. Through the Parnell family debacle, he'd remained on friendly terms with the boy in order to glean information about the Parnells in general, and Ashley in particular. Now that the Parnells knew where Ashley was and, in fact, had her in their custody, Terry might know the plan.

"Terry, it's Conrad." Conrad listened for any negativity, but detected none.

"Conrad, I'm so glad you called. We've found Ashley. Did you know?"

"Yes, she's been trying to get in touch," he lied.

"Well, she's on her way here. You were right all along. Posttraumatic stress syndrome. I mean, buildings crumbling down. People jumping out of windows. Body parts. People buried alive —"

"Washington?" Welton interrupted. Senators had bunkers in the bowels of the D.C. buildings, didn't they? If they'd taken Ashley there, it was the worst possible scenario. Welton's heart began to flip in his chest.

"No, Longboat Key, Florida. Dad's picking her up in Albuquerque, and they're flying into Sarasota. We'll all be there. You ought to be there, too, man."

"She needs time alone with her family," Welton said once he'd taken a reassuring breath. "I'll see her soon enough." He disconnected, and without putting down the handset, called the airport to charter a plane to Sarasota. Expensive, but soon the money would no longer be a problem and he'd own a jet. By the time Crane called with the Parnell flight plan, Welton was halfway to the Philadelphia airport. With any luck he'd arrive in Florida before Ashley.

⚜

Even before Monica Monroe had won her first talent contest at age twelve, she'd been a member of Cardinal Sean Parnell's cathedral choir, and continued to be a frequent soloist when she was in Detroit. Her parents were devout Catholics and it meant a lot to her father, especially since her mother's death. So dutifully, as requested this time, she'd sung her favorite, Schubert's "Ave Maria," at the ten o'clock Thanksgiving Day Mass. Now, as the cardinal thanked her profusely, she was anxious to join Patrick, go home, and eat herself into oblivion.

"Is Patrick here?" the cardinal asked as she turned to leave.

"Waiting in the back with my brothers' families. I guess I should get back to them. The usher mentioned you wanted to talk to me about something?"

"Could you step into the sacristy for a moment?" They closed the door just in time to avoid a group of parishioners who either wanted to kiss the Cardinal's ring or to ask Monica for an autograph.

"I know you have family obligations," Cardinal Parnell said. "But I have quite an extraordinary request."

"Yes?" she asked, truly curious.

I talked to Carl Schiller yesterday." His paper-thin, wrinkled face grimaced. "About Ashley."

"About Ashley?" Monica's eyebrows arched. She had only been with her biological half sister three times. Each time Ashley had seemed remote, detached.

"She's alive," he said in a whisper.

"My God," Monica blurted. "I mean, my goodness. That's wonderful."

"Yes." He bowed his head and made the sign of the cross.

"Where is she?"

Cardinal Parnell stood wringing his age-mottled hands. "She's being taken to Florida," he finally answered. "And I think that I should be there. And that brings me to my request. I was wondering if you could lend me the use of your aircraft?"

Monica was taken aback, and looked it.

"Your dad keeps bragging about your plane." Cardinal Parnell looked uncomfortable. "How it can be ready to go at a moment's notice."

"Um…" Her pilots had the day off. "Let me check with Patrick and the pilots." Monica punched the speed dial on her cell and left the sacristy. The cathedral was empty except for her family, her nephews clowning around the baptismal font. Quickly, she conferred with Patrick. No question, the cardinal could use the plane, but should they accompany him? They'd both noted how frail he'd looked on the altar. Ashley, alive, was big news, and maybe she could be of some help to the Parnells in this extraordinary circumstance. And while she was there, she could catch up with hot gossip about her niece Jenna and Terry Parnell.

"Dad, what do you think?" she asked, knowing how much having the family together for holidays meant to him.

"Yes, you should go." Nick Monroe put his arms around Monica and Patrick. "We owe Cardinal Parnell so much."

"Thank you, my children," Cardinal Parnell said when Monica and Patrick returned with the good news. He bowed his head and gave them a blessing.

Monica knew she'd never get over the awe of being this man's niece. She thought of Paul Parnell's letter to her — "My request is that you share your identity with the Parnells . . . all I ask is that you embrace the family . . . even though, I'm not worthy, I am so proud of you. I pray that you can forgive me . . ."

She had renounced the money, but perhaps she could be helpful to the family.

CHAPTER THIRTY-NINE

Rory knew that something was going on. Something important. Why else would Frank be spending a holiday with them? He'd never made a secret about how he felt about her noisy kids. But now he seemed so genuinely caring. What was he up to? And what about Gina and Terry driving across the state for Thanksgiving? And Dan to join them later? Still, a nagging concern clouded this togetherness. Were they doing this for her, knowing this would be her last holiday? If so, she was pleased because she considered the effort a tribute. So much better to have her loved ones here while she was still alive. She grieved for Carla and Ashley and her parents, but took comfort in knowing she'd see them soon. Today, despite the gnawing pain in every bone and her exhaustion, she'd be thankful.

Rory got around mostly by wheelchair now, and just as she was wheeling herself into her dressing room, she heard the roar of an engine, followed by excited barking. From her bedroom window, she watched two large dogs leap out of the back of a shiny red truck. Labs, one black, the other yellow. Beautiful dogs, but — Tyler was allergic. Before she could call Chan, nine kids, including Tyler, surrounded the animals. Maybe Tyler would be okay now that Chan had started him on allergy shots.

As Rory selected among her robes for something cheerful, she heard a tentative knock, and Gina asked, "Rory, is it okay if I come in?"

Gina walked in and the two women embraced. Rory was free of intravenous lines and feeding tubes, but down to ninety pounds. Gina, the picture of health, helped Rory select matching sandals and a festive scarf.

"You're a very special person, Gina." Rory's voice was almost drowned out by boisterous kids and friendly barks. "Your dogs?"

"They come with Dan. Lucy and Lucky. They're great with kids, so not to worry. Anyway, Terry's out there to keep them in line, assisted by Carrie, Where Matt is these days, you'll find my daughter." Gina smiled. "I think they're a super couple."

"That's great," Rory said, a shadow crossing her hopeful spirit. Four daughters and she'd never see them develop romantic relationships. But they'd have Chan, she kept reminding herself.

"So," Gina said, "let's talk about today. Sounds like the Tallys have the dinner under control, so could I ask if we could all meet in the library in a little while for a discussion?"

"Why?" Rory asked. It had to be something about Dad's trust. What else could they want to discuss? Of course, that was why Frank had come to Florida. He must have found a legal away around the test approach. "I don't think I'm up to it," she said. Money and property and wills and trusts were the last things she waned to discuss.

"Chan can sit in for me."

"Rory, please, join us. It's important."

Rory looked into Gina's dark eyes and saw the crinkle of a smile. What was going on? Had the kids prepared some kind of performance and Gina was the adult sent to insure her presence?

"Okay," she said. "Let's face the music."

In the library, Chan, Frank, Matt, Terry, and Carrie were already seated. Frank cleared his throat as if he were to address the Senate. "I have some phenomenal news," he said. "I think it will come as a surprise to you, Rory and Chan, and to you, Terry. Ashley is alive," Frank said with no more preamble.

While Rory gasped, Frank explained about Ashley and Welton. He also informed the group that Monica, Patrick, and Cardinal Sean were on their way.

"What took her so long?" Chan demanded. "Rory needed her and she's too scared to show herself? That doesn't cut it with me."

"Chan," Gina said, "she was pregnant. She would have been concerned for the baby."

"And now she's lost the baby." Rory gently massaged Chan's arm, calming him.

"Oh, shit!" Terry jumped up, his eyes darting around the room. He repeated, "Oh, shit."

Gina rose and spun Terry around to face her. "Terry, such language. Why—?"

"Why?" he shouted. "Because Conrad called me. Because of me, he knows that Ashley is headed here. I didn't know he was persona non grata and took for granted that he'd want to be with her. He said she'd need to spend time with her family and that he'd see— God, I feel like such an idiot."

"Don't worry," Frank reassured the young man. "Dan and the private investigator are with her. Our security will keep her safe until we decide if we need to take further precautions. This is not your fault. We should have told you all. Not left anybody in the dark."

Rory lowered her head and smiled. "Ashley is alive. She's coming here. I have one of my sisters back."

For the first time in many months, Rory felt a pang of hope. She could almost feel Ashley's bone marrow trickling into her system, Ashley's cells replacing her diseased ones. The process would be long and demanding and she'd be isolated from her kids for weeks to prepare for the graft. But maybe, with Ashley's HLA match, she'd be one of the lucky ones with leukemia to see her children grow up. She'd hardly dared wish for a complete remission, but now—

"Chan," she said, "let's tell the kids!"

CHAPTER FORTY

When Welton was honest with himself, he'd always known that it would come to this. Too much duplicity, avarice, disrespect. He had no choice. They had underestimated him, a being of superior intelligence.

Welton had met Buzz Riley years earlier when he'd been on staff at the Menninger Clinic, and Buzz an inmate at Leavenworth. Conrad's research in hypnosis had included a study of the criminally insane, and it had introduced him to Buzz. Buzz was one of the smartest human beings that Welton had ever met, and Buzz was completely without a sense of right and wrong. But, he was the perfect hypnosis subject. Thanks to Welton's skill, Buzz Riley won parole long before the completion of a thirty-year sentence for homicide.

Other than genius, Buzz and Welton had something else in common. They had both executed their fathers, Welton, opportunistically in a hospital elevator, Buzz with a baseball bat as the old man slept. And Buzz had come in handy as a mastermind and executioner of Lenore, Stanley Welton's first wife, and Crissy.

Welton had multiple contingency plans in place for Buzz when it came to the Parnells, but with a fortuitous stroke of fate, they were consolidating. Except for Monica — not a concern as she'd already renounced the Parnell money — all the family would be together on Longboat Key for Thanksgiving. An unexpected bonus for Welton. All were innocently gathering for the family holiday, awaiting Ashley's return. All in one place, at one time.

Now as Welton waited for Buzz to join him in the private terminal at Philadelphia International Airport, he checked his watch. If his plane took off as scheduled, they'd be in Sarasota at 3:10 p.m., almost two hours before Ashley was to arrive. Buzz had everything he needed in place, and Welton had no desire to know the details. Buzz had never come close to being caught, but if he were, his brain would be empty of any association with Conrad Welton. The wonders of hypnosis harnessed.

"Dr. Welton, sorry I'm late." A wiry guy, his gray hair in a pony tail, rushed to the doctor, the lone passenger in the departure lounge. He wore black jeans, a black long-sleeved pullover shirt, and black running shoes. "Let me get your bag, doc," Buzz said, easily hoisting Welton's luggage. "I ain't got much stuff. I'll be outta there tonight, a night on the road and back home tomorrow."

Welton didn't ask his hit man where *home* was. A telephone number was all that connected them. And that number would be changed tomorrow.

"Let's get on that plane. Your name on the manifest is Bernie Reed."

"Same initials as mine. Cool, doc."

Welton planned to deepen Buzz's hypnotic state once they settled into the small jet. He had no doubt that Buzz would perform. He had before, and would again. Longboat Key would be treated to spectacular fireworks that night.

CHAPTER FORTY-ONE

Monica showed up at the Executive Terminal at Detroit Metropolitan Airport without makeup except for lip gloss, a ticket to anonymity. Patrick looked his casual best in chinos and a golf shirt, and the cardinal was in uniform. The starched Roman collar with the clerical black suit and crimson skullcap looked anything but casual.

"Where does he think we're headed?" Patrick stage-whispered into Monica's ear as the old man walked down the aisle in front of them. "A religious service? Maybe to dedicate a basilica?"

"Cardinal Parnell, let me help you with that," Patrick said, taking the black valise and the slim garment bag and setting it on a vacant seat.

"Traveling light," Monica said, taking the seat across the aisle from the cardinal.

"Yes, and thank you both, again," he said.

Monica heard the tremor in his voice, once famous for powerful orations, a voice that inspired and motivated. Monica attempted small talk, but the cardinal seemed preoccupied. Perhaps he was exhausted from the two Masses, one at dawn for the nuns and the high Mass that she'd attended. But she was eager to use this private audience to get some questions answered.

"Cardinal Parnell," she began reverently. "Did you know my mother well?"

"No," he answered, with only a blank stare.

Monica found that strange, since the Parnell brothers had been close. Or had Paul confessed to his brother, thus the vow of secrecy?

Finally, he said, "Your father told me that she was a very beautiful woman, Monica. She had long black hair and very dark eyes — like you. He told me that you look just like her."

"I do have another question, Your Eminence. When you took me to the Monroes, I was three months old. Why wait three months? Why not an immediate adoption right from the hospital?"

His voice grew weaker. "Perhaps she wanted to keep you, but found it too difficult — a child — a career?"

Monica felt deflated. "What kind of woman was she?" she asked, pressing the old man.

The cardinal's shoulders sagged and his head drooped. "Carl knew her. You should ask him. I really don't know much. He's the one who made the deal."

"Deal?"

The old man blinked, and his eyes fluttered closed. "Ask Carl for the details if you wish. Paul always regretted not just telling Vivian about you. There was no need to arrange an adoption. Vivian was a dear woman."

"My parents always wondered why you, personally, arranged my adoption. Mom figured that I must have been related to a wealthy donor to the church. Still, I owe you so much."

As the old man's eyelids drooped and he lowered his face into his hands, Monica pressed one more question. "Could you tell me how my birth mother died?"

Silence. Maybe he hadn't heard her. She was about to ask again when she saw tears trickling down the wrinkled cheeks. "So many memories," he whispered. "She contracted AIDS and died in 1995."

"What got him all teary eyed?" Patrick whispered once the old man began to snore lightly.

"The Parnell family is totally dysfunctional," she said. "Thank God, I'm a Monroe."

The tarmac serving private flights at the Sarasota airport was empty when the Gulfstream landed, and Monica and Patrick each took one of Cardinal Parnell's elbows as they headed toward the terminal.

"No media," Monica remarked to Patrick as she glanced about. "That's a relief."

"No one knows we're here," Patrick said. "Until this morning, we didn't even know we would be here."

"Uh-oh," Monica whispered, as a man emerged from the terminal and headed toward them.

CHAPTER FORTY-TWO

Rory had settled on the sofa in the family room as Gina prepared a nebulizer treatment for Tyler.

"Mom, I'm okay." Tyler wheezed. "It wasn't the dogs' fault."

"It's nobody's fault," Rory said. "We're lucky Aunt Gina's here to give you a treatment. I guess those shots haven't started to work yet. You're going to have to stay away from those dogs."

Gina was measuring the proper dose of Ventolin. "Should we call Chan?" she asked.

"We can let him know," Rory said, "but it's okay to repeat the Ventolin three times."

"Mrs. Stevens," Leo Tally stood at the entrance to the room, wringing his large, dark hands. "I hate to interrupt. But it's the twins, ma'am."

"Chip and Charlie?"

"Yes, ma'am. The kids have been comin' and goin' like normal from the pool all afternoon. But I haven't seen Chip or Charlie for an hour. They were horsing around the pool when the dogs started barking something fierce." He paused for a breath. "The boys said they were going out to investigate. I told them not to go beyond the fence. Not to go down to the beach. I put the dogs in the garage. And I waited down by the pool. But the twins are not back. I called security at the main gate and at the private gate. Nobody has seen them. They're not in the house either. Those two are full of their pranks, but I'm worried —"

Tally's voice terrified Rory. At five o'clock on Thanksgiving night, this unflappable man seemed way too concerned. She directed him to take another look.

"I'd like to send a security guard off the property to look around," Tally said in parting, "just in case they wandered off."

Welton's plane arrived in Sarasota at 3:05 p.m. Buzz Riley deplaned first and headed directly for a rental van. In the meantime Welton gave the pilot instructions to refuel, get something to eat, and be ready for departure shortly after five. The flight plan would be Sarasota to Las Vegas. Once he had Ashley on board, he intended to marry in Vegas the following day. They'd be man and wife by the time Ashley learned that the rest of her family had been killed in a major explosion.

From then on she would have him to lean on. There'd be no more intercourse, of course. Since pregnancy no longer offered an advantage, he could avoid the problem of his painful penis disorder. Instead, he could easily program Ashley's mind to feel sexually satisfied.

Welton was a world expert in hypnosis. His indirect, authoritative techniques, pioneered by Milton Erickson, founding president of the American Society for Clinical Hypnosis, and a mentor, had now excelled the older man's. Welton knew that the subconscious mind is neither logical nor analytical, and that Ashley had a favorable proclivity for hypnotic suggestion. She'd been adequately programmed that life with him was her destiny, that she needed him for her very survival. All he needed was physical proximity to reinforce his implanted induction techniques.

He went over his plan one more time. Ashley would arrive with Dan and the private investigator in two hours. He would greet her with flowers and a loving welcome. If Dan gave him any flack, Welton would remind him that he was the one who'd insisted that Ashley was alive. And that he was the obvious choice to oversee her recovery. He was sure that once close to Ashley — close enough to physically touch her — she'd readily agree.

Welton heard men's voices outside the terminal. One he recognized. It was Frank Parnell, talking to an attendant. Here to meet Ashley. That surprised him. Keeping his head down, Welton stepped into a small hall leading to the restrooms. Shielding his face with a newspaper, he glanced around the corner. Frank stood with Chandler Stevens. He heard one of their cell phones ring, then Chan's voice. "Rory wants me back at the house," he said. "Tyler's having an asthma attack and she's worried that he might need oxygen. I'll jump in a cab."

"No," Frank said, in a tone worthy of a senatorial vote. "Take the Rover and have Leo Tally come back for us."

Welton remembered what Ashley had told him. That her father kept three vehicles at each property, a Mercedes sedan, a Porshe 911, and a Land Rover. The same model and color at both places.

"Okay," Chan said with no argument. "I'm sure Tyler will be fine, I just want Rory not to worry."

Chan left, and Frank lingered just outside the door to the terminal.

Welton stayed in the small corridor until he heard the approach of a plane and he saw Frank head toward the door leading to the tarmac. He checked his watch. Four fifty-five. Showtime.

"We arranged to have you taken directly to the house," Monica told the cardinal. "Even though you'll be staying at the rectory on Longboat. Oh, that's Frank over there, isn't it?" Monica pointed to the man walking out onto the tarmac.

As the cardinal responded, Monica was distracted by the roar of a small jet about to land. She felt strangely unprotected.

"What a coincidence." Frank strode toward them. "I figured your plane was Ashley and Dan's."

Patrick shaded his eyes to follow Monica's gaze to the arriving plane. "A Lear. Isn't that the Parnell aircraft?"

CHAPTER FORTY-THREE

Ashley and Dan had fallen into an easy conversation that revealed how kind and gentle her stranger-brother was. So different in every way from Frank. They looked a lot alike, but Dan had none of Frank's hard-driving ambition. He told her that he lived on a dirt road in the middle of nothing but palm trees.

"My barn is four times bigger than my house. Big enough for all that heavy equipment including my favorite toy, a new John Deere."

"I never knew much about you, Dan," Ashley said. "Naturally I saw you at some of the family affairs, but you were always in and out so fast. And I was sort of shy."

"Only thing I knew to talk about was soil and insects and rain and my palm trees. The queen palms are my favorites. I like them even better than coconuts, the signature palm of —" Dan stopped. "But I'm boring you with all this. You, with everything that's on your mind."

"I can't tell you how wonderful it is to be talking about simple, ordinary things," Ashley said, curling her feet under her in the oversized seat.

Ashley felt a pang of envy when Dan spoke of his remarriage to Gina. Dan was so happy and she was so miserable. Sad, confused, scared, ashamed. She patted her flat abdomen. But Dan had lost everything once and now he was so vibrant and alive. Would that ever happen to her?

"Dan, what happened between you and Gina?" Ashley asked, needing to find something to keep her mind off what may lie ahead.

"We were students in Miami when we fell in love and married. I told her that I was an orphan."

"You did?" Ashley's look was wide-eyed.

"I was selfish and I wanted her to love me for myself, not because I was a Parnell. I worked for a messenger service, and I never told her about the money that Dad sent as an allowance. Gina graduated from the nursing school just one month before the twins were born. She took a night-shift job in the emergency room when the babies were six weeks old. I still had one more year of school, but I was so exhausted taking care of the babies when Gina worked, that I quit going to classes and didn't tell her."

Ashley had never seen this side of Dan. He'd always been so aloof and remote.

"Then everything collapsed. Uncle Carl showed up at our place. The issue was an inheritance I was to get on my twenty-third birthday, a trust fund left by my mother. It came as a lump sum of one and a half million dollars. The babies were then three months old. No one at home even knew I was married. Gina was about to leave for her shift at the hospital that day when Uncle Carl showed up at the door of our rented apartment. That's when she found out that I'd built our life on a lie."

"Oh, how horrible," Ashley said, for the first time her mind fixed on a problem not her own.

"Gina simply left with the babies. I had betrayed her. She assumed that I thought she wasn't good enough for my family."

Dan looked so distraught that Ashley leaned across the aisle to touch his shoulder.

"Did you go after her?" Ashley asked.

"No," he said, lowering his head and pausing for a moment. "Cowardice. Pride. They say that pride is the worst of all the sins. But, Gina and I are together again."

"How about your son and daughter? Are they pleased about you and Gina?"

"Yes," Dan said, sounding tentative. "But Terry had a reaction that concerns me, shames me even. All those years the twins were growing up, I'd never considered that Gina's rejection of the Parnell money might not have extended to them. Terry thinks that I should have made an effort to help them financially."

"That's all changed now," Ashley said, feeling inadequate to advise anybody.

"Terry most definitely wants his share of the trust. I told him I'd do whatever it takes to pass Dad's test. Frankly, I don't have a clue as to what to do."

Ashley gave him a sympathetic pat on the arm. "Dad's test, Dan, is at the root of what's happened to me. Conrad is desperate for *me* to pass that test. And after I do, I'm afraid he will destroy me."

"We won't let him near you, I swear. The compound in Florida has several layers of security." Dan glanced back at Preston sitting in the row behind them. "Jack will see that it's reinforced like Fort Knox."

Ashley tried to accept Dan's confident promise. But she knew that Conrad would not give up on controlling her. But if she could stay safe for the next six weeks, until the money was dispersed, she'd look for a pediatric residency starting in January. Maybe in Tampa, so she could be close to Rory. Or New Mexico, near Ruthie. Still, she could not shake the image of Crissy. In the undertaker's limousine at the cemetery.

Welton headed toward the tarmac, two dozen yellow roses in his arms. But the plane was a Gulfstream, not the Parnell Learjet. He saw a second plane was approaching the runway — the Parnell aircraft this time. Clutching the bouquet to his chest, he watched as three individuals deplaned the Gulfstream — Monica Monroe and Patrick Nelson helping Ashley's uncle, the cardinal.

Welton watched as Frank Parnell walked over to greet the trio. Lightheaded now, he gasped as he felt a wild flipping in his chest — paroxysmal superventricular tachycardia. Once he'd lost consciousness with an attack. *That could not happen now.* Welton told himself to breath slowly, not to hyperventilate. Use your mantra. "I will not give up." He repeated this five times. Once between each labored breath.

CHAPTER FORTY-FOUR

Rory waited in the family room, rigid with fear over the missing twins. Carrie and Gina flanked her on the sofa, each trying to distract her with small talk. She'd sent Tyler to his room, his breathing much improved with the treatment. Chan was on the way back from the airport. She needed him, not for Tyler now, but to help find Chip and Charlie. Leo Tally had been gone for ten minutes, searching for the boys. Terry had ended a long phone conversation with Jenna, Monica's niece, who'd surprised him with the news that Monica and Patrick would be flying in later in the day. She didn't know why they'd made such sudden plans, but to Terry's delight, Jenna would be driving in from Tampa that evening. When Terry came in to inform Rory, she'd been too distracted to hear him out, immediately asking him to go out and look for the twins.

Terry had been gone only a few moments when he ran back inside. "They found Mr. Tally," he shouted.

"How about Chip? Charlie?" Carrie asked, jumping up.

"Are they okay?" When Rory tried to pull herself out of the wheelchair, her body buckled.

"The property security man found Mr. Tally in the dune grass by the beach," Terry said in a rush. "Rory, he's been shot! We've called the police — an ambulance." Rory could hear sirens in the background.

"Where are my boys?" Rory rasped.

"We don't know. The police are on their way. "

"Chip and Charlie are out there. And there's a gunman on the loose?" Rory's voice was hoarse with strain. "The rest of the kids?"

Carrie answered. "Tyler and Rick are in their room. The girls were with Ann, setting the table."

"Ann just ran out to be with Leo," Terry reported. "Emily and Becky gathered the younger girls in the library. There's a security guard with them. Rory, I promise you, they're okay, but the twins —"

"Please bring them in here, all the kids," Rory said. "I need to have them with me."

Carrie and Gina returned with the two younger boys, all the Stevens girls, and Elise. They all surrounded Rory with terrified expressions on their innocent faces.

"They were in the pool fooling around, and all of a sudden they were gone." Becky said. "I didn't pay much attention."

"From what you're telling me," Rory recapped, "they were last seen about four o'clock." She stared at her watch. "An hour ago."

The doorbell chimed, followed by a loud pounding.

"The police," Carrie bolted for the front door.

Monica and Patrick stood with the cardinal on the tarmac, waiting for the passengers on the Lear to deplane, surprised that Frank had met their plane, and also relieved that Ashley was aboard the second jet. They had thought to make their way to the terminal to allow Ashley a private reunion with Frank, but the cardinal made no effort to move on.

"There's Dan," Frank pointed to the first to step off the plane. "And Ashley with dark, short hair. She looks shaky. We should have arranged a wheelchair."

Monica glanced back toward the terminal. A man was walking directly toward them, carrying a bunch of yellow roses that obscured his face. She felt a trickle of annoyance. No one was supposed to know she was here, but the paparazzi had their networks.

The pounding in his chest diminishing, Welton tried to focus on the scene playing out on the tarmac. Too many Parnells milling about. He had to extract Ashley from the group, get her out quickly, efficiently, onto his waiting jet. He strode out, roses in his arms, like a one-man welcoming party. Ashley looked horrible. Her hair was chopped off and she was very, very pale. For a moment he wondered whether she'd been so traumatized on September eleven that her physical health had deteriorated. Well, no matter, he'd have her happy and fit in no time. He would easily erase the New York City atrocities from her mind.

All eyes focused on Ashley, Dan, and the private investigator who looked hefty enough to double as security detail. Crane may have been right. This big man could be trouble. But Welton would not let even a giant prevent Ashley leaving with her future husband.

As the passengers from both aircrafts and Frank converged in a group hug, Welton approached. Then Ashley spotted him. Her scream pierced the air.

For an instant, Welton panicked. This was not the response he'd hoped for. He stepped toward her with a brisk step, nevertheless. "For you, my love," he blurted, offering her the flowers. With one shoulder, he nudged Dan aside to get close enough to squeeze her arm, to fling an arm around her, gather her body to his. Then, pulled back into his induction mode, she would come without complaint.

Ashley pulled away. "No!" she screamed again.

In an instant the huge man pulled her out of Conrad's reach. And in the same instant, Welton felt a tug and a frail hand grasp his pant pocket. Ashley's uncle, the cardinal, his face oddly contorted, canted forward against Welton. Welton elbowed the old man back. Words were coming out of the cardinal's mouth. "Your mother must have loved you so."

"The fuck about my mother."

"Stand back, you." The huge man spoke in a deep, commanding tone. Welton dropped the flowers.

In his head he heard Winston Churchill say, "Don't give up!" He forced himself to breathe slowly, just as he'd trained so many others to do. He had to keep the heart rate steady with mind control. Deep breaths, he coached himself — in and out — a type of self-hypnosis. Consider your choices. But there was only one. Welton reached for his weapon.

CHAPTER FORTY-FIVE

The first detective to arrive at the house assured the family that the Longboat Key chief of police was on his way. The Sarasota Police Department had also been notified. Rory thrust a picture in front of the detective — two freckle-faced boys with auburn hair and brown eyes ready to tackle a birthday cake with ten candles. Then she heard the roar of motors that signaled the arrival of three more police cars, followed by the familiar engine of the Land Rover.

The family was still in the family room and Chan bolted past it, heading for the boys' bedroom. What must he be thinking with the police vehicles out there?

"Chan, no," Rory called, and Carrie ran out to catch up with him.

"Tyler's fine, Chan, but we need you here."

Chan turned to gape, and Carrie grabbed his arm and pulled him into the family room.

"Dad, Chip and Charlie are missing." Emily had attached herself to him, tugging on his shirt. "Mr. Tally's shot. We don't know where the twins are —"

"Rory?" Chan asked as four uniformed and two plainclothes officers stepped toward him, everyone talking at once over the chatter of radios.

Carrie stepped up. She briefed both the police and Chan. How they'd found Mr. Tally lying in the dune grass on the beach.

"Tyler's okay?" Chan touched his youngest son's cheek.

"We're starting a manhunt," a more senior police officer announced. "Do you have a blueprint of the property?"

"I don't know," Chan said. "And I don't have time to mess around trying to find one. I'm going to find my kids. It'll be dark soon."

"We'll take the dogs," Carrie said. "They love those kids. If anybody can find them right away, it'll be Lucky and Lucy."

Rory slumped in the wheelchair, her four daughters and two sons fidgeting at her side. Terry and Carrie had gotten the dogs, and Chan, with a local police officer and a detective were searching the property perimeter. To the rear of the estate was the road, effectively blocked by fencing. To the front, the ocean. To either side, similar estates, all isolated by fencing hidden in lush landscape. A burly plainclothes policeman announced to the group that security was down across the entire estate. The state of the art security surrounding the outside perimeter, each of the buildings, and motion detectors throughout were all non-functional.

The chaotic scene was further interrupted by raucous barking. Dan's dogs were going crazy over something or somebody. In response, the family moved from the family room to the patio outside, Gina guiding Rory's chair.

"Mom, are you okay?" Rory heard a familiar young voice call out over the barking dogs. "Mom!" coming from the direction of the beach.

The dogs barked harder and strained at their leashes.

"Mom!" Karen screamed, running out. "That's Charlie!"

Rory grimaced. So this had all been a trick. The twins had been hiding, planning a joke on all of them. Now, with the dogs barking, they must have crawled out of their hiding places. She felt relief *and* anger.

"Mom, Mom?" Charlie ran to her side. "We heard the sirens —"

Rory opened her eyes. "Charlie, you had us terrified —" Then she remembered the security system. Disabling such a sophisticated system would be far too complicated for ten-year-olds.

"Where's Chip?"

"He's still dragging the guy. I ran up to make sure that you were okay. We got scared, Mom, when we saw the ambulance."

"Guy? What guy?"

A cacophony of voices rose from the front of the house. Rory tried to stand, teetered, then slipped back into the wheelchair, as Chip, in his bathing suit, ran to her side.

"Mom, you're not going to believe this," Chip began. "Me and Charlie tracked him in the sand. He was crawling like a dog."

"More like a snake," his twin corrected.

"Then we tied him up, right, Charlie?"

"Yup. Wait'll we tell Dad."

Rory put an arm around each wet, sturdy body and pulled them close to her, confused, but no longer terrified. When she looked up, four sheriff's deputies were dragging a man dressed in black, a cap over his head, a ski mask obscuring his face, across the lawn. The man was tied up, hands and feet with strips of beach towel. Chip and Charlie joined the others standing over their prisoner; both were clearly proud of themselves.

"Chip, Charlie," Chan's voice shouted from the driveway amid the barking dogs.

"I'll put the dogs in the garage," Carrie said, patting Tyler on the head.

As soon as the family gathered on the front deck, Chan began his story. "First of all, Mr. Tally is going to be okay. Before going into surgery, he said that he'd gone out to look for the boys, and he found a man wearing all black circling the house. He was laying out some wires. Mr. Tally followed him when he went out toward the beach. In the tall dunes, the man had opened a box hidden under a tarp, and Mr. Tally asked the man what he was doing. And the man turned around and shot him. But Mr. Tally had a stun gun behind his back. Even after he'd been hit, he'd got a shot off. Then he passed out."

"It turned out the boys were wandering on the beach, where they were not supposed to be without adult supervision, and found the man — still with residual effects of the Taser — crawling along the dunes."

"We knew he was a bad guy 'cause of the mask," Chip said. "So we jumped on him."

"Yeah, he had a knife and we used it to cut up our towels so we could tie him up," Charlie concluded with a wide grin. "So you're not gonna punish us now that we're heroes, right?"

CHAPTER FORTY-SIX

Welton yanked the Colt out of his pants pocket. He'd never fired it, not even in target practice.

"Stand back," he yelled, waving the gun, wildly. "Ashley, come with me. Now, my love!"

He almost smirked as Frank and Dan stood dumbfounded. Monica and Patrick stared. But the big man, Preston, did not release Ashley.

"Let her go," Welton ordered. "Or I will shoot. Not her, but —" He swung the gun to target Monica. "Come to me, Ashley."

She made as if to step forward, but Preston held her back. "I'll go with him," she said. "I can do it —"

The cardinal came at Welton again, stumbling into him, grabbing him in the awkward clutch of an older person. Maybe it was the feeble tug or maybe just the distraction, but Welton's grasp loosened, and the gun fell to the pavement with a thud.

"Welton stared at his empty hand an instant before plunging to the ground, desperate to retrieve the weapon, ignoring the old cardinal who kept flailing at him with weak, but purposeful blows. Then he heard a woman's name, "Jessica."

By the time his hand touched steel, he heard a voice boom. "Stop right there or I'll shoot." It was Preston.

Bent over, but without hesitation, Conrad turned toward Preston and pulled the trigger. A grunt. The gun in the big man's hand fell onto the blacktop.

Welton got to his feet, seeming more dazed than amazed that he'd hit his target. He'd disarmed the only professional in the crowd, and blood began to saturate the big man's sports coat. The Parnells, except for the cardinal, who lay on the ground panting, seemed in shock.

All Welton had to do now was get Ashley out. He reached her and grabbed for her arm, but not soon enough. Frank inserted himself, pulling his sister just beyond Welton's reach. The cardinal was mumbling words that distracted Welton so that he did not see Dan lean over to pick up Preston's gun. "Jessica, my love, why didn't you tell me? Our son — we could have —" Welton cringed at the tears streaming down the old man's wrinkled face as he slowly rose and grasped the sleeve of Welton's jacket. There was the blast of a gun and the cardinal fell forward, forcing Welton to take a step back. A second blast. Welton's eyes widened, fixated on Ashley as he fell over the cardinal's body.

Dan grimaced after his second shot. How could he have anticipated Cardinal Sean thrusting himself in front of Welton? He gazed dully ahead, the gun still in his hand, heavy as a boulder. Patrick, having grabbed Monica, shielded her with his body, Ashley had knelt to tend to Preston, and Frank stood staring at the ground at Welton sprawled on top of Cardinal Sean. Dan choked back a cry and gasped. He'd shot his own uncle, a helpless, innocent old man. He dropped to his knees, brushing against the fallen crimson skullcap. Was Cardinal Sean dead? No, he was saying something. Dan hefted Welton's body off his uncle as he heard feet running in the background. The cardinal reached out, managing to clutch a handful of Welton's shirt, now soaked in blood. "Conrad, my boy," he sobbed.

"What's he saying?" Frank had joined Dan on the ground, Monica and Patrick, on their feet, staring down.

Cardinal Sean struggled to sit up while refusing to let go of Welton's shirt. He kept repeating. "Please . . . forgive me . . . oh, my God . . ."

"Dan, can you figure out what he's saying?" Frank said.

"No!" Reality overtook shock, and Dan yelled, "Get an ambulance, for God's sake." Patrick began to dial 911. Dan turned back to Cardinal Sean, leaning over him protectively. He was still refusing to let go of Welton's shirt. "Cardinal Sean, please, stop." Dan took the veined hand, prying it free from Welton. "You're hurt. Lie still." He felt a sticky warmth seeping through the black clerical suit.

"Dan, don't let him die." Cardinal Sean's voice was barely audible. "He is my son. Help him."

Dan looked to Frank for his reaction. But his brother was directing the arriving paramedics, who surrounded the cardinal and began their lifesaving duties. Dan stepped back and breathed a sigh of relief as Ashley knelt at Preston's side, pressing her jacket against his shoulder. Two more paramedics headed their way. To Dan, it seemed as if the only fatality was Welton.

The entire area was swarming with cops, who took the gun away from Dan and led him into the terminal. Glancing back, he saw Welton's body lying on the blacktop. He was being left for the medical examiner. Monica and Patrick gave statements and left, but Frank and Ashley stayed by Dan's side during his lengthy interrogation. Pending further investigation, Dan was released and helped into the car by the shaken Frank and Ashley.

CHAPTER FORTY-SEVEN

As the three siblings left the charter terminal, heading toward the Longboat Key compound, Ashley's emotions went from guilt to relief to sadness to a glimmer of hope. Conrad could threaten her no more. She would make the bone marrow gift to Rory as soon as possible. She would dedicate herself to medicine. She would spend her holidays with Ruthie. She was feeling positive for the first time in weeks, until they all gasped at the sight of at least five police cars gathered at the compound.

Chan, surrounded by his children, ushered her out of the car. They were all talking at once. I'm taking Aunt Ashley in to see Mom first," Chan said to them. "We can get caught up later."

It was Rory who related to Ashley how Chip and Charlie had apprehended a man who had planted explosives to dynamite the compound. Ashley didn't have to be told that the villain was Conrad. She had loved and gotten pregnant by a madman. The thought of her vulnerability over the past weeks made her shiver. This was all her fault. Because of her weakness, her whole family could have been killed.

"He's dead, Ashley. He'll never be able to hurt you again." Rory kept saying.

Once the police had left and the younger children were put to bed, Chan took the phone call they were all awaiting. All were silent as he spoke to the doctor at Sarasota Memorial Hospital. "Jack Preston's wound was superficial and they'll release him tomorrow morning," Chan reported to concerned faces. "And Cardinal Sean is doing as well as can be expected. The bullet lodged in his lung, but it missed the major blood vessels. They had to take out a section of the lung. There may be complications. That's all we know. He's in intensive care and we can't see him until tomorrow."

Dan moaned, "It was an accident. He got in the way —" And, as if reliving the scene, he said, "Cardinal Sean kept saying something very strange. That Conrad was his son —"

Ashley frowned. "Naturally, all priests call sinners 'my son.'"

Cardinal Sean spent three days in intensive care. He tolerated the lung surgery amazingly well, and by the fourth day, the doctors had him up and about. When he insisted on saying Mass in the nondenominational chapel, the family agreed to attend. In borrowed vestments with no trace of ceremonial crimson, the cardinal celebrated Mass from his wheelchair. The service was short, and afterward the family gathered in the hospital's executive conference room for brunch.

The cardinal, now in a golf shirt and slacks, began. "Thank you all for being here. I can't tell you how much it means to me." Between the wheezes, he reminded the group that he had offered Mass for the souls of Carla and Meredith. As well as for my brother, Paul, and Conrad Welton — the son I never knew I had."

A loud, collective gasp followed, but no one said a word. Ashley buried her head in her hands. The father of her baby — her uncle's son — her cousin.

The old man continued. "Did you know that we were not always rich? That my father, your grandfather, was the youngest of seventeen children?" More gasps. "Only nine survived childhood. And somehow my father got an education at Penn, married my mother, whose father, your great-grandfather, was an immigrant and one of the founders of the stock exchange in Boston."

Cardinal Sean continued. "Dad made a name for himself in the banking business so Paul and I never experienced poverty, to say the least. I remember when Paul went off to the army, right out of high school. It was the Second World War and mother was inconsolable. He got sent to Guam right after boot camp. That's when my mother extracted from me a promise — a promise that I would be a priest. That I'd never have to go to war. I explained over and over that priests were chaplains, that they died on battlefields. She didn't want to hear it. To placate her, I promised. I was sixteen when I started the seminary."

Dan glanced around the table: everybody spellbound. Where the hell was the old man going with this?

"Sort of like the medieval days," he went on, attempting a chuckle. "Eldest son inherits. Second son goes to the Church. Anyway, your father made it back from the Pacific, and you know the rest."

After a dry cough, and a sip of water, Cardinal Sean proceeded. "I was twenty-five that summer. My last summer vacation at home in Philadelphia before I was to be ordained a priest. Actually, it started early for me because I came down with appendicitis and had to have emergency surgery. Jefferson Hospital. I had a nurse. Something quite shocking happened between me and this particular nurse. It was a bond, an attraction I couldn't explain even to myself. Other than my mother, I had never been close to a woman. I had no sisters. I'd been in the seminary since age sixteen. I had never had a date. I had never even held hands with a girl."

Dan realized that he'd never known this man, his uncle.

"It was the same year that your father was dating Kay. I recovered from the operation with horrible reluctance." Cardinal Sean cast a wistful smile as he toyed with his water glass. "On the day that I was discharged, Paul and Kay came to pick me up. They were young and fun and very happy. My nurse was there, and I introduced her to them. Paul said that they were taking me to a place they had rented on the Jersey shore. So I threw out an invitation for Jessica to come with us. Jessica Long, R.N. 'I might need a nurse,' I said, all the while pleading with my eyes that she understand my need to continue to see her. My heart leapt as she accepted. We grew so close so quickly. For the first time, I shared my doubts about my vocation. That I wasn't sure. That I didn't know if I had a true vocation, or if I was doing this to please my mother — Paul used to joke that I went to the seminary to be Mama's pet. And Jessica told me about her life. How she'd grown up in Ohio, graduated tops in her nursing class, and was at Jefferson to finish off a bachelor's degree. She also told me she was about to become engaged to an orthopedic surgeon in Cincinnati. Did she love him, she kept wondering. She said she didn't know. We became lovers. At the end of the second week, Mother showed up as we lay on a blanket on the beach — in an intimate embrace."

"What did you do, Cardinal Sean?" Ashley prompted.

Cardinal Sean's voice trembled as he continued, "Ashamed to be caught by my mother. Ashamed that I did not know my own mind. Just tasting what I now know was love, yet afraid to veer from the path laid out for me. Not knowing where to go, I went home with Mother. I finished the seminary. Was ordained. Never saw Jessica again. Never — ever — held a woman again. Never — ever — forgot Jessica."

"Cardinal Parnell, how difficult." Monica dabbed at tears. "Did you ever try to contact her? The nurse? Jessica?"

"I called the hospital. I was told she'd gone back to Ohio. Much later I found out that she had married that orthopedic doctor and that she had children. Nothing more. What could be gained? I had had my one chance. There would be no other."

Dan looked at Gina, tears welling in his eyes. He, too, had blown a chance, but for him things had turned out so much differently.

"When Carl Schiller called, and told me what the private investigator had found about Conrad and about Jessica, I knew. I felt it like a profound blow. The days, the months, the year — they all fit. Jessica had given birth to my child. If I had known, I would have quit the seminary and married her. And the child, Conrad, was treated so cruelly by a father who was not his own." The old man cast his eyes down. "And then Jessica took her own life. How can I ever forgive myself? How can God forgive me?"

"Cardinal Parnell," Monica murmured, sympathy pouring out of her dark eyes.

"There is no excuse," he preempted her. "My son has been the cause of so much anguish." He bowed his head as if to pray, but no more words came forth.

Finally Ashley said, "Cardinal Sean, the anguish is over; you can't help Conrad now; and it is for the best that our child was not born."

"There's one more thing," Cardinal Sean said, his voice assuming a more authoritative tone. "When they took the bullet out of my lung, they found something else. "Cancer," he said. "Metastatic from somewhere. They want to do more tests, but I told them no. I don't want chemotherapy. I don't want more tests. I'm going back to Detroit. I'll announce my retirement. Get my affairs together."

Everyone locked their eyes on the old man, who seemed to have more to say.

"But, I must tell the story of Conrad. I want people to understand the hardship, the deprivation he suffered because of me, a selfish, spineless man."

"No way," Monica blurted. "That's not going to help anything. It'll only bring more problems to the family, and think of the impact on the church."

"We can't let embarrassment for the family or the church get in the way of the truth," he countered. But the family finally convinced the old man that, in this case, truth would be folly. Dan was the spokesperson. "Cardinal Sean, you've been an exemplary leader. Maybe you weren't sure about your vocation, but I think God was sure. Look at all the good you've done. All the people you've helped." Dan took a break to consider his next move. "Despite all the horrors of the last year," he continued, "our family has survived. We have become closer and stronger. And I, for one, want to put at the top of my agenda, that we, as a family, do everything we can to elect a Parnell president. We owe it to Meredith and to Dad. It was their dream, and now it's up to us to see it through. I'm just a tree farmer, but I intend to throw myself into Frank's campaign."

As Frank registered shock, Ashley said, "We'll all pitch in. Maybe Monica could do one of her fabulous concerts."

Dan's idea elicited excited suggestions for an hour before the nurse wheeled the cardinal away. Afterward, Dan brought up the last piece of unfinished business. "Next month will be the one-year anniversary of Dad's death. Thought I'd check to see what everybody's doing about that inheritance test." One year ago, he'd not have given it a second thought, but he'd promised Terry.

"Forget me," said Monica. "Remember, I renounced it from the beginning."

"I just want to forget it and get on with my life," Ashley said.

"Same for us," said Chan. "We have everything we need except what money can't buy."

"No matter, I think we all owe it to Dad to show up for the test," said Frank, dropping back into command mode, "to respect his legacy. Including Rory, Chan, and Monica."

EPILOGUE

Carl Schiller scheduled the test one year and a day after the reading of Paul Parnell's will. He chose the Devon homestead, where Frank and Elise lived.

Much had happened that year: a botched presidential election, terrorist attacks, homeland security, congressional reaction. A year had passed since Frank had fumed over his father's will. How dare his father impose a test period on his inheritance, he had thought then. How embarrassing that he'd tried to challenge it, he thought now. He still felt every day the fathomless loss of Meredith, Rory's illness, Carla's pointless death, and the psychopath cousin who had tried to kill off the family.

Frank noted that when Monica arrived, she had dyed her hair with red streaks. Elise had read about her new hair in *People* magazine. "Monica, Patrick, good to see you." Frank greeted them. "Caught your show last night — had to sneak off the dais during another fund-raiser. Steve Spurrier was great on the show, but it's not a slam dunk to go from college to the pros."

"Please don't get him started!" Monica said as Frank led them inside. "Are the others here yet?"

"Gina and Dan are coming in on the Lear, Chan with them. Rory's in isolation getting ready for the bone marrow transplant."

"And how is Elise?" Monica asked, settling on the plush sofa.

"If she had her way, we'd live in Florida with the Stevens kids. But we're going to be fine here. I'm keeping the farm so Elise can have horses. And when Chan brings the kids up, they can use the house. I think that's what Meredith would have wanted."

"I'm sure it is," Monica said. She looked at the family portraits. Some with Frank's mother, Kay. Some with Vivian. None with her mother. "You know, I still feel weird about this. I really don't want the trust money. I'm happy just being part of the family."

Family had become important to Frank, too, so he didn't contradict her. Instead, he said, "Here's Ashley!"

"You look so much better." Monica embraced her sister. "Back to your natural hair color."

Ashley, now living in Tampa, could not let that statement go unremarked. "Speaking of hair color —" She looked at her sister quizzically, and Monica grinned.

Everyone had gathered in the living room by the time Carl arrived. They talked first of personal events: Carrie and Matt were engaged, and Terry was still seeing Monica's niece Jenna.

Monica spoke up. "She's crazy about him. But then she's just plain crazy."

The conversation stopped when Carl shuffled to the Sheraton desk in the middle of the room. Frank tried not to notice the palsy as Carl removed some papers from his briefcase. The old man looked sad, defeated, but he had been loyal to Dad up to the end, Frank thought. He glanced about the room. Everyone seemed relaxed, at peace with themselves and each other. A year ago they'd all been strangers.

"I'll get straight to the point," Carl began. "The trust distribution will be based on the stipulations your father set. He provided each of you with written, individual guidance. Your father felt you each needed to make certain life adjustments to bring you into harmony with his personal credo." He bowed his head, then went on, "I will read verbatim what he wanted for you."

"For Dan, involvement in the family. Reconciliation with Gina and his children. I score that a pass."

"For Frank, involvement in the family. Moral leadership in family and government affairs. I score that a pass."

"For Monica, involvement in the family. Forgiveness. A pass."

"For Rory, just be your wonderful self. A definite pass."

"For Ashley, balance of family and medicine. I think we'd all agree, a pass. And Ashley, as special thanks for your gift of bone marrow to Rory."

Carl seemed to have finished. So this was the test that had so shaped their lives?

"And for Carla, Uncle Carl?" Ashley asked softly. "What did Dad want for Carla?"

"For Carla, that she seek help to find inner peace." Carl read. "And for Carla, her inheritance was to be held in trust until I, as the trustee, saw fit to release it."

Dan spoke up. "Is that all there is? No actual test? No number two lead pencils? Proof of performance?"

Carl returned the papers to the briefcase. "I can now distribute a sum of one point eight billion in equal portions to Dan, Frank, Rory, Monica, and Ashley. That's three hundred sixty million each. Congratulations."

"So there was no real test?" Frank looked disappointed.

"Yes, there was, Frank," Carl replied, holding his head high. "When your father knew he was dying, he created this incentive to urge you to accept the moral credo that he himself had embraced. The 'wisdom of age' he kept saying. He felt that in life he had failed you, and perhaps in death he would be more successful. 'If they follow my credo, they'll be truly happy.'" Carl ended his statement with, "Your father could not have anticipated the tragic consequences."

"We mustn't blame him." Gina looked from face to face. "He did what he thought was right. What happened is not his fault."

"Let's make a pact," Dan suggested. "No more speaking of faults. We've all made mistakes, but we must move forward. We have each other; that's what Dad wanted for us. Now how about we head for the airport and take the Lear to pay Cardinal Sean a visit. He's bound to need some cheering up in that nursing home where he insists on staying."

"Not so fast," said Carl. "You have to sign papers, and pick up your millions."

"The papers can wait," Frank said. "I agree with Dan. Let's head for Detroit."

Dan jumped up, pulling Gina with him. "On the way, let's get started on 'Parnell for President.' How about we plan some strategy?"

"Whoa." Frank laughed. "We've unleashed a political machine."

"Family's got a lot of connections," Dan said with a grin. "And a lot of money. If we pool it, we should be able to pull this off."

"I just hope having a brother as president won't bring on more paparazzi, Monica said."

Meredith, if only you were here. Frank had to steel himself not to cry.

"We're going to have to start in your state. Get those voting machines fixed," Frank said to Dan, as he slung an arm around his brother's shoulder.

"Come on, everybody." Dan opened his arms and they all gathered for a group hug. Paul Parnell's dream, come true.